Deborah Armstrong

Library of Congress Control Number:		2012905988
ISBN:	Hardcover	978-1-4691-9390-8
	Softcover	978-1-4691-9389-2
	Ebook	978-1-4691-9391-5

To order additional copies of this book, contact:
Xlibris Corporation
1-888-795-4274
www.Xlibris.com
Orders@Xlibris.com
102221

Dedication

This book is dedicated to the Ladies, both four-legged and two, who are a constant and beloved presence in my life. To my four-legged ladies—I thank you for providing me with a wonderful life, a storyline, and chocolate milk. To my two-legged ladies—I thank you for your love and friendship. I thank you for your encouragement and support of my writing, without which I would have stopped long ago.

Prologue

♥

Quinn Thomas opened the back door to the waiting limo and got in. He was eager to get back to his hotel room, away from the drunks and the hookers.

"Anytime," he grumbled.

"Just waiting on one more," the driver answered him. "I can see him coming now, and it looks like he's got company." He smiled knowingly.

"Damn," Quinn swore under his breath as he saw the other passengers approaching.

Tom Braden, a fellow actor who was not as famous as Quinn, stumbled to the limo as a woman pulled him toward their ride. Quinn had seen the woman before and had stayed away from her. She was known to make the rounds at all of the best film festival parties, making sure the men were well taken care of, especially the stars. Apparently, Tom was on her to-do list tonight.

"Hey, buddy!" Tom said drunkenly as he fell onto the backseat. "Great party, eh?"

Quinn was tired of the nonstop poke at the Canadian vernacular. He ignored Tom and the woman as he leaned his head back against the headrest. Maybe if he ignored them, they'd do the same.

He could hear their moans from wild groping and drunken kissing. He had no urge to look. He'd seen it all before and didn't need to see a repeat performance. He tried not to judge, but Tom should know better. He was married with kids.

"Hey, Quinnie, wanna join us?" the woman asked as she put her hand on his crotch.

Quinn grimaced as he opened his eyes and removed the uninvited hand. "Thanks, but I think Tom wants you all to himself."

"Hell, Quinn, join in. There's lots to share!" Tom said enthusiastically as he undid his belt and worked his pants down to his ankles.

The woman was already naked. There wasn't much to take off. It was clear that her skintight dress was the only garment she wore to the party.

"Come on, Quinnie, you can have first choice. What do you want?"

"Thanks, but not tonight. You two have fun. I'm going to close my eyes. Pretend I'm not here."

"Your loss." Tom shrugged as he mounted the woman.

"Aren't you gonna watch?" The woman seemed disappointed in not having an audience.

"No." Quinn put his head back and closed his eyes.

Quinn tuned the couple out. It wasn't hard to do. He had years of practice. He could sit through any uncomfortable situation and think of something completely different. He always timed it perfectly, coming out of his thoughts just as the torture ended. No one ever knew he was gone.

Calculus and statistics were the usual standbys, but not tonight. Tonight Quinn wanted something better to take his mind off the live sex show happening across from him. Tonight he thought of her, the woman he had dreamed of for what seemed like forever. He envisioned her long brown hair hanging down past her shoulders, shining in the sunlight as the wind blew through it. He could see her smile and the sparkle in her eyes as she laughed. Her lips were full and sensuous, kissable and irresistible. Quinn knew what that mouth could do. Her kisses were torture and ecstasy all at once. No woman could compare to the kisses she gave him.

Quinn hardened at the thought of her. He imagined his hands caressing her body, running over the soft curves, the full breasts, and her long legs. He could feel her as she reacted to his touch, the electricity that sparked between them, and the way she arched her back when he entered her, pulling all of him into her. He could feel her nails raking up over his back, finding his hair and pulling him tight and never letting go. He focused on that image. He remembered every detail—her taste, her smell, and her touch. Damn, how he wanted her. He ached for her.

He took her slow and easy, and she loved every minute of it. He was in no rush, and neither was she.

"Quinn buddy, we're here. It's time to wake up." Tom shook Quinn's shoulder, assuming he was asleep.

Quinn kissed his dream good-bye. *Soon*, she promised him, and then he opened his eyes.

"You missed a helluva party, buddy." Tom smiled broadly as he tucked himself back into his pants.

Quinn couldn't help but notice the lipstick smeared over Tom's swollen lips. He handed him a handkerchief. "Clean up before you get out, man, if you don't want your wife to see a picture of this."

He ignored the woman. She'd make sure she looked good when she stepped out of the limo. She probably had another star on her list waiting for her.

He looked out the tinted windows and was instantly relieved to see they were in the underground parking garage of the hotel. There would be no crowds to push through tonight. Quinn got out of the limo quickly and headed for the elevator. He didn't wait for the others. The elevator door opened, and he stepped in, pushing the button for his floor and the Close Door button at the same time.

"Quinn!" Tom called out to him.

They could take the next one. *Fuck them.*

A quick swipe of his key and he was in his hotel suite. Quinn dropped the key on the desk and headed for the bar. He poured himself a full glass of scotch before he stripped. Damn, he was still hard for her. It served him right for thinking of her for an hour. The things they did . . .

Quinn's cell phone rang a familiar ring.

"Mother," he drawled as he answered it.

"Bad timing? Are you with someone?" his mother teased.

"Not tonight, Mother. Perhaps you'll catch me another time." He took a long drink from his glass.

"I wish." She laughed lightly. "Hollywood's most eligible bachelor and I can never catch you with anyone. You're sure you don't have something to tell me?"

Quinn groaned, "I'm as straight as an arrow, Mother. I thought you'd be happy that I'm not sleeping my way through Hollywood."

"But you need to have sex, Quinn. A man as handsome and as virile as you needs to get laid."

Quinn was used to frank conversations with his parents, especially his mother. Before his first date in high school, she presented him with a box of condoms, certain he'd get lucky. She knew the girls would want him.

"I'm the master of my own domain, Mom. Don't worry about me. How's Dad?" It was definitely time to go to the default topic.

"He's sitting with me in the living room. We watched one of those entertainment shows. You were on it, of course."

"I didn't do it. Whatever they say I did, it never happened." Quinn headed for the bathroom and started the shower.

"They say you're hooking up with Rene. I thought she was history."

"She is. There's nothing going on between us. I told you that."

"Yes, but—"

"Mom, we've gone over this. Who are you going to believe? Your son or the television shows?"

"But it's so convincing."

"Professor Thomas, you should have your doctorate rescinded for believing such lies. I think I'll write to the dean of the faculty."

"You could, but I don't think it would help. I'm sleeping with him. I think he'd side with me. I give excellent head."

Quinn choked on his drink. She always had to have the last word. "May I speak with him?"

Quinn could hear his father admonishing his wife. He smiled at their banter.

"Hello, son. Sorry about that. You know how she gets when she sees you on television. How are you?"

"It's okay. Just stick up for me, will you? And tell her it's not true. She knows me better than that."

"She loves you. We both do. How are things in Toronto? Meet any real stars?"

Quinn appreciated his dad's humor. Quinn would always be his son first. Being a movie star was just like any other occupation. It didn't matter to him as long as Quinn was happy.

"I'm flying to LA tomorrow. I have a meeting scheduled with the studio. Then I'm back to New York to finish this damned movie."

Quinn's father knew that not talking about Toronto meant that it was the same as any other film festival—long, tortuous, and extremely lonely for his son.

"I've got to go. I'll phone tomorrow. Tell Mom for me."

"Good night, son."

Quinn ended the call and put his phone on the bathroom counter. He looked at himself in the mirror. His hard-on was gone. There was no better way to lose it than by having a phone conversation with his mother about sex. The shower was hot, just the way he liked it. Quinn cleared his mind of all thoughts. He was tired, and he had an early flight in the morning.

"I'm mad at you," the voice on the other end of the phone admonished him.

Quinn looked at the clock on the bedside table and groaned. "Rene, it's four o'clock in the fucking morning."

"You weren't sleeping, were you? Who's with you?"

Quinn could hear the drunken jealousy in her voice. "Why are you mad at me?" He sat up in the bed and reached for his unfinished drink. "I haven't done anything." He swallowed the drink in one gulp.

"That's the point, Quinn. You haven't done anything. I keep waiting for you to make a move, and you don't. We should be lovers," she sobbed. "We should be making love right now. Instead, you're with some bimbo, and I'm here all alone. Bastard!"

"I am in bed by myself, Rene. There has been no sex on this trip, not that it's any of your business."

"Liar."

There was no reasoning with her. Rene was Quinn's costar in his current movie, *Untitled*, and they had filmed two other movies together. Their on-screen chemistry was unmatched by any other couple in Hollywood, but that's all there was. Away from the cameras, they had nothing in common, not even between the sheets.

"I don't lie."

"All men lie. It's your nature to lie." She sniffed and then noisily gulped down a drink.

"I've never lied to you, and I won't start now. Come on, Rene, you know nothing's going to happen with us. We tried it, got the T-shirt, and moved on."

"I don't want a damned T-shirt. I want you."

"Look, I've got an early flight to LA. Then I'll be back to New York on Monday. We'll talk it out then. Go to bed, Rene. Get some sleep. You'll feel better in the morning."

"I love you."

"Good night, Rene."

He put his phone down on the bedside table and made himself comfortable. There would be no more sleeping tonight. Quinn closed his eyes and focused on her, the woman of his dreams, the woman he had never met.

Chapter 1

♥

Davina Stuart walked through the Toronto Pearson International Airport terminal 1 with a feeling of foreboding. *What am I doing?* she asked herself as she got in line for the Air Canada flight to Los Angeles. *It's not too late. I can just turn around and go back to the farm.*

Last night, Davina's best friend, Maggie, had insisted on reading Davina's tarot cards before she left for LA. Davina rarely gave the readings much credit, but Maggie lived her life by them and wanted to make sure that Davina was going to have a successful trip. It was a shock to Davina when Maggie saw success and romance in the cards, all happening while Davina was in California.

"I hope the success part comes true, but I'm really not looking for romance," she told Maggie. "I think I've already had my shot at that."

"Oh, never say that, Davi," Maggie argued. "It's never too late for romance, and you still have a lot of love to give someone. Look at what the cards say! Your heart is full of love!"

Oh, if that were only true, she thought. Davina shook her head and came back to reality.

The ticket agent greeted her warmly, "Good morning. May I have your ticket and passport, please?"

Davina handed over her airline ticket with her passport.

"Do you have any baggage to put through?"

"No, I have a bag for carry-on." She didn't plan on staying long—fly in for the meeting with the Hollywood executives, spend a day or two sightseeing, and then head home to the farm.

"You're flying executive first class. Here is your ticket and your seat assignment. You can check through these gates and wait in the Maple Leaf Lounge if you would like. Your flight will be called in an hour. Enjoy your flight."

Davina took her ticket and walked toward the departure area. She wanted to clear customs and get settled in the lounge so that she could collect her thoughts. Apex Studios was flying her to Los Angeles to talk with her about the filming of her best-selling novel, *Second Harvest.* A meeting with the cast was planned for tomorrow, and the studio invited her to sit in. She was thrilled for the invitation but thought it just a publicity gimmick.

It was only two years ago that Davina was a happily married mother of three. Then unexpectedly, her husband of twenty-five years died in his sleep from a brain aneurysm, leaving her to run the family farm and raise three children by herself. For three months, as she grieved the loss of her husband, Davina kept a journal. Although it was meant to be a private outlet for her grief, when the journal was completed, it was a novel and a damn good one. Maggie convinced her to send it in to have it published. Within a year, Davina was a published author with a book on the New York Times Best Sellers list that was still going strong and was now going to be made into a movie.

Davina breezed through customs and headed toward the Maple Leaf Lounge. *Might as well make use of it,* she thought. *The chance may never happen again.* She helped herself to a coffee and muffin and then settled comfortably into an oversized leather armchair.

Within seconds, the quiet was disrupted by shouting outside the lounge entrance. She looked toward the door and saw through the frosted glass a large crowd with cameras flashing.

Paparazzi.

The lounge door burst open; and Quinn Thomas, Hollywood's latest heartthrob, barged in. He looked around the lounge quickly and then headed over to a leather armchair far away from the other patrons. He hid his physical attributes—his six-foot-three-inch frame with broad shoulders and rock-hard body, his thick dark shaggy hair, his famous baby blue bedroom eyes, and his sensuous, kissable lips—well under his trademark jeans, faded T-shirt, and gray hooded jacket. Since Quinn's last movie, his photos had been published in every entertainment magazine and Internet celebrity gossip Web site. He was romantically linked to almost every Hollywood starlet, with a new romance every month.

Davina tried her best not to stare at him, but what did it matter? His face was hidden; he couldn't see her. She found herself fantasizing about him sitting next to her on the flight. *Oh, give it up, Davi,* she said to herself. *You're old enough to be his mother.*

She may have been older by about fifteen years, but in no way did she look her age. She was tall, about five feet ten inches, with a slender, well-toned body from working on the farm. Her dark brunette hair fell past her shoulders, and the style enhanced her youthful face. She wore her favorite dress that tastefully showed off her curves and brought attention to her long slender legs.

Davina smiled to herself as she thought of the first time she met her daughter at the airport, arriving on a flight home from Europe. There she was, that bubbly teenager walking through customs in her pink pajama bottoms and white hooded jacket, not caring what she looked like, just comfortable. Maybe that's why Quinn always looked like that in the tabloids. Was he being comfortable or hiding from the world? *No. He looks like he's hiding.*

The boarding of the flight was announced. Davina finished her coffee and gathered her purse and travel bag. She noticed that Quinn didn't show any sign of following the group out of the lounge. She smiled to herself as she realized the silliness of her fantasy. *He's on another flight.*

"Welcome aboard. Your seat number is 3A. Enjoy your flight," said the attendant.

"Thank you," Davina replied. She walked to her seat and put her travel bag in the overhead bin above her seat and then sat down. Davina looked out the window and thought, *So many planes with so many adventures waiting to take flight.* She reached into her bag and pulled out a pen and the manuscript of her latest project. She jotted the words down on the front cover. They sounded corny, but maybe she could make use of them.

While she was writing, she heard the snap of the overhead bin close as someone stored gear overhead. She felt her seat move as a body fell into the seat beside her. She turned her head to say hello. It was the polite thing to do. Davina opened her mouth to speak, but no words came out. Sitting in seat 3B was Quinn Thomas.

Chapter 2

♥

Everything about him said, *Don't bother me.* His seat belt was fastened, his arms were crossed across his chest, and his hood was pulled down over his forehead, covering his eyes. Davina knew there was no way he was going to acknowledge her. *Fine,* she thought. *With my luck, he's probably an asshole anyway—gorgeous, but still an asshole.*

Watching him, Davina thought of her late husband who could fall asleep anytime and anywhere. She sighed as she thought of him. She missed him. The pain of losing him still stabbed at her heart. *I needed more time.* Davina closed her eyes and pushed all thoughts of her husband away. No more grieving for what should have been.

Once the plane was in the air, Davina pulled out her iPod, put in her earplugs, and started listening to her favorite tunes. She opened the dog-eared, coffee-stained manuscript of her second novel. This was her first draft, and the ending wasn't coming to her as she had hoped. She was aiming for somewhere between the fairy-tale ending of true love and bittersweet love of the real world. She tried to concentrate, but she couldn't. Quinn Thomas was sitting beside her, and he was impossible to ignore.

You're an idiot, Davi. You should be talking to him, having a drink with him, and gazing into those baby blues. What if he's sleeping? Stare at him and fantasize. There's no law against that, and you're due for a good fantasy. You know it's been way too long since you've had a really good one. He was in that one. Remember?

She scribbled in the margin as she argued with herself. Davina stopped when she realized she had scribbled the words "Quinn Thomas Hot Sex Now" in the margin of the funeral scene.

Davina turned her head to look at Quinn. He was awake, possibly had been for a while, and was staring at her. A smile worked its way across his gorgeous face. She turned off her iPod and pulled out her earplugs.

"You caught me," he said guiltily. "I hope I didn't disturb you, but I was enjoying watching you work. You're very sexy when you're reading."

"Excuse me?" Davina felt the heat from her blushing. "I haven't heard that one before." She prayed that he hadn't read what she had just written.

Quinn's blue eyes gazed into hers and caused her heart to jump. "I'm sorry if I'm embarrassing you. I think that you are an incredible-looking woman, and I couldn't help but watch you while you read." He smiled at her and extended his right hand. "Hi. I'm Quinn Thomas."

"Hi. Davina Stuart." She shook his hand firmly. *Breathe, Davi, breathe,* she told herself. She realized she hadn't let go of his hand, then quickly let go.

"Nice to meet you, Davina," he said, his voice warm and sexy, his eyes sparkling. "I apologize for my entrance into the lounge earlier. I thought I was going to get trampled out there! Stuff like that's not supposed to happen in Toronto."

"That's where you're wrong. The world thinks we're very civilized and polite, but when a rock star or movie star hits town, we go crazy. Very few celebrities like to come up our way because of all the ice and snow."

Quinn laughed. "It's September. There is no ice and snow this time of year."

"Obviously, you didn't notice the dome over the city. It keeps the cold and snow out of Toronto while the film festival is on."

Quinn's smile touched his eyes. "You should be a storyteller. I'd believe anything you told me even when I knew it wasn't true."

Davina smiled back at him. "Thank you. I don't think you could go anywhere without being recognized and mobbed. I saw some photos on the Internet from your last location shoot in New York. Those fans were maniacs. I don't know how you ever got the movie made."

"I don't know if we did get it filmed." Quinn chuckled. "I think the director's going to put some scenes together, add a few shots of me, and that will be it. I don't think the fans care about the movie as long as I'm in it. It's really sad."

"Oh, I don't think that's true," Davina protested. "Your movies are great. I have to admit I've seen them all more than once or twice. My daughter and I get together once a month to watch movies. There's usually one of yours on the list."

"Your daughter is old enough to see my movies?" Quinn moved in closer to Davina, keenly interested.

"She has been for a while." She wasn't sure if he was being polite or if Quinn had no clue about Davina's age. He was very charming and definitely not an asshole, not yet anyway.

Their conversation was interrupted when the flight attendant served them wine. Davina took a long sip from her glass as she gazed at Quinn's face. He was definitely more handsome in person. His skin was flawless—no acne scars or blemishes. His eyebrows were groomed perfectly, arching over his sparkling baby blue eyes. His lips were as kissable as she had imagined, and his smile really did touch his eyes. Thick shaggy brown hair framed his perfect face. Davi resisted the urge to run her fingers through it.

"Is it your first time to Los Angeles?" Quinn asked her once the attendant left.

"First trip to LA, but I've been to California before."

"So is there a lucky man waiting for you in LA or back in Toronto?"

"There's no man waiting for me in either place," Davina said softly.

"I can't believe there's no one waiting for you." He looked at her left hand. There was no ring on her third finger. "Are you divorced or never married or—"

"Widowed," she said quickly. "For two years now."

The silence enveloped them. Davina looked down at her bare finger where her wedding band and diamond engagement ring used to be. Their indentation marks were no longer visible. She rubbed at the empty space.

Quinn took her hand in his, and she looked at him. His eyes held her in his power as his warmth flowed through her.

"I'm sorry for your loss. I apologize if I upset you."

Davina shook her head. "You didn't upset me. You had no way of knowing." She smiled at Quinn. "I miss him, but I'm not in mourning."

"So does that mean that you're—"

Davi didn't let Quinn finish. "Not looking."

"You have plenty of love left in your heart for one more man. I can see that. It's in your eyes. And no, you aren't too old for me, if that's what you are thinking."

"How do you know that?" Davina gasped. Davina had many fantasies about Quinn, but this was not one of them. She wanted hot sex with lots of hot kisses and an orgasm that would make her scream into next week. She wanted to be taken. She didn't want words of love or need them. She pulled her hand away.

Quinn's eyes locked with hers. "You know, the man you see in the movies isn't the real me. What the press says about me isn't true."

"So you're not a Hollywood heartthrob then?" Davina joked weakly as she felt herself being pulled into him.

"I don't care about that. It's not who I am inside."

The sincerity of his words caught her breath.

"Do you believe in love at first sight?" His voice was soft and full of hope.

"I don't, but my husband did." Davina laughed nervously. "He said that was how he fell in love with me. It took him a while to convince me that his feelings were true."

"So you know it happens then?"

"Mr. Thomas," Davina said in frustration, wishing for any conversation but this.

"Call me Quinn."

"We've just met. You don't know me. I don't know you."

"Tell me the truth. When I sat beside you, did you fantasize about me?" He moved closer to her, trapping her.

Davina didn't answer.

"I'll take that as a 'yes' then."

"It doesn't mean anything," she protested. "Fantasies are normal."

"So is falling in love."

"Not like this." Davina shook her head. "Believe me. Once was enough."

"Why? Why can one man fall in love with you at first sight but another can't?"

"Because I don't want it to happen," Davina said, exasperated. "I'm past that stage of wanting to be loved. Hot and heavy sex is all I want now." She groaned as soon as she heard the words leave her mouth, silently cursing his baby blues for pulling her in.

Quinn murmured lustfully, "How hot and heavy?"

Davina knew she was caught. There was no way out of this conversation. *Play with him, Davi. Show him the old broad still has it in her. What have you got to lose?*

She leaned toward him and murmured sexily, "Unbelievably hot and heavy, soaked in sweat and totally exhausted."

"Here on the plane?" His eyebrow arched mischievously.

"I didn't get that far. I take my time when I fantasize."

"Care to tell me about it?"

"I don't kiss and tell, Quinn. Not even with my fantasies." Davi sat back in her seat as she winked at him.

"I want to get to know you, Davina Stuart. I want to know all about you." Quinn looked at his watch. "We have plenty of time to get to know each other."

"What if we end up not liking each other?"

"That won't happen, but on the off chance it does, we arrive in Los Angeles and never see each other once we get off the plane. What do we have to lose? Are you up for it?"

"It sounds like mile-high speed dating." Davina couldn't resist joking. *I must be insane.*

Quinn winked at her. "We could join the club, if you'd like."

"Let's stick to the speed dating part, shall we?"

Chapter 3

♥

"You first," Davina told Quinn, "and nothing from your Web site unless what's posted is untrue."

He waited for the flight attendant to refill their wineglasses before he spoke. "If it's on my Web site, it's all true." He paused and then smiled. "You've checked me out."

"I check out a lot of people," she said casually. "Okay then. Tell me what I don't already know." She took a long sip of her wine.

"I have a photographic memory. I remember everything I've ever seen or read."

"Everything?"

"Everything," he assured her with a low voice, "including the handwritten fantasy of a beautiful woman."

Davina's mouth dropped open. *No!*

"'Quinn Thomas Hot Sex Now.'" He made the words sound more sinful and sexy than she could have ever imagined.

"Not fair! You were encroaching on my personal space."

"It wasn't hard to miss."

"You didn't have to look," Davina protested halfheartedly.

"Yes, I did," he said, obviously not regretting his actions. "It's my turn. Do you date?"

"I've been on a few in the last year, but nothing that turned into anything serious."

"Why?" he asked before he took a sip of his wine.

"The men were okay, but I didn't know if they were interested in my spread or me."

Quinn choked on his drink. "Excuse me?"

"I'm a farmer, Quinn. I wasn't sure if they liked my land or me. What did you think I meant?" she asked, smiling at him knowingly.

"Nothing." He shook his head. "What kind of farmer?"

"I'm a dairy farmer. I run the farm with my three children."

"But you were working on a manuscript."

"I was editing for a friend," she lied. Davina wasn't comfortable with saying she was an author. She thought *Second Harvest* was a one-hit wonder. If she published a second book, then she would call herself an author. Until then, Davina Stuart was a dairy farmer from Canada.

"You wrote my name and 'hot sex' in the margin."

"It's for the funeral scene. I thought it would spice it up a bit. What do you think?"

"I think you Canadians have a sick sense of humor."

"It's the long cold winters. It does things to our brains and our libido."

Damn, he loved the sound of her voice. It was soft and feminine, caressing him with a tenderness he had longed for far too long. "Like what?" he asked, eager to hear more.

"I don't kiss and tell, remember?"

"Why are you going to California?"

"I'm taking a few days holiday before we get busy with the harvest. I told you that I'd never been to LA. I thought now would be the perfect time."

"There's no one waiting for you?"

"No lover, if that's what you're asking. I'm on my own."

"Do you drive the tractors?"

"I can do it all. If there's a job that needs to be done, I do it. Right now, my focus is on the cattle and the paperwork. My son and the hired men look after most of the machinery work."

"I'm impressed."

"Why?" she asked, serious. "And you'd better not say it's because I'm a woman."

"I'm impressed because farming is a business. You grow food for people to eat, and what you do is dependent on the weather, the price of seed and fertilizer, and so much more. There is so much that works against you."

"And for us," Davina added. "I prefer to look at the positive side."

"With everything?"

"I try. There's not much good that comes from negative thinking."

The pilot's announcement interrupted them. "Ladies and gentlemen, please buckle up and secure your trays in the upright position. Prepare for landing. Thank you for flying Air Canada flight 789 to Los Angeles. We hope you enjoyed your flight."

"Wow, that was fast," Quinn said, shaking his head. "I'm not done."

"Not done what?" Davina asked as she put her tray away.

"I'm not done getting to know you."

"That's speed dating for you." Davina smiled. "Sorry."

"Okay, then, did I pass? Will you go out with me?" His eyes burned into hers.

She could feel herself melting into him. "I'm only here for a couple of days. Then I'm heading home. I don't know if I can." *Don't be a fool, Davi.*

Quinn persisted, "Do you have plans for tonight?"

"No," she said reluctantly.

"Then give me your cell phone number or the name of your hotel, and I'll give you a call later today."

"I'll give you my business card. It has my cell phone number on it." Davina fished through her wallet and handed Quinn her card. "Here you go."

Quinn looked at the card quickly and then tucked it safely into his wallet. By now, the plane had landed and was taxiing to the arrival area.

Quinn leaned over to Davina and whispered to her, "Now when I get into the airport, it's going to be hell again. The paparazzi will be there in full force, worse than in Toronto. I have my security there to get me out as fast as possible. I won't be able to walk out with you, but I'll see you later tonight. Okay?"

"Sure. I'll see you later." *This was fun, but I won't see you again.*

Quinn could see the doubt in her eyes. "I will call you, you know. You'll see." He gave her a quick hug.

Davina felt the heat of her blush. She was too old to be blushing.

"We haven't finished our date," he reminded her. "I don't lie. I will see you again."

The door to the plane opened. They both got out of their seats and retrieved their bags from the overhead bin. Once they made it out the door, he hurried down the ramp, looking back at Davina one last time. By the time Davina got to customs, there was a mob scene outside the doors. She couldn't see Quinn, but she was sure that was his mob.

The customs agent asked her, "Reason for your visit?"

"Business," Davina replied. "I'm only here for two days."

"What kind of business?" The customs agent scanned her passport.

"I'm a writer." *And I have a date with Quinn Thomas.*

"Good luck with that," he said as he handed back her passport. "Next!" he called to the next person in line.

"Thanks," Davina said. *I don't think I'll need it. I think it's already in the cards.* With that, she sent a little prayer of thanks for Maggie and headed out through customs.

Davina looked to her right and thought she could make out the mob of paparazzi attached to Quinn. It was moving slowly out toward the exit, cameras flashing away. She wondered how he could live with that day after day. *I'd go crazy.*

Then she looked straight ahead and saw a man standing with a card that read D. L. Stuart.

"Hello, I'm Davina Stuart. Are you looking for me?"

"Yes, hello, Ms. Stuart. I'm Bert. Do you have any luggage, or is this everything?" he asked as he pointed to her travel bag.

"This is it."

"Let me take your bag," he offered.

Davina followed Bert out the doors to the limousine parking. Bert opened the back door of the limousine, and Davina slid into the spacious backseat. The air was nice and cool.

"So where are we off to?" she asked him.

"The Crown Plaza Beverly Hills Hotel. My instructions are to drive you to the hotel. Unless you need my services for the rest of the day, I'll be back at ten tomorrow morning to take you to the Apex office."

"Thanks, Bert. I don't think that I'll need your services again today. I think I'll just relax a bit." *And wait for a phone call.*

Davina relaxed in the comfort of the limousine's leather seat and closed her eyes. The scenery didn't matter to her. Her thoughts were of what had happened with Quinn on the plane. No one would ever believe their conversation. She didn't even believe it happened. *Maybe he's on drugs or is sleep deprived,* Davina wondered. *Who in his right mind talks like that to a perfect stranger? Someone who knows how to act,* she answered back. Quinn wasn't a star on looks alone. He could act, and he was definitely giving Davina quite the performance. *Reality check, Davi, you've been played. Love at first sight. Give your head a shake.*

Chapter 4

♥

Davina checked into her suite. It was spacious with a spectacular view of the city. She quickly unpacked her travel bag. She checked her cell phone service. Yes, she could receive calls here. That was good to know, just in case Quinn did intend to call her. She pulled out her manuscript and thought she'd try another round of editing. After the second page, she knew her concentration was shot.

"Forget it," she groaned in frustration.

Quickly, Davina stripped and put on her workout clothes. She didn't travel anywhere without her runners, shorts, and T-shirt. She pocketed her room key and cell phone and left for the hotel gym.

The gym was empty. Davina headed to her favorite cardio machine, the elliptical cross trainer. She grabbed a towel from the rack, set the timer to one hour and got to work. The television screen overhead was set to the news channel. Davina concentrated on the screen, pushing Quinn out of her mind. World news occupied her thoughts. For the first thirty minutes, her plan was working. She was breaking out in a good sweat, the stiffness from traveling was gone, and her body felt good.

Then there on the screen was Quinn, surrounded by reporters and flashing cameras as his security guards tried to herd him out of the airport. The reporter spoke about Quinn's return from the Toronto Film Festival and speculated as to which starlet he would be with while in LA. Photos of two women were flashed on the screen. One showed him in a very compromising situation with his latest leading lady, Rene Adams. She was hanging off him, but he didn't look happy. Davina could see it in his eyes. Quinn looked embarrassed. The other was of him with Natasha Ward. Quinn didn't look happy with her either.

Davina's cell phone rang.

She slowed down her pace and breathed heavily into the phone. "Hello?"

"Davina, it's me, Quinn. Are you okay?" His voice was filled with concern.

"Oh, sorry," she apologized quickly, "I'm in the gym, and you caught me while I'm doing cardio. I'm watching you on the news right now."

"Really?" he asked, clearly embarrassed. "What am I up to?"

"I'm watching your exit from the airport today. Do you have to go through that every time you travel?"

"Unfortunately, yes."

"You poor man, I really feel for you. Honest."

There it was again, that voice so soft and tender.

"Thanks." There was a brief silence, and then he said, "So I'm phoning about our date tonight."

"You're cancelling," Davina interrupted him.

"No! I'm phoning to make the arrangements. You're not getting out of it. I told you that."

"But you're supposed to be going out with Natasha Ward or Rene Adams while you're in LA. That's what the reporter is saying right now," she teased. "If it's in the news, it has to be true, doesn't it?"

Quinn caught on to her. "Very funny," he said dryly. "Rene's in New York, and I have no idea where Natasha is. Where are you staying?"

"The Crown Plaza Beverly Hills, do you know where it is?"

Without hesitating, Quinn answered, "I'll be at your door at six o'clock."

"I'll be ready. I'll see you soon."

By 5:45 p.m., Davina was dressed and ready to go. She wore a simple black dress with black pumps. No need for stockings; her legs were tanned nicely. A simple diamond pendant and matching studs finished her look.

At six o'clock, there was a light rap at the door. Quinn was on time. Davina opened the door and was pleasantly surprised by the gorgeous man standing before her, dressed in black pants and a black button shirt.

"For you, my lady," he murmured as he offered her a single red rose.

"Thank you. It's lovely." She inhaled the rose's perfume.

"You look even lovelier than you did this morning, if such a thing could be possible."

Davina blushed at the compliment. "Thank you."

"Shall we go?" he asked as he offered her his arm.

"Yes." Davina picked up her evening bag and walked with Quinn to the elevator. "May I ask where we're going?"

"It's my favorite place in all of LA, someplace very secluded and private. I hope you like it."

They entered the elevator, and Quinn pressed the button for the penthouse floor.

"I didn't know there was a restaurant on the top floor. What is it called?"

"Chez Quinn," he answered as he gazed down at her.

She held his gaze. "Oh, really?" she said slowly as she realized where they were going. "Is it a popular spot?"

"It's not well known, but the chef is brilliant and the ambiance is very romantic. You can only get in by invitation."

"I must be very lucky then," she said, smiling at him.

By this time, they were out of the elevator and walking to the end of the hall. Quinn slipped his key through the slot and opened the door for Davina. This was Quinn's suite—two bedrooms, two bathrooms, a living room, and a full kitchen. It was a perfect hangout for a star away from home or, in Quinn's case, a star without a home. Dimmed lights shone throughout the suite. Soft music played in the background. The mood was definitely set for romance.

Quinn led Davina to the kitchen and motioned for her to sit in one of the high-backed stools at the counter.

"Tonight, my lovely, you are dining at Chez Quinn. Tonight's menu is a mixed salad with a light raspberry dressing, Arroz con polo, and for dessert, we have an ice wine served with dark chocolate and raspberries. You can sit here, and I will cook for you. Would you like a drink? I have white wine or perhaps you would prefer something else. We have almost everything at Chez Quinn."

"I wouldn't mind a single malt scotch, neat, if you have it."

"Oh, the lady likes the hard stuff! Don't you know it puts hair on your chest?"

"It does?" Davina asked with mild surprise. "I haven't noticed. I'll have to check myself out later."

"Perhaps I'll get the chance to check you out myself, later." He winked at her. "Scotch for the lady, coming up." Quinn poured drinks for the two of them. "Actually," he confided, with a warm voice that sent shivers up her spine, "this is my drink of choice. I love the burn, and you can take your time with it. There's no need to rush. Just like great sex."

"I've never thought about the sex part, but you could be right." She took a slow sip of her drink. "So where are we with our date? What's next on our list of discussion topics?" she asked as she made herself comfortable on the stool.

"Well, let me think," Quinn said as he put on his chef's apron and started to prepare the meal. "We could talk about politics and religion, but that could cut the evening short, if we disagree. I guess we're at family, sports, music, and sex in any particular order. How about we cover one topic per course?"

"So are you planning for us to be talking about sex by the time we have dessert, or are you planning on us having sex by the time we get to dessert?" Davina asked with feigned innocence.

"Davina, you shock me! That never crossed my mind." Quinn smiled knowingly. "We'll just have to see what happens, won't we?"

"Please call me Davi, if you prefer. My friends call me that. Davina's my business name."

"What do your lovers call you?" Quinn gazed into Davi's eyes.

She felt herself being pulled into him as she held his gaze. "I don't kiss and tell. Do you?"

"Someday, Davi, you will tell me."

"Perhaps," Davi murmured softly, "you never know what's in the cards."

Quinn smiled and then went back to preparing the meal. "What does Davina mean? I've never heard it before. It's lovely."

"Thank you. It's the Gaelic feminine of David, and it means beauty. I'm named after a great aunt. What about Quinn? What does it mean?"

"It means descendant of Cuinn. It's not very exciting, I'm afraid."

"True, but it sounds so masculine. It's very sexy."

"You think so?"

"Honestly. It's very manly. It makes me think of Quinn the Hunter."

She watched him as he prepared the meal. She shifted on her seat, aroused by watching his large hands handling the fresh vegetables, almost caressing them. Davi wondered if he knew what he was doing to her. Was this how she affected him when he watched her read on the plane?

"Okay, you first with family," she prompted him.

Quinn took a drink from his glass. "I am the only child of John and Margaret Thomas. My parents are university professors currently teaching at Harvard. I see them whenever our schedules allow, mostly Christmas and birthdays. I have no cousins, so it is just me. My close friends are few, and they are scattered across the country. I try to meet up with them whenever I can. We grab a beer and catch a baseball game or hockey game, depending on the season. They're all getting married, having kids, and I'm still the pitiful bachelor friend they have to console."

"Pitiful? I don't think so. You mean to say none of them would like to be in your shoes?"

"Maybe *pitiful* isn't quite the right word. They envy the traveling and the starlets and want to wear my designer clothes and drive my Porsche, but they don't want my loneliness. They know there's no one for me to come home to at the end of the day, and they know that I envy them that."

Quinn mixed the salad together and offered Davi her plate and then sat down next to her.

"You're young, Quinn. There is plenty of time for you to settle down. You should be enjoying yourself." She took a forkful of her salad.

"Believe me, I have enjoyed myself, but it's time for something more. I want to share my life with someone. I am ready." Quinn stabbed at his salad.

"Mmm, great salad," Davi offered. "Is this your own dressing?"

"Yes. I'll give you the recipe later. Now it's your turn."

"Family . . . I am the youngest of four children. My parents, Jack and Jill . . ."

Quinn tried not to choke on his food as he stifled a laugh.

"Don't laugh!" Davi lightly slapped Quinn's arm. "Anyway, they were very loving and supportive. My siblings are all crazy and wonderful in their own way. They all have children and grandchildren, and we get together for all of the holidays. I have three children, two girls and a boy, all in their twenties.

"Tigger is my baby. She's the one who watches your films with me. She is the romantic. Rich is my son. He has always wanted to farm and is taking over the business. He's the athlete and comedian. Cat is my eldest daughter. She is smart, loving, and very talented. She was the one who helped me keep it together when her dad died. And that's it for family."

"You named your daughters after felines?" Quinn asked, incredulous. "Tigger and Cat?"

Davi laughed. "No, silly, those are their nicknames. They are Tamara and Catherine, but they prefer to go by Tigger and Cat. Is that better?"

"Much better."

Quinn cleared away their empty salad plates and started to serve the main course for them.

"What about your husband?"

"What would you like to know?"

"You said he believed in love at first sight. I'd like to know more about him. Where did the two of you meet?"

Quinn placed another plate in front of her and then removed his apron.

"This smells wonderful," she complimented him and then took a bite of chicken. "Where did you learn to cook like this?"

"My mother taught me. We spent a lot of time together in the kitchen. You haven't answered my question," he reminded her as he poured them both a glass of wine.

"Okay, sorry. We met at university in an English class. Ross sat beside me on the very first day."

"Is that when he fell in love with you?"

"That's what he told me." Davi smiled as she remembered that day.

"And what was it about you that he fell in love with at first sight?"

Davi stuck her legs out from under the stool for Quinn to look at. "My legs. I think you like them too."

Quinn put his hand on her leg and caressed it. "Oh yes, I like them too," he murmured hungrily as his gaze burned into her. Davi felt a slight tingle.

"So what are the spices in the chicken dish? It's very tasty," Davi asked as she tucked her legs back under the stool.

Quinn cleared his throat. "It's a different variation than normal. I left the garlic out. I didn't want to take a chance on having garlic breath later."

Davi gave Quinn a knowing smile. "So we're almost done with the main course, and we haven't discussed sports or music. We might have to skip the whole sex thing completely."

"Not a chance," Quinn said emphatically. "So here it goes. I can watch almost any sport on television if I have to. I like to swim, but I don't have much time for anything else. The gym is where I get my workout, and I only run when it's from the fans and paparazzi. That's it for me."

"Ditto for me, except for running from the fans and paparazzi. That hasn't happened yet."

"Oh, are you expecting fans and paparazzi?"

"Possibly, you never know."

"True," Quinn agreed. "Next is music. I play the piano and guitar, and some people think I can sing. My iPod is full of everything and anything, as you can tell from what is playing now." There was a soft jazz melody playing.

"Not quite a ditto here, although I can tinker at the piano, and some people tell me I have a nice singing voice. As far as music goes, I will try anything once. My iPod has a mixture of everything—classical, country, some rock, and love songs. Like I said, I will try anything once."

"Anything?"

Davi didn't answer. She looked down at her empty plate. Quinn's plate was empty too.

"Is it time for dessert already?" she asked innocently as she finished her wine.

"How did you like your meal?"

"It was delicious. Give my compliments to the chef. I hope his dessert is as good as his main course."

"Oh, I think you'll find it is."

"What about the dishes? Do you need any help?" Davi asked as she reached for her dirty plate.

"Madam, we don't ask the guests to do the dishes at Chez Quinn." Quinn pretended to be offended.

"I apologize, sir."

The dishes remained untouched. Quinn led Davi to the living room, where they sat beside each other on the overstuffed couch. He opened a bottle of ice wine and poured them each a glass. On the table was a plate of raspberries and small chunks of Belgian dark chocolate.

"Dessert," he said as he offered her a glass.

Davi took a sip. The ice wine was very sweet and cold. She looked at the label.

"It's from Niagara. Where did you get this?"

"It came with my gift bag from the Toronto Film Festival. I thought I'd put it to good use." Quinn put his glass down. "Now it's time for sex," Quinn murmured as he leaned in toward her. "You go first."

"Go first?"

"Talk."

"What do you want to know?" Davi asked softly as she reached for a raspberry. She knew where this was heading.

"Your first time, what was it like?"

"It's not very exciting. Sorry. It was with my husband before we were married. I wanted to make sure we were sexually compatible before we said 'I do.' It was a prerequisite to my marrying him."

"Really?" Quinn asked, amused by her answer. "It must have been good, if you still married him."

"It was better than good, and it kept getting better." Davi smiled at Quinn. "And your first time?"

Quinn cringed and took a sip of his wine. "I was eighteen. It was prom and my girlfriend at the time wanted to give me something to remember her by. I was heading off to Harvard, and she was trying to hold on to me.

The sex was awful. Neither of us knew what we were doing. We tried a few times after that, but we just couldn't click. I couldn't wait to head off to school to get away from her. It sounds awful, but it's the truth."

Davi's face showed mock horror. "I hope you got better at sex!"

"Of course I did, woman!" Quinn reddened from embarrassment. "It just took some time. Sometimes it's just not as easy as it should be."

"What is that supposed to mean?"

"There's a big difference between making love and having sex with someone. In my experience, women want me to make love to them, but it always turns out to be like an audition for a porn movie starring Quinn and the wannabe girlfriend. There's no feeling or tenderness. They only want to show me all the things they can do in bed. I'm tired of it. I want more than that."

"You tired of sex? I find that a bit hard to believe. I thought guys thought that even bad sex was better than no sex at all."

"Maybe, but I'd rather sleep alone than deal with that crap."

"So is there no truth in the stories about you and your leading ladies?"

"Almost none, but lately I've been managing on my own." Quinn touched Davi's cheek. "What about you? How have you handled the past two years?"

"Oh, I've been able to look after myself too."

Quinn topped up Davi's wineglass. Davi took another piece of chocolate. She bit into it and savored the bitterness.

"So what do you look for in a woman, Quinn? What will it take to win your heart?"

She leaned into him as he continued to caress her cheek. His hand was soft and warm. Quinn gazed at Davi. She was all that he wanted, and his eyes told her that.

"You," he answered.

Davi took another sip of her wine and then put the glass down on the table. Her mind was racing. She should leave now before she got in too deep. *This is crazy. I'm old enough to be his mother, but it's Quinn Thomas and he wants me! It's only for one night. Who will it hurt? No one. I can handle it. Admit it, Davi. You've been hot for him all night. Go for it.*

"Would you like me to tell you what I look for in a man?" Without waiting for his reply, Davi moved closer to Quinn and nestled into his neck. "First, he has to have the right smell. I'm very much a smell person, and his scent has to turn me on." She inhaled his scent and sighed. "You smell very good."

Quinn responded by wrapping his arms around her.

"Second, he has to taste right."

Davi pulled herself up even to his face, her lips lightly brushing his. She started with a soft kiss and then pressed harder. Both of them could feel each other's heat. Their lips parted and their tongues explored each other's mouth.

A deep moan escaped from Quinn.

Davi pulled away and looked into his eyes. "Third . . ."

"There's a third? How many things do you look for, woman?" he asked impatiently.

"Just wait." Davi slid her hand down Quinn's hard flat stomach until she felt the hard bulge in his pants and gave it a squeeze. "He has to have that."

Quinn's lips pressed hard against Davi's as he pulled her to him. A soft moan escaped from Davi as she submitted to him. Quinn's hand searched for the zipper on the back of Davi's dress. With one smooth stroke, her dress was undone. Not releasing her from his kiss, he deftly slid the dress off her shoulders, exposing her black lace bra. His fingers traced across her collarbone and then slowly down to her nipples. He felt their hardness and massaged them through the fine lace. Davi moaned and dug deeper into his kiss. Her hands reached up to his hair and laced her fingers through its thickness. She pulled him in tight to her.

Quinn released Davi from his kiss. The lust flaming in his eyes mirrored hers. "I want you, Davina Stuart. I want you now."

"Quinn . . ." Davi hesitated. She wanted to tell him that this was insane and that she was too old for him, but instead, all she could say was, "I'm not on any birth control."

"Not a problem." He scooped her up into his arms and carried her off to his bedroom.

Their lovemaking began tenderly. Quinn undressed Davi slowly, kissing her body as it became revealed to him. He removed his clothing quickly, discarding them on the floor. Quinn took his time with her. His hands caressed her face and then slowly moved down over her breasts and to her stomach. They could both feel the electricity flowing between them. When he finally touched between her legs, Davi gasped. She was hot, wet, and ready for him.

"Now, Quinn, now," she begged him.

He stopped and reached for a condom on his bedside table, quickly tore open the wrapper and put the condom on. Quinn slipped slowly into Davi. He sighed as he entered her. She was hot and tight as her core enveloped him. Davi's nails dug into his back. Her back arched and her legs wrapped around him. She was pulling him into her, and he had no resistance. Quinn's thrusts became deeper and more urgent. Davi's mouth searched for his and locked on to his lips with an intensity that was torture and ecstasy all at once. She released him and brought her mouth to his nipple. She licked it and then suckled it hard. He groaned louder and deeper. Davi nipped him. A low moan escaped from Quinn. His thrusts intensified. She touched herself where he entered her; her moans increased as her body began to shudder.

"Yes, Quinn, yes," she encouraged him.

Quinn exploded into Davi just as her orgasm swept through her. He crumpled onto her. Davi hugged him closely and kissed his sweat-covered brow. Remembering the condom, Quinn gently rolled off Davi and disposed of it quickly.

"You were right," he laughed softly. "You do look after yourself."

"I'm sorry."

"Don't apologize. I've never been made love to like that before. You had complete control over me. It was amazing."

"Really?"

Quinn kissed Davi on her forehead. "It was unbelievable. Next time it's my turn."

"Next time?"

"You didn't think I'd be happy with having you just once, did you?" Quinn asked as his finger caressed her cheek. "Unless you're thinking this was a mistake. You aren't, are you?"

"No. It wasn't a mistake."

Davi opened her arms to Quinn, and he obediently nestled into her breasts.

"You're so soft," he murmured. "I love your breasts. They feel so natural."

"They are natural."

"Promise me you'll never have any part of you fixed. No boob job, no tummy tuck, no face lift, no Botox or collagen—nothing."

"I never thought of it," Davi admitted. "Why?"

Quinn raised his head and kissed Davi gently. "Nothing compares to the feel of real lips. I shudder every time I have to kiss someone's injected lips. There's nothing sensual about them at all." Then he gently kissed her eyelids and forehead. "Your wrinkles and lines tell your life's story. They belong on your face. Your breasts are soft and lovable." He kissed them both and nuzzled into them. "It's not easy cuddling with oversized bowling balls."

"I like to bowl." Davi smiled as she enjoyed the attention being given to her breasts.

"You can bowl. Just don't use the balls for boobs."

"Okay, I promise. What about you, though? Is everything on you natural? No enhancements?"

"The only thing that comes and goes on me is facial hair. The rest is all natural, baby."

"No chest hair from drinking scotch, I see."

"And none on you either. That's a relief." He grinned playfully at her.

"Gee, thanks." Davi thought for a minute and then asked, "So when our date is over . . ."

"What do you mean by 'over'?" Quinn interrupted her as he pushed himself up to search her face for an answer.

"When my fantasy date is over," she said softly, "and I leave your bed tonight."

"You're not leaving." He lowered his head to kiss her. "This is not a fantasy. It's real, Davi. I'm in love with you."

Davi trembled as she felt the tingle flow through her from his kiss. She wanted this more than she had ever wanted anything before. She wanted to be devoured by him. She wanted his hands to touch her, to make her tingle all over. She wanted his body but not his heart.

"No, Quinn," she gasped as she broke away from his kiss.

"Why are you being difficult?" he murmured as his kisses moved down to her breasts.

"I'm not being difficult. I'm being realistic. We're not falling in love. This is just one night together. It's nothing more."

"To you maybe," he said as he kissed her belly button and then looked up at her, his blue eyes sizzling with desire. "No more talking, Davi. I told you I was going to make love to you again. It's my turn."

"Now?" she gasped as his hand touched her sex.

"Now."

Davi closed her eyes, enjoying Quinn's touch. How long had it been since a man touched her in this way? How long had it been since she'd actually enjoyed sex?

"Remember when I told you that my fantasy about you was hot and heavy, sweaty and totally exhausted?"

"Yes," he answered as he slid down her body, leaving hot kisses along the way.

"Give it to me, Quinn, now."

Chapter 5

♥

The nagging awareness of her morning meeting caused Davi to waken on time. She and Quinn had spent the night talking and making love. She didn't know when they finally fell asleep. Davi couldn't bear to wake Quinn, desperate to avoid any possible awkwardness resulting from their night spent together. She slipped out of bed and dressed quickly. Davi returned to her room after leaving a note on Quinn's pillow, thanking him for a very memorable date.

Davi had time to get ready for her meeting. She was exhausted but happy. It was nothing that a long cold shower and a few cups of strong coffee wouldn't cure. At precisely 10:00 a.m., Davi was picked up at her hotel by Bert, the limo driver. He was very cheerful and complimented Davi on her appearance. She was glowing.

Within twenty minutes, Davi was in the large office of the producers overseeing the movie. Good mornings and other pleasantries were exchanged, and coffee was served to everyone.

"We're so glad you could join us today, Ms. Stuart. We're excited to show you our project."

"Thank you. I'm happy to be here. I'm looking forward to meeting the cast. You've done an excellent job at keeping it a secret. My friends and family don't believe me when I tell them I don't know who will be in the movie. It's driving them crazy."

"Well, that will be over soon. This is the agenda for today's meeting. We'll introduce you to the director and cast, then fill you in on our plans for the film. We've flown them in for today so that they can ask you any questions about the characters, if they have any, and you are free to ask questions too. There will also be some photos taken of you with the cast."

"That sounds great." It was hard for Davi to conceal her excitement. She wondered what to say to the cast when she met them. *Hi, I love your work,* sounded so lame. She'd have to think of something better than that.

There was a light rap on the door, and then the director and cast entered the room. They were laughing and joking. Everyone but the last man to enter was happy to be there. One of the producers introduced the director, Chris Whyte, known for his flair for filming dramas. Chris then introduced Davi to the cast. She recognized them all, including Quinn Thomas.

Quinn and Davi stared at each other. For an instant, time stood still. Davi's heart pounded as she waited for Quinn's reaction, a sign that last night was not a mistake. Quinn's face was emotionless as his eyes burned into hers. Then Quinn's face broke out into a thin smile as he walked over to Davi and offered her his hand.

"It's nice to meet you, Davina. I read your book. It was so believable."

Davi felt the sting from his comment. "Thank you," she said softly. *So this is the way it's going to be. You told him you only wanted a one-night stand, Davi. Looks like you got it. He's moved on.*

Quinn took a seat across the table from Davi. He kept his eyes focused on her, his face expressionless. Davi struggled to keep her mind on the meeting.

Davi learned about the shooting schedule and the location shoots. They had found a farm in northern New York State that would do the trick for the majority of the film. If all went well, they hoped to start in November of this year for some harvest shots and then complete the rest in the next year. The release date was yet to be determined. Publicity appearances would work around that date as well.

"All right then, does anyone have questions?"

"I would like to thank all of you for wanting to make my story into a movie." Davi was most sincere. Her eyes began to tear up.

"Is this actually a true story, an autobiography? I can't believe all of this has happened to one person or to one family," one of the actors asked with disbelief.

"Yes, it's true."

Quinn spoke for the first time during the meeting. "I have a question. The ending in the book isn't the true ending to your story, is it? It's a great ending, but you didn't get married in real life. You're still single?"

"You are right. It's not the real ending, but I thought I had to give that ending to my readers. Is that all right with you?"

"Yes. Thank you."

"So if there are no more questions, we'll have a few pictures taken, and then we'll call it a day."

The studio photographer entered the room and arranged everyone for the photo. Quinn managed to get himself beside Davi. He stood as close to her as possible on her left side. His right arm hugged her waist, and his hand rested on her hip. His body heat was penetrating Davi's clothing. She was afraid of breaking into a sweat before the picture taking was finished. Her heart began to race. She could feel his arousal pressing against her left hip. The others gathered around them.

"Smile, everyone," the photographer sang. "Just one more . . ."

Davi tried not to faint. *What the hell is he doing?*

"Don't worry, love," he whispered in her ear, "I've got you."

"And we're done."

"Thanks, everyone, for coming. We'll see you in a few months."

"If Ms. Stuart doesn't have plans, I'd like to take her to lunch," Quinn announced.

Davi looked at Quinn with surprise. He ignored her through the entire meeting, and now he wanted to take her out? "That would be nice. Thank you." She smiled sweetly.

The producers didn't mind. Having their lead actor take out the author for lunch was great publicity. Everyone left the room slowly, most of them whispering about Quinn and his odd behavior. Quinn stayed next to Davi until his arousal abated.

"That was interesting," Quinn chuckled as the last person left the room.

"What were you thinking, Quinn!"

"I wasn't thinking anything. You know that part thinks all by itself." He smiled his wicked smile at her. Then with a serious tone, he said, "You left me. Why?"

"I had this meeting."

"Your note made me think you didn't want to see me again."

"Last night was a great fantasy for me. I'm not expecting anything else from you."

"What about what I expect? What I want?" His voice betrayed the longing he was trying to conceal.

"Don't," Davi said as she touched his lips with her finger. "Don't ask me to fall in love with you. I can't do that."

Quinn stared at her for the longest time, as though he were willing her to change her mind. Davi stared back at him, challenging him.

"I won't ask you, but you will fall in love with me, Davina Stuart," he said with conviction.

"What makes you so sure of yourself, Quinn Thomas?" She didn't dare look away from him.

"Because I know in here," he said as he touched his chest over his heart. "And I know here," he said as he pointed to his head. Quinn didn't wait for Davi to respond. "I'd like you to meet someone."

"Don't tell me it's your mother," Davi deadpanned as Quinn took her hand and walked out of the building with her.

Quinn laughed.

"You're not going to answer me?"

"It's not my mother, not yet anyway. She lives in Boston."

"Quinn, this isn't funny." Davi stopped when they reached his car. "This love-at-first-sight thing is not happening."

"Are you sure your name isn't Cleopatra?" Quinn asked her as he opened the passenger door of his black Porsche for her. "Because you sure are the queen of denial."

Quinn didn't wait for her answer. Once she was seated, he closed the door and walked around to the driver's door. Davi watched him as he moved. He was 100 percent man, sexual and confident. She had never met a man so sure of himself. She'd share his bed, but she wouldn't give him her heart, not now, not ever.

Quinn's phone buzzed.

Quinn answered it, "Hey, Luke. I found her. How about meeting at our usual place in about fifteen minutes? You're already there. Great. We're on our way." Quinn pocketed his phone and then drove out of the lot.

"So where are we off to, and who are we meeting?"

"We're going to Le Café. It's an outdoor eatery here in the city. It's not secluded, but the paparazzi aren't so bad here. We're meeting up with Luke. He's my best friend and my manager. We usually have lunch together on Saturdays."

Quinn maneuvered the Porsche expertly through the heavy traffic.

"Why didn't you tell me you were an author? You said you were a farmer."

"I am a farmer, one who happened to write a best seller. When and if I get my second story published, then I'll call myself an author. Until then, I'm just a farmer who writes."

"You are an author. *Second Harvest* is amazing."

"You said it was believable," Davi said, remembering the slight he had given her earlier.

"I was pissed," he said as he looked at her. "I thought you had lied to me."

"I don't lie." She could feel her face redden with indignation.

"Maybe not to others . . ."

Quinn didn't finish his statement as he brought the Porsche to a stop in front of the café. He was greeted on his side by the parking valet. Paparazzi lined the sidewalk. Quinn slid out of the driver's side and walked around to help Davi out of the car. Cameras were focused on him as he was bombarded with questions. He put his arm around Davi's waist and stopped to smile at the cameras. Davi didn't know where to look. There were cameras everywhere. The noise was unbelievable.

"Quinn! Who's with you? We haven't seen her before. Got a new lady friend?"

Quinn answered happily, "Be nice, guys. This is D. L. Stuart. She wrote *Second Harvest*. She's here for a visit, and we're having lunch." With that said, Quinn turned and led Davi into the café.

They were led to a table where Luke waited for them. Luke got up as they approached. "Hello!" He held out his hand to her.

"Hi, I'm Davi Stuart." Davi smiled as she squeezed Luke's hand. She liked a man with a firm handshake.

"Luke, this is Davi, the love of my life," Quinn said seriously.

"Quinn!" Davi admonished him. "Don't say that."

"It's true."

"Hold on here, you two. Fill me in on what's going on."

Luke offered a chair to Davi. "Sit down and start at the beginning. Don't leave out any details."

Davi sat down and took a long drink of water from her glass.

"I've already ordered a bottle of wine for us. I hope you don't mind. I ordered our usual, Quinn. Do you like red, Davina?"

"Davi, please, Luke. Yes, red is fine," she answered.

Their waiter appeared with three glasses and a bottle of wine. He uncorked the bottle and poured them each a glass. "I'll be back to take your order in a few minutes."

"May I propose a toast?" Luke asked. "To love at first sight. May our eyes always be open to see it and our hearts open to accept it."

"You told him?" Davi sputtered as she glared at Quinn. "Are you insane?"

"Sorry, Luke," Quinn said dryly. "I didn't mention that I'm the only one in love right now. Davi's holding out on me."

"Excuse me?" Luke asked before he took a drink from his glass.

"She only wants to have hot and heavy sex with me."

Luke choked on his drink. "What?"

"I fell in love with this woman as soon as I sat beside her on the plane, and she won't believe me. Her late husband could fall in love with her at first sight, but apparently no other man can." Quinn downed his glass of wine and motioned for the waiter to bring another bottle.

"What's wrong with just wanting sex?" Davi asked as she kept her emotions in check. *What game is he playing?*

"You should want more for yourself, Davi. You're bright and beautiful and the sexiest woman I've ever known. You deserve to be loved."

"You're right. I deserve to be loved, but it doesn't mean that I want to be loved. I don't need the heartbreak. It's my choice."

"What heartbreak? Being widowed again?" Quinn asked, surprised at her answer.

Quinn looked at Luke and explained, "Davi wrote *Second Harvest*."

"I thought I recognized your name." Luke smiled. "Great book, and it's going to be a great movie."

"Thank you."

"So is that why?" Quinn pressed her. "Is that why you don't want us to fall in love? Are you afraid of losing me?"

"No. That's not it." *Let's not go there,* Davi prayed. *Drop it, Quinn.*

She could tell he was getting pissed. The man had a short fuse, at least that's what she had read in the celebrity magazines. Davi didn't have a fuse. It took a lot to get her to blow, and Quinn was doing his best to get her to do just that.

"Is he the only man who could ever love you like you deserved? Was he so damned special?"

"Hey, you two, why don't we order lunch? Then can we start at the beginning. I'm lost here." Luke knew his friend all too well. In another minute, he would be swarmed by the paparazzi, eager to broadcast his latest public outburst.

Davi ignored Luke. She was mad now. If Quinn didn't care where they had this conversation, then neither would she.

"No, Quinn, I deserved better than what I got. I deserved to have a husband who loved me completely. I deserved to have a husband who was faithful and who came home to me every night. I didn't deserve a husband who bedded anyone who was willing and able. But that's what I got, and I won't be pressured into making the same mistake."

Davi reached for her glass and downed its contents. Their waiter arrived immediately to refresh it with a new bottle. Quinn sat back in his chair, staring at Davi while Luke gave their lunch order to their waiter.

"We'll have three burgers with everything." Luke looked at Davi. "It's what we always have."

"That's fine." Davi waved off their waiter.

"Is your book a lie?"

"Of course it's not a lie! Everything I wrote about happened. We loved each other, and we were damned good at raising our kids and running a business together. I loved him, but it wasn't enough to keep him faithful. Do you think I'd write about that in the book? For Pete's sake, Quinn, not even my kids know about it!"

"Was he always unfaithful?" Luke asked, now curious for details.

"No. He cheated on me once when we were first married, and then he cheated on me six months before he died." *What the hell*, Davi thought, *might as well get it all out in the open.*

"How did you know he was cheating?"

"He smelled of White Diamonds when he'd come back to me. I only wear Hypnotic. It's easy to tell the two fragrances apart."

"Why did you stay with him?" Quinn asked roughly. "Why would you put up with it?"

"I didn't put up with it. I gave him a choice, counseling or the divorce court. He chose counseling. We were working on our marriage when he died."

"Did you forgive him?"

"I was working on it."

"I'm sorry," Quinn apologized as he took Davi's hand.

"What for?"

"For not being there to kick his ass for you. He was an idiot for cheating on you. He didn't know what he had."

Davi smiled appreciatively at Quinn. "He did know what he had, Quinn. That's the sad part. He knew what he had, and he still couldn't help himself."

The waiter arrived with their meals.

Davi groaned when she saw the size of her burger. "I can't eat all of this. Do you guys have this every Saturday?"

"What's the problem?" Quinn asked.

"I'd have to slaughter a cow every other month to keep you two fed!"

Davi picked at her burger as she thought about what Quinn had said.

"Thank you for wanting to kick his ass. I think you would have set Ross straight if he'd met you."

"I might have killed him," Quinn said with complete seriousness.

"That wouldn't have been good for you. I'd hate to be responsible for ruining your movie career," she teased.

"Not to mention mine," Luke added. "He's my best client!"

"I'm your only client, asshole," Quinn laughed.

"Isn't that what I said?" Luke laughed back. "So, Davi, does that mean you're a big fan of Quinn's?"

"I love his movies. I think he's a very talented actor, but I wouldn't say I'm a big fan of his."

"Really?" Quinn asked, curious by her response. "I thought you knew everything about me. You told me not to tell you things that were posted on my Web site. You told me you and your daughter watched my movies every month."

Davi could feel her blush. She was never good at lying.

"You told me you fantasized about me. Hot and heavy, soaked with sweat and totally exhausted. That's what you begged for last night."

Davi put her finger over his lips. "Quinn, we don't kiss and tell."

"I love you," he said softly, his gaze burning into hers. "I know you don't want me to but I do."

"Please don't." She couldn't look away from him. His eyes were so blue.

"Okay, I'll shut up about it if you let me date you for the rest of the weekend. Let me give you the fantasy you've always wanted. If nothing else, I'll have the memories from this weekend."

"Is that a line from one of your movies, Quinn?" Luke teased. "I'm sure I heard it from somewhere."

"You can always be replaced," Quinn mumbled.

"I'd love to have another date with you," she said softly as his gaze still held her captive.

"We can have dessert back at my hotel suite. I have chocolate and raspberries."

Chapter 6

♥

It didn't take long to get back to the hotel. Quinn parked his Porsche without incident from the paparazzi. They entered the penthouse elevator, and within seconds, they were behind the closed doors of Quinn's suite.

The chocolate and raspberries remained untouched. A trail of clothing led from the suite entranceway to the bedroom. Quinn and Davi lay facing each other on the bed, their fingers tracing invisible patterns on each other. Each stroke sent a sexual tingle through their bodies. Davi's hand slowly worked its way down to Quinn's arousal. She stroked him gently.

"That feels so good," he murmured. "Keep going."

Davi kissed Quinn long and hard. "Mmm, you taste so good. I want to taste you all over." She slid down his body and took him into her mouth. Her tongue worked its way over his tip and down his shaft. He tasted delicious, and she let him know it by her moans.

Quinn dug his hands into her hair. His body rocked with the pleasure he was receiving. "Harder, woman, harder," he begged.

Davi worked her tongue and lips expertly on him, encouraged by his moans of pleasure. She could tell he was about to climax. She released him and gazed up into his eyes.

"I want you. Now," he groaned.

Davi reached for the last of the condoms and put it on Quinn. She straddled him and let herself down onto him. His heat penetrated her, and she shuddered from it. She rode him slowly as she leaned over him to kiss his mouth. Their tongues touched and tasted each other. Davi pulled away and let her breasts touch Quinn's lips. He pulled on her nipples and suckled them. His hands clamped on to her buttocks, pushing his cock deeper into her. Davi's excitement rose, bringing her close to the edge. With a loud moan, Quinn climaxed, and she came soon after. She lay down on him and sighed and then slid off him and removed the condom.

"Amazing," Quinn sighed softly as he closed his eyes and reached for her. "Come here, woman."

Davi nestled into Quinn's waiting arms. Her fantasies never felt like this, the feeling of being safe and loved. Davi closed her eyes. *Don't think of love.* She pulled away from Quinn. "I'm ready for some real dessert, but I think I'll have a shower first."

"Good idea. I'll put the coffee on, and then I'll join you."

Davi slipped out of bed and made her way to the bathroom. The shower was enormous. It was all glass and tile. It could easily hold six people, not that she thought Quinn ever tried that, but she would ask him. On the wall, there was a stereo panel. Davi turned it on. Davi turned the shower on and stood under the cascade of cold water falling from the ceiling like a waterfall. She closed her eyes and enjoyed the sensation as she moved slowly to the music.

"What the hell!" Quinn yelled as he felt the cold water on his skin.

Davi screamed from being startled.

"The water's freezing, Davi. What are you doing?"

"Sorry, Quinn," Davi apologized. "I like cold showers." She quickly turned the dial to hot. "Let me warm you up," she cooed as she wrapped her arms around him and kissed him softly. "Feeling warmer?"

"Almost," Quinn grumbled.

She ran her hands over his body and stopped at his cock. "That water was cold, wasn't it?" She laughed as she looked at his shrunken member. "We'll have to fix that, won't we?"

"Please do," he encouraged her.

Davi knelt down and took Quinn into her mouth, working on him slowly. The hot water fell gently over them. Quinn relaxed and leaned against the glass wall. Davi took all of him into her mouth, applying the right amount of pressure to inflame his arousal. Her tongue worked on him as her hands massaged his shaft and scrotum. Quinn's hands grabbed on to Davi's hair and pushed her down further onto him. Her throat took all of him as she sucked harder. She worked with a steady rhythm, and Quinn moved his hips to match hers. Davi could hear a deep moan coming from the back of Quinn's throat. He was getting closer. She could feel Quinn tense for his release. Davi swallowed and then rose up to meet Quinn's waiting mouth.

"I love you," he gasped as he broke away from her kiss. "I know you don't want me to, but I do."

Davi buried her head into his chest and closed her eyes as she fought back tears of regret.

Quinn took Davi out for a walk for some evening sightseeing. Quinn liked the evening. It gave him a better chance of being unnoticed, free from fans and paparazzi. They came across an outdoor cinema/restaurant where one of Quinn's movies was playing.

"Come on, Quinn. Let's see it. It will be fun," Davi begged as she pulled on his sleeve.

"It will be embarrassing. I don't like to see myself on-screen."

"For me, please? It's a beautiful night. We can have something to eat while we're watching it. It will be a perfect ending to our second date."

"How can I say no to you, woman?"

"Don't start now." She gave him a quick kiss.

Davi allowed Quinn to pick a table that was out of the way from the main dining crowd but was still in good viewing distance of the gigantic video screen. He sat with his back to the screen. He looked uncomfortable, but Davi was determined to get him to relax.

"Let's order some drinks, Quinn. What would you like?"

"Do we have to sit through the whole thing? If so, I'll start with a double scotch."

Their waiter approached them and recognized Quinn immediately. "What a wonderful surprise! It's so nice of you to join us tonight, Mr. Thomas. I guess you know that we're playing one of your films tonight. It's one of my favorites—*The Engagement*."

"Thanks. We'll both have a double scotch, single malt, no ice." Quinn was polite but didn't want to talk to anyone.

"I'll be back with your menus."

Davi looked around the dining area. They were being watched, and she could see whispering going on, but no one was about to intrude on them. That was a relief.

The waiter came back with their drinks and handed them the menus. "The special for tonight is our Quinn Special."

Quinn choked on his drink. "Oh my god, what is it?"

"Strip sirloin steak with potato of choice, garlic mushrooms, and mixed green salad."

"We can't say no to that, Quinn." Davi smiled at the waiter. "I'll have mine medium well, please, with fries."

"Make mine rare, please. And bring another round of drinks while you're at it."

The lights dimmed and the opening credits began to show on the screen.

Davi motioned for Quinn to move his chair beside hers. "Please," she asked sweetly. He obeyed reluctantly.

"This is my favorite of your movies. You are such a stud. The first time I saw this, as soon as I got home from the theater, I had to run to my bedroom and pull out my vibrator."

Quinn choked on his drink again. "Are you trying to kill me tonight? I can't believe you said that!"

"It's true, and I thought you might enjoy hearing it." Davi whispered lustfully in Quinn's ear, "Maybe I could count it as the first time I had sex with you without knowing I would be having sex with you eventually. That would mean that I've had sex with you more times than you've had sex with me."

Quinn turned his head to face Davi, giving her a wry smile. "I don't think that counts, but it's an interesting idea."

"Doesn't count by whose rules? In my book, I think it counts, and I so beat you in that category then."

It was Quinn's turn to whisper in Davi's ear. "That movie's been out for a year and a half now, so if you use that logic, my jacking-off while fantasizing about the love of my life beats you without question. You've been my fantasy for as long as I can remember, and I can remember for a very long time. Don't you see that's why it was love at first sight when you sat down beside me on the plane? I knew who you were."

Her heart skipped a beat. She turned to Quinn and said, "You had to say that."

"It's the truth and you know it."

The waiter appeared with their meals and then made a hasty retreat. Davi laughed through the movie and held Quinn's hand through the sad parts. Through the corner of her eye, she caught him smiling during some of the scenes. At other times, his hand covered his eyes as he cursed quietly.

"I can't believe I did this," Quinn groaned as the final credits ran. He looked at Davi, who was wiping tears from her eyes. "You're crying? Why?" He tried not to laugh at her.

"I always cry at this ending. It gets to me." Davi sniffled. "But it's a good cry."

"What can I do for you?"

"Keep making those movies and I'll be happy." Davi kissed Quinn on his cheek.

Quinn paid the bill, and the couple made their way back to the hotel.

"I don't want to be out too late, and we have a busy day tomorrow."

"Oh? What are we doing tomorrow?"

"I'm showing you the sights. Now let's get going. We have one more stop to make on the way back to the hotel."

"Where's that?"

"The drugstore. We're out of condoms. Remember?"

Chapter 7

♥

The next morning, Davi awoke alone. She could hear the shower. She looked at the bedside clock. It was 8:00 a.m. Davi couldn't remember what time she finally went to sleep last night. Quinn had kept her very busy. He wanted to try out the assortment of condoms he had purchased at the drugstore. He hated wearing them, but if he had to, he was going to make it enjoyable for both of them. Davi got out of bed and headed for the bathroom. She could see the steam escaping from the shower.

She opened the door. "Mind if I join you?"

"Of course you can," he said as he gave her a welcoming smile.

"Have you ever had a party in here, Quinn? This shower is enormous."

"I never thought about it, Davi. We could have our own little party now, if you want." Quinn winked playfully at her.

How she loved that wink. "I'm afraid I'm all partied out from last night. I'm surprised I can walk this morning. You were very naughty last night."

"But was I good?" he asked as he pulled her in close to him.

"You were better than good." She kissed him on the mouth. "Excellent, I'd say." She reached for the bar of soap and began to wash Quinn. She started at his back from his shoulders down to his round, hard buttocks. "You have a nice bum," she told him. Then she washed between his legs and moved to his front. Davi was greeted by a huge erection. She batted at it. "I haven't finished washing you yet."

"I already did the front," he told her.

"Then you can do me now," she said as she handed him the soap. "Mind turning the water down a bit? It's really hot. This is when his-and-hers showers would come in handy."

"No his and hers, woman!" Quinn bristled at her suggestion. "You'll just have to get used to slightly warmer water, and I'll get used to it being cooler. It's called compromise."

Quinn turned the dial down slightly. He proceeded to wash Davi. He started at her breasts and gently massaged them with the bar of soap. Then he rubbed the soap down to her belly and between her legs. Davi opened her legs for him. He gave her sex special attention. Davi moaned at the sensation. Quinn moved to her back and started at her shoulder blades, working his way down to her buttocks.

"You have a beautiful bum," he murmured. "And your legs just keep on going."

Quinn put the bar of soap in the soap tray and held Davi from behind. He massaged her breasts and nibbled on her ear. His arousal pressed against her back. Davi moaned with pleasure. He dropped one hand and touched her between her legs. His fingers played with her folds, searching for the nub that gave her so much pleasure. Davi gasped when he found it. Her hips backed into him. Quinn pressed harder into her back. Davi flattened her palms against the shower wall to give her support as she let Quinn press against her. She ached for Quinn to be inside her, but she couldn't take the risk. Quinn brought himself close to her opening.

"No, Quinn, please don't," she cautioned.

"Damn it, Davi."

He continued to make love to Davi with his hand as he made use of her buttocks and back. She gave him so much pleasure he could hardly contain himself. He waited for her orgasm before he released himself.

Quinn brought his lips to Davi's neck and kissed her. "I love you, woman."

Quinn released her and then left the shower, leaving Davi alone.

You're an idiot, she argued with herself. *Why won't you love him? Because loving him could be the worst mistake I've ever made. Or the best mistake you'll ever make. Did you consider that?*

Quinn took Davi to Macy's and Bloomingdales. He acted as if he were a child let loose in a toy store, looking at and touching everything.

Davi couldn't help but share in his excitement. Quinn had that effect on her.

"Isn't there anything you want, Davi? Something I can buy for you?" he asked excitedly.

"No. I'm fine, Quinn. I don't need anything. I just like to look."

"Are you sure? I really want to get you something, something to remind you of me."

"I don't think I'll be forgetting you." She laughed. "I think you've made that almost impossible."

"I've got an idea. Come on, let's go."

Quinn took her hand and led her through the mall. He stopped when he reached the store.

"Promise me you won't put up a fuss?" Quinn looked down at her with his blue bedroom eyes, working his Quinn magic.

"I don't like promising when I don't know what it is for."

"It will be fun. Trust me, please. Promise me you'll be good."

"Okay. I promise," she said reluctantly.

Davi looked up over Quinn's shoulder and read the store's sign, Victoria's Secret. "Quinn, no, you wouldn't." Davi could feel the blush come to her cheeks.

"Come on, Davi, you promised," Quinn encouraged her as he practically dragged her into the store.

The store manager spotted Quinn and greeted him instantly, "Hello, Mr. Thomas. It's a pleasure to have you visit our store. Is there anything I can help you with today?" She took a long look at Davi and smiled sweetly at her.

"Hello. I'm not quite sure what we're looking for," Davi said softly, trying to hide her embarrassment.

"Why don't you tell me your size and we'll show you a variety of our lingerie. I'm sure you'll find something that you like."

"My bra size is thirty-six D, though you may want to take my measurements. I'm a size eight to ten, and I like my bottoms on the large side just for comfort."

"Excellent. Thank you. Come with me and I'll show you a few things." She looked at Quinn. "Mr. Thomas, would you like to come with us or have a seat over there, and we'll let you know when we have a selection ready?"

Davi gave Quinn the look that warned him to sit.

"I think I'll go sit over there and wait." Quinn excused himself and left.

Davi followed the manager around the store as she pulled items off the rack and held them up to her. "You're in very good shape, my dear. You can really show off your assets in most of our lingerie. Is there anything in particular that you want?"

"Thank you."

The manager's compliments put Davi at ease. Quinn thought she was beautiful too. What more did she need to build her confidence to try on lingerie?

"I really don't know what I want, but let's just see what works, if you don't mind, and maybe one or two things for fun."

"That's the spirit, dear."

Davi was intrigued with the chosen lingerie and was eager to try on the selection.

"Now do you want privacy while you try these on, or does Mr. Thomas get to see you model them?"

"Oh, this is all for him. I don't mind if he wants to have a look."

Davi and the manager approached Quinn, who was busy chatting to a couple of the sales girls who quickly left as they saw their employer near.

"Having fun, Quinn?"

"I will now. Do you have something to show me?"

"Mr. Thomas, if you'll come with us. We have a private fitting room where you can view our selection."

They were led to a closed-off section of the store. Davi's selection was hung neatly on a rack in a spacious fitting room. Quinn was ushered to a large armchair outside of the fitting room.

"I'll leave you two alone. If you need anything, press the button here, and I'll be right with you."

Quinn made himself comfortable. His eyes were on fire.

"I like this chair. Front-row seat. Perfect."

"I don't trust you, Quinn. This could be very dangerous for me."

"I promise not to ravish you while we are in the store. However, I will not promise anything for what happens when we get back to the hotel. Is that good enough?"

"Yes. You stay there. I'll be right out."

Davi looked at the items, most of which were extremely revealing. She was so glad that she had gone to the spa before she came out to California. There were no unwanted hairs anywhere. She'd have to thank Maggie once again for taking her there.

She tried on what she called safe lingerie. They were pretty and feminine, but nothing that screamed sex. Quinn liked what he saw and behaved like the perfect gentleman as she modeled for him. Then Davi tried on a black pleated baby doll with very skimpy panties. Davi opened the curtain.

"Wow."

"You like it?"

"What's not to like?"

"It comes in a burgundy, if you prefer."

"No. Black is perfect on you. It goes in the keep pile."

Davi could see the bulge in Quinn's jeans. She scooted back into the fitting room to give him time to recover. She took the next item off the rack.

"Oh god," she mumbled to herself. "Please give me strength."

This item was truly revealing. It was a cutout teddy that barely covered the breasts and then ran down the torso in a narrow piece only to join with a very skimpy thong. It was surprisingly easy to get into. Davi knew that it wouldn't be hard to get off. She only hoped it would last for more than one wearing.

Davi pulled back the curtain and met Quinn's lusty stare. He got up from his chair quickly and took her in his arms.

"Let's do it now, woman. You've driven me to the edge." His mouth came down hard on hers. He forced her mouth open and plunged his tongue into her mouth. Davi sighed as she welcomed the invasion. Quinn's hands caressed Davi's body. Davi felt Quinn's arousal through his jeans. She broke away from him, pushing him back.

"No, Quinn. Behave. Save it for later, okay? Now let me get dressed. Be good and sit there and chill."

Quinn let out a deep growl as he fell back into the chair. Davi took her time changing. She had to give Quinn time to cool down. They couldn't walk out of there with Quinn's arousal pushing out of his pants. She had to take some pity on the man.

"There, I'm ready. You may purchase whatever you would like and surprise me with your choice. How does that sound?"

"Great. I can do that. I know exactly what I want."

"I bet you do," Davi chuckled and then gave him a kiss. "I'll get coffee for us at the coffee bar right across from here."

Davi ordered two coffees and a couple of muffins. She was hungry, and she was sure Quinn would want something. She settled in at a table and waited for Quinn. What she thought would take five or ten minutes took more than twenty. Davi was becoming concerned.

Then Quinn emerged from Victoria's Secret with not one bag but three large ones. At the same time, he was stopped by the paparazzi wanting to take his photo while they asked him what he had in the bags. Davi brought her hand to her mouth to stifle a laugh. Quinn's face reddened, and then he smiled as he spoke to the photographers. He posed for a couple of shots and then walked away. Davi waved to him.

"I won't ask you what's in there, Quinn," she said as she pointed to his purchases. "I'm sure I'll read about it or hear about it on television."

Quinn took a long drink of his cold coffee. "I thought I was going to die. Then I thought, 'What the hell,' and told them the truth. I hope you don't mind, love."

Davi choked on her muffin. "What did you tell them, Quinn? What was the truth?"

"That I bought them for my fiancée." Quinn looked seriously at Davi.

"Your fiancée? Why?"

"I figured that whoever bought you these outfits and expected to see you in them better be married to you or engaged to you."

"Because you bought lingerie for me? Are you crazy?"

"Not any kind of lingerie." He winked at her.

"We agreed, Quinn, to date this weekend, nothing more."

"Woman, stop lying to yourself. It's been more than a date since the moment we met. I knew it, and I know you did too. You just won't admit it."

Davi and Quinn stared into each other's eyes. Davi felt herself melting into him again. She felt warm and loved.

"I can't," she said weakly.

"I promise to love you forever. I will never cheat on you or break your heart. I will be your fantasy man every hour of every day if that's what you want. All I ask is that you love me. Marry me."

"I'm too old for you."

"You wear me out in bed, woman. You're not too old."

"Did I tell you about my best friend, Maggie?" Davi stroked Quinn's hand.

"Would she tell you to say yes?" Quinn took her hand and kissed it.

Davi smiled. "Maggie believes in reading cards. They guide her in life and have never steered her wrong. She read mine before I flew out to LA."

"Sounds interesting," he said cautiously. "She only reads the good stuff, right?"

Davi smiled. "Yes, only the good stuff. She told me I would find success and romance while I was out here."

"I like her cards."

"When I met you, I thought the romance meant sex. That's all I wanted. That's all I could possibly hope for."

"Why was it all you could hope for?"

"Look at me, Quinn. I'm older than you, much older. What could you possibly see in me to fall in love with?"

"Other than how great you are in bed?"

"Be serious."

"I love the way you laugh. I love the way you make me laugh. Your sense of humor is wicked and brutally honest."

"There will be a day when you won't laugh. You'll need more."

"I love the way you run your fingers through your hair when you're thinking. I love how your tongue pokes out of your mouth and licks your lips as you're reading. That was such a turn on when I first saw you."

"I can't always be reading."

"Davi, it's how you make me feel. You make me happy. I love everything about you. I want you in my life forever. Is it so wrong to want that?"

Davi closed her eyes. She knew she'd been fooling herself, trying to convince herself that it wasn't love. She knew she was in love with him. She loved everything about him too. He was more than a fantasy. Fantasies didn't keep her warm at night or hold her tight when the lovemaking was over. Fantasies didn't tell her they would love her forever.

Davi opened her eyes. "Ask me then," she said softly.

"Davina, my love, will you marry me? Will you be my wife forever?"

"Yes."

Quinn leaned over the table and kissed Davi on the lips. When he finally let go to take a breath, he noticed they were not alone.

"Davi, I think you'd better phone home. Your family may want to hear the news from you before it's on tonight's news."

Davi looked around at the crowd. She could feel herself blush as the crowd started to applaud. Was nothing private in Hollywood?

"I won't phone them from here."

"Okay, but we've got one more stop to make and then we're heading back to the hotel."

"Tell me it's the drugstore for some ibuprofen or the liquor store for a big bottle of scotch."

"I've got that stuff at my place. No, this next stop will take away the need for any pain medication. Let's go."

Fifteen minutes later, Davi and Quinn walked out of Tiffany's, with Davi wearing her diamond engagement ring.

Chapter 8

♥

Quinn and Davi made it back to their hotel in record time. Quinn's excitement from Davi's acceptance of his proposal was evident in his driving. Not that he was reckless but Davi had to remind him to slow down and watch for red lights all the way back. She was a nervous wreck by the time she got out of the car.

"I'm heading for the shower," she announced. "I need to unwind a bit before I call my kids."

They had already decided for a night in with pizza and beer. Quinn picked up the hotel phone and placed the order. Then smiling to himself, Quinn took the Victoria's Secret bags to the bedroom and carefully laid out one of his purchases on the bed before returning to the living room.

Davi could feel the fatigue leave her body and wash down the drain. If anyone had told her she would be engaged to marry Quinn Thomas, let alone any man, after only three days of knowing him, she would have said they were crazy. *I'm the one being crazy, crazy in love.* How the man made her smile and laugh. He made her feel beautiful again and loved. Quinn filled a void in her that she hadn't known existed. It was like not knowing you had a bruise until you banged it again and felt the pain. This bruise wasn't painful. It was quite the opposite. It was pleasurable and addictive. The more she was with Quinn, the more she realized she couldn't be without him. She hoped her kids would understand.

Davi dried herself off and then walked into the bedroom and saw the black cutout teddy lying on the bed. She laughed aloud seeing that he wanted her to wear it while eating pizza. She hoped it would last through one wearing.

Davi sat on the edge of the bed and phoned home. Tigger answered on the third ring.

"Hello?"

"Tigger, it's Mom."

"Mom! Is it true? Are you engaged to Quinn Thomas?" Her daughter shrieked at her over the phone.

"You heard?" Davi asked nervously as she raked her fingers through her hair.

"It's on the Internet, Mom. Is it true?"

"Yes, it's true. It's a long story."

"Do you love him, Mom?" Her daughter's voice was suddenly soft.

"Yes, I love him." Davi looked down and touched her new engagement ring.

"And he makes you happy?"

Davi sighed. "Yes. He makes me very happy."

"You need to be happy, Mom. It's time."

Davi felt like crying. When had her baby girl grown up?

"What about Cat and Rich?"

"They're not home, but I'm sure they'll be hearing about this very soon."

"Tell them I'll call them tomorrow, okay?"

"Okay, Mom. Give Quinn a hug from me. Tell him he better not 'fuck up.'"

"Tigger!"

"Mom, it's his line from *The Engagement*, remember?

Davi smiled. "Yes, I remember."

"Good night, Mom. I love you."

"Love you back."

The pizza and beer had been delivered. Quinn sat in an armchair, waiting for Davi. He liked this, sitting and waiting for her. He loved the anticipation. After finally finding the woman of his dreams, he didn't mind waiting for her, knowing that she was coming to him.

Davi walked in quietly and stopped in front of him. "If this doesn't survive tonight, I'll be very upset."

"Don't worry, love, I bought more than one." Quinn smiled as he pulled Davi down onto him. He kissed her long and hard. She tasted sweet. He breathed in her scent as he held her close. "It's time to finish what we started back at the store."

Quinn stood up and carried Davi in his arms to the bedroom. Davi had already pulled back the comforter.

"Looks like you were thinking the same thing, love," he whispered in her ear as he placed her on the bed.

Davi melted into Quinn. His kisses were hot everywhere they touched her. His loving hands caressed every part of her, especially her long legs. She sighed as he caressed the soft flesh of her inner thighs. She was ready for him. Davi was amazed at how quickly her body responded to Quinn. She wove her hands through his hair and pulled him closer. Their kiss was long and deep. Quinn rolled onto his back and pulled Davi with him so that she was straddling him.

"Let me look at you." His blue eyes burned into her.

Davi didn't take her eyes off Quinn. She felt a blush coming on. His face was serious, and his eyes were filled with love. Davi caught her breath. She could see his heart in his eyes. She finally understood what Quinn had told her on the airplane.

Davi's hands went to Quinn's chest, and she massaged his nipples until they were hard. Then she leaned over and playfully suckled them. Quinn moaned with pleasure. She could feel him throbbing underneath her. Davi moved her hips slowly over Quinn's hardness. The silk from the teddy was soft and slippery against him. A moan escaped from further down Quinn's throat.

Quinn reached for Davi's breasts and massaged them through the silkiness of the teddy. Her nipples were already hard and erect.

Davi moaned with pleasure. "I didn't know shopping could be so much fun," she whispered.

"Welcome to my fantasy, woman," Quinn whispered back.

"Nice fantasy."

Their bodies rocked together. Quinn held off as long as he could before he peeled the teddy off Davi. It was surprisingly easy for his large hands. Davi smiled as she watched him remove the delicate garment.

"I thought you said you had more, just in case," she teased.

"I know, but this is the practice one, just in case." He winked at her. Quinn reached for the box of condoms on the bedside table. He pulled out a package and tore it open. "Now that we're engaged, I shouldn't need this."

"We'll talk about it later. Put it on, Quinn."

Davi raised her hips to allow Quinn to enter her. He shuddered at her heat. He moved in and out with a deliberate slowness, putting pressure on just the right spot. He could feel Davi respond to him. She moved with his thrusts and arched her back. Her hands dug into Quinn's thighs. Quinn lost himself in her. She had that power over him. Their rocking became faster and harder, each of them building up to that final moment when they came together. Davi collapsed onto Quinn, his arms wrapped around her. Silence enveloped them for the longest time.

Davi remembered the condom. "Quinn," she poked him, "the condom." She rolled off him and peeled it off. "I think we're okay."

Quinn groaned.

"I phoned home and spoke with Tigger."

"What did she say?" Quinn held his breath, waiting to hear her reaction.

"Don't 'fuck up' and that's a direct quote."

Quinn laughed. "She won't quote all of my movie lines to me, will she?"

"I have no idea."

They got out of bed and dressed. Within minutes, they were sitting on the sofa with their pizza and beer.

Davi reached for the television's remote. "Mind if we watch a late movie? We haven't really dated until we stay up late and watch a movie together."

"What kind of movie?"

"A horror movie in black and white would be good."

"Why horror?"

"So I can hold on to you and bury my face in your shoulder when the scary parts come on. You hold me close, and we cuddle all through the movie. It's a great date."

"You've done this before?"

"Never. That's why I want to do it with you. This whole weekend has been a fantasy. I might as well have another one."

Quinn's phone rang. Quinn picked it up from the table.

"Luke, it's late. What's up?" There was a long silence. "Thanks, man. I think she's finally convinced. She's wearing my ring." Quinn rubbed his finger gently over the ring on her finger. He chuckled as Luke said something. "We should be in bed, but we're on a date. We're watching an old horror movie in black and white. Davi's nails are digging into my skin, and she's holding on tight." Quinn laughed. "It's her fantasy date, man. She wants this." Quinn listened to Luke. "Tomorrow? It's short notice. Hold on."

He looked at Davi. "Will you change your plans and fly with me to New York tomorrow? The studio needs me back ASAP. Luke will look after your ticket."

"I have to get home, Quinn."

"You'll head home from New York on Monday. You'll even get home earlier than if you left from here and flew direct."

"Sure, why not?"

"Luke, go ahead. Davi's fine with it. So let me know when we're flying out. Talk to you later."

Quinn pulled Davi in tight. "Thanks for coming with me. I'm not ready to say good-bye."

They continued to watch the movie until Quinn's phone rang again.

"Hey, Luke. What time's the flight? Eight a.m. Ben will be here at six to pick us up. Got it. Thanks. Good night."

"I guess we'd better get packed," suggested Davi. "Unless you want to watch the rest of the movie."

"I've seen it before."

"Me too. The ending sucks."

"Then why are we watching it?"

"I told you. It was a fantasy of mine. You played your role as the protective boyfriend very well. Thank you." Davi kissed him on the forehead.

"You dug your nails into me. I'm going to have scars." Quinn watched Davi's face. "You weren't even scared."

"But you liked being there for me, didn't you, Quinn? You liked being my protector. You liked my fantasy. Admit it."

"You're wicked."

Davi turned off the television. "I'd better get back to my room and pack my stuff. It's a good thing I don't have much. Well, at least I didn't until someone bought me a lot of lingerie."

"I'll come with you," Quinn offered as he stood up. "You shouldn't walk the halls alone at this hour." Quinn led Davi out the door to the elevator. "I haven't seen your room. I'd like to know what the studio provided for you."

They walked into the elevator. Quinn pushed the button for Davi's floor.

"I think it's nice, but then I haven't spent much time in it. I don't think it compares to the penthouse."

The elevator door opened, and Quinn led Davi to her room. He held out his hand for her key, took it, and then swiped the lock. He opened the door for Davi to enter.

"After you."

"Yes, it doesn't compare to your place," Davi teased. "At least in looks, but we can always try out the bed for a final comparison." Davi stood beside the bed and looked up at Quinn. "It's my room, my bed, my way. Are you up for it?" Davi held out a condom package.

"Davina Stuart," Quinn said with a voice low and lustful, "you really are wicked."

He unzipped his jeans.

"Quinn Thomas, you are mine, now, right here." Davi pulled off her T-shirt, unzipped her jeans, and kicked them off. "We have a bed to mess up."

Davi was true to her word. She made love to Quinn her way. She kept him on the edge for what seemed like an eternity. Every time Quinn was ready to come, Davi would change positions and do something different to him. She made his body feel things he never dreamed possible. Finally, Quinn begged for release, and Davi obliged him. Quinn collapsed on the bed in a sweat.

Davi smiled triumphantly at her exhausted lover. "Poor Quinn," she teased as she got out of bed.

Davi packed her bag quickly. There wasn't much to pack—her gym gear, her dresses and shoes, and a few items of underwear and shirts.

"I'm ready."

"I'm not. What's your shower like?"

"Small, if I remember correctly."

"Let's try it out."

"I only brought one condom."

"I brought one too." Quinn got out of bed and pulled a condom out of his jeans pocket. Quinn took Davi by the hand and led her to the bathroom.

"There's no room, Quinn. It's a small tub."

"We'll fit," he promised.

Quinn turned on the water and let it run until it was warm. He took Davi into his arms and kissed her. Instantly, Davi could feel his arousal press against her belly.

"You're fast," she murmured.

"You're hot," he replied.

He put the condom on and helped Davi into the shower. He lifted her up so that her legs wrapped around his waist. Her arms wrapped around his neck as his hands supported her weight at the hips. Quinn guided his length into Davi.

"I like your shower better," she said. "There is more to hang on to, and yours has a stereo."

"This one will do."

Quinn kissed Davi long and hard. His thrusts pushed deep within her. Davi moaned softly into Quinn. She squeezed him tight between her legs. Her hands found his hair, her fingers weaving through it, pulling gently on him. The warm water ran over her back. Davi's skin tingled from Quinn's touch. She pulled him in closer.

"I love you," she moaned as she climaxed.

Quinn's thrusts increased harder and longer. Davi closed her eyes and held on tight. Quinn responded by tightening his grip on her. She gasped as his fingers dug into her buttocks. Davi didn't try to move. Quinn had her pinned to his body. She held on for the rest of the ride. Quinn moaned into Davi's ear as he climaxed. Davi kissed Quinn's shoulder and nipped him gently. A long sigh escaped from Quinn, and then he released her and let her feet touch the floor. He continued to hold her close. Davi could hear his heart beating. She loved the sound. He kissed her softly and then remembered to take the condom off. He opened the shower door and threw the used condom into the trashcan.

"I hate these things," he said with disgust. "They take the spontaneity out of lovemaking, love."

Davi laughed. "What's more spontaneous than what we just did?"

"When you're on something, I'll show you spontaneous, woman."

Chapter 9

♥

The drive to the airport was quiet. Davi and Quinn were exhausted from their long night. When they finally made their way back to his suite, Quinn thought of more ways to make love. Despite Davi's pleas for sleep, Quinn convinced her that she could always sleep on the plane and making love was more important. Davi got her revenge when a very tired Quinn stepped into the shower with her and the water was ice cold.

Davi didn't fully appreciate what Quinn had to go through every time he went to the airport. Despite Quinn's warnings to her, it was a real eye-opener. Ben, Quinn's driver and security guard, parked the limo and escorted the couple through the airport. Ben was heavier than Quinn by about seventy-five pounds and taller by two inches. He navigated the airport like a Mack truck pushing through the crowd.

Quinn was without his usual shield for getting through the airport. Gone were his hooded jacket and baggy clothes. He was dressed in dress pants, shirt, and jacket. He and Davi made an attractive couple, with Davi wearing the dress that first caught Quinn's eye. Quinn had his arm around Davi's waist as they walked close behind Ben. The paparazzi and various fans moved around them, pushing for a closer look. Airport security was having a difficult time holding back the crowd. Someone was going to get hurt. Camera flashes were everywhere, and the noise level was painful.

Quinn told Ben to stop.

"Hey, guys," he called out to the mob, "let us get checked in and I promise I'll give you some time. Just let us get through, okay?"

The mob calmed down enough so that the couple could make it to the airline's kiosk. Airport security ushered them to the front of the line. The paperwork was all in order. Davi and Quinn were given their boarding passes.

Quinn whispered to Davi, "Do you mind giving a quick interview to keep the fans happy?"

"Not at all. Lead the way."

Quinn led Davi off to an open area. Ben stayed with them. The mob quickly enclosed them.

"Okay, guys, you've got ten minutes before we have to leave. If this works out, I promise we'll do this again next time. If there is any trouble, there will be no second chance."

The crowd got quiet. Davi could feel the tension leaving Quinn's body.

"As you know, D. L. Stuart and I became engaged yesterday. We are extremely happy. Her book, *Second Harvest*, is being made into a movie, and filming will begin in November. I am fortunate to have a role in the movie, and I hope I do it justice. Thank you."

"Davina, will you say something to the press?" yelled out a reporter.

Quinn gave Davi a squeeze for encouragement.

"What would you like to know?"

"What's it like nabbing Hollywood's most eligible bachelor?"

"I didn't know he was the most eligible bachelor," she answered. "And I don't think I nabbed him. He nabbed me. He really took me by surprise."

"So you don't consider yourself a cougar then?"

Davi felt Quinn tense. "No, I'm not a cougar. A cougar is someone who actively hunts a younger male and uses everything she has to get him. Correct? I definitely did not hunt Quinn, nor have I been on the prowl for any man. If anything, I was pursued by Quinn. He's the hunter." Davi winked at Quinn.

"Okay, that's it for questions. I'll sign a few autographs. Then we have to go." Quinn was seething. How dare someone call Davi a cougar? Davi's composure when answering the question was the only thing that kept him from losing it. He couldn't wait to get her away from the crowd.

"That cougar comment was uncalled for, Davi. I apologize," Quinn said to her as they walked away.

"It was bound to come out sooner or later. People are going to think that about me, Quinn. It is obvious that I am older than you are. I'm okay with it. I learned that from you."

"I love you, woman."

"I love you too."

Once on the plane and settled in their seats, Davi said to Quinn, "Do you realize that I don't have a comeback for you calling me 'woman'? Quinn is the only thing I can think of that sounds manly enough for you."

"I've got one I'd love to hear you call me, but you can't use it yet."

"Tell me."

"No. When the time is right, you'll come up with it all by yourself." Quinn gave her another of his winks and then kissed her on the forehead.

Soon after takeoff, breakfast was served. Davi was more tired than hungry. She gave her croissant to Quinn and passed on the coffee. She needed to sleep. Quinn called for the attendant to take their trays away.

"Come, cuddle with me, love, and go to sleep." Quinn opened his arms to Davi, and she nestled into his chest. She was asleep instantly.

Davi woke to soft kisses on her forehead. She opened her eyes to see Quinn's gorgeous face looking down at her.

"You've slept through the flight. We're getting ready to land."

Quinn's security met them at the arrival gate. They formed a protective circle around the couple and escorted them out to the waiting limo. This time, the paparazzi and fans were brushed off. Quinn didn't have the time to stop for them.

Davi and Quinn slid into the backseat. Jake, Quinn's head of security in New York, got in behind the steering wheel and drove off.

"How are you, Jake? Anything new happen?"

"Nothing much when compared to what you've been up to."

"Quinn, you haven't introduced us," Davi reminded him.

"Oh, sorry. Jake, this is Davi. Davi, this is Jake. He's one of my best friends. He's also my driver and head of security. He's the best."

"It's nice to meet you, Jake."

"Same here, Davi. You're even prettier in person."

"Thank you."

"So? What's the story, Quinn?"

"We met on the plane, Jake. It was love at first sight for me. Davi played hard to get. It took a shopping trip to Victoria's Secret to win her over."

"Quinn." Davi gasped, mortified.

Jake laughed. "You do realize that Sue will want details. Meeting on a plane and falling in love won't cut it with her."

Quinn laughed knowingly. "Tell her she'll have to wait." Quinn put his arm around Davi. "Davi's coming with us to the set. Let's make sure she gets settled and isn't bothered."

"Not a problem."

They arrived at the set within the hour. The crew was almost ready for the afternoon shoot. Quinn headed right for the set manager and director to find out what the plan was. Jake put on his security ID badge. He ushered Davi toward Sally, the public relations representative.

"Hey, Jake, how are you? Thanks for getting Quinn here on such short notice. Something came up and we had to film this scene today." Sally looked over at Davi and gave her a broad welcoming smile.

Davi held out her hand to Sally. "Hi, Sally. I'm Davi."

"I know who you are. Congratulations! You have this whole place talking! Many women cried when that announcement came out last night. I was one of them, I have to admit."

"Sally, Davi needs a badge and somewhere to hang out. You'll help us with that," Jake reminded her.

"Sorry, you've got me all excited here. Jake, take Davi over to where they are setting up. There are seats for you right behind Quinn's. I'll pop over to the trailer and get a badge for Davi. Would you like a drink of any kind, Davi?"

"Coffee with cream would be great. Thanks."

Jake led Davi over to where the filming was to occur. She smiled when she saw Quinn's director's chair with his name on it.

"We can sit behind him here," Jake told her. "It could take a while for makeup and wardrobe to get him ready. Will you be okay?"

"When I get my coffee, I'll go through my manuscript here. I'll be fine, Jake. Do you need to go somewhere?"

"I need to check on Quinn and make sure no one's made it past the guards. I'll come back with him."

Davi looked around her. There were people everywhere, all hurrying to get themselves and their equipment ready right away. There were cameras and microphones suspended from booms. She looked at the set in front of her where Quinn would be soon. There were three false walls to give the look of a bedroom. A king-sized bed with nightstands on each side of the bed completed the set.

Davi racked her brain to recall anything that Quinn may have told her about the movie. He called it a dramex—a drama with some sex thrown in for good measure. Quinn wasn't sure where the movie was heading because the scenes were being filmed completely out of order and the director was constantly rewriting the story. He didn't tell her he was coming back today for this sex scene. *This will be interesting*, Davi thought to herself.

Quinn stormed through the studio, pulling his director's chair around to face Davi and threw himself into it. "That bitch!" he roared.

Davi rubbed his arm to soothe him. "What's the matter?"

"It's Rene, my costar." Quinn practically spit the words out. "She's doing this out of spite. I know it!"

"Calm down. What is she doing?"

"She's demanded that our sex scene be filmed today. She's upset about our engagement, Davi. She's been trying to hook up with me for months. She wants to cause problems between us."

"How can she do that?"

"She's asked for a closed set, and that's okay for what we're filming. It's on the line between rape and rough sex. It's up to us to play it out."

Davi knew what a closed set meant. It meant that all unnecessary personnel had to leave the set. It gave the actors and director license to go beyond the script if they wanted to, including having sex.

"Rene's going to do her damnedest to cause something to happen between us on film. She's getting back at me. This will be in the press as soon as the director yells cut."

"If I weren't in the picture, do you think she'd ask for a closed set?"

"Who knows with Rene?"

"If she did ask for a closed set, would you end up having sex with her?"

"Of course not, Davi. Are you crazy?"

"Then nothing is going to happen. If you wouldn't have sex with her with me out of the picture, how is she going to get you to do it with me in the picture? It just won't happen. Do whatever you have to do to get you through this. It's only acting, right?" Davi smiled at him with complete understanding.

Quinn took a deep breath and slowly let it out. "Remember what I told you about breasts and bowling balls? She has tenpin balls. I could get a black eye or a concussion with her." He could feel himself start to relax as the sound of Davi's voice soothed him.

"You'll heal." Davi caressed his cheek. "Feeling better now?"

"I feel like a little kid who needed a time-out. Thanks."

"We all need a time-out every once in a while. I'm glad I could help. Do you want me to leave, or would you like me to stay? Whatever will help you get through it, I'll do it."

"Stay, please. Having you here will keep me focused." He raked his hands through his hair and then sighed heavily. "I'll go tell them you're staying and that I want to get this over with as soon as possible."

"Say it nicely, Quinn. Stay on top in every way," she teased him.

Quinn leaned over toward Davi and cupped her face with his hands. "I love you."

"And I love you. Now go back there and get to work." She kissed him lightly on the lips, but he kissed back hungrily.

"I needed that for strength. See you when it's over."

"I'll be here."

Davi closed her eyes and took a deep breath. She could hear movement around her as the crew settled in for the shoot. She concentrated on Quinn. *He'll get through this. We'll get through this.*

"Davi?" Jake stood in front of her, holding her coffee and her badge.

"Hi, Jake. I forgot about the coffee." She clipped the badge to her jacket and then accepted the offered coffee cup.

"Oh, Sally got called away for something, and I thought I'd better bring this to you before it got cold."

Davi took a sip. "It's just right. Thanks, Jake."

"Uh, Davi, may I ask you something?"

"Go ahead, Jake. What is it?"

"What did you say to Quinn? He's done a full 180 in the last five minutes. He's all smiles and back to his old self."

"You mean he hasn't been?" Davi teased.

"You know what I mean."

"Sorry. I told him what he already knew. He just needed me to say it to him."

"You didn't put him under a spell or anything?"

"No!" she laughed. "Why would you say that?"

"Quinn hasn't been his old self in almost a year. I almost forgot what he used to be like. You've changed him, Davi. Thanks."

"I've only been with him for a few days. I won't take credit for changing him. Maybe he was ready to get back to his old self." Davi smiled warmly at Jake. "He's lucky to have someone care about him the way you do."

"We've been friends since before he got into this business. He's helped me out many times, and now I'm looking after him. It looks like you're going to be looking after him too."

"I'm not a babysitter, Jake."

"Oh, I'm not saying you are. I meant that he's going to do great because of you. Does that make any sense?"

"I think so. Thanks."

"Here they come now. You sure you want to be here?" Jake couldn't conceal his nervousness about what was about to happen.

"I'm okay. Do you want to sit with me?" Davi pointed to the chair beside her.

"If you don't mind, I'll go find something else to do while they're at it." Jake reddened at the double meaning of what he said. "What I meant, while they're . . ."

"Pretend fucking? Not to worry, I'll be here."

Jake laughed at Davi. Quinn was lucky to have her. She was one cool lady.

Davi took a long sip of her coffee and settled into the chair. Quinn, Rene, and the director walked over to the bed. They talked about the scene.

Davi recognized the director, Guy Tremblant. He was known for his off-the-wall brilliance behind the camera but his personal life was what she thought of right away. Guy had only recently returned to the States after serving a self-imposed exile resulting from a sex scandal involving the underage daughter of a well-known movie producer. Davi wondered why Quinn hadn't mentioned his name.

"Just be natural, you two—make it real," she heard him say.

Someone walked over and took a light reading off them. Setting up took hours, so it seemed. Patience was mandatory in this line of work. Guy Tremblant turned from them and looked over to where Davi was sitting. For a brief moment, their eyes locked. Davi felt a cold shiver run up her spine. Quinn and Rene got into position.

"And action!" called the director.

There was no dialogue. Rene slapped Quinn across the face, and he retaliated by picking her up and throwing her on the bed. Davi didn't know whether to watch or look away. For Quinn's sake, she had to watch. She owed him that much. Davi watched as the couple wrestled on the bed. Clothing was torn off. In minutes, they were both down to their underwear. Quinn kept Rene pinned to the bed. He kept control of her hands while he kissed her roughly. Rene was squirming under his grip. Whether she was trying to break free so she could undermine Quinn or it was part of the role, Davi couldn't tell. Quinn made it look real. Quinn ignored Rene as she screamed at him. He secured both of her hands on the pillow above her head with his left hand and then moved his right hand down to his crotch. He made it look like he was releasing his cock for the rape. His hips started to move as he simulated penetration. Rene was still struggling. Quinn put his mouth over hers to stifle her screams. His thrusting intensified as Rene's body went limp. Moments later, Quinn roared a terrifying orgasm. Davi jumped in her seat. She watched Quinn slump and whisper something in Rene's ear. Rene's eyes opened in shock.

"And cut!" called the director. "That was excellent! There's no need to do that again. Thank you, Quinn, Rene, and everyone for a great job. We'll call that a wrap, and we'll be back here tomorrow for 7:00 a.m."

Quinn pushed himself off Rene, glancing quickly at Davi before he put his pants back on. Then he walked off the set to change his clothes.

Jake came over to check on Davi. "How are you?" he asked, concerned about her reaction to what she had just witnessed.

"I'm okay. That was a tough scene to act. Didn't they do a great job? It looked so real. Quinn looks exhausted, and Rene looks like she's in shock. I really feel for them. It's a good thing they only needed one take."

"You are amazing. I could barely watch that. Never mind how realistic the rape looked. How could you watch Quinn having sex with another woman, even pretend sex?"

"I don't know, Jake. I just could."

Quinn came up on them without them noticing. His face grim, his blue eyes dull.

"Lets' go."

Davi gave him her hand, and the three of them left the studio in silence. Jake drove them to Quinn's hotel. He unloaded their bags and then gave Davi a hug before he left them.

Davi followed Quinn up to his suite. He pulled the key out of his pocket and let them both in. She closed the door behind them. Quinn dropped his bag and headed to the bathroom and closed the door. Davi heard the shower start.

This suite was similar to the one in Los Angeles. Davi went to the kitchen and easily found the scotch. She found glasses and then filled them. Davi made her way to the bathroom. She tried the door. It wasn't locked. She opened it slowly and walked in.

"Quinn?"

He didn't answer. Davi took a sip of her drink and then put both glasses on the counter. She stripped off her clothing and then put the glasses in one hand and opened the shower door.

"Here," she offered him the drink. "You'll feel better."

Quinn took the offered glass and drained it in one gulp. Davi offered him hers. He shook his head no. Davi took a large gulp herself and then put the unfinished glass on the bathroom counter.

Davi joined Quinn in the shower and took him into her arms. Quinn wrapped his arms around her. Davi could feel him shake as the stress and tension from the session made its way through him. She held him until the shaking stopped. She didn't know how long they were there. It didn't matter. Quinn needed her, and that was all that mattered.

Quinn gave out one long sigh. "I'm okay now. Thanks." He kissed the top of Davi's head.

"If you want to talk about it, we can."

"No, it's over. Tomorrow's a new day." Quinn took the bar of soap and started to wash himself. Davi offered to do his back.

"Quinn, may I ask you something? You don't have to tell me if you don't want to."

"Go ahead. Ask me."

"What did you say to Rene at the end of the scene? I saw you whisper in her ear, and her eyes almost popped out of her head. She left the set upset."

Quinn took a deep breath before he answered her, "It wasn't nice. I'm embarrassed that I said it. I told her if she tried a stunt like that again, I'd never work with her again and I'd make sure no one else would, although I didn't say it as nicely."

"You may not want to hear this, Quinn, but that was amazing acting in that rape scene. It was so real. I was scared for Rene. She looked terrified too."

"She thought it was going to turn into a love scene, but I preferred not to have it that way. I had to keep control of the scene, and this was the only way I could do it. Let's not talk about it anymore. I'm hungry."

Davi turned off the shower and handed Quinn a towel. She looked at the clock in the bathroom.

"It's late. Do you know if there's anything in your kitchen?"

"It should be fully stocked."

"I'll see what I can make for us. Go get dressed and relax. I'll be out shortly." Davi wrapped a towel around her head then quickly dried herself off. She went into the bedroom and found one of Quinn's T-shirts to wear, and then she made her way to the kitchen. The fridge was full.

"Would you like a Western omelet? Will that do?"

"Perfect. Thanks."

Quinn wore only his jeans. He worked on his second scotch as he sat in a large armchair and watched her. Within ten minutes, Davi had made an omelet for them. She brought their plates into the living room. Quinn took his plate and devoured his meal quickly while Davi took her time.

She hated to break the silence, but something just occurred to her. "What time is my flight tomorrow morning?"

Quinn reached into his pocket and took out his phone. He pressed a few buttons and had the answer for her. "Ten o'clock. Jake will pick us up at six thirty, drop me off at the studio, and then take you on to the airport. You'll get there in plenty of time."

"Thanks."

Quinn was exhausted. "Come, Davi, it's time for bed." He stood up and offered her his hand.

They turned off the lights and went to bed. She held him close to her heart while he slept. She didn't realize how hard today would be on him, how much he needed her support. Her heart ached for him.

Davi whispered, "I love you," to Quinn before sleep finally came.

She enjoyed her dream. She could feel Quinn's hair between her fingers as she pulled him close to her, giving him hot wet kisses. She tingled as his hands caressed her body while his warm breath brushed against her ear. Davi felt the heat of Quinn's body as she wrapped her legs around his back. Her nails scraped across his shoulders, digging in when she felt the first hard thrust as he entered her. A soft moan escaped from her as the pleasure flowed through her. Davi wanted this dream to last. She loved how it felt to have Quinn inside her, to be joined to him. Davi held on to Quinn, feeling his muscles tense as he neared orgasm. She felt his seed flow into her. Davi woke with a start as Quinn collapsed onto her still asleep.

Chapter 10

Davi cursed herself for allowing this to happen. Not again! Davi knew her body. She was ovulating. She knew there was a good chance she would be pregnant.

Quinn and Davi had not discussed having children. They hadn't had the opportunity. Davi had three adult children. She was looking forward to becoming a grandmother, and now she was possibly going to be a mother again. She knew that her age played a major role in conceiving. She was in excellent health and menopause hadn't started. Quinn was young. She knew the odds were in her favor to have another healthy child. Did she want another child? Tears welled up in her eyes. Davi cried softly with no one to comfort her while Quinn slept soundly in her arms.

Quinn awoke early feeling well rested. He looked at Davi sleeping soundly beside him. Quinn resisted the urge to wake her and make love to her. Yesterday had been such a stressful day for both of them. Davi needed her sleep. Her support yesterday was the only thing that got him through his scene with Rene and the aftermath. He was so thankful for her. Quinn kissed her on her forehead.

Quinn made his way to the shower and let the hot water run over him. He washed away all thoughts of yesterday and concentrated on today. He was not looking forward to saying good-bye to Davi after finding her so soon. A week or two without having her close to him would be torture.

How someone could make such a change to his life in such a short time was amazing to him.

The past two years had been difficult for Quinn. He was lonely and miserable. The studio wanted to make full use of their talented heartthrob, so they paired him with their most beautiful and talented starlets, especially Rene Adams and Natasha Ward. When he wasn't filming, Quinn's schedule was filled with public appearances where Rene, Natasha, or some other starlet would be hanging on his arm. Quinn would date them casually, even sleep with them, but he knew deep down that he wouldn't ever fall in love with them. The more time he spent with them, the more miserable he became. Eventually Quinn started wearing his trademark hooded jacket, T-shirt, and baggie jeans in attempt to hide his unhappiness.

For years, the image of his dream woman haunted Quinn—the long brown hair that fell in soft waves past her shoulders, the smile that touched her sparkling eyes, and the lips so soft and sensuous. She made it impossible for him to want another woman the way he wanted her. Every night she made love to him in his dreams. She filled every waking fantasy, kissing him and whispering words of love. Lately, every visit had ended with her promising that she'd be with him soon. Quinn believed her.

When Quinn sat beside Davi on the plane, he knew he had found her. It was torture sitting next to her, watching her read as she ignored him. He sat motionless, taking in every inch of her. In his dreams, he knew her—the feel of her soft skin, the taste of her mouth, and the fragrant scent of her hair. He ached to reach out and touch her to make sure that she was real and not a dream. Quinn knew without a second thought that he had to make the woman sitting beside him his.

Quinn finished his shower and then made his way back to bed. Thoughts of Davi had made him hard. He ached to feel her in his arms one more time before they had to say good-bye.

Davi opened her eyes slowly. Quinn could see that they were puffy and bloodshot.

"Davi, sweetheart, are you all right?"

Davi rubbed her eyes. She was too tired to try to make the words come out right. "I'm in heat."

Quinn tried not to laugh. "You're what?"

"I'm ovulating," she groaned.

"Okay," Quinn said, confused by her admission. "Does that mean you didn't sleep well?"

Davi forced herself awake. She had to explain what she meant. She motioned for Quinn to sit up with her in the bed.

"When I ovulate, I can get really horny."

"Are you telling me you want sex now?" Quinn's voice was immediately low and sexy.

"No, Quinn, what I'm telling you is that I've been ovulating this weekend. Last night we had unprotected sex. I thought it was a dream until I felt you come inside me."

"Oh." Quinn knew immediately what Davi meant, why she was so adamant about using condoms. "Did I force myself on you?"

"No. This was all my doing."

"Can you—"

"Get pregnant? I don't know. We didn't discuss having a family, and now it's a possibility. You deserve to have your own children. I just don't know if I want to start a family again."

"Will you have my child, Davi?" Quinn pulled her close to him.

Davi shook her head. "I can't give you my answer now. I'm sorry."

"When will you give me an answer?"

"I don't know. When I've thought this out," she said brusquely.

"You realize that I'm going to go insane?" Quinn held her tighter.

"Quinn," Davi said seriously as she moved out of his grip to face him. "You need to think this out too. Decide what you want, what you really want. Do you want children, or do you want me? If you want children, then maybe it's time to call it quits now."

"Why can't I have you and children?" Quinn asked, confused.

"What if you can only have me? Will I be enough to keep you happy? Or do you need children to do that? If you do, then we both know what we have to do."

Quinn's phone rang.

Quinn answered it. "Hey, Jake, hold on." Quinn clamped his hand over his phone. "We have to talk about this, Davi. Jake's waiting for us. I'll tell him to go away."

"No!" Davi said quickly. "We need to think this through by ourselves. Tell him we'll be down in five minutes."

"Sorry, Jake, something came up. Give us five minutes, and we'll be down."

The ride to the movie set was too short. Davi didn't get to stay in Quinn's arms for very long. Jake had closed the divider between them to give them privacy. Quinn felt the limo stop and heard Jake get out.

"I hate your leaving like this. We should be talking about us, not saying good-bye," Quinn said when he released Davi from his kiss.

"Think about what you want, Quinn, and I'll do the same, and we'll talk about this when I know if I'm pregnant."

Davi cupped his face with her hands. She loved him. She knew that with all of her heart. She also knew that she couldn't keep him if he wanted more than what she could give him. She'd already had one husband whose needs she couldn't satisfy. She'd be damned if she put herself through that again.

There was a light rap on the window. Jake had to get Quinn in to work and Davi to the airport in time.

"Go," she whispered.

Quinn left the limo reluctantly. Jake escorted him to the studio door and made sure he went in. Quinn was making it difficult for Jake to do his job this morning. Jake returned to the limo and opened the back door to talk to Davi.

"Would you like me to drop the divider, or would you like some privacy?"

"Please drop the divider and talk to me. I don't want to be alone right now." She smiled weakly at him.

Jake did most of the talking as he drove Davi to the airport. He could tell that Davi's mind wasn't on the conversation. He assumed she was missing Quinn already, so he kept it light and told himself not to take offense if she didn't remember anything they had said to each other.

Jake parked the limo and escorted Davi through the airport. It was a relief to walk through the airport without being mobbed. He helped her through check in and offered to stay with her until she had to go through customs.

"Let's have coffee," he suggested as he steered her toward a coffee bar. He bought two coffees. "Do you want to talk about it? You're not missing him already, are you?" Jake said with a hint of seriousness.

"I'm tired. This whole weekend has been crazy."

"Not having second thoughts, are you?" Jake teased.

"No, but I do have a lot to think about. So much has happened."

"All good, I hope," Jake said with concern.

Davi answered him with a smile.

Jake looked at his watch. It was time to get Davi to customs. He stood up.

"Come on, lovely lady. It's time to get you to your plane."

Davi stood up and hugged Jake. "It was nice to meet you, Jake. I know we're going to be great friends."

"You can count on it. Now go catch your plane and look after yourself."

Davi's flight home was quiet. Luke had booked her a business class ticket, for which she was very thankful. She had the row to herself. Davi settled in with her iPod and a pillow and closed her eyes. She didn't have the energy to read or eat. She slept.

Davi forgot that there could be press waiting for her when she came through customs at the airport. She associated the press with Quinn not her. For a few moments, she was blinded by the camera flashes and overwhelmed by the noise, but once things settled, she was able to focus on getting through it.

"Ms. Stuart, congratulations on your engagement! Any wedding plans you can tell us about?"

"We haven't made any plans."

"Have you and Quinn Thomas been seeing each other for a long time?"

"No."

"Will you be moving to the States?"

"I doubt it. If you'll excuse me, I really need to get going."

The crowd parted and let her through. To her relief, she wasn't followed. She checked out her truck from the parking lot and headed home.

Davi pulled out her cell phone and pressed speed dial. "Maggie, it's me. I'm on my way home. Yes, please. Put the coffee on. I have lots to tell you. Bye." Davi closed her phone and headed for the farm. She was only half an hour away from the sanity of home.

Chapter 11

♥

Davi pulled up the long driveway to her farm. It felt so good to be home. The house was a century farmhouse that had been well maintained. The exterior brickwork and woodwork were kept in mint condition. There had been an extension added on to give the growing family more living space, but it retained its country charm. Davi had looked after the landscaping. With Maggie's keen eye for detail, Davi created an idyllic refuge in the backyard. A saltwater swimming pool and hot tub were surrounded by massive flower gardens and trees. The pool had been closed a few weeks ago, but the hot tub was kept open all year. Davi longed to go for a soak. Maybe Maggie would join her.

Maggie's car was parked at the side by the kitchen door. Davi parked her truck beside Maggie's, grabbed her travel bag, and headed into the house. The smell of freshly brewed coffee and fresh muffins welcomed her. Maggie got up from the kitchen table and gave Davi a big hug.

"Davi, what have you been up to? The cards said romance, girl, not meet a movie star and get engaged!" Maggie's Irish laugh put Davi at ease instantly.

"Pour me a cup of coffee and I'll tell you all about it. Actually, I could do with a soak in the hot tub. Would you care to join me?"

"I can't today. Sounds like you've got a lot to tell me."

"I do. I'll have a soak later then. I have to go pee."

Davi headed for the washroom.

"How about some Bailey's for your coffee? Do you want some?" Maggie called through the bathroom door. Bailey's was Maggie's special ingredient for heart-to-heart conversations over coffee.

"No! It's too early for that. I'll just have the usual, please."

Davi washed her face, refreshed her lipstick, and ran her brush through her hair. She was now ready to talk to Maggie and tell her everything. Davi took the offered coffee as she sat down at the table and inhaled its aroma. She picked at a muffin.

"What's wrong, Davi? You should be bouncing off the walls, but you're too quiet even for you. Out with it." Maggie took Davi's hand and gave it a squeeze for encouragement.

"Nothing's wrong, Maggie. It's all good, really." Davi sipped slowly from her coffee cup.

"Davi, out with it," Maggie said as she squeezed Davi's hand harder.

Davi put her coffee cup down on the table. She looked at Maggie and smiled wickedly.

"The sex is fantastic! I knew you were dying to find out since the cards don't tell you everything."

Maggie laughed at her friend's teasing. "Thank you. Now tell me everything."

Davi proceeded to give Maggie a detailed account of her weekend with Quinn. From their first meeting on the plane to their last kiss good-bye.

"I must be crazy, Maggie."

"You're not crazy, Davi. You're in love. Now show me what he bought you. Let's see if the man has taste."

Davi opened up her travel bag and showed Maggie every item from Victoria's Secret. Maggie's eyes opened wide, and Davi was sure she swore in Irish.

"Quinn said that whoever sees me in these has to be married to me or at least engaged to me. So the next thing I know I'm leaving Tiffany's wearing this." Davi held up her left hand and showed Maggie the ring.

"Very nice," Maggie said as she examined the ring, nodding her head in appreciation. "Now what is it that you haven't told me? I know there's more to the story, Davi."

Davi gazed at her best friend. Maggie always knew when something happened or was about to happen. It was more than a woman's intuition and more than reading the cards. Maggie had a gift, one that Davi didn't take lightly.

"I think I'm pregnant," she whispered.

"Obviously not planned."

"Obviously."

"Details, Davi. Did the condom break? You wouldn't have unprotected sex. I know you too well."

"It was one of those making love while you're still asleep scenarios."

"Ah, I see," Maggie replied knowingly. "Raging hormones again, was it? I seem to recall this happening to you before and nine months later . . ."

"We were so careful, Maggie. I wouldn't let him near me unless he wore a condom. Then I have this stupid dream, and I'm all over him."

"Are you sure about being pregnant?"

Davi raked her fingers through her hair and breathed in deeply before answering. "Maggie, my cows have the highest pregnancy rate in the county. Do you know why that is? It's because I can tell when they're ovulating and when it's the best time to breed them. I know my own body the same way I know my cows. It was definitely the right time to get pregnant when I had unprotected sex with Quinn."

"So what's the plan?"

"I'll make a doctor's appointment for next week and have a blood pregnancy test done. There's an early test available now that should let me know if I'm pregnant."

"Does Mr. Hollywood Heartthrob know?"

"Of course he knows! It's just that . . ." Davi found it hard to say the words.

"What is it?"

"He really wants to have a family."

"And you? What do you want?"

"I have to think about this. Having another child at my age was not in my plans. I'm ready for the kids to marry and make me a grandmother. You know how much I've wanted that."

"What if you say no and Quinn wants children?"

"We have to talk about it, Maggie. Worst-case scenario would be that we call it quits before we go any further. He deserves to have a family."

"Could you give him up that easily?"

"No! I'm crazy about him, but if I can't accept becoming a mother again, there may be no other choice. I'll just have to work it out. I've never had to think about something like this before."

"So in the meantime, what happens?"

"Life goes on. I'll finish my book, run the farm, and look after my family."

Maggie got up from the table and refilled both of their cups. She added some Bailey's to her coffee and then sat down.

"So what do the kids think about you and Quinn?"

"I spoke with Tigger. We both know what a romantic she is. She's all for it. I have to sit down with all of them tonight to make sure they are okay with this. Maggie, I'm old enough to be Quinn's mother. Am I crazy to want to have a life with him?"

"Davi, you are the most loving and giving person I know. You are full of love and you lost your husband too soon. There is nothing wrong or crazy about loving someone who is younger than you are. This will work out."

"Thanks."

"What about your wedding? Was anything discussed?"

"We didn't have time. I don't want to rush things. We need time to make sure we're doing the right thing."

"Is that both of you talking or just you?" Maggie looked knowingly at Davi.

"I need to make sure. Cards or no cards, I need to know in my heart and in my head that I'm doing the right thing."

"Listen to your heart, Davi." Maggie squeezed her hand. "The head will agree eventually."

Maggie left and Davi found ways to keep busy. Thoughts of having a soak in the hot tub were quickly forgotten. Davi changed into her jeans and cowboy boots then went to her office and checked her voice mail and e-mails. An hour passed quickly. Her kids would be home by 6:30 p.m. She had plenty of time to think of what to make for supper. She'd make one of their favorites.

Davi walked out to her truck to retrieve her cell phone. As she did so, she thought it would be a good idea for her to take pictures of her world, the same world she wrote about in her book. The farm was large, situated on two hundred and fifty acres. It housed over five hundred head of dairy cattle and grew some of the crops needed to feed the herd.

Davi headed for the maternity barn first. This was her favorite place on the entire farm. She always liked to check on the cows who were about to give birth. Davi lovingly called them the Ladies. Many times, she had assisted in bringing a new calf into the world. It was such an uplifting experience. Davi peered into the main birthing pen. A cow was in labor, and by the looks of it, the calf would be born soon. Davi stayed to watch. She would take pictures of the birth.

It didn't take long for the calf to be born. Davi climbed into the stall and had a look at its belly—a girl. That's what they wanted. Davi checked the calf's nostrils to make sure it could breathe. It could, so she pulled the calf around to its mother so the cow could lick the calf dry.

"Good job, Mom," she said to the cow and then left the pen.

She took another picture for Quinn. He'd like this one.

Davi then headed off to the calf barn, where the newborns were housed. The calves were so tiny and delicate-looking even though they weighed over one hundred pounds at birth. Davi watched as the calves nursed from their bottles. It made her think of baby bottles and getting back into that routine again. Davi closed her eyes to clear her thoughts. She took shots of the calves nursing from the automatic feeders. Quinn would find this interesting.

Then Davi made her way to the main barn. The men would be milking by this time. She poured herself a cup of coffee from the lunchroom and then walked to the observation deck and sat down. She watched as the cows entered the parlor and got into position to be milked. Everything was so quiet and orderly. Davi could watch for hours. She took more pictures and enjoyed her coffee. Then she headed to the main barn, where the cattle were housed. Davi took more pictures to show Quinn what the cows ate and how they were treated. She was sure he had never seen a barn like this before.

Her cell phone rang.

"Hello?"

"Mom, you're home! How was your flight?" It was her son, Rich, calling.

"It was good. I slept all the way home. There was a change of plan. I flew in from New York. Where are you?"

"I'm driving home from a farm conference. I should be home by suppertime. Do you want me to pick something up for supper?"

"That's a great idea. I'll try to get some work done before you get back. I guess we have lots to talk about."

"We sure do. I love you, Mom."

"Love you too. Bye."

Davi left the barn and headed down the driveway to the mailbox. There were only bills waiting for her. Back to the photo shoot. The corn had already been harvested for silage. She took pictures of the empty fields to show the size of the farm. She took pictures of the buildings and the machinery—the tractors, the combine, the trucks, and everything else that was a part of her world.

Davi made her way back to the farmhouse. She took a picture of her beloved truck in the driveway. Davi stood back and tried to fit the entire house into one shot. It was difficult. She took a picture of her country kitchen. She left the two empty coffee cups on the table to show Quinn her and Maggie's favorite gossip spot. She took a picture of her large screen television to show Quinn where she and her daughter watched his movies. The last room on the main floor to show him was her office. She took a picture of her computer, where she created *Second Harvest.* Davi took a picture of the office wall covered in family photos.

Her family would be home soon. She'd make another pot of coffee and set the table for supper. Davi browsed through the pictures. She was happy with all of them. She pressed on the messenger icon and sent the pictures to Quinn's phone with the message, "Quinn, for your eyes only—pictures of my spread. Love, Davi."

The kitchen door opened. Rich was home with supper. He brought his favorite takeout—pizza. This meant they'd be having beer with it. Some things always stayed the same. Davi checked the fridge. Rich had thought ahead and made sure it was well stocked.

"Hey, Momsie," he crooned. Rich put the pizza boxes down on the table and then grabbed Davi and gave her a big bear hug. "So how was California?" He smiled mischievously at her.

"Oh, not much happened. It was kind of boring."

"You're right. It was getting boring seeing you and—what's his name?—on television all of the time."

"Really? Were we on all the time?"

"No, of course not," he teased. "We only saw you on all of the entertainment shows and then on the local news, and then there was the shopping channel."

"The shopping channel?" Davi asked, mortified.

"They were showing your ring and selling the knockoffs." Rich took hold of his mother's left hand to look at the engagement ring. "Nice." He then helped himself to a beer and sat at the table.

"This is embarrassing."

"Tell me about it," Rich groaned playfully.

"You're not embarrassed by me and all of this?"

"Not in the least. We think it's funny that our mom is hot enough to pull in the big guy. Meowwww," he roared the meow.

"That better not be the sound of a cougar. I can still ground you!"

Rich laughed. "You are in no way a cougar. I think you need to be at least one year older for you to qualify."

Davi stood behind Rich and rubbed his head.

"What about the age difference? He's only a few years older than you."

"That could be a problem. But if it is, it's mine, and I'll deal with it. Don't worry, Momsie. We're all very happy for you. You need to be with someone."

Davi leaned over her son and hugged him tight. He reminded her so much of his father. Rich was tall—six feet four inches, with a broad shoulders and a lean body. His arms were well muscled from the manual labor on the farm. He had the dark Stuart hair, but with Davi's wave. No one knew that though. Rich kept his hair short. His eyes were a deep chocolate brown, another Stuart trait, but his smile was all Davi's, with the slight dimple in his cheeks. Rich still lived at home with Davi and the girls, but his plans were to marry his girlfriend of two years next year and live in another house on the farm.

The kitchen door opened again. Davi's two daughters walked in. To the untrained eye, the sisters looked like twins. Their resemblance to each other and to Davi was remarkable. They were slightly taller than Davi, and their hair was the same length and color as hers. Their only distinction was their choice of colors. Tigger preferred purples and greens, while Cat liked reds and blacks. Both girls still lived at home. Cat taught at the local elementary school. Tigger was training for a management position at the local hotel.

"Hey, Mom, congratulations!" They both took their turn giving her a hug and a kiss.

"Don't you want to hear the details?" Davi asked dumbfounded.

The girls helped themselves to a beer.

"Is he good to you?" Cat asked her.

"And he loves you and you love him?" Tigger added.

"Yes to everything." Davi smiled. They were giving her the same talk she'd given them when they'd found love.

"Then that's all that matters," the girls chorused.

"Don't you want to meet him before you accept him so fast? You kids have surprised me in a good way, but I'm still in shock." She sat down heavily in her chair.

"Mom, your happiness is all we want, just like you want happiness for us. It goes both ways." Rich put his hand on her shoulder. "We trust you to know what you're doing. You're old enough to make that decision. Aren't you?"

Chapter 12

Later that night, Davi felt lost in her bed. She'd only spent three nights with Quinn, but her body ached for his company. She missed his warmth, his smell, and his strong arms around her. She marveled that after two years of being used to sleeping alone, she would suddenly miss the company of another. Davi picked up a book from her nightstand. A favorite romance kept her company when she couldn't sleep. After reading the same paragraph over three times, Davi put the book down and got out of bed, wrapping her housecoat around her.

She could feel the start of a headache. She felt anxious. She knew this feeling, and she didn't like it. When her husband, Ross, was late coming home from his farm meetings, she would feel this way, wondering what he was up to, wondering whose bed he was sharing. She hated the mistrust and the anger that filled her. She hated the jealousy and the resentment that ate at her.

She didn't want to feel this way with Quinn. He loved her and swore that there was no one else. She wanted to believe him, but her confidence hadn't fully recovered from what she had gone through with Ross. What was she thinking? She'd only just met the man. Who in their right mind skips dating and jumps right into an engagement in three days? She was setting herself up for heartache, and she didn't know what to do.

"You're an idiot," Davi said aloud as she looked out the bedroom window into the darkness, her reflection staring back at her. "We don't have an ice cube's chance in hell of making it work. You're too old for him, you've had your chance, and you have a family. He's young, and he wants children of his own."

Davi closed her eyes as the realization hit her. *He wants your spread.* He didn't want her farm, but he wanted everything that came with it, the wife, the family, and the sense of security.

The phone rang, interrupting her thoughts. Davi took her time answering it.

"Hello?" her voice was soft and quiet.

"Davi, I know it's late but I had to call you. Did I wake you?"

"No. I couldn't sleep. I've been thinking."

"I don't like the sound of that." He waited for her to respond.

"I can't do this, Quinn. I've been thinking about us, and I just can't do this. It's not fair to you."

"What do you mean you can't do this?" Quinn kept his voice calm as he felt a knot form in his stomach.

"I can't marry you or have your baby." Davi looked out into the darkness, feeling lost and alone.

"I thought it was just the baby part that was up for discussion. You already said you'd marry me." Quinn tried desperately to keep his voice light.

"They go together."

"No. They don't have to. Besides, I thought we were to hold off on this discussion until you knew if you were pregnant or not."

"Does it matter?"

"Of course it matters. What's really going on, Davi?"

"I'm used to being on my own."

"You may be used to it but you don't like it. Admit it, Davi."

"I was happy."

"I make you happier." His voice was deep and lusty.

"I'll still be alone. Marrying you won't change anything except make things worse."

"What?" he asked, stunned.

"You'll be away working, and I'll be here alone, wondering who you're with and what you're doing. I won't put myself through that again, Quinn. I promised myself that."

"Who said you'd be alone, and what the hell makes you think I'll be cheating on you? I'm not Ross."

Davi could hear the anger and the hurt in his voice. She couldn't let it stop her. She had to tell him the truth.

"There's something I haven't told you," she said softly.

"Tell me." Quinn held his breath.

Davi closed her eyes tight, forcing the words from her mouth, "Ross wasn't totally to blame. I made him cheat on me."

"No one can make someone cheat on them, Davi. What are you talking about?"

"We stopped having sex months before he started cheating." Davi breathed out.

Quinn waited for her to continue.

"It's not that I wanted him to cheat on me. It's just that I wasn't interested in having sex with my husband anymore."

Quinn wanted to say he didn't believe her but swallowed the words. "You're a livewire in bed, Davi."

"With you, but I wasn't with him. Not for a long time."

"It's no excuse to cheat on your wife, Davi," Quinn said tenderly.

"But it wasn't much incentive to stay faithful either."

Quinn wasn't sure what she was trying to tell him. "Are you telling me that our sex life will be short-lived?"

"I don't know. I don't want it to be," Davi stammered.

"You had a great sex life for twenty-four years before you stopped. Am I right?" Quinn pressed her.

"Yes. It was great."

"So can I assume that we should have great sex for at least the next twenty-four years?"

Davi didn't answer him.

"Davi?"

"I'll be really old by then," she said slowly.

"I'll be old too. Maybe I'll be the one who loses interest and not you."

"I don't think so, stud." Davi smiled.

"I don't believe you'll stop wanting me, but it's a chance I'm willing to take."

"The odds are against us."

"Damn the odds," he groaned, exasperated. "I don't care about what people think about us. I don't care if we stop having sex now or in twenty-four years. I love you and that's all that matters. I want to spend the rest of my life with you." Quinn paused before he continued, "You love me too, Davi. Why this sudden change of heart?"

"Because right now I am alone and I don't like it. I want you here in my bed, Quinn. I want you with me, holding me close, making love to me. I don't want you hours away in another country doing whatever. So it's better we stop this now before it's too late."

"Don't you think I want to be with you too? Don't you think I feel incredibly lonely right now? I've had you in my bed for three nights, and now I feel lost without you here. Why do you think I'm calling you in the middle of the night?"

"Regret?"

"Don't."

"I'm giving you an out, Quinn. You should take it." Her voice was shaky.

"I don't want it. I want you forever and nothing less."

"Why?" Davi sat down in her armchair and pulled her robe tight around her.

Quinn sighed. "Honest?"

"Nothing but the truth."

"You turn me on. Everything about you turns me on. I've been hard for you since I sat beside you on the plane."

"Liar! You ignored me as soon as you sat down beside me."

"How long did I ignore you?"

"An hour."

"Ten minutes. I opened my eyes after takeoff, and that is when I saw you. Believe me. I did not ignore you. You ignored me, and I waited for you to notice me."

A smile touched Davi's face. "Really?"

"I had a great fantasy while I watched you read, woman, and the whole time I kept thinking she's the one. I have to get her to talk to me."

"Why wouldn't I have talked to you?" Davi relaxed in the chair, pulling her knees up under her, making herself comfortable.

"You are so out of my league. I knew if I didn't play it right, you'd shoot me down."

Davi laughed. Her headache was fading. "You're playing me now, Quinn Thomas."

"Never. I swear."

"Why would I shoot you down, even though I am out of your league?" she asked, intrigued.

"You looked so incredibly beautiful and smart and sophisticated. I thought there was no way on earth you were single. Some lucky bastard had you, and I sat there jealous. For some reason I thought coming onto you as Quinn Thomas the actor wouldn't work. For all I knew you had no idea who I was, and so I had to be me, the real me."

"I thought you were playing me," Davi said softly, "but I didn't care."

"Why didn't you shoot me down?"

"I told you. You were my fantasy. I'd have been the biggest fool on earth if I didn't talk to you."

"I'm real, Davi, and my love for you is real."

There it was again. His warm voice was caressing her and causing her body to tingle. He was pulling her in.

"You love me too. You're fighting it, but the more you do, the harder it's becoming."

"Quinn, you're distracting me."

"From what?"

"From breaking up with you."

"You don't want to break up with me. You're just getting used to wanting someone again. You need me, Davi Stuart, and your body's letting your head know it. That's all it is."

"I don't like to feel this way," she groaned.

"Neither do I, but we'll make this work." His voice caressed her, calming her.

"How?"

"We'll talk to each other every night. We'll tell each other our fantasies. We'll stay on the phone until we both fall asleep."

Davi got up from her chair and walked to her bed. She shrugged off her robe and got into bed. She dimmed the lights and nestled into her pillows.

"Talk to me, Quinn. Tell me a fantasy of yours."

"We're on a secluded beach. It's hot. The sun is beating down on us. You're lying down on one of those beach beds, looking so sexy and inviting. I'm covering your body with suntan lotion. I'm massaging it onto your soft skin."

"Where's the beach?"

"Does it matter?"

"Yes. I want to know where you've taken me."

"Aruba. Have you ever been there?"

"No, but I hear it's beautiful. Go on please."

"Your skin feels so good. You love the massage I'm giving you. You're purring with delight."

"I don't purr, Quinn."

"This is my fantasy and in it you purr. Stop interrupting, woman."

"Sorry."

"You're purring and you start to squirm with delight. I undo your bikini top."

"I don't wear bikinis."

"You should and you will and you do in this fantasy. Let me continue. I undo your top and start to massage your breasts. They feel so soft. Your nipples are so hard and so inviting. You reach out your arms and pull me to you and you whisper—"

"I have to go, Quinn," she interrupted him again.

"No, that is not what you say."

"No really, I have to go. The farm phone is ringing. There must be an emergency out at the barn. I have to go. I'm sorry."

"Can I call you in the morning?"

"Yes. I have to go. Bye."

Davi ended the call and answered her telephone. There was a calving at the barn. The vet had to do a cesarean section and needed Davi's assistance. An hour and a half later, Davi was back in bed, freshly showered and tired. She put her head down on her pillow and went to sleep, dreaming of Quinn. He was holding her tight and making love to her. Davi called out his name as she slept.

Chapter 13

♥

The next morning, Davi lay in bed, waiting for Quinn's call. Her heart beat faster in anticipation. She felt like a teenager all over again. Her phone rang.

"Quinn," she breathed into the phone.

"You missed a really good fantasy, woman," he teased.

"I'm sorry. You'll have to tell me about it sometime."

"I have a better plan. I'll take you there, and you can experience it firsthand."

"I'd like that."

"I thought you would."

"So how was yesterday? We didn't get a chance to talk about it."

"We worked around the sex scene from last Sunday."

Davi took in a deep breath. "How did that go? Was it difficult for you?"

"No, Davi, it was fine. We filmed the before and after scenes. Rene handled herself well. She can really act when she keeps it professional. Today we're heading to a location shoot somewhere downtown. It's probably going to be a madhouse, but then that's all part of the job." Quinn paused. "So what happened last night?"

"One of the cows was having a difficult labor. The vet needed assistance with a C-section. I'm the assistant on call. Mother and calf are both doing well. Where are you now?"

"Jake's driving me to the location. We're stuck in traffic. It's your turn."

"My turn?"

"Tell me a fantasy while I'm here staring out at traffic."

"I'm not going to say anything while Jake's with you."

"I'll close the divider. Then you can talk in complete privacy. How's that?"

Davi overheard Quinn telling Jake something about telephone sex and needing privacy.

"Why would you say that?" she asked, embarrassed.

"It's the truth, isn't it?"

"Yes, but . . ."

"I don't lie, Davi, and Jake would wonder why I would close the divider if I didn't have anyone in the backseat with me."

"What?"

"Forget it," Quinn brushed her off quickly.

"You've had sex with women in your limo?" Davi pressed him.

"Let's not go there. It was a long time ago."

Davi knew she had him. He didn't lie.

"Is it good in the backseat?"

Quinn hesitated. "It can be. We can try it out next time you're here if you want."

"No, thank you. I've got something better than your limo," she replied lustily.

"Tell me about it."

"It's summer, and we're going through one of the worst heat waves. It's humid and sticky, and everyone's sweating."

"You have a thing about heat and sweat, don't you?" he chuckled.

Davi ignored him. "It's nighttime, and I drive you up to the escarpment in my pickup truck to show you the city lights below us. We park way out in the middle of a field. I have an air mattress in the back and a cooler of cold Canadian beer. You and I get comfortable in the back of the truck. You're sweating through your shirt, so I help you take it off."

"What kind of shirt is it?"

"It's your blue T-shirt. It's my favorite."

"I thought so. Continue."

"I take my bottle of beer, and before I open it, I touch your nipples with it. Immediately, they harden, and then I start to play with them with my tongue. You run your hands through my hair, pulling me in close. You want me, but I resist."

"What happens next?"

"I take the bottle and trace it down your chest to your abs, and I outline each one with it. Your stomach tightens, and you moan with desire. I look down at your crotch, and it's easy to tell you are fully aroused."

"I'm aroused now, woman," Quinn murmured softly.

"You're wearing your tight jeans, and your cock is throbbing to be set free. I undo your button and zipper and release you. Then I stroke you. You're so hard, and you feel like velvet. I love to stroke you."

"I know."

"Then I take a long drink of my beer, letting it cool my mouth. I take a sip and don't swallow while I take you in my mouth. You jerk as the cold beer wraps around your cock, but you like it. My tongue caresses you, and my lips hold you tight. Your hands rake through my hair while you tell me how good it feels."

"It does feel good," Quinn agreed.

"I can feel you tense. You want to come, but I won't let you, so I release you."

"Then what?"

"I lift up my skirt, and I mount you. I'm hot and wet for you."

"What about your panties?"

"I'm not wearing any underwear. It's too hot. Remember? I undo my shirt, and you pull me forward and fondle my breasts. You want to taste me, but I won't let you. I pull back. I touch my breasts to tease you. Then you take your bottle of beer and touch my breasts with it. It's cold, but it feels so good against my hot skin."

"Then what happens?" his voice was rough from arousal.

"I ride you. You're thrusting hard, and I'm taking all of you. I close my eyes and focus on your cock. It's unbelievable. I've never felt anything like it before. I scream out my orgasm. Then you pull out and put me on my back. You reach for your beer bottle and pour some of it in my belly button, then start to lap it up. Then you take the bottle and you . . ."

"Momsie! Get up. We have our meeting now. Remember?" Rich's voice boomed from behind the bedroom door.

"Coming!" Davi yelled back.

"What?" Quinn rasped in disbelief.

"I'm sorry, Quinn. I forgot the time. I have a meeting with our banker. He's waiting for me in the kitchen. I have to go."

Quinn was in sexual agony. "You can't leave me like this, Davi. Not again."

"I have to."

"At least tell me the ending. What happens with the bottle?" he asked in desperation.

"You figure it out, cowboy. It's not that difficult. I'll talk to you later. Bye. I love you."

Chapter 14

♥

"I'm beginning to think you like leaving me high and dry, Davina Stuart," Quinn Thomas growled into the phone later that night. "I had to spend half an hour locked in my limo until I could jack off. Jake was in hysterics."

"I'm sorry," Davi cooed. "How can I make it up to you?"

"Come to New York."

"I can't, Quinn. My calendar is full. I've got meetings every day this week."

"What about the weekend?"

"I can give you Friday night and Saturday, but I have to be home for Sunday. We're having a special afternoon service at church."

"You can't miss it?"

"No. I've made a commitment. I have to go." Davi listened to the silence. "We said we'd try to make this work, Quinn. It's the best I can do for this weekend." *Don't make it difficult so soon, please.* She waited for his response.

"Friday it is then. I'll take whatever I can get. Thanks, Davi."

"You're mad."

"No, I'm disappointed, but it's not your fault. I promised you we could do this and we will. Be patient with me, okay?"

"I will."

"I love you. Good night, woman."

Davi woke from a restful sleep. Dreams of Quinn kept her company through the night. Davi went through her daily routine of walking around the farm, checking on the work plans for the day, and then checking her e-mails. There was an e-mail from Quinn. He had sent her open e-tickets for her trips to visit him.

Davi picked up her office phone and called Maggie. She didn't wait for Maggie to say hello when she answered.

"So when am I getting married?"

"And good morning to you too," Maggie said cheerfully.

"I know you've looked at the cards, Maggie. I thought I'd enter the date on my calendar so that I don't double book it." Davi's tone was somewhat serious.

"I don't have an exact date, Davi, but it will be this year. I can feel it."

"It doesn't give me much time to plan a wedding. Can you check the cards again?"

"No, but it will happen. You know it will. What's going on?"

Davi closed her eyes. She wanted to be sure that she was doing the right thing. She wanted Quinn to make sure. He was the one who started the whole marriage thing after all.

"It hasn't been a week yet. Quinn could change his mind."

"He won't and neither will you, but it will have to be you who finally decides to trust him and make the commitment. Your head will come around eventually. You know your heart is already there."

"Sometimes I don't like you very much," she sighed.

"It's not me—it's the cards that you don't like. The truth can be a bitch, can't it, Davi?" Maggie laughed.

"I'll talk to you later, Maggie. Bye."

Davi's cell phone rang.

"Hello?"

"Hey, woman."

"Hey, Quinn, I received the e-tickets. Thank you. Does that mean you still want to see me?"

Quinn laughed. "My parents want to meet you. They are flying up this weekend. We'll have dinner with them on Saturday. I'll be working Friday night, but I'd like you to come to the set with me."

"They're flying up so soon? Isn't it rushing things?"

"Davi, they think our engagement was rushed. I don't think wanting to meet you is rushing things. But if you're not up to it, I'll tell them to hold off for a while."

"You're right," Davi agreed. "I would love to meet your parents."

"That's the spirit! Jake will pick you up at the airport. Oh, and bring some of your presents. We didn't get to finish trying them out. Look, I have to run. I'm getting dirty looks from the crew. I love you. Bye."

"Great," Davi said aloud. "I'm forty-seven years old, and I'm about to meet my boyfriend's parents. Kill me now."

Chapter 15

♥

The flight to New York was peaceful. Davi watched one of Quinn's movies. She could never get enough of him. She watched his face and his movements and the way he held his on-screen lover. Nothing he did on-screen was what he did with her. She marveled at how he had two very different personas, both equally attractive and intoxicating. She thought that Quinn would bring something of his real self to the screen, but he didn't. Of course, he was gorgeous and charming, but it was how he touched women and kissed them. The subtle differences showed Davi that he was genuine with her.

Davi collected her bag and walked through customs without any fuss. She had called ahead to Quinn to let him know her flight's arrival time. He assured her that someone would be there to meet her. Davi looked around. She didn't see Quinn or Jake. As she moved down the line, she saw a young man holding a sign with the word *Woman* on it. Davi laughed. Only Quinn would do this. Davi walked up to him. He looked embarrassed.

"Hi. I think I'm the woman you're looking for. I'm Davi."

"Oh, hi, I'm Will. Jake sent me here to pick you up. I hope you don't mind the sign. Quinn insisted it would work to get your attention without letting the paparazzi know that I was waiting for you."

Will took Davi's bag from her.

"Oh, it did. I hope you weren't too embarrassed to hold it."

"Not at all. I got lots of offers and some business cards in case I was interested. I'm just happy I wasn't arrested for soliciting. Now that would have been embarrassing." He shook his head and laughed as he thought about it.

Davi laughed with him. "It's good to know you've got a great sense of humor. It looks like you need it with Quinn."

"He's been great this last week. I was told we have to thank you for that. So thanks."

"Don't thank me. He was due to turn around. I happened to be there when he did."

"If you say so."

Davi and Will made it to the parking lot.

"Quinn's working late tonight. They're filming outside in the downtown area. It's a real madhouse. Jake's had to put on extra security to keep the fans back. That's why he's not here to meet you. You'll see for yourself what's going on."

Traffic was heavy. It took almost an hour for them to get to the location. Security waved Will through the gates. He parked the limo close to the trailers where Jake was waiting for them. He looked very tired and stressed, but a smile lit up his face when he saw Davi.

"It's great to see you, Davi. We've all been waiting for you. Quinn's over the moon."

"Thanks, Jake. It's great to see you too." Davi kissed him on the cheek.

"Let's get you to his trailer. Quinn's finishing a fight scene. Then he has to clean up for the next one. We'll probably beat him to his trailer."

The two of them walked together to an enormous RV. The sign on the door read Quinn Thomas. Quinn sat waiting on the step for them.

"Word had it that an incredibly gorgeous woman was walking this way with Jake. I figured I'd wait here and check her out. I'm so glad to see it's you." Quinn winked at her. "I can't touch you, Davi. I'm covered in crap. Give me a rain check in five minutes?"

"Of course." Davi smiled lovingly at him. Even when dirty, the man was gorgeous.

"I'll stay out here and you two go in," suggested Jake.

Quinn walked up the steps and opened the door for Davi. "After you," he murmured.

Meeting the couple head-on was Sarah, who was in charge of Quinn's clothes and makeup.

"Quinn, you look awful, sweetheart!" She stepped toward him. "You stink! Hurry and get a quick shower and shave. They want you clean-shaven for this scene. We've got fifteen minutes."

"Sarah, I want you to meet—"

"Davi, I know, Quinn. We'll get to know each other while you get ready. Now go!" Sarah slapped at Quinn's butt while he turned and headed off to the bedroom.

Davi looked at Sarah. She was slight in build and very pretty. She may have been close to Davi's age. It was hard to tell. Her makeup was applied perfectly, and her hair was pulled back in a messy ponytail. Her smile was friendly and inviting.

"Come, Davi, have a seat here." Sarah pointed to one of the two barber's chairs in front of a large mirror and makeup counter. "Would you like a drink? I have a fresh pot of coffee, juice, and water."

"Water would be great, thanks."

Sarah walked over to the kitchen fridge and pulled out two bottles of water and then offered one to Davi.

"It is so nice to meet the one who captured Quinn's heart. You are beautiful."

Davi could tell Sarah was checking her out.

"Thank you." Davi took the offered drink. "But I think Quinn did the capturing. He took me totally by surprise."

"Tell me about it," Sarah drawled. "I've known Quinn for ages. He likes to surprise people." Her eyes were focused on Davi. "We're all surprised."

Davi sipped from her water bottle and then put it down on the counter.

"How surprised?" Davi asked softly, suddenly feeling uncomfortable. *What has Quinn done?* "Is there something I'm missing? Am I replacing someone?"

"Replacing someone?" Sarah asked innocently.

"A girlfriend that Quinn didn't tell me about, someone that everyone likes. Someone like you, perhaps?"

Sarah smiled appreciatively. "Thanks for the compliment, Davi, but Quinn and I are strictly friends."

"Is there someone else?" Davi asked her again.

"There's no one, Davi, and there hasn't been. You're the only woman Quinn has ever wanted his friends to meet."

"Then why do I suddenly feel like I'm on the hot seat?"

"She's making sure Jake's not making up stories about you. Sarah's my overprotective studio mother, Davi," Quinn said as he walked into the room with a towel wrapped around his waist. His hair was wet and disheveled. His face was clean-shaven.

"I'm allowed to be, Quinn. Someone has to look out for you." Sarah smiled, but her concern still showed in her eyes.

"I love her, and you'll love her too, Sarah bear. You know I'm right." Quinn pulled Sarah into his arms. "What's your husband going to think if I tell him you're jealous of my fiancée?"

"He'll say, 'What's new?'" Sarah laughed into his chest. "Now let me go. We've got work to do."

Sarah held out her hand to Davi. "I'm sorry if I made you feel uncomfortable. It's just that—"

"No need to explain," Davi interrupted her. "I'd be protective of him too. He's lucky to have friends like you, Luke, and Jake."

Sarah smiled at Davi and then picked up a pile of clothing from the counter.

"Here, Quinn, put these on."

Quinn dropped his towel and proceeded to get dressed.

"Quinn!" Sarah gasped in mock shock. "There are women present. Have you no modesty?"

"Not around you two lovelies. You've seen me naked more times than anyone I know, Sarah, and I don't think Davi minds. Do you, Davi?" He smiled wickedly at her.

"Not at all." She chuckled.

Quinn sat in the barber's chair next to Davi.

"Do your magic, Sarah. What do I have to look like now?"

"Let's have a look at you." Sarah spun the chair around to have a close look at Quinn's face. "You're perfect. There's not much for me to do."

Sarah worked quickly and efficiently on Quinn. His mop of hair was dried and styled to his classic shaggy look in no time. Then she went to work on his face with ease.

"Quinn's got perfect skin, Davi. You probably noticed that already. I don't need to do much. Just get him ready for the camera lights and draw attention to those baby blues."

Sarah gave special attention to Quinn's eyes. She was fast with the brush and powder. She made it look so easy. By the time she was finished, Quinn was his perfect self. His bedroom baby blues were sizzling.

"All done," Sarah announced.

It was perfect timing. There was a light rap on the door before Jake walked in.

"Ready?"

"Let's go," announced Quinn. He rose from his chair and gave Davi a quick kiss on the lips. "Jake will look after you now, love. I'll see you later." Then he was gone.

Jake kept the door open for Davi.

"I guess that's my cue to leave," she said. "I'd like us to be friends, Sarah."

"We are friends," Sarah said as she hugged Davi. "Don't mind me, Davi. I've been looking after Quinn since he started in this business. I've never heard him talk about anyone the way he does you. He's so happy. It's hard to let go."

"You don't have to let go. Just share."

"She's been with him forever," Jake explained as he walked Davi to the shoot. "Sarah's been Quinn's makeup artist and dresser since he came to Hollywood."

"She loves him," Davi said knowingly.

"Like a son or best friend. There's nothing going on there, Davi. One thing you'll discover is that Quinn doesn't have many friends, but the ones he does have are his best friends. We love him and watch out for him. We're Quinn's gang."

"Where does that leave me?"

"Right where you should be—with Quinn."

Jake pointed out to the roped-off area across the street where hundreds of bystanders were lined up to watch the production. Davi had seen pictures on the Internet of the crowds that gathered at location shoots. The photos didn't do the enormity of the mob justice. Security guards lined the rope. People were pushing and shoving to get a better view of Quinn. The screams were deafening. Davi felt slightly afraid. She looked for Quinn. He was standing over by the director with another actor running through the scene. Quinn didn't have his script in his hand. His photographic memory made that unnecessary. If there were ever changes made to the script, he would only have to be told once, and he made the changes. He made acting look so natural.

Jake ushered Davi to a seating area off to the side.

"We can stay here and watch. It's almost suppertime. They'll make a few test runs before they break for something to eat. Then they'll do the filming for real. The canteen is over there." Jake pointed to a fenced-in area with a catering truck and picnic tables. "The food is great."

Break time was called. Quinn slapped the other actor's shoulder and laughed. Both of them walked over to the crowd. The crowd went wild. Quinn offered to have his picture taken with a few people and then signed some autographs. He apologized to them when he broke away to get something to eat and promised to come back after the shoot was finished.

Davi, Jake, and Quinn headed off to the canteen.

"I'm starved," Quinn remarked as he wrapped his arm around Davi.

The threesome went through the food line. Davi chose a mixed salad and chicken breast, Quinn had pasta, and Jake had a sandwich. Quinn's pasta was devoured in seconds. Davi passed him her barely touched salad and chicken.

"I'll get something later," she offered.

"Thank you."

"Let me get it for you now," offered Jake as he got out of his chair. "It will give you two a minute alone." He smiled at them.

"He's a great guy. So is Sarah. They love you."

"Sometimes I don't know how they put up with me." Quinn stared at his plate, playing with his food and then looked up at Davi. "There's nothing going on between Sarah and me."

"I know."

"She took me under her wing when I first started working. She knows everything about me. We're best friends."

"I can see that, Quinn."

"I want to make sure . . ."

"Make sure of what?"

His eyes searched her face for understanding. "I don't have a thing for older women. You are the only woman I have eyes for, Davi. And I don't consider you old."

"Don't," Davi said quietly, shaking her head. "Don't say another word."

"It's just that—"

Davi put her finger over his lips. "Quinn. Shut up before you dig yourself into a hole you'll never get out of."

"I'm an idiot," he said against her finger.

"My gorgeous idiot," Davi corrected him.

"Time to head back," announced Jake as he returned with Davi's food.

"See you later." Quinn leaned forward and kissed Davi good-bye.

Quinn walked off and Davi could hear the screams from the crowd. Jake placed the salad in front of Davi.

"Thanks," she said. "I'll stay here and enjoy whatever quiet there may be."

"No such luck. Finish your salad. Quinn will want to see you watching him. He settles knowing you're around. We've all noticed it. You have the magic."

"Jake," Davi started to protest.

"Don't argue with me, Davi. You don't know what he was like before, but since he met you, he's changed for the better. Although you haven't been here this week, knowing he can talk to you settles him. I've seen him calling you or texting you. The moods are gone, and the bad behavior has disappeared. You've changed him, Davi."

"Maybe he was ready to change. Did you consider that?"

"He had to change, but he wasn't ready." A mischievous smile worked its way across Jake's face.

"What is it?" Davi asked cautiously.

"I was thinking of your phone conversation with Quinn in the limo the other day. I've never laughed so hard." He laughed as he thought about it.

"Tell me you didn't hear it." Davi could feel the heat of her blush.

"Oh, I didn't have to hear it, Davi. The look on Quinn's face told me everything I needed to know. You definitely have the magic."

Chapter 16

Quinn worked late into the night while Davi sat in her director's chair, bundled in a blanket and drinking café mochas to keep her warm. Neither one was tired by the time they made it back to Quinn's hotel suite.

"You didn't tell me you had a franchise," Davi commented as she entered the suite.

Quinn looked at Davi, not understanding her.

"Chez Quinn, New York. It's identical to your LA suite."

"Of course! It's the same. It makes it easy for me. I have two of everything on both sides of the country. Well, almost everything."

"What is it that you don't have two of? Is it your Porsche?" Davi teased him.

"No. It's you," he said. "There will only be one Davi." Quinn closed the door behind him and took Davi in his arms. "I'm sorry for what I said earlier."

"Don't be. It's forgotten."

Quinn leaned down and kissed her. "You don't know how much I've missed this," he breathed into her ear as he released her from his kiss.

"I brought my lingerie. Would you like me to put something on?"

"Not this time. It's all coming off. I have a fantasy I'd like to try out."

He took his time with her, slowly undoing the buttons of her shirt while giving her hot kisses. His large hands slid the shirt off Davi's shoulders and let it fall to the floor.

"I like this bra," he murmured as his mouth made its way to the delicate lace barely covering her soft round breasts.

"You should," Davi gasped as he took her nipple into his mouth. "You bought it for me."

Davi ran her hands through Quinn's hair. She loved the feel of it, pulling gently on it. She released him when he undid her bra and let him take it off her. Quinn fell to his knees and kissed Davi's belly. Slowly he undid her jeans and pulled them down over her hips to the floor. Davi stepped out of them.

"You're beautiful," he said with reverence, "so beautiful."

Quinn took a condom package out of his jeans pocket. "Until you tell me not to, we'll use these."

"Do you always carry condoms with you?"

"Only when I'm with you," Quinn murmured. "I'd hate to miss an opportunity to make love to you."

Quinn picked Davi up and carried her into the living room. He put Davi down by the floor to the ceiling window that overlooked New York City.

"I want to make love to you while we both look down on the city lights."

Quinn kicked off his jeans then put the condom on. He cradled her body from behind. Davi molded into him; she knew what she had to do. She pressed her hands against the window for support. The glass was cool and felt good against her skin. Quinn's hands cradled Davi's breasts. He kissed her neck, his breath hot against her skin. Slowly, Quinn slid into Davi. As always, she was ready for him.

"Isn't it a beautiful view?" he murmured in her ear.

"Yes," she breathed.

Davi found it difficult to concentrate. Quinn's thrusts were slow and deliberate, the pressure causing her to tingle all over. She was melting into him. Her legs were going weak, but Quinn held her in place. Davi wanted to turn around and kiss Quinn. Her lips ached for him. She closed her eyes and ran her tongue over her lips, imagining Quinn kissing them.

Quinn could see her reflection in the window. "Keep your eyes open, Davi. I want to see your face against the lights."

"When did you come up with this one?" her voice was almost a whisper.

"When I talked to you on the phone the first night we were apart. I was looking out this window and missing you, and all I had to look at was the lights. Now when I look out this window, I'll see your face too."

Quinn's pace quickened. Davi moved her hips to accommodate him. Quinn's right hand left her breast and found her nub. He applied pressure as his strokes increased. Davi pushed her rump into Quinn. She wanted all of him, enjoying the overwhelming pleasure he was giving her. Davi gasped. Her orgasm was close to coming, but she was fighting it.

"Let it come, Davi," Quinn coaxed her. "Don't fight it."

"But it feels so good. I don't want it to end."

"Let it go," he said softly.

The sound of his voice sent shivers through her. Davi moaned the loudest and longest release she had ever experienced. Quinn released himself soon after. He shuddered as he held on to her. They stayed joined until their breathing eased.

Quinn turned Davi around and picked her up. "Now it's time for sleep, my love."

After breakfast, Quinn and Davi headed down to the hotel's underground parking. Quinn's car was parked in the reserved section. Davi looked around. She saw various cars: Porsche, BMW, Ferrari, Audi, and domestic. They approached a black Volkswagen convertible Beetle.

"Here she is, Davi, my little bug," Quinn said with pride.

"She's beautiful!" Davi gushed as she ran her hands over it. "I love it! I never thought you'd have one of these. They look like they're so much fun."

"They are. No one expects to see me in something like this. We've seen many places together. Come on, get in," Quinn said excitedly as he opened the passenger door for her. "I know it's kind of cool outside, but I want you to feel her with her top down."

Quinn started the car and put the top down. Then he reached into the glove compartment and pulled out a Yankees baseball cap for himself. "Now I know you are particular about your caps, so I sent away for this. I hope you like it." Quinn pulled out a package from under the seat.

Davi smiled when she opened the package. It was a John Deere Owners cap. She put the cap on and smiled at Quinn. "Thank you. I love it!"

Quinn pulled out into the morning traffic. The air was cool on Davi's face, but she didn't mind. She was having a ball and loving it. Quinn touched his iPod. "The Theme Song" from *Rocky* came on full blast.

Davi laughed. "You're a child of the eighties, aren't you?"

"I love the eighties music—great beat and terrific sound. And the dance music—there's nothing better!"

"You and my kids will get along famously. They are definitely lovers of the eighties."

Quinn moved expertly through the traffic. He ignored the occasional rude driver and smiled when he was cut off. No one was going to ruin his mood. Eventually they made it to the studio. The sidewalk was already lined with fans and paparazzi waiting to get a glimpse of him. No one knew he had a black Beetle. He wondered if he could drive past the mob and make it to the gate without being recognized. No such luck.

"Smile," he said, "we're about to get mobbed."

Photographers descended upon the open Beetle like vultures. Quinn slowed the car down to a stop. They were surrounded.

"Hey, guys!" he greeted them. "How's it going?"

"Quinn, give a look over here! Smile! Davina! Smile!" Commands were coming at them from all directions.

"Want to give them a nice picture, Davi, and show off your hat?"

"Sure, why not?"

Quinn leaned over to Davi and put his arm around her, pulling her close. They smiled for the cameras. He counted to ten. "Okay, that's it! Please let us through now."

The paparazzi pulled away. "Thanks! Catch you later!"

Quinn drove past security. Jake stood waiting for them. Quinn pulled up beside him.

"You handled that well, Quinn. You're getting your touch back." He looked at Davi and smiled broadly. "And here's the reason why. Good morning, lovely lady."

"Good morning, Jake."

Quinn got out of the car and walked around to let Davi out. He was always the perfect gentleman. Jake escorted them to Quinn's trailer.

"Good morning, gorgeous!" Sarah met him at the door and hugged him. "You're going to love what we have for you today!" Sarah moved on to Davi and gave her a hug. "Good morning, Davi! It's going to be a great day today." Then she gave Jake a hug. "Hey, big guy."

"He's all yours. I have to check on security. See you later." Jake left as quickly as he had entered.

Sarah ushered Davi to the unoccupied barber's chair. Quinn was already seated and looking at the clipboard on the counter.

"Ah," Quinn said, "I'm getting all dolled up today and going dancing. I'm also going to find myself a bad guy or two while I'm at it. Perfect."

"It sounds like you're filming a Bond movie, Quinn."

"Not even close, Davi."

Quinn got up and started to undress. Sarah folded his clothes as he handed them to her.

"Take note as to how well Sarah looks after me, woman. I expect this when we're married." He winked at Davi and smiled wickedly.

"Don't you dare expect that of her, Quinn, or I'll be giving you what for!" Sarah scolded him.

Davi couldn't help but laugh at the two of them. The tension from last night was gone.

"Here, put this on." Sarah handed him his tuxedo shirt and pants. "Here are your shoes, and make sure you put on the black socks this time. I'm not going to get yelled at by the director because you think it looks better to wear white athletic socks."

"He wouldn't," she gasped in mock horror.

"Oh, he did, and I got chewed out for letting him sneak that by me. You have to watch this man constantly." Sarah ruffled Quinn's hair as she spoke. "Now sit still and let me do your face." Sarah inspected Quinn. "You look tired, hon. Not much sleep last night?" She looked at Davi.

"I tried, Sarah, but he just wouldn't stop."

Quinn winked. "You should have been there, Sarah. It was the best! Oh, on second thought, it was a good thing you weren't."

All three of them laughed. Sarah finished with Quinn's makeup and then helped him with his bow tie and jacket.

"How do I look?" He turned to face Davi.

"I'm speechless." She kissed him lightly on the lips. "I'm jealous of your dance partner."

"Don't be." He took Davi by the hand. "Come on, let's go! There's a movie to be made."

They made their way to a different set. This one was made up like a ballroom. It had the chandeliers, the dance floor, and the tables and chairs. The orchestra was setting up on the stage. Quinn led Davi to her chair where Jake waited with a coffee.

"You spoil me, Jake. Thanks."

"You're welcome. See you later, Quinn." Jake smiled broadly as he waved his friend away.

Quinn snorted. "I'm going once I kiss my lady good-bye." He kissed Davi lightly on the lips. "See you later."

"Bye. Have fun."

Davi settled into her director's chair and enjoyed her coffee. "So what's this movie about, Jake? Quinn wouldn't say much."

"I have no idea, Davi. I've been on the set since day one, and I still don't know. If you figure it out, let me know. They could be a while before they start. Do you want me to stick around and keep you company?"

"Only if you want to, Jake, but I can keep myself busy with some reading."

"Okay. I'll go check on things outside and see how it's going. See you later."

"See you."

Davi pulled out a magazine from her purse. She didn't want to read anything too heavy. She knew her focus would be needed elsewhere. It didn't take long for the orchestra to get settled and start warming up. Davi put the magazine away. Her coffee was cold. She got up to get a refill before the filming started. She remembered seeing a refreshment table when she walked in, so she headed off that way.

Sally stood by the table, sipping her coffee.

"Hi, Davi, how are you?"

"Hi, Sally. I'm great and you?"

"I'm well, thanks. Are you looking forward to seeing the ballroom scene? I hear Quinn's quite the dancer. All the women are going to be hanging around to watch that man in action."

"I've seen him dance on-screen," Davi confessed. "And you're right, he is amazing to watch. But I've never danced with him."

"You've never danced with him?" Sally's eyes opened wide in surprise.

"We haven't had the chance, Sally. Sorry to disappoint you there." Davi chuckled. *Didn't Sally know that she and Quinn had only been together for a week?*

"Well, maybe you'll get the chance soon."

"I hope so." Davi smiled at Sally as she thought of dancing with Quinn. *Another fantasy to make real.* "I'm going to head back to my seat. I'll see you later, Sally."

Davi made it back to her seat. Cast members dressed in ball gowns and tuxedos were assembling on the dance floor. The director and choreographer were going over the scene. The director marked off where he did not want them to go on the dance floor. That would be Quinn and Rene's spot. They checked for spacing and lighting. The cameras were set up in the right positions.

Quinn and Rene came onto the dance floor. Quinn, always the gentleman, escorted Rene to their spot. She was dazzling. Her long dress sparkled under the lights. The cut of the front showed off her amazing breasts, or bowling balls according to Quinn. Her hair was coiled on top of her head, accentuating her long graceful neck. Quinn looked his gorgeous self. They were a striking pair.

As the director talked to them, Quinn took Rene in his arms and danced with her. There was no music, but Quinn waltzed perfectly with Rene. He followed the director's cues exactly. He looked in the right direction, turned in the right direction, and smiled at the right time. Every move was perfectly choreographed.

When the director yelled, "Stop!" Quinn halted and released Rene. "That's perfect, Quinn. Do you think you can remember it when we film?"

Everyone around them laughed. Quinn only had to be told once and it was burned into his memory. If there were to be more than one take, it wouldn't be because of Quinn.

The orchestra was cued to play and the dancing began. Quinn took Rene in his arms and they began to waltz. They were so graceful together. Davi's mouth dropped open as she watched them expertly stay away from the other dancers and stay in their area of the dance floor. Quinn dipped at the right time, smiled, and looked in the right direction. They kept dancing as the cameras moved around them, getting all of the different angles. Davi looked at her watch. They had been waltzing for fifteen minutes straight. Quinn didn't even look tired. Rene, however, was looking weary. Finally, she just stopped.

"Cut!" yelled the director. "Rene, sweetheart, what's the matter?"

"My feet are killing me! No one can dance for that long! Except for Quinn and that doesn't count. He's not wearing five-inch heels!"

Quinn released Rene and smiled. He sympathized with his costar. He knew she was struggling to keep up with him no matter how easy he tried to make it for her.

"Take a break everyone! We'll have a look at what we filmed and see if it's sufficient. Stay close by."

Quinn turned and headed straight for Davi. She noticed he hadn't even broken into a sweat. He turned his chair toward her and sat down.

"Hey, beautiful."

"Hey, yourself. That was amazing dancing. You are such a professional!" She leaned into him and whispered, "Did you notice all the women on the sidelines watching you? You are the highlight to their day."

"I didn't see anyone." He turned to have a quick look at his audience. "Honest. I didn't see them. I don't see anyone when I know you're here." He reached for her hand and gave it a squeeze. He pointed to her coffee cup. "May I?" he asked.

"It's probably cold by now." She offered him her cup.

"It doesn't matter. I'm thirsty." He took a long drink from her cup.

"When I'm not here, do you see them?"

"No. I only think of you."

"Smooth answer."

"But true. So do you dance? I never thought to ask you. Not that it matters."

"What do you mean it doesn't matter? If you can dance like that, you'll want a partner who can dance too."

"So can you?"

"Not like that, though I wish I could."

"You will. You just need me," he said with unabashed confidence.

"Rene can dance beautifully."

Quinn shook his head and smiled. "She doesn't dance. She learned a few steps yesterday to help her get through this. That's why her feet hurt so much. I just carried her through it, but don't tell anyone. It's a secret." He winked at her.

"I won't say a word," she promised.

"Okay, everyone, back to the dance floor, please. Quinn, Rene, we're going to do your close-ups now. Makeup! Let's do a touch-up please!"

"I've got to go. See you at the next break." He kissed Davi on her head and then left to meet up with Sarah.

The rest of the morning went by slowly. Quinn and Rene danced while the camera zoomed in on their faces. They did this take several times, and then they had to do it with their dialogue. From what Davi understood, Quinn was looking for Rene's boyfriend and was trying not to let Rene find out about it. There was verbal fencing going on between them. This was to lead up to the rape scene.

Davi looked at her watch. It was almost lunchtime. She wondered if they took a break at noon. Davi looked around and saw Jake standing near the exit. She got up and walked over to him.

"Hey, Davi, how's it going?"

"I'm bored, Jake. I can't take much more of this. It's one thing being an actual part of the production, but sitting on the sidelines is a killer," she said quietly to him, cautious of being overheard.

"Tell me about it," Jake nodded his head in agreement. "I'm glad I can walk around and check on the security and chat with people. Otherwise, I'd be in the loony bin."

"You think they'll break for lunch soon? It's almost noon."

"Getting hungry or are you ready to leave?" Jake could read Davi so well.

"Do you think he'll mind?"

Jake put his hand on her shoulder. "Of course he'll mind. You're his muse, but if you need a break from this, he won't stop you. He'll understand."

"Maybe I could hang out in his trailer. It's quiet there, and I could work on my book. I have my draft and a memory stick with me. If I had a computer I could work on, it would really help."

"Good idea. I'll see what I can rustle up for you. Do you need Mac or Windows?"

"Anything with Word will work. I'll make sure I bring my own laptop next time."

"Let me walk you to Quinn's trailer. You get settled, and I'll find you a computer. Sally will get one for me, I'm sure."

"What about Quinn?"

"He'll be fine. I'll make sure someone lets him know where you are if they break for lunch before I'm back."

"Thanks, Jake." Jake and Davi had arrived at the trailer. "I'll take it from here."

"See you later." Jake turned and walked back toward the set.

Davi made herself familiar with the trailer. It was a man's trailer. On one side, it had all the comforts of home and more. A large overstuffed couch, a gigantic flat-screen television, game systems, and a sound system filled the living area. The kitchen was small, but it had everything—microwave, large refrigerator, and dishwasher. Behind the living room was Quinn's bedroom. It was decorated tastefully in masculine colors of beige, brown, and black, complete with a king-sized bed. Davi checked out the bathroom. It had a huge shower in it, another one that could host a party. Quinn's wardrobe racks and his makeup counter were neatly organized for him on the other side.

Davi settled on the couch. She turned on her iTunes and put in her earplugs. Davi pulled out her manuscript and a pen and then started reading the second last chapter to get her into the flow of the story. She really wanted to get this book ended. It nagged at her constantly in the back of her mind.

The story is about modern-day lovers trying to find their way in the world. The heroine is the country girl trying to find her way in the big city. The hero is the country boy waiting for the country girl to find her way back to him. The heroine is successful in the city, overcoming the obstacles of the proverbial glass ceiling, but something is missing from her life. A family tragedy brings her back to the country. There she reconnects with her ex-lover and becomes torn between staying with him and returning to the city. She wants the best from both worlds, and the story concentrates on her struggle to achieve that through compromise.

Davi cursed that she didn't have a computer to write her final chapter. *This will have to do*, she thought as she turned the manuscript over and wrote on the back of the pages. Her chapter flowed out of her. The words came easily and with the feeling she had been desperate to find. Davi was oblivious to time passing. When she finished the last sentence, she put down her pen and let out a triumphant sigh. Her book was finished. At least the first draft was.

Davi looked at her watch. It was almost three o'clock. Her stomach started to growl. She went to the kitchen and looked for something to eat. The fridge was full of beverages and cucumber. The cucumber was Sarah's. She saw Sarah use it on Quinn's puffy eyes. Davi took out a diet Coke and then opened the freezer. It was filled with frozen dinners. She took one out and popped it into the microwave. In two minutes, it was ready. Davi pulled off the cellophane, got a fork from the drawer, and sat down in the living room to eat her lunch.

Davi enjoyed the quiet. It let her pull her thoughts together. *Quinn and I will have to compromise and it's going to hurt a bit, but I know we can make this work. He'll have to be the one that comes to the country. There's no way I'm doing this!*

"Jake!" Davi suddenly remembered him. He didn't return with the computer. Something must have happened. He wouldn't have left her for this long. Davi panicked. She opened the door, ran down the stairs, and headed toward the set. Her mind raced with thoughts of something going horribly wrong. She opened the door to the set and saw Jake talking with Sally.

"Jake!" she gasped.

"Davi, what's wrong?"

"I was worried. You didn't come back. Has something happened?" her voice faltered.

Jake smiled and put a comforting arm around her shoulders. "Davi, I did come back to the trailer, but you were so engrossed in your work I didn't want to disturb you. I left the laptop on the counter and came back here. Quinn knew how much you needed to work so he left you alone too. How did it go?"

Davi let out a sigh of relief. "I finished it, Jake. The first draft is done. I'm so excited!"

"Way to go! Does that mean you'll be celebrating tonight?"

"You don't usually celebrate the first draft, but I guess it wouldn't hurt. The ending to this has been a real struggle. Being here really helped me put the pieces together." Davi looked around. "How's Quinn? What is he up to now?"

"He finished filming the dance scene then went on to the fight sequence. Quinn should be ready for makeup soon. He's got to get bloodied up." Jake looked over Davi's shoulder. "Here he comes now."

"There she is!" Quinn grabbed Davi from behind and gave her a big hug. "I heard you were hard at it. How did the book writing go?"

"I finished it, at least the first draft. I'm really excited about it."

Quinn turned Davi around. "That's great! Congratulations!" He kissed her tenderly on the lips. "We'll have to celebrate. Once we're done with the fight scene, we'll be finished here." Quinn put his arm around Davi's waist and led her back to the trailer.

Sarah was already inside waiting for him.

"Now I get to do ugly on you, Quinn. I've been looking forward to this all week!"

"Be gentle, please. We don't want to scare off Davi," Quinn teased.

"I think she's made of harder stuff," Sarah chuckled.

Davi tidied up the mess she had left behind in the living room.

"So what's the book about, Davi?" Sarah asked. "Everyone's talking about the next best seller being written right here in Quinn's trailer."

"I don't know if it's going to be a best seller. It's a romance about people from different worlds, trying to make their love work for them. The ending just came to me today. It's been a tough go."

"I wonder why that is?" Sarah winked at her. "Does anyone we know have anything to do with it?"

Davi looked at Quinn, who was watching her through the mirror. "Oh, Quinn interrupted the thought process, that's for sure, but he also helped me with the ending. I don't know if it would have come to me if I hadn't been here."

"So maybe you'll dedicate the book to him?"

"You never know." Davi smiled lovingly at Quinn. *Yes, this book will be dedicated to him.*

"You're all done, Quinn. I'll have to add to it gradually. Try not to get hurt for real." She patted his shoulder.

"I will try. How do I look, Davi? Do I look kissable?" He puckered his bloodied lips at her.

Davi planted a kiss on his forehead. "That's about all I can do."

"Then that's all I need. See you later, love."

Quinn got out of his chair and left the trailer.

"Am I supposed to go with him? He didn't say anything this time."

"You can do whatever you want. Stay here or watch him beat up some poor guy. What would you like to do?"

"I'd really like to go for a walk. I need to get some exercise." Davi stretched her arms as she spoke.

"I'd go with you, but I have to do his makeup. Ask Jake. He can help you with that. Come on, let's go."

Sarah opened the door, and the two of them left the trailer.

Chapter 17

♥

Davi was overjoyed to have her freedom even if it was only for an hour or two. It didn't take much convincing to get Jake to agree to let her go for a walk outside the confines of the studio. He would be her bodyguard. That was his only condition.

"What about Quinn? Do we have to tell him?" She felt like a teenager planning to sneak out after curfew.

"No. We'll tell him afterward. There's no need to worry him. And besides, you're with me."

Jake was happy to have Davi as an excuse to leave the studio. He hadn't been on the outside for a long time. This would be refreshing and stressful at the same time. Getting Davi through the mob outside would be the hardest part. They made their way to the gates. The sidewalks were filled with eager fans waiting for a glimpse of their favorite star. The paparazzi lounged on the curb, waiting for a photo opportunity.

"Just smile, Davi. You don't have to talk to them. I'll get you through this." Jake took Davi by the hand and led her across the street to the sidewalk.

The mob started screaming.

"Do they even know who I am?" Davi asked in bemusement.

"You bet they do." Jake turned to the approaching paparazzi. "Back off, guys. Give the lady some room."

The cameras flashed as microphones were pushed in front of her face.

"Where are you off to, Davina? How are things going with the film?"

Davi smiled at the cameras. "Hey, guys. I'm going for a walk. I need to stretch my legs."

"And what's Quinn up to?" one of them asked her.

"Last I heard, he was busy beating up people."

"You don't like violence? Is that it?"

"No, I just want to go for a walk."

Jake guided her expertly through the mob. They were cooperative in letting her through. She thanked them as they let her pass.

"Well, done, Davi," Jake praised her. "You make it look so easy."

"Thanks. Where are we heading? I have no idea where we are."

"Nowhere in particular. There isn't much in this area except for the old buildings. The architecture is quite amazing."

"You're into architecture?"

"I almost studied it, but things happened. I still appreciate a beautiful building, though."

"Isn't it funny how our plans can change? We never know for certain what the cards have in store for us. Even if they tell us good things are coming."

Jake kept hold of Davi's hand. She didn't mind. She felt secure with him, and she knew that he felt better knowing that he had hold of her.

"You're a good walker, Davi. You've got a good pace."

"Thanks. I try to walk every day around the farm. It's good for the body and helps clear the mind. I haven't had a chance to take a walk while I've been here."

"Do you miss home? I know this is nothing close to it."

"You're right. There are no similarities between New York and home. I don't really miss home until I drive up the driveway, and then it hits me that I've been away. I miss the openness and the fresh air. I miss seeing my cows. I miss my kids, but they are busy with their own lives, so I know they are okay without me for a while. I miss my bed. It's hard getting used to a hotel bed no matter how comfortable it is and with whom I'm sharing it."

"He's hard to sleep with, is he?"

"I didn't say that. Actually, he's like a big teddy bear. There's so much to cuddle. Your wife must love sharing the bed with you. You're huge."

"I haven't heard her complain, although I don't think she thinks of me as a teddy bear." Jake motioned for them to sit down on a bench. "Quinn said that you sent him pictures of your farm. May I see them?"

"Of course you can!"

Davi pulled out her cell phone and handed it to Jake.

"I know nothing about cows," Jake said sheepishly. "I love all dairy products, but I have no idea where milk comes from."

Davi pointed to the first picture. "This is a newborn calf. It weighs around one hundred pounds when it's born."

"How many calves does a cow have?"

"They're just like people, Jake. I call them the Ladies. They can have one or twins or sometimes triplets, but that is rare. We prefer they have just one at a time. It's easier on the cow."

Jake could tell by the animation in her voice that Davi loved talking about the Ladies. He could sense the deep affection she had for them.

"How often do they have calves?"

"Their pregnancy is just like ours—nine months and nine days. And they have to have a calf to be able to give us milk, so they have a calf every year."

"Do you have a bull on the farm?"

"No, it's too dangerous. We use artificial insemination, and we pick the bulls that will improve our herd production. It's very scientific now."

"No sex?"

"No sex and to make it worse, we don't keep the male calves. We sell them, and they get raised for beef."

"That sucks." Jake shook his head as he looked at the rest of the pictures.

"The Ladies rule when it comes to dairy farming," Davi said proudly. "That's Buddy," Davi said when the picture of her truck appeared.

"Nice," Jake whistled his appreciation. "V8?"

"Yes. He's fully loaded. I love driving him. What do you drive when you're not Quinn's chauffeur and bodyguard?" Davi asked him as she pocketed her cell phone.

Jake chuckled. "I drive a minivan, but don't tell anyone. It's bad for my image as badass security guard."

"You look more like the biker type to me," Davi said as she looked at Jake. It was hard to ignore his size. He was about six feet five inches tall with a bodybuilder's physique. Jake's black leather jacket fit snugly across his broad shoulders and massive chest. His hair was cropped close to the scalp. Davi wouldn't be surprised if he sported a tattoo or two.

Jake smiled as he thought of his bike. "I have a Hog, a nineteen ninety-three Fat Boy. I take her out every chance I get." Jake looked at his watch. "It's time to get you back. Quinn should be wrapping up soon."

"This has been nice, Jake. Next time can we talk more about you?"

"There isn't much to tell, but next time we'll talk about me."

Jake walked Davi back through the crowd to Quinn's trailer. "He should be here any minute."

"How do you know that?" Davi asked.

Jake pointed to an earpiece in his right ear. "Hands-free communication."

Jake and Davi entered the trailer.

"May I get you a drink, Jake? I think I'll have some water."

"Water will be great. Thanks."

Davi went to the fridge and took out two bottles. She handed one to Jake. She walked over to the couch and sat down, picked up the remote, and switched on the television.

The television station blared, "And coming up next, our entertainment reporter has the latest on Quinn Thomas and D. L. Stuart. Please join us after this commercial."

"This should be interesting." Davi sat back on the couch and had a long drink of water. "I wonder what we've done today."

It was a long two-minute wait, but finally the reporter came on. "Today, D. L. Stuart toured New York City with her very own bodyguard. While her fiancé, Hollywood heartthrob Quinn Thomas, was busy filming his latest movie which is still untitled, Davina Stuart toured the streets of New York."

The film footage of Davi and Jake showed them holding hands while Jake led her across the street. It was a very innocent shot, but of course, this reporter couldn't leave it alone.

"The last time we saw a bodyguard holding a star's hand, they ended up dating! Is there something going on that Quinn doesn't know about? This is something that this reporter will look into."

"Well, that was interesting," Quinn drawled from behind them.

Jake and Davi startled. They hadn't noticed him coming in.

"What have you two been up to while I've been working?"

Davi's face went white. Tears came to her eyes.

"Damn press," Jake cursed. "They take something purely innocent and turn it into something sordid. I'm sorry, Davi, I should have known this would happen."

Jake looked at Quinn and got up. "I'll leave you to it. I'll wait for you to leave to make sure you get out okay."

"Thanks, Jake." Quinn clapped Jake on the shoulder as he walked by him.

"Davi, sweetheart, please don't cry." Quinn sat on the couch beside her and took her in his arms. "She's just an idiot reporter. She says stupid stuff like that all of the time. No one takes her seriously."

"But that was hurtful. Jake and I took an innocent walk and she made it look ugly. It's embarrassing and insulting."

"You'll have to get used to it. At least half the stuff you read in the entertainment magazines is made up. We rarely give interviews, yet they have pictures of us and inside information that they print every week." Quinn kissed her forehead.

"I don't know how you can be so cool about it."

"It's easy when you know it's not the truth. When you do speak to the press, be nice, give a short answer, and don't rise to the bait. They'll respect you if you give them respect. Now dry those eyes. We've been invited to Jake and Sue's to meet the gang, if you are feeling up to it. They are dying to spend some time with you."

"Are we going back to change?"

"No, it's casual. I'll have a quick shower before we head out." Quinn got up and started to undress.

"Mind if I join you? I know your shower is big enough for both of us."

"There's nothing I'd like more," he said lustfully as Davi started to undress on her way to the bathroom.

The water was hot and so was their lovemaking. The two of them had become very adept at having sex while standing up. They were the perfect fit for each other. Davi wrapped her arms around Quinn's neck and her legs around his waist while he supported her hips with his strong arms. His thrusts were deep and powerful. Davi tingled with the electricity that flowed between them. She dug in deep and held on to him. Quinn crushed her to his body, his thrusts getting faster and harder. A low moan escaped from him. Davi came right after him. She loosened her grip on him and slowly let her feet down until she could stand.

"Wow," they said in unison and then kissed each other.

"Jake's waiting for us," Davi reminded Quinn.

"He knows what we're doing. He won't mind." Quinn nuzzled her ear.

"This is embarrassing."

"No, it's not. He's happy for us, so don't be embarrassed. Now let's get dressed. We don't want to be too late."

Quinn dressed, ran his hands through his hair, and was ready. He sat in one of the barber's chairs and watched Davi as she dressed and then dried her hair. He loved how her hair fell past her shoulders and framed her face. She was truly beautiful.

"All done," she announced. "I'm ready."

Quinn got up and kissed her softly on the lips. "I am so happy. Thank you for coming into my life, woman."

"Thank you for wanting me in your life."

Chapter 18

♥

Jake and Sue lived in an old brownstone in an old part of the city. Quinn parked his car in front of the house. Quinn opened the car door for Davi and walked her up the long stairway to the front door. Before he could knock, Sue had the door wide open and was hugging Davi and pulling her into the house at the same time. Quinn followed close behind and shut the door behind him.

"Davi, how are you?"

Davi was surprised by Sue's strength for someone so tiny. Davi didn't think Sue weighed more than one hundred pounds. Sue kept her brunette hair stylishly short to frame her cute pixie face.

"I'm fine. Thanks for inviting us over."

"Davi, this is Sue." Quinn laughed. "Don't let her size fool you. She can put any one of us on the floor before we know it. That's how she keeps Jake in line."

"Shut up, you!" Sue swatted at him. "Everyone's here."

Sue led Davi to the kitchen. "Jake's in charge of the bar. Just give him your order."

The spacious kitchen was at the back of the house. Off to the side, in front of a large window was an enormous harvest table that easily seated the gang of ten. The group stood as Davi entered and each man gave her a bear hug as she made the round of introductions to all of them. The women all smiled warm hellos to Davi as they kissed her cheek.

Quinn stood back and waited for Davi's welcome to finish and then gave a hey-guys to all of them.

"Quinn," was their response in unison.

Quinn and Davi sat at the two offered seats. Jake placed a beer in front of Quinn.

"What's your pleasure, Davi?"

"I'll have a soda please, Jake. It doesn't matter what it is." Davi noticed the looks she got by not asking for an alcoholic beverage.

The group settled into a lively discussion focused on Davi. Quinn kept an arm draped around Davi's shoulders, making sure he was always in physical contact with her. She gave them an abridged story of her life, her family, and her farm. She pulled out her cell phone and let them see the pictures of where she lived.

"Jake, it's time to put the barbeque on. Why don't you take the men out with you and let the women get the food together." Sue gave Jake the nod.

"Come on, guys, it's time to do men's work. Anyone want another beer?"

All the men but Quinn got up and went out to the backyard.

"Mind if I hang out with you lovelies?"

Davi took Quinn's hand. "Are you afraid they're going to gang up on me?"

"No. I want to stay in here with you."

"Go, Quinn," Davi ordered. "You'll be fine without me. Go be with the men. They're waiting for you."

Quinn gave Davi a long kiss and then left her with the other women. Davi could hear the women sigh as he left the room.

"Okay," she announced, "you have about ten minutes before he makes his way back here. Ask whatever you were going to ask me and everything stays among us here. It doesn't go any further. Agreed?"

"Agreed," they chorused.

"What was all of that about? Quinn not wanting to leave you," Sarah asked.

"He's always touching you," Sue added.

"I think he's making sure I'm real and not a dream. Maybe he's afraid that I'll disappear if he leaves me."

"Isn't that cute?" one of them said.

"What's he like?" Sue asked boldly.

Davi gasped in surprise, "You want to know what one of your best friends is like in bed?"

Sue answered her honestly, "I want to know if his ability equals his looks. That's all."

"I didn't know that looks had anything to do with it, but if you really want to know . . ."

"Yes!" they all shouted together.

"Better than you'd ever imagine, and he's like that battery bunny—he keeps on going." Davi winked at them.

"I knew it!" Sue exclaimed.

"Did you really meet last week?"

"Yes. We met on a plane flying to LA."

"You're not drinking."

Davi gulped. *Here it comes*, she thought.

"Are you pregnant?" Sue asked quietly.

The other women gasped.

"I hope to find out soon. Quinn knows about it."

"It's his?" someone asked surprised.

"Of course it's his," Sue defended Davi. "Don't be silly."

"If I'm pregnant, the baby is most definitely his."

"Wow," Sarah breathed. "That was really fast. You meet Quinn on a plane, and within a day or two, you're engaged and possibly pregnant."

"I'm having trouble dealing with being pregnant. Please don't tell anyone. We haven't decided what we're going to do."

"Everything's happened too fast," Sarah said softly.

"Tell me about it," Davi sighed. "This could be a movie. I just don't know what kind yet."

"Romance," Sue chirped in. "It will work out. Don't worry." She hugged Davi.

"Do you ladies need any help?" Quinn poked his head through the door.

The women laughed.

"You know him so well, Davi," Sue said, impressed. "Come on in, lover boy, we know how hard this is on you. Come keep us company." Sue motioned for Quinn to have a seat at the table. "Davi, sit with Quinn, and the rest of us will get the food organized."

"Am I that obvious?" Quinn asked with mock surprise.

"Not at all, love." Davi mussed his shaggy hair.

"So about whom or what have you been talking? Was it anything of interest?"

Sarah laughed. "Wouldn't you just like to know? What an ego!"

"It's not ego, my dear. I just know you ladies too well. You were pumping Davi for info on me, weren't you?"

"What kind of info?" Sarah asked.

"You know. The kind that everyone wants to know: Boxers or briefs? Does he snore in his sleep? Does he leave the toilet seat up or put it down? The real juicy stuff." Quinn winked at Davi.

"I think Sarah would already know if you're a boxers or briefs guy, Quinn," Davi said dryly.

"Sometimes he's commando, and sometimes it's the boxer briefs. He likes to surprise me."

"Commando's her favorite, though. I catch her looking," Quinn laughed.

The women joined him.

"No to the snoring, and the toilet seat is always down." Davi finished answering the questions for Quinn.

"Would anyone like to take the steaks out to Jake?" Sue asked as she pulled a large tray of raw meat out of the refrigerator.

"I'll do it," offered Davi. "I'll leave you ladies to look after Quinn." She smiled broadly, took the offered tray, and went outside to the barbeque.

"I brought something for you," Davi announced as she appeared with the tray.

Jake took the tray. "Thanks, Davi. How's it going in there?" He nodded toward the house.

"I think they've got it all under control. They had less than ten minutes with me before Quinn returned to claim me. I thought I'd head out here and see how long he lasts."

"Not even five minutes this time. He's got it bad for you, lady." Jake chuckled as he put the steaks on the grill. "We made him have another beer with us before he could head back in. I hope you like your steak medium well—that's the only way I do it."

"Medium is fine." Davi and Jake stared at the steaks sizzling on the grill. "Do you think he'll make it through the week, Jake?"

"I'll give him until Friday before he's on the plane to see you."

"That's what I was thinking too."

"What were you thinking?" Quinn asked.

"He didn't even last five minutes," Jake remarked.

"Jake and I were thinking that you could make it through to Friday before you jumped on a plane to come see me. That would be our longest separation since we met."

Quinn hugged Davi. "I only hope I can make it that long. You've got a lot of confidence in me, both of you."

"I'm appointing Jake to keep you thoroughly occupied for as long as possible. If I had an in with the movie producer and director, I'd have them keep you busy too."

"Keeping busy isn't the problem," Quinn sighed.

"I know." She kissed him on the cheek and then turned to Jake. "Do you and Sue have children?"

"We have two—a boy and a girl."

"Do you have pictures of them?"

"I've some on my phone." Quinn took out his phone, touched it, and produced a recent photo of Jake's children. "The little girl is four and her name is Rachel and the little boy is Connor and he's two and a half."

"They're beautiful, Jake."

Jake smiled with pride. "Thanks, but they are so exhausting at times. I don't know how Sue manages by herself. Do you have a picture of your children?"

"I have one in my wallet. I'll show it to you sometime. They're a bit older than yours, not as cute perhaps, but I love them to bits."

"I haven't even seen a picture of your family, Davi. You sent me pictures of your cows but not of your kids. Go get the picture for us. Please," Quinn insisted.

Davi went in search of her purse. She knew it was somewhere in the kitchen. Davi found it on the chair where she had sat. She pulled a picture out of her wallet.

"Are the steaks almost ready, Davi?" Sue asked.

"I'm sure they are. I'll ask Jake for you."

Davi left the kitchen with her photo. It was a family picture taken of Davi, her husband, and her children.

"Here," she said as she handed the picture to Quinn. Jake stood beside him to have a look. "This picture was taken about three years ago. This is Rich. He's twenty-five now. This is Cat. She's twenty-four. And this is my baby, Tigger, she's twenty. And this is my late husband, Ross, and me, of course."

"Nice family," Jake said.

Quinn didn't say anything. He passed the photo back to Davi. Davi looked at Quinn but couldn't read his face.

She turned to Jake. "Sue wants to know if the steaks are almost ready."

"Tell her we'll be eating in five minutes. Thanks."

Davi turned and headed off to the kitchen. She didn't know what to make of Quinn's reaction and now was not the time to talk to him about it.

"Steaks will be ready in five minutes, according to the cook." Davi breathed in deeply. "It smells so good in here."

"Thanks. We're ready to eat as soon as the steaks arrive."

Jake entered the kitchen with the men following close behind him. Sue had quite the spread laid out for her guests: baked potatoes, various salads, and fresh bread. Quinn spoke very little. Everyone noticed his silence and tried their best to keep the conversation light.

After their meal, the group went outside to sit by a fire, enjoy their coffee, and listen to music. The air was unusually warm for late September. Slow dance music played in the background.

"Let's dance, Quinn," suggested Davi. She took his hand and pulled him toward the patio. Quinn pulled her in close and started dancing. "I'm sorry," she whispered. "I've upset you, and I didn't mean to."

"No, you didn't upset me. I did it to myself. I apologize for being an idiot."

"Why are you an idiot?"

"I saw that picture of you and your family and I became extremely jealous. That's what I want with you, but you have it already. You don't need to go through it again. Why would you?"

"Because I love you, and it would be something wonderful for the two of us." Davi put a finger over Quinn's lips. "But my heart and head aren't in agreement yet. I'm still working it out. Let's wait to see what happens next week. I love you."

"I love you too."

The music changed into lively disco music. Quinn released Davi from his embrace, and the couple started to dance to the music. Quinn kept his eyes on Davi the entire time. His smile reached his eyes; he laughed as she teased him with her dance moves. Everyone noticed the change in Quinn. He was happy again. The other couples decided to join in the fun on the patio.

Sue shimmied her way over to Davi and whispered in her ear, "You really do have the magic touch with him. Good job!"

Sue danced her way back to Jake.

Davi had a great time dancing. She got to dance with all of the men. It gave her the opportunity to get to know them better. Jake was the last of the friends to dance with Davi. They laughed and smiled at each other. They were both thinking of the same thing—Quinn.

Quinn tried to cut in. Jake wouldn't let him.

"I get my dance with the lady, Quinn. You'll have to wait your turn." He took Davi in his arms and danced her away from Quinn.

Davi laughed, thoroughly enjoying the men's behavior. "I don't think he liked that, Jake."

"He'll get me back, and then he'll get over it."

"How will he get you back?"

"Just watch."

In seconds, Quinn came twirling by with Sue in his arms. Quinn was holding her tight. Jake and Davi could see the blush in Sue's cheeks.

"See, I told you. That's how he gets back at me. He gets Sue all hot and bothered, and then I have to deal with her the rest of the night."

"You say that like it's a bad thing."

"It's not. Not for me anyway," he said happily as he winked at her.

"You're awful. I can see why you two are such close friends."

The music ended.

Jake released Davi from his arms and pointed her in the direction of Quinn. "Go keep him happy."

Sue was already making her way to Jake. Her cheeks were still glowing. Slow dance music started to play. Quinn held his arms open for Davi.

"May I have this dance, woman?" His eyes sparkled in the outdoor lights.

"Nice move on the dance floor there, stud."

"Jake doesn't mind. I'm not Sue's type anyway."

"What makes you think that?"

"He didn't tell you? We met Sue at a bar years ago while we were still nobodies. She could have hooked up with either one of us, but she chose Jake. They've been together ever since. It was love at first sight for her."

"Another romantic," she sighed.

"They both are. That is why they are so accepting of us. They all love you, you know. I think you've kicked me out of first place with them."

"Have I?"

"Didn't they tell you? While you were in visiting with the women, Jake and the boys were threatening me with bodily harm if I broke your heart. They were very graphic in their description of what they would do to me."

Davi laughed. "You poor man," she teased.

"That's not all of it! Then the ladies cornered me in the kitchen and told me that if I screwed up my relationship with you, they would castrate me and feed my balls to the guys."

"They didn't," she said with feigned shock.

"You are truly number one now, where you should be forever."

Chapter 19

♥

Their drive back to the hotel started in silence. Both Quinn and Davi were lost in their own thoughts. Quinn thought of Sunday when Davi would be back at home and he'd be left alone. Davi thought about the events of the night. Quinn's friends were truly close and devoted to Quinn. She laughed aloud as she thought of their threatening him with castration if he should break her heart.

"What's so funny?" he asked as he squeezed her hand.

"I was thinking of you being castrated and what a waste that would be, although I don't think the women would ever carry it out. They lust after you too much."

"That's a comforting thought. Thank you. However, I don't plan on testing it to see if you are right." He smiled. "By the way, what were my lady friends talking to you about in the kitchen?"

"We promised that what was said in the kitchen stayed in the kitchen. My lips are sealed." Davi made the motion of zipping her lips closed.

"May I hazard a guess and you'll tell me if I'm right?"

"Go ahead."

"They asked you if I was good in bed. That's the only thing they don't know about me."

"They're your friends! I can understand them thinking about it because you are incredibly gorgeous and a movie star, but you'd think they'd also not think about it because they are your friends."

"So what did you tell them?"

"That you are better than they could ever imagine and that you are like that battery bunny—you keep on going."

Quinn smiled appreciatively. "And how did they take that information?"

"I only confirmed what they already believed. Apparently being handsome means you should be great in bed. I don't know what they would have done if I had said that you were awful. I hope you don't mind me telling them about you. It was just part of the female bonding. I had to give them the goods on you." Davi tried to give Quinn her best innocent look.

"Guys don't ask guys about their girlfriends. It's so different with women," Quinn said seriously.

"Of course it is. Admit it. If the sex between us were lousy, you wouldn't be here now. You would already be looking for your next true love. Your friends naturally assume you like what you're getting between the sheets. There's no other reason for you to be with me."

Quinn shook his head in disagreement. "Sex isn't everything, Davi. I don't know if I would have walked away. You're comparing me to Ross."

"I'm not comparing you to Ross. Let me finish. Women, not all women mind you—we can put up with lousy sex if there are fringe benefits. Hanging on to your arm on the red carpet would be a very nice fringe benefit."

"You put up with lousy sex with Ross," Quinn reminded her.

"Yes, because our marriage was about more than sex. I would have put up with lousy sex with you too because you were my fantasy, remember? It wouldn't have mattered what the sex was like. It was only going to be one night. I didn't care about red carpets then, and I still don't. That's why I wouldn't be with you now if the sex wasn't great."

"Are you saying you're only with me because of great sex?"

"No, it's not the only reason, but it sure helped in convincing me to stay with you."

"How can you say that? Doesn't love have anything to do with it?"

"Yes, love has a lot to do with it, but great sex is the glue that holds a relationship together in the beginning. Physical and sexual attractions are natural. We need them to procreate. I'm proof that sex can dwindle in a relationship after a long period of time, but usually, other strengths in the relationship make up for that." Davi chuckled as she thought of it. "Except in my case, where my husband cheated on me. But for there to be no spark in the beginning, I think the relationship is in trouble."

"So are you saying we have a spark?" he asked, arching his eyebrow perfectly.

Davi loved how he could do that.

"No, Quinn, I'm saying we have an inferno. Nothing's going to put this fire out for a long, long time."

By the time they got back to the hotel, it was well past midnight. Neither one was tired. Quinn poured himself a scotch while Davi turned on the television.

"Oh, look, Quinn, *Smashed* is on. Let's watch it!"

"We're not watching one of my movies," Quinn groaned.

"Oh, come on, this is one of your best macho movies yet! How can you not want to watch yourself smash cars and faces to smithereens and bed all those women? What guy wouldn't kill to be you in this movie?" Davi patted the seat beside her. "Come on, Quinn, pretty please?" Davi smiled wickedly at him. "I might make it worth your while."

"All right, you win. You know I can't say no to you, woman." Quinn plunked himself down on the couch beside Davi. "This movie was a pain in the ass to film. There were too many stunts, and they wouldn't let me do any of mine. I don't like this movie because it's so phony."

"Quiet. It's starting," she said as she nestled into his chest.

Quinn had never watched any of his movies in their entirety until he met Davi. He found it difficult to watch himself on-screen. He loved making movies. He just didn't like the result. Attending opening nights for his films was always torture. If he couldn't sneak out of the theater, he usually focused on some mathematical task as the movie played, usually solving statistics problems he recalled from his university days. Tonight, things were different. He was with someone who truly enjoyed his movies and wanted to share that enjoyment with him. This was the second time that she had convinced him to watch one of his movies. The first time was definitely torture, but he survived. This time, it didn't feel as painful.

Quinn started to relax. His left arm draped over Davi's shoulder with his hand caressing her breast. He kissed the top of her head while he watched the movie. A loud bang came through the sound system. Both of them jumped.

Davi laughed. "That part always gets me. I know that it's coming, but it makes me jump every time."

Smashed was one of Quinn's earliest movies. He played a big buff good guy who wreaked destruction on a gang that killed his family. The movie appealed to men, but women loved it too because Quinn was shirtless through most of it and he had a memorable love scene with more than one woman. He was nominated sexiest man and best kisser of the year after this movie was released.

"Quinn, your first love scene is coming up. It's so hot."

Quinn covered his eyes. "I can't watch this. It's embarrassing."

"But it's so good." Davi was serious. "Not many men can make that look so real and so romantic. I bet a lot of guys got lucky after taking their girlfriend or wife to that movie." Davi stared at the screen and watched Quinn's moves closely. "I've noticed that you are a different lover on-screen to what you are with me. Should I be jealous?" Davi turned her head to look up at him.

Quinn looked at the screen and watched his love scene. He smiled at Davi. "You will never get that from me. I promise you that."

"Why?"

"Would you like me to show you why? It's easier to show you than to tell you."

"Please, I want to know."

Quinn pulled Davi up onto the floor and held her in his arms. "This is how I'm holding her. Correct?"

"Yes."

"And this is how I'm kissing her." Quinn brought his lips to Davi's and kissed her hard for ten seconds. He then released her. "How was that?"

"It was great, but . . ."

"Not what you're used to?" he finished her sentence.

"No, not what I'm used to."

"Okay. I'll kiss you again the same way, and then I'll move into my kiss for you. You let me know however you want when you notice the difference."

Quinn took Davi in his arms again. He kissed her hard while his hands pressed lightly against her back. This was the movie kiss. It was nice. Then it changed. Quinn pushed open Davi's lips with his tongue and gently explored her mouth. His hands moved down her back, applying pressure on her lower spine as he pulled her into him. Davi could feel her legs weaken and her heart race. She wanted to melt into Quinn's kiss. She moaned with pleasure. Quinn held her up and pressed her harder against his body. She could feel his muscles through his shirt and his heart beating. Davi's arms wrapped around Quinn's neck, and she pulled him deeper into her. Her moans increased. Quinn pulled away from her.

"That kiss is for you and no one else. Whatever you see me do on the screen with the women, I can guarantee you'll not get from me."

"But it looks so hot on the screen."

"That's why it's called acting, love." Quinn smiled. "It may look hot, but it's nothing compared to what we have."

Davi took the remote and turned off the television.

"Let's go to bed." She offered her hand to Quinn. "I feel an inferno coming on."

Chapter 20

♥

Quinn's phone rang. With Davi nestled into his chest, Quinn reached awkwardly for his phone.

"Morning, Mother," he grunted into the phone. There was a long silence. "What time? Okay we'll see you then."

He put the phone back down on the bedside table. Davi stirred and began to rub her hand along Quinn's chest and stomach.

"Who was that?" she asked sleepily.

"My mom. She wants us to meet for lunch now instead of dinner. They've been invited out to visit friends tonight. Go back to sleep." Quinn yawned noisily.

Davi's eyes popped open. For a brief moment, she'd forgotten the reason for her visit with Quinn. His parents had asked for a meeting with their only son's fiancée. For his sake, she hoped that this would be a happy occasion. Davi couldn't settle. She tossed and turned. She tried to stay far away from Quinn in the king-sized bed to let him sleep. Quinn reached for her and pulled her back to him. He nuzzled into her breasts.

"It's only lunch with my parents," he mumbled. "Don't worry about it."

"I'll try."

"There is no try. There is only do or do not," he mumbled deeper into her chest.

"You're quoting *Star Wars*?" She giggled as his whiskers tickled her.

Quinn propped himself on one elbow to look at Davi. He was not too tired for his bedroom eyes or his cock to be fully functional.

"Woman, have you not heard tales of my conquests with my light saber?"

"No, I have not," she replied demurely as she reached down to stroke him. "But if you'd like to tell me now, I am all yours."

"I think I'll show you, if you don't mind, my own version of *Star Wars.*"

"Do I have a role to play, or is this just a Quinn Thomas production?"

"You're the extra. You just have to lie there and wait for my direction." Quinn winked at her and then dove under the covers.

Davi held her breath. She had no idea what her sleep-deprived lover was up to. It didn't take long to find out. Davi let out a soft moan as she felt Quinn come up between her legs and plant his lips on her sex. She lifted her hips to receive his tender kisses. Her hands reached for him but could only grab the sheet covering him. Quinn's hands pulled her in closer to his mouth. Davi moaned as the pleasure moved up her belly. She raised her hips higher to accommodate him as she writhed against the sheets. She felt his tongue working on her, darting in and out of her, flicking her tender spot.

Just as Davi thought she was going to climax, Quinn stopped and replaced his tongue with his fingers. Another sensation took over. Quinn worked his way up Davi's belly to her breasts. He sucked on one nipple as his fingers played with the other. He switched back and forth, knowing when to release and work on another body part. Davi was kept on the edge. Quinn would not let her fall until he was ready to join her.

"Quinn," Davi moaned, "please."

He rolled onto his back and pulled her with him. Davi reached for the box of condoms.

"We're getting low." She ripped open the package and put the condom on Quinn's erection. "I thought you bought a month's worth."

"I did. I think we make love more than the average couple."

"You're not average, Quinn."

"And neither are you. Shall I continue my story?"

Pushing her legs apart, Quinn entered her. Davi pushed herself upright, looking deep into his eyes. Her hips moved in rhythm with his.

"I don't remember this part," she gasped.

"You won't. It was left on the cutting room floor."

"I can see why."

Quinn pulled Davi down to his face. His lips covered hers. His large hands caressed her back, feeling her curves. Davi pulled away from his lips.

"I'm coming."

She closed her eyes and tilted her head back. Her mouth opened slightly as she softly moaned while she fell off the edge. Davi kept her hips moving to get every ounce of pleasure from her fall. Quinn held on to Davi's hips and plunged deeper into her. He raced to catch up with her. A loud groan forced its way out of him as he exploded into her. Davi collapsed onto his chest.

"Who were you supposed to be? You never said."

"Just another extra."

Davi was taken aback. "You weren't Luke Skywalker or Han Solo or even Darth Vader?"

"No. I never wanted to be them. I only wanted the light saber and to have my own adventures."

"How'd that work for you?"

"Pretty good. I got the girl, and that's all I wanted." Quinn kissed Davi.

"I love you."

"That's the plan. Forever."

Davi rolled off Quinn, and he disposed of the condom.

"Shower time," Davi announced. "Alone shower time," she added as Quinn made an effort to get out of bed. "You stay put and rest."

"I won't argue," Quinn said as he fell back into his pillow. "Wake me by eleven."

Quinn held Davi's hand while they walked to the restaurant. The fall air was refreshing. The sidewalks were overflowing with pedestrians. It felt good for both of them to be free from being noticed. They would stop and look through shop windows, but neither one had any interest in shopping. They were expected elsewhere.

They arrived at the restaurant in good time. The maître d' led them to their table, a secluded table tucked away from nosey patrons. Quinn sat down beside Davi. His parents had not yet arrived.

"They won't be late," he told her. "For once I'm early. Would you like a drink?"

"I'll have decaf coffee, please."

Quinn placed an order with their waiter. "Two decafs please."

"You're drinking decaf now?"

"I thought I'd give it a try. See what it's like. If you have to go on it for the next nine months, I'll do it too."

"You'll do what for the next nine months?" a voice asked from behind him.

"Mom!" Quinn jumped to his feet and turned to give his mother a hug.

Davi stood up and waited for the introductions.

"Mom, Dad, I'd like you to meet Davina Stuart. Davi, I'd like you to meet my mom, Margaret, and my dad, John."

Margaret offered her hand to Davi.

"It's so nice to meet you," Davi said with sincerity.

"It's a pleasure."

Margaret released Davi's hand to allow John to hug Davi.

"We've been looking forward to this all week. You're a beauty, Davi."

"Thank you." Davi could feel the heat from her blush.

Everyone sat down. Quinn put his arm around Davi's shoulders. When the waiter arrived with the two coffees, Quinn's parents added another two to the order.

"So what did I not fully hear concerning the next nine months?" pressed Margaret.

Davi looked at Quinn. This was his mother. He could tell her.

"Davi's trying a new detox diet. I told her I might go on it with her to keep her company."

Despite being a great actor, Quinn was a terrible liar. Davi looked at him in disbelief. She knew his mother wouldn't believe him.

"You've never gone on a detox diet, Quinn. You don't believe in them," Margaret said knowingly.

She stared at her son. Quinn returned the stare unflinching.

Davi jumped in. "I might be pregnant, so I'm watching what I drink. I haven't fully accepted the pregnancy. Quinn's trying to cover for me. I'm sorry."

"Don't apologize, Davi. Obviously, this wasn't planned. Is this why you're engaged?"

"No. This happened after the engagement, Mother. Davi has three children, and she wasn't planning on a fourth. The earliest she can have the test is next week. In the meantime, I'm giving Davi the time and space to figure out what she wants to do."

Davi felt Quinn's arm tighten around her. She wasn't sure if it was to give her support or him.

"But what do you want? Doesn't that matter?"

Davi could see the fire in Margaret's eyes. Quinn had the same intensity when he was on the attack.

"Margaret, it's none of our business," Quinn's father whispered as he patted her hand.

"It is our business. You could be pregnant with my grandchild and you're telling me you may not want it?"

"Mother, don't start. Please." Quinn shifted uncomfortably in his seat.

"No, Quinn, it's okay." Davi wanted to get this over with now. If Margaret Thomas had something to say to her, she wanted to hear it now.

Their waiter appeared to take their lunch orders. Quinn appreciated the reprieve from his mother's inquisition. He watched as his mother placed her order. She usually took her time, pointing to various items on the menu, asking how the chef prepared each dish. This time, she didn't bother. Margaret Thomas was chomping at the bit to grill Davi.

She placed her order. "Grilled salmon with salad, no dressing."

The rest of them placed their orders. Quinn ordered a burger with fries. He smiled at his mother when their waiter left.

"You still eat like a teenager," Margaret commented once the waiter left. "I hope you don't still act like one. Perhaps that's what Davi sees in you." She turned her attention to Davi. "How old are you, Davi?"

Davi could feel Quinn tense beside her.

Here it comes. Davi thought before she answered Margaret. "I'm forty-seven."

Davi heard the slight hitch in Margaret's breath when she heard Davi's age.

"Would you have his baby, though, if you could?"

"In a perfect world, I would have Quinn's baby without a second thought. But this is not a perfect world, and it does require a great deal of thought."

"How much thought do you need to make a baby? Don't you just have to fuck?"

For a brief moment, it felt as though time had stood still. Margaret stared at Davi. John's mouth dropped open as he stared at his wife in disbelief. Quinn pulled Davi in close as though he were shielding her from his mother. Davi smiled.

"You're right, Margaret, it doesn't take any thought to make a baby, but it will take a lot of thought if Quinn decides he wants children, and I decide that I don't. If I'm not pregnant and Quinn decides that he wants children, then I think this is a very opportune accident. We can say good-bye before we say I do. Then Quinn can find himself someone else and start a family."

"Mother, what are you doing?" Quinn asked through clenched teeth.

"She's looking out for you, Quinn. She's being a mother." Davi didn't take her eyes off Margaret. "I can tell who gave you the acting gene."

"What the hell?" Quinn asked, confused.

"She's making sure I love you enough to let you go." Davi smiled at Margaret as she spoke.

"You don't have to prove anything to her, Davi. There is no one else for me but you. Baby or no baby, we are getting married."

"May I say something?" Quinn's father asked, hoping to diffuse the situation. "Margaret, this is their decision not ours. We need to stay out of it and we will."

"Yes, but . . ."

"But nothing. Our son has never disappointed us with his decisions. He has always made the right choice, and now is not the time to doubt him. We will accept whatever Davi and Quinn decide, and we won't talk about it again unless it's to give them our congratulations and suggest names for our grandchild. Have I made myself clear?"

Davi watched Quinn's father. He was older than Davi, possibly in his mid-fifties. He was gorgeous too. It was evident Quinn got his looks from his father. He had the same smile, kissable lips, and the charm.

It was obvious that Quinn and his mother had the same fire and temperament. She could see the fire in Margaret's eyes when she argued for her son and her unborn grandchild.

Quinn's mother took a deep breath and gazed thoughtfully at her husband. Davi could tell that he was the calming influence in the relationship. Margaret smiled at him and then nodded her head in agreement.

Margaret looked at Quinn and Davi. "My methods may not be rational, but my reasons are. I had to make sure you were the one, Davi. Quinn, I've been having terrible nightmares about you. You married some blonde bimbo who only wanted you for your name and your money. I tried to talk you out of it, but you wouldn't listen to me. You said the sex was great."

"At least the sex was great," Quinn smiled.

Margaret grimaced. "Actually, it was terrible. She turned out being a closet lesbian and made you sleep in the guest bedroom."

"So that's why you've been grumpy all this week. I thought it was something I did, but all along, it's been Quinn's fault." John laughed.

"Actually, it's Davi's fault," Quinn teased. "After all, she's the bimbo."

"Hey," Davi said, feigning indignation, "I'll have you know that I'm a true brunette."

Chapter 21

♥

Quinn and Davi walked hand in hand from the restaurant. They had no particular destination in mind as they enjoyed the beautiful Saturday afternoon. Both were on an emotional high after having a wonderful time with Quinn's parents. John and Margaret had given the couple their blessing and welcomed Davi into the family.

"Could this day be any better?" Davi said happily as she looked around her. "When I'm with you, I feel like I'm on holiday. It's so hard to go back home to reality."

"Can you stay with me and go back to the farm when you need to?"

"No, I can't see that working. The paperwork is too much to let slide. I have commitments at home too. People depend on me to be there. We'll make this work." Davi squeezed Quinn's hand. "You'll have to make the trip my way when you can."

"It will be home base. I want that so much."

"Wait until you actually come and see it. The farm life doesn't appeal to everyone. I won't be offended if you don't like it."

"I'm not planning on being a visitor. That's not the plan."

When they came to a park, Quinn stopped to watch the children playing. He held Davi close to him.

"You want that, don't you?" Davi asked, knowing the answer.

"I didn't realize how much until right now." His voice was almost desperate.

"Quinn, I . . ."

"No. You don't have to say anything. We'll wait until you get the test results. I want a child, Davi, more than anything—except for you. You come first."

The couple stood in silence as they watched the children play.

Davi decided she had to ask Quinn something that weighed heavily on her mind. "What are your thoughts on abortion?"

"I've never really thought about it. It wasn't something that touched my life. I guess I was pro-choice."

"Was?"

"I don't know if I could agree to the abortion of my child. Not when I want one so much."

"What if the baby had problems? Would you agree to it then?"

"I don't know, Davi. I honestly don't know. What about you?"

Davi sighed. "Maybe it's because of my age. I raised three healthy children, and some days I found it all exhausting. I'd be forty-eight by the time this child arrived. I need it to be healthy for me to have enough energy to raise it."

"But you wouldn't be alone. I'd be there to help," he said with confidence.

Davi cupped his face with her hand and smiled. "It doesn't work that way, love. No matter what you promise, the load of the responsibility falls on the mother."

"It doesn't have to be that way." His eyes held her gaze.

"You're sweet but so naive. You have a successful career. You won't give that up for a child. You can't."

"You don't know that. I don't have to be making movies all the time. I've made enough money to last for a very long time."

"But you love to act," Davi said softly.

"And I'd also love to raise a child. Doesn't what I want matter?"

"You're right, it does."

Davi started to walk away. Quinn caught up with her and took her hand. He pulled her to a stop.

"Aren't you excited in the least to think you might be pregnant?"

"I'm terrified and I'm embarrassed." She looked away from him.

Quinn turned her face to him. "Do I embarrass you?"

"I didn't say that. It's being pregnant at my age. My kids will be over twenty years apart. I should be a grandmother soon not a mother again!"

"You'll be the sexiest mother around. There's nothing to be embarrassed about, so what terrifies you?"

"Going through it all over again and worrying about the health of the baby. This time, I'm older. I know the odds are against me."

"But not totally. I've read up on this, Davi. Things could be fine for you and the baby. We can have this baby."

"I may not even be pregnant."

"But you know your body. You are pregnant, aren't you?"

Quinn's gaze filled her with warmth, calming her.

"Yes, but I don't know if I want to be, Quinn. Will you give me time to think about it?"

"Think about it but don't do anything until we talk about it. I've told you my feelings. You come first, but the baby is a close second. Really close."

Chapter 22

Back in his hotel suite, Quinn and Davi cuddled on the couch, listening to light jazz music.

"Tell me about how you make memories," Davi murmured as she stroked his chest.

"My mind takes pictures with all of my senses. I memorize every moment we spend together. I can recall your scent and your taste. I can recall how it feels to be touched by you and how you feel to my touch. I remember everything we've ever said to each other. It's very much like having my own video recording machine in my head."

"Do you do that with everything?"

"Right now, it's only you I want to memorize."

"Your mom said that you chose acting over medicine. Were you planning on becoming a doctor?"

"No, not really. With my photographic memory, it made it rather easy to get good grades in school. I did well in science, but I didn't trust myself. I didn't know whether I was really good at it and that I had a calling for medicine or if it was just my ability to recall everything that I read that made me a good student. In theater, I knew everyone's parts. I could step into any role as a stand in, I could help out if someone flubbed their lines, I could concentrate more on the acting than just reciting my lines. I knew that it was something I was genuinely good at, and I loved to act."

"Did she want you to become a doctor?"

Quinn chuckled. "Whose mom wouldn't want them to become a doctor? She would have loved it, but she supported the choice I made."

"My mom always wanted me to marry a farmer. She thought it was the best life anyone could have."

"Were you from a farm?"

"No, but that didn't stop my mom from loving the farm life."

"I've always wanted to marry a farmer," Quinn said softly.

"No, you haven't, liar."

"Always within the last week then," he said as he kissed the top of her head.

"Don't say that until you know what it actually means. It's like me saying I've always wanted to marry a movie star. I have no idea what that means and what that would do to my life."

"What it will do to your life," Quinn corrected her.

"Okay then, tell me what it will do to my life. Prepare me." Davi sat up and fixed her gaze on Quinn.

"It will do absolutely nothing and everything to your life. You decide. You can get caught up in all the hoopla and go to all the galas and award ceremonies and openings and wear designer clothes and jewelry offered to you, or you can do absolutely nothing and stay on the farm, raise our children, and wait for me to come home. It is your choice, woman."

"May I have a bit of both?"

"Like what?"

"I'd love to be all dressed up and be sparkly while I accompany you to some big Hollywood event. Once would be enough to make a great memory."

"Only once?" Quinn raised an eyebrow.

"Once would be enough, but I'm entitled to change my mind. Let's wait and see what happens the first time."

Davi was dreaming of Quinn. He was holding her close and whispering words of love in her ear. She could feel his warm breath against her face. Her body tingled. A pleasurable sensation started between her legs and worked its way to her breasts. She squirmed with delight. Davi felt a gradual pressure between her legs and with it brought more pleasure.

"Oh, Quinn," she murmured.

"I'm right here," he whispered in her ear.

Slowly Davi opened her eyes. Quinn lay on his side next to her, smiling at her. She could feel him in her, thrusting gently.

"Oh no," Davi groaned. "Not again!"

"It's okay, love. I'm covered." Quinn kissed Davi. "You were calling my name in your sleep and rubbing against me. I thought I'd help you out. Is this what you were dreaming about?"

Davi answered Quinn by wrapping her arms around him and pulling him in closer. Her hips moved in sync with his. Her head fell back as she enjoyed the pleasure. Quinn's mouth found her neck and covered it with hot kisses. Davi moaned at the sensation. Quinn did not rush himself, taking his time with her. Quietly Davi climaxed and Quinn soon followed. He disposed of the condom, and then they lay together in each other's arms.

"Thank you."

"For what, love?" Quinn asked as he nuzzled her ear.

"For making my dream much better."

"Anytime."

"And thank you for using protection. You're being very good about it."

"I told you, Davi, until you tell me otherwise, we'll use it."

They lay in silence. Neither one of them wanted to talk about Davi having to fly home today. Ignoring it wouldn't make it any easier.

Davi sighed. "It's time to get up, isn't it?"

"We have to leave in fifteen minutes. Unless you've changed your mind and want to stay." Quinn nuzzled Davi's neck. "I could give you more of this and some of this." His hand caressed her breast.

"I have to go, Quinn."

Quinn groaned in response as Davi extricated herself from his embrace. She got out of bed and walked to the bathroom, closing the door behind her.

"If only I could stay," she whispered as she wiped the tears from her eyes.

Quinn wrapped his arm around Davi's waist as they walked in silence to the airport security gate. As they got to the gate, Quinn stopped and pulled Davi into his arms.

"I don't want you to go."

"I have to," she said as she fought back tears.

"I'll miss you," his warm voice caressed her.

"Me too."

"Call me after church. We can have coffee over the phone."

"I'd like that." Davi smiled. "Now give me my kiss."

Quinn brought his mouth down to Davi's and kissed her hard. His hand moved down to her lower spine and applied just the right pressure. Davi felt her legs go weak as her heart started to beat faster. She pulled Quinn in tighter, pressing her body into his. The tingle started instantly moving down her arms to her fingers, down from her breasts to her stomach. Davi moaned as the tingle touched her sex.

"Wow," Quinn whispered as he released her.

"Wow, yourself." Davi picked up her bag. "Talk to you soon, stud."

"Real soon," Quinn murmured.

Davi turned and walked through the customs gate. Quinn stayed and watched her until she was out of sight. When he turned to head for his car, he found himself surrounded by adoring female fans.

"Hi, ladies, how are you today?" Quinn asked as he accepted an offered pen and started to sign his autograph. "I'm having a great day today, how about you?"

He chatted with the fans as he slowly made his way out of the airport. "Don't get too close now," he said as a fan tried to kiss him. "You don't want to make my fiancée jealous, do you?"

Davi stopped at one of the newsstands in the departure area. She thought she'd see what the latest gossip was on Quinn and her. On the front cover of *What's Happening* was a picture of the two of them with the heading, "Weeklong Engagement on Rocks." The next magazine had their picture on the front cover with the heading, "Kids Embarrassed over Mom's Engagement: 'He's our age!'"

"So not true," Davi said aloud.

She scanned all of the popular celebrity magazines, finally coming across one that had a picture of Quinn proposing to Davi at the mall. The caption was simple: "Quinn Thomas proposing to D. L. Stuart at coffee bar." Finally, something that was true. Davi bought the magazine.

Chapter 23

♥

Davi waited impatiently in her doctor's waiting room. Fortunately, her ob-gyn kept up to date magazines for her patients to read while waiting. It was no surprise to Davi to see pictures of Quinn and her on most of the magazines on the table. She picked one up and browsed through it. She caught one of the other patients in the office staring at her.

"That's you," the woman commented as she pointed to the magazine's cover.

"Yes, it is."

"Congratulations."

"Thank you."

"Is any of that true? What they've written?"

"I don't know. I'm having a look at it now. Give me a second and I'll let you know." Davi read the article quickly. She laughed at some parts. "We met on a plane, that is true, and we are engaged. My age isn't quite right, and I was not interviewed by the magazine, so everything they have me saying is definitely not true. Would you like to have a look?" She offered the magazine to the woman.

"No, thanks. I have that one at home. You two look so good together."

"Thank you."

The nurse stepped into the waiting room. "Ms. Stuart, you can come in now."

Davi got up and followed the nurse into the doctor's office. Davi had known her doctor for years. She had delivered all of Davi's children.

"Hi, Davi. I haven't seen you in a long time. What brings you here?" Dr. Marsh asked as she greeted her from behind her desk.

She opened the file and read the note posted inside.

"Request for pregnancy test. Oh my. Care to tell me about it?"

"We had an accident while I was ovulating. I know the signs. That's why I have three children. I read that I can have a blood pregnancy test eight days after conception. I'd like to have one if I can."

"Before we discuss that, do you mind filling me in on what you've been up to, Davi?" The doctor folded her arms on the desk and listened intently.

Davi told her the abridged story of meeting on a plane, a romantic weekend ending with a proposal.

"And this pregnancy?"

Davi played nervously with her engagement ring. "I don't know. He really wants the baby. I think I'm too old to go through this again. Would I be crazy to have a baby at my age?"

"Why don't I have the test run? Then we can talk about your concerns. I'll have the results in an hour."

"You can do it while I wait? I thought it would take a day or two."

"I'll let the nurse take the sample. I'll see to my next patient. Then we'll have our talk," the doctor said before she left the room.

A few minutes went by before the nurse came in.

"How are you today, Davi? It's good to see you again." She was quite pleasant as she rolled up Davi's sleeve and prepped her arm for the blood sample.

Davi smiled at the nurse. "I'm well, thanks."

"It looks like you've been busy. Your face is plastered everywhere."

Davi could feel the blush burn her cheeks. "Everyone knows my business now, but don't believe everything you read. It's not all true." She winced as the needle pricked her arm.

"Oh, I don't believe all of it."

"Thanks."

"We're all done. Keep some pressure here, and you'll be fine. The doctor will be right back when she's finished with her other patient."

Davi reached for a book on the doctor's table, *Having Babies after 40*. She flipped through the pages. It was hard to concentrate. Davi had no idea how much time had passed when the doctor finally walked in. She had a broad smile on her face.

"Congratulations, Davi. You are pregnant."

Davi sat in her truck and thought about what to do next. She was definitely pregnant. There was no more avoiding its reality. She thought about how much Quinn wanted a child. She tried not to picture a future of them with a baby, but the images forced their way into her thoughts. Davi smiled. The baby had Quinn's hair and his eyes.

"Don't get carried away, Davi. Quinn's the romantic, not you. Be rational," Davi said aloud.

There was no rational when it came to Quinn. Davi loved him completely as he did her. She couldn't explain why, it just was. Just like this baby. It wasn't planned, but it didn't make it any less real, any less wanted. Yes, it was wanted and loved. Davi placed her hands on her abdomen.

"How can I not want you or love you? You're a part of me. You're a part of Quinn. It took a while for me to accept you. Everything's happened so fast. But that's not your fault."

Davi reached for her cell phone. She typed in a text message for Quinn:

> D. L. Stuart, in cooperation with Quinn Thomas, is pleased to announce their first joint project due June 20th. The name of the project is yet to be decided but will be known as BABY until a name has been chosen.

Davi pressed the Send button. She would be home in twenty minutes and was sure she'd hear from Quinn by the time she arrived home.

Chapter 24

♥

Quinn didn't call. Jake did.

"We lost the bet," he announced before she could say hello.

Davi understood immediately. "What's his flight number?"

"Air Canada arriving at four thirty."

"Thanks, Jake, I'd better go."

"Congratulations," Jake blurted out.

"Has he told anyone else?"

"Just Sarah and me. Sarah told him not to tell anyone else. She said it's too early. He didn't understand her. You can explain it to him."

Davi had half an hour before she had to leave for the airport. She decided to put fresh linen on the bed. She tidied up her bathroom and had enough time to leave a note for her family: "Gone to airport to pick up Quinn—love, Mom."

Davi arrived at the airport with time to spare. She texted Quinn to let him know she was there waiting for him. Fortunately, all of the arrivals came out of the same customs area. Davi found a spot with a clear view of the exit. Quinn would be sure to see her as soon as he came through the sliding doors.

As she waited, Davi could feel eyes on her. She looked around and saw people staring at her. Some of them had the celebrity magazines in their hands, comparing her to the photo on the front page. *Wonderful,* she groaned to herself.

Davi looked up at the information screen. Quinn's plane had arrived. She hoped he'd be out soon. People started to gather around her. Normally, she'd think it was so they could see their loved ones come through the sliding doors, but this time Davi knew it was to see someone else. She could feel the excitement in the crowd. The doors started to open. Passengers started to file through and were greeted by friends or loved ones as they made it down the ramp. Every time the doors opened, she strained to catch a glimpse of Quinn. She wondered what he was wearing. Would it be his old standby of hooded jacket and jeans? Passengers were coming through now at a steadier pace. Davi prayed for the crowd to lessen but it didn't. She looked around her. Cameras were being held high above people's heads, waiting for a shot of Quinn.

The doors opened. Quinn appeared looking handsome in jeans, white shirt, and leather jacket. Davi's heart skipped a beat when he looked right at her and smiled. Cameras started flashing, and people were calling out his name. Quinn headed right for Davi, his eyes only on her. When he reached her, he picked her up and kissed her.

"I had to come."

"I know." She smiled at him. "It's a madhouse here. How did they know you were coming here?"

"We're connected. If you're at the airport, I must be coming to you. Let's go. Lead the way."

Davi led the way toward the parking garage. Quinn stopped to sign a few autographs but kept it to a minimum. The paparazzi yelled questions at him, but they were nothing he could answer. He only told them that he was here for a short visit. There was no security to help them out of the airport, but the crowd left them alone by the time they reached the parking garage.

"They're a much tamer group than last time. That wasn't too bad."

Davi paid the parking fee and then led Quinn to the truck. She got in behind the wheel as he threw his travel bag into the backseat and then got into the passenger seat. Quinn leaned over and pulled Davi toward him for a kiss.

"Hope you don't mind. I'm glad you found out I was coming."

"Jake called to tell me we'd lost the bet."

"So we're having a baby," he exclaimed with pure joy.

"Yes, we are." She couldn't help but be pulled into his excitement.

"What did your doctor say about you having a baby at your age?"

"Long story short?"

"Yes."

"We can do it."

"Yes!" Quinn shouted as he pumped the air with his fist in celebration.

"When I'm in my second trimester, I can have an amniocentesis done to see if the baby has any birth defects. If it does, we can decide if we want to terminate the pregnancy or not."

"You're still considering abortion?"

"I've never had to think about abortion before, Quinn. We'll have to talk about this later, but for now, let's just enjoy the moment. Anyway, this is our production. We'll make all decisions together."

"So you want this baby then. You're okay with being pregnant." Quinn had to be sure.

"Yes, I am. I'm sorry to have made you wait for my decision. But if all goes well, you'll be a dad in nine months."

"I'm going to be a dad," Quinn said proudly. He looked out the passenger window. "When will we get to your farm?"

"Ten minutes to go."

"But look at all of this development. You're not in the middle of the city, are you?"

"Some days it feels like it, but no, we're just outside of the city limits. You'll see."

Davi stayed on the main road, driving through an industrial section and then through a housing development. At the next main intersection, the contrast between city and country was shockingly apparent. On the south side of the road, houses were jammed together in a high-density neighborhood. Across the road to the north was open space. No houses, no factories, only farmland.

"Wow," said Quinn.

"Wow is right."

Davi continued through the intersection and drove north for another five minutes.

"This part of the country isn't slated for development for years to come. We can only hope that it stays that way."

Davi turned into the long farm driveway. Tall maples in their full autumn splendor made a welcoming arch over the entrance.

"We're home," Davi announced as she parked the truck.

"It's beautiful, Davi. Your pictures didn't do this place justice."

Quinn got out of the truck. "Will you show me around the farm while there is still daylight?"

"Can I get you a change of clothes first? You'll pick up the barn smell. It will go right through your clothes."

"Is it a bad smell?"

"No, it's just that it stays with you. If you brought a change of clothes, you can shower afterward and you'll be fine."

"I'll take the risk. Let's go."

Davi took Quinn's hand. "I want you to meet the Ladies."

They walked to a large barn. Davi opened the door. Quinn was greeted by a sweet smell, a combination of cow, feed, and manure. There was pop music playing in the background.

"They listen to music?"

"Twenty-four hours a day. They like the light pop. It has a calming effect. The heifers, the younger females, listen to a rock station. They seem to like that one best."

Quinn laughed as he noticed the size of the cows. "Wow. They're huge."

"Of course they are. They're all about to have babies, one-hundred-pound babies." Davi walked Quinn through the barn. "These Ladies are due to give birth in a week or two. Over here, these Ladies are due anytime."

"They look really comfortable. How do you know when they're in labor?"

"They're very much like women. They give off the same signs. They'll get restless and sometimes they even let you know that it hurts. Some are very stoic and don't make a sound." Davi inspected the pens. "No one seems to be doing anything right now."

Davi led Quinn out a different door to another barn.

"Here are the babies."

"They are cute. How old are they?"

"They are newborn to three months. They are fed bottled milk and are gradually weaned onto grain. Once they are weaned, they go over to another barn."

She took him to the next barn.

"How many barns do you have?"

"Lots. Here's where we keep the teenagers."

Davi opened another door where rock music played.

"I love that song." Quinn laughed as he heard U2 playing in the background. "They really like this music? You're not pulling my leg?"

"Wait until you hear what the milking cows like to listen to."

Quinn looked around at various pens with animals ranging from small to almost fully grown. They were all clean and looking very calm.

"The girls or heifers come in here around six months of age, and by the time they reach thirteen months of age, they should be pregnant."

"They're just babies at thirteen months!"

"Not in cow years. They're ready to be moms."

"What about the dads? Where do you keep them?"

"The bulls? We don't have any on the farm. It's all done artificially. We choose the dad for the cow."

"No sex?" Quinn asked in surprise.

"Never." Davi laughed, remembering Jake had the same reaction. "I don't think the Ladies mind one bit. Maybe that's why they are so happy."

Quinn pulled Davi in close. "You'd mind, though, wouldn't you?"

Davi could see the mischief in his eyes. She could feel his arousal pressing against her. He would take her now if she'd let him.

"Later, stud."

Davi led Quinn out the barn and took him to another barn. "This is where the pregnant heifers stay until they have their calf. Once they do, we take them over to the main milking barn."

"It's quite a system you have."

"You haven't seen it all yet."

Davi led Quinn to a much larger building. It stood by itself apart from the other buildings.

"This is where we milk the cows."

It was a huge building, bright with natural daylight. Light rock was playing in the background. Some cows were lying down in the stalls, while others were standing and eating at the manger.

"They're very quiet."

"Of course they are. They're happy. Or should I say content? They have great food, clean water to drink. They have a soft bed to lie down on, they're clean, and they have room to move around in."

Davi led Quinn through a passageway to the milking parlor.

"This is where we milk them. The cows will be milked later tonight. We can always come out again if you want to see how that is done. It's quite amazing if you've never seen it before."

"I'd like that."

Davi led Quinn through the parlor and outside.

"That's about it for the buildings and the cows. This is where I spend my time."

They walked back toward the house.

"I can see why you want to be here, Davi. It seems so peaceful."

"What about the smell? You haven't mentioned the smell."

"Actually, I like it. It doesn't bother me. Should it?"

"No, I'm glad it doesn't. We'd be taking too many showers if it did." Davi looked at her watch. "The kids should be home by now. I'm feeling nervous."

"Why?" Quinn stopped and pulled Davi around to face him.

"Another reality check, I guess, with you meeting them for the first time."

"It will be fine. You'll see." He kissed her forehead.

Davi wrapped her arms around him. "I hope so."

Davi and Quinn walked into the kitchen. Rich sat at the kitchen table, having a beer while the girls were getting supper ready. The girls stopped what they were doing and ran to Quinn, both of them throwing their arms around him at the same time.

"Finally!" they exclaimed together.

"We've been wondering when you'd finally come for a visit," Tigger said happily.

Neither one of the girls let go of Quinn. He hugged them back. Quinn was amazed at how alike the girls were. They could be twins for all he knew. They had the same rich brunette color as their mother. Their build was similar to Davi's, but they were two inches taller.

"I came as soon as I could."

The girls finally let go of Quinn and stepped back to make room for their brother.

Rich got up from the table and offered Quinn his hand. "Good to meet you, Quinn."

"Thanks. It's good to finally meet all of you."

"Supper's almost ready," Tigger announced.

"Quinn, I'll take you upstairs and show you where you can wash up, if you want."

"Do I smell?"

"Both of us do. Let's go and let them finish getting supper ready."

Quinn picked up his travel bag and followed Davi through the house to the upstairs. The stairway was massive with ornate carved spindles. It wound its way to the second floor. There were five bedrooms upstairs and one main bathroom. Davi's master bedroom was the first door on the right. She turned on the light. The room was massive.

"This used to be two bedrooms. After Ross died, I had my bedroom enlarged and I added a master bathroom. I needed to start over again."

The room was decorated tastefully. Antique furniture filled the room, including a king-sized four-poster bed. Farm prints decorated the walls. There were two armchairs in a corner by a gas fireplace. The bathroom had a large walk-in shower and a Jacuzzi bathtub.

"Nice," Quinn said. "Do you use the Jacuzzi much?"

"Not really. I hate to waste water, but sometimes it's nice to have a soak when the world seems to be a bit too much for me."

Quinn put his arms around her. "I hope that hasn't happened lately, love."

"No. It's been a long time since I felt that way."

"So is there a guest room for me?"

"Don't be silly. You're in here with me. My kids are old enough to understand. It goes both ways. It's a bit late now, anyway, don't you think?"

"I was just making sure."

Davi stripped off her top and put on a clean shirt from her closet. She went to the bathroom to wash up. Quinn sat in one of the armchairs, waiting for her.

"I want this, Davi. It feels right," he called out to her.

Davi walked out of the bathroom.

"I'm glad. I want this to feel right for you. I want you to feel like you belong here."

"How long do we have before we're expected downstairs?" His blue eyes burned into her.

"They are waiting on us. I'm surprised I haven't heard them yelling from the bottom of the stairs."

"Give me a minute."

Quinn went into the bathroom and closed the door. Davi sat down and closed her eyes. *Could this day be any better?* She didn't want the day to end.

Quinn came out of the bathroom shirtless.

"My shirt smells. I know what you mean now."

He rummaged through his bag and pulled out a T-shirt to put on.

"You had to bring that one, didn't you?"

"I know you like me in blue. I brought it for you."

"It's not just the color, you know. It's the way you wear it."

"Are you coming, Mom? Supper's ready!" Cat yelled up the stairs.

"Want a beer?" Rich asked Quinn when they returned to the kitchen.

"Sure. Thanks."

Rich retrieved a beer from the fridge, opened it, and handed it to Quinn. He motioned for him to have a seat at the table. Quinn and Davi sat down across from the girls.

"Are you here for long? Mom didn't tell us you were coming," asked Rich.

"She didn't know I was either. It was a spur-of-the-moment decision. I have to head back tomorrow morning. I've got to be at the studio by noon."

The girls stared at Quinn.

"You came for the night?" Cat asked. "Why would you do that?"

The three of them looked at Davi and Quinn. Quinn looked at Davi. They were her family. She could tell them the news.

"I found out today that I'm pregnant."

The room went silent. Her children looked at each other and then back at Quinn and Davi. Immediately, Cat and Tigger pounced on Davi and gave her kisses and hugs.

"Congratulations, Mom. This is great news!"

"What about all of our talks on safe sex?" Rich's voice was filled with indignation. He stood up from the table. "You made damn sure that we wouldn't do anything stupid. I guess it didn't apply to you." His large hands gripped the edge of the table as he leaned in toward his mother. "Did you not care, Mom, or did you think you were too old to get knocked up?"

Quinn stood up quickly from the table.

"Rich," he said calmly, "it's not what you think."

"I'm not talking to you." Rich glared at Quinn. "You're not family. Yet."

"Rich," Tigger cried, "what's got into you?"

Davi didn't move as she stared at her son. He'd never shown his temper before. He was always quiet and thoughtful, careful with his words.

"Settle down, Rich," Cat said as she put a hand on his arm.

Rich ignored his sister, his eyes locked on his mother.

"Mom!" He was furious and demanded that she answer him.

"I cared," she answered in the calmest voice she could muster. "I made sure we used protection every time. It just happened."

Quinn sat down and wrapped his arm around Davi's waist, pulling her close to him.

"I'm the one to blame. Don't take it out on your mother."

Rich laughed mockingly. "Sure, take the blame, Quinn. But it doesn't matter. It falls back on my mother. She's the one stuck with a baby when you leave her."

"I thought you supported our engagement?" Davi asked, dumbfounded.

"Of course I supported it. I wanted you to be happy. I never thought you'd bring a baby into it."

"Why does that matter?" Tigger asked, confused.

"I'm committed to your mother," Quinn said, his voice still calm. "I'm not leaving her."

"For how long will your promise last—a few weeks or months, maybe even a year or two? Come on, Quinn, tell the truth. My mom's just a bit of fun. You have a thing for older women, but it won't last."

"What the hell's gotten into you?" Cat yelled at him. "How can you say such a thing?"

"Someone needs to look out for Mom!" Rich said angrily.

Davi rose from her chair and walked over to her son. Her hands cupped his face.

"Thank you for looking out for me, hon, but I know what I'm doing."

Rich started to speak, but Davi put her finger over his lips.

"I never expected to find love again, not after being with your father for so long. I thought my time for that was gone. I had the three of you and the farm. I thought I was happy." Davi looked back at Quinn. "But Quinn found me. He loves me, and he makes me very happy."

"But for how long?" Rich said against her finger.

"Quinn promised me forever, but it doesn't matter. I'm thankful for every day I have with him." Davi removed her finger from Rich's lips. "Please don't let this come between us."

"Mom, I'm worried for you. What if it doesn't work out for the two of you? I don't want to see your life ruined."

"Quinn won't ruin my life, nor will this baby. I had the three of you, and I never once thought my life was ruined." Davi smiled at her son.

"That's different. We were wanted."

"And so is this one," Davi said as she placed her hand on her abdomen. "You always said you wanted a baby brother." She smiled up at him, trying to coax a smile from him.

"That was twenty years ago." Rich shook his head. "You gave me a puppy instead."

"Better late than never."

Rich sighed heavily. "I love you, Mom."

"I love you too." Davi lifted her face to kiss him on the cheek.

Rich wrapped his strong arms around his mother. "I want you to be happy."

"I am," Davi said with confidence.

Rich looked over at Quinn. "Be good to her. She deserves nothing but the best."

Quinn got up from his chair and walked over to Davi and Rich.

He held out his hand to Rich. "You've got my word.

The two men shook hands.

"Well, if that's all settled, can we eat now? Supper's getting cold." Tigger announced as she started to fill her plate.

Chapter 25

♥

Quinn heard Rich get up for morning chores. He eased out of bed and pulled on his jeans and then quietly slipped out of the bedroom. He caught up with Rich in the kitchen.

Rich looked up at Quinn. "You're up early."

"We need to have a talk," Quinn said as he poured himself a cup of coffee.

Rich nodded to a chair at the table. "Sure."

Quinn sat down and took a long drink from his cup. "I realized last night that there was something I forgot to do. I forgot to apologize to you."

Rich snorted. "You want to apologize for getting my mom pregnant?"

"No. I want to apologize for not being the guy you probably wanted her to fall in love with."

Rich looked at Quinn and then smiled. "You are a bit young for her. I don't mind the movie star bit, but you are close to me in age."

"Believe me, if I could be ten years older even fifteen years, I'd do it in a heartbeat if it made it easier for you to accept me." Quinn ran his hands through his messy hair. "I'm in love with her, Rich. She's the most amazing woman I've ever met. She's smart, funny, and beautiful. I don't see her age. She's—"

Rich held up his hand to stop him. "She's my mother, Quinn. I've known her for twenty-five years."

"I want to be married to her for at least that." Quinn's face was serious. "I promised her forever, Rich, and I intend to keep that promise."

"It's not the two of you being a couple that's weird. It's having a baby. Mom was talking about wanting grandkids a month ago."

Rich got up from the table and put his dirty dishes in the dishwasher.

"She'll be the sexiest mother and grandmother around," Quinn said with conviction.

Rich grimaced. "I don't want to even think about that. The words *sex* and *mother* shouldn't ever be in the same sentence."

Quinn nodded in agreement. "I know what you mean." He got up from his chair. "So we're good then, Rich?"

"Yes, we're good. Love her, Quinn, and keep her happy."

Davi woke to find Quinn taking off his jeans.

"Good morning," he said with a voice warm and sexy.

"Good morning." Davi smiled back at him. "Have you been somewhere?"

He pulled back the covers and slid into bed beside her.

"I spoke with Rich. I wanted to have the chance to talk to him privately."

"And?" Davi asked, curious at the outcome.

"We're good."

"Care to elaborate?"

"No, it's guy stuff," Quinn said as he wrapped his arms around Davi and hugged her tight.

"It's time for you to go," Davi said softly.

"We've got time," Quinn said as he kissed her hair.

"Time for what?" Davi giggled as his whiskers rubbed against her face.

"This," Quinn murmured as he began to make love to her

Later that day, Davi made her way back to the house from the barn. She liked to help with afternoon chores when she could. Her cell phone rang.

"Hey, Quinn."

"Woman, I've been thinking about something most of the day, and I think we can do it."

"What do you think we can do?" Davi closed her eyes as she waited for his reply.

"I want to get married in the next two weeks. I can't wait any longer or I'll go crazy. I've worked it out in my head. I think we can pull it off."

"Two weeks? That's our Thanksgiving!" Davi went quiet. Quinn waited for her to say more. When she spoke, it was not what he expected. "Give me three reasons why."

"What?"

"You heard me. Give me three reasons why I should marry you sooner than later."

"Davi, I've thought about this. Believe me. We don't need much—just the license, the minister, and your family. Everything else is a bonus."

"Three reasons, Quinn."

Quinn took a deep breath. "I want the ring, Davi. I want to know that I'm yours and you're mine. I want the piece of paper that says we're married. I want to know that I have a home and a family waiting for me when I'm finished work. I want that now before I start anything else in my life, including my next movie."

"I knew it! You want my spread," Davi teased.

"Be serious, please."

There was a long silence. Davi kicked the gravel with the toe of her boot. She closed her eyes and thought. Quinn could hear her breathing.

"We don't have to get married. We can stay engaged until . . ."

"The cows come home? Davi, it's time. We love each other, we have a baby on the way, and living apart is torture for both of us."

"I can't do it on my own. I'll have to ask Maggie to help me. There's so much to do. There's the church, the reception, the license . . ."

"You can do it, Davi. I know you can."

"If we can do it, you'll owe Maggie big time, maybe forever."

"I can do forever. You know that."

"You say that you can. We'll just have to make sure you stick around to mean it."

By the end of the week, all of the arrangements for the wedding had been made. Every detail had been covered, at least Davi and Maggie thought so.

"There's something we've forgotten, Maggie. Can you think of what we've left out? I can't put my finger on it."

Davi got up from the kitchen table to refill their coffee cups.

"Let's go through the list. We have the church, a guest list, a minister, the bride and groom, wedding party, organist, flowers, DJ, reception, dresses and . . ." Maggie's face went white.

"What is it?" Davi dropped down into her chair, almost spilling the full cups of coffee.

Maggie grabbed Davi's arm. "We don't have a photographer. There's no one to take the pictures. You don't want anybody taking them, Davi. It's got to be someone who knows what they are doing."

Davi smiled with confidence. "I know someone who gets his picture taken all of the time. He can look after this. I'm sure he can find a photographer."

"Quinn," Davi said excitedly when he called her that night. "I need you to do something. It's very last minute and important."

"I'm listening."

"We forgot to hire a photographer. I have no idea who to ask. I haven't been to a wedding in ages, so I wouldn't even know who to ask for a referral. You've had your picture taken a gazillion times. I thought there might be someone you could ask who might know someone who could do the photographs. Can you help out with this?"

"Consider it done. Is that it?"

"The dresses."

"Your fitting is for Tuesday, and the tuxedos have been looked after."

"Great, but it will be just Maggie and me. The girls can't afford to take a day off work. If we find something for them, I'll bring them out on Saturday so they can get fitted."

"But you're coming out on Friday for the cast party, aren't you? I am really hoping you'll make it out for that."

"Oh, right. I'll come out Friday, and they can follow on Saturday. We'll have a shopping day."

"Sounds like fun. May I come along?"

"Rings, Quinn, I forgot about wedding rings. We have to do that too."

"Then I definitely get to come along with you. Good. Is there anything else that you need me to do?"

"I'm thinking—church, reception, flowers, dress, limos, photographer, rings, music . . . We need our song."

"We need our song?"

"For our first dance, we need to have a song. Does anything come to mind?"

"Yes."

"Great! What is it?"

"I won't tell you. I'll let it be a surprise for you. Is there anything else?"

"Our honeymoon—we won't have time for one, will we?"

"Do you mind if we postpone it until Christmas? I start work on your movie right after the wedding. Come stay with me for a week or two. I promise we'll have a great time."

"I was planning on coming with you. You're not getting rid of me that fast!"

"Now do we have everything looked after? I want to talk about something else."

"That's everything. Go ahead."

Quinn's voice was instantly low and lusty, "I want to tell you about a fantasy I'd love to try out with you, woman."

"Are we in Aruba?" Davi asked, intrigued.

"No, we're in the backseat of my limo."

"Is Jake driving?"

"I don't know. Does it matter?"

"I'm not having sex with you if Jake is in the front seat. That's just wrong." Davi was adamant.

"Trust me. He wouldn't care." The low and lusty voice was fading.

"You've done it when he's been driving?" she asked, shocked.

"That's not the point. We're talking about you and me." Quinn knew immediately he'd lost control of his fantasy.

"You've had sex in your limo with other women, and now you want to add me to the list? I don't think so, stud." Her tone was suddenly cool.

"You've got this all wrong, Davi," he sputtered.

"How many women have you had in your limo?"

"I've given lots of women a ride in my limo." He cringed as he realized how that sounded. "No. That's not what I meant."

"How many?"

"Fewer than you're thinking."

"You have no idea what I'm thinking."

Quinn listened to the heavy silence. He closed his eyes and prayed she wouldn't hang up on him, let along break up with him over something so stupid. *Idiot.*

"*What's Happening* says you're known for your backseat workouts. All of your costars have had at least one session with you."

"All of them?"

"All of the female ones. There's no mention of the males. I think Rene has had the most. She says you're amazing with what you can do with an armrest and a seat belt."

Quinn swore under his breath as he realized he'd been had. "You are wicked, Davi. That was not nice. I thought I'd upset you."

"Just keeping you on your toes, lover," she breathed lustily. "Do you have another fantasy in mind?"

"Well, there is one that involves a plane . . ."

Chapter 26

♥

Maggie and Davi caught the first morning flight to New York on Tuesday morning. Quinn had made all of the arrangements, including getting a tuxedo for Rich, who had flown out on Monday for his own fitting.

Sarah greeted them at the arrival gate. "Davi, over here!" She waved to get their attention.

Davi and Maggie walked over to her.

Sarah hugged Davi. "I have missed you!"

"Hi, Sarah, this is my best friend, Maggie. Maggie, this is Sarah, Quinn's right-hand woman. She's responsible for his looks."

"I make him pretty for the camera," Sarah explained.

"How did you get away for the day, Sarah? I didn't think you could do that."

"Oh, it's a slow day today. My husband, Pete, is filling in for me today. Jake's at the limo, waiting for us. Let's go."

"Jake? I thought it would be Will."

"It was, but Quinn got antsy and thought it would be best if Jake looked after you for the day."

The three women exited the airport.

Jake stood by the limo, smiling broadly at them. "Davi, it's good to see you again." He gave her a big bear hug, let her go, and then shook Maggie's hand. "Hello, Maggie."

"Hi, Jake, it's so nice to meet you."

Jake opened the back door for them, and the women got in.

"Ooh, this is nice. Are you going to have one of these at home? It could come in handy, Davi," Maggie teased.

"No way. I'm doing my own driving at home. No offense, Jake. So where are we off to, Sarah? Quinn wouldn't tell me anything."

Sarah's eyes sparkled with excitement. "We're going to the design house of an up-and-coming designer, David Paul. Quinn really likes his menswear. He designed the tuxedos for the wedding. David Paul wants to break into women's fashion and asked Quinn for the chance to dress you and the girls for the wedding. If you don't like his work, say so. We have a plan B and C waiting if we're not successful here."

"David Paul. I've read about him, Davi. His work is amazing," said Maggie. "I'd love to have a dress of his!"

Sarah looked at Maggie and smiled. "You're on the list too, Maggie. It's a thank-you from Quinn."

Maggie smiled with delight. "He makes it so hard to stay mad at him."

"You're mad at Quinn? Why?"

Davi explained, "She's not mad at him. She just wants him to think that she is because of all of the hoops he's had her jump through to get this wedding organized. Maggie's never met Quinn, but she wants him to be indebted to her forever."

"Maggie, if you are Davi's best friend, Quinn will be yours forever. He'll give you whatever you want. It's just the way he is."

The limo stopped. Jake got out and opened the door for them.

"I'm staying out here. The less I see, the less I'll be forced to tell him."

David Paul greeted the threesome as they entered his studio, kissing their cheeks. "Welcome. Come with me and I will show you what I have in mind for you. Please don't hesitate to tell me if you don't like it. I don't want to waste your time, and you won't hurt my feelings."

The women were shown into a large room. Dresses were displayed on mannequins, and many more were hanging on racks. There were mirrors everywhere. David Paul showed the women to their chairs. Immediately, models began to make their way out from behind an archway, each one wearing a different wedding gown and each one lovelier than the first. Davi could hear Maggie and Sarah sighing over the dresses, but none of them called out to her. David Paul watched her expressionless face. He knew that she needed something different, something that would show off her understated elegance. He walked through the archway and returned with a dress in his arms.

"This is the dress for you. No one has worn it. I finished the work on it myself this morning. Please try it on for me."

The three women stood up and followed David Paul to a back room. Davi began to undress while Maggie and Sarah prepared the dress for her. Davi stepped into the gown and carefully pulled the long sleeves up her arms. Sarah and Maggie did up the back for her. The room went silent as the three women looked at Davi's reflection in the mirror. The long dress was form fitting but allowed Davi to move and breathe. The neckline had a deep plunge that accentuated Davi's breasts without flaunting them. There was no train, but the dress gently flowed from Davi's hips. The dress was made of white brocade that gave the dress elegance in its simplicity.

"How is everything in there? May I see you?"

Sarah opened the door for David Paul.

He brought his hands to his mouth and gasped, "You make that dress. It's fantastic on you! What do you think?"

"I love it. It's beautiful," exclaimed Davi. Tears came to her eyes.

Sarah came up beside Davi and lifted her hair gently up off her neck. "If you wear your hair something like this, you'll show off the neckline and the dress will show you off perfectly."

David Paul made a close inspection of the dress. "It fits perfectly. I must have been thinking of you when I designed it. I'd be honored if you wore my dress, Davi."

"Thank you, David Paul. I would love to wear this dress."

"Well, that was easy," Sarah said, relieved. "Now let's see if you have anything for the bridesmaids and Maggie."

"How old are your daughters?" asked David Paul.

"They are in their early twenties."

"Do they like to dance?"

"They love to dance. They're disco divas," Maggie answered for her.

"Then may I suggest that we do something fun for them. Give them something they can wear again if they choose. No one likes to be stuck with a bridesmaid's dress."

"What do you have in mind?" asked Davi.

David Paul clapped his hands again. Models came out wearing variations of the same party dress with spaghetti straps. One was a burnished gold, another in pewter, one in silver, and one in bronze, all shimmering. They came to a couple of inches above the knee. They were perfect for dancing and having fun.

"I like them. What do you two think?" asked Davi.

"They certainly aren't your ordinary bridesmaid dresses," observed Sarah.

"I like this one," Maggie pointed to it. "Cat would look gorgeous in this color, and this is Tigger's color definitely.

"Try it on," urged David Paul. "Let us see what it looks like on you."

Maggie blushed. "I can't wear the same thing the girls are wearing. Don't be ridiculous!"

"Try it on, Maggie. You are the youngest-looking forty-year-old I know! And besides, you're part of the bridal party anyway."

Maggie looked at Davi in shock. "I am not in your bridal party. You never asked me, and I don't want to be in it. You've got your two girls, and that's all you need."

"Will you be my matron of honor, then? Pick any title you want, just be a part of this day for me."

"I'll be the odd woman out. It won't look right."

"You won't be." Davi stared at Maggie. "Try the dress on. That's all I'm asking. Please."

"Do it, Maggie," Sarah encouraged her. "What have you got to lose?"

Maggie sighed. "Fine. I'll try on the damn dress."

"Excellent," said David Paul as he led Maggie to the fitting room.

Jake poked his head through the archway and called out, "Is everything okay in there? Hello?"

"Jake! I forgot about him!" cried Davi. "Sarah, go look after him, please. He can't see me in this dress."

Sarah left quickly to let him know that everyone was fine. She asked someone to bring him a coffee. By the time she returned, Maggie appeared wearing the dress.

"Wow," Sarah and Davi said in unison.

"It's too much."

"Too much what?" Davi asked. "It's beautiful.

"I know. That's the problem. I shouldn't wear something like this."

David Paul wouldn't let her refuse. "You, dear lady, are just what this dress needs to show it off. This wedding will be a showcase for some of my creations. If you do not wear it, I will be so disappointed. You will be doing me a huge favor by agreeing to wear it. So please reconsider."

"But the girls . . ."

"Never mind the girls. We will have them in these dresses, or we will find something else for them to wear. Don't worry about them. We have this dress for you, and that is all that matters." David Paul was final in his verdict. "Sarah has already picked out a dress for herself, so we are done here. Go find your shoes then return for the final fitting."

"So you found your dress?" Jake asked as he saw three smiling women exit the studio.

"I found my dress, Jake. It's all coming together."

Finding the right shoes for the outfits was simple but expensive. Maggie cringed at the price of the shoes, even knowing that Quinn was paying for them. Davi found a beautiful pair of shoes in which she'd be able to dance all night long. The foursome then made their way back to David Paul's for the final fitting.

"You'll bring your daughters here on Saturday, and we will find them a dress. Don't worry about it, Davi."

"I won't, David Paul. I know you will have something for them. Thank you."

David Paul handed Davi a garment bag. "This is for you, Davi. I know it will fit you. It's a thank-you gift from me to you."

"You don't have to thank me, David Paul. I'm the one who should be thanking you!"

"Perhaps the next time you need a dress, you will think of me first. That is all the thanks I need, dear lady." He kissed her on the cheek and walked the women back to the limo.

"I'm starved," announced Sarah. "Let's get something to eat."

"That's an excellent idea," agreed Maggie. "Where should we go?"

"Your reservation has already been made, ladies. We're on our way now," Jake announced.

Davi looked out the window. She recognized the area. They were heading to the studio. She smiled. She knew there was no way Quinn would let her visit New York without seeing him.

The limo turned into the studio parking lot.

Maggie looked out the window. "This looks interesting, Davi. Will there be any big stars here for me to meet?"

"It all depends on what you mean by big, Maggie."

The three women giggled. Jake shook his head. The limo stopped. Jake got out and opened the door for the women. Davi and Maggie both looked around. Sarah started walking toward the canteen.

"Is he free, Jake?"

"He will be shortly. He wants you to get some lunch, and he'll join you. Come on, ladies, let's go."

Jake stood back and let Davi lead the way through the food line. Everything smelled delicious. She helped herself to salad and a small serving of pasta. Maggie did the same. Jake followed with a burger and salad.

"Mmm, this is delicious. Is the food always this good?"

"I think it has to be or else the crew and cast would go on strike. They put in long hours here, and they have to be well fed," explained Davi.

Davi looked at Jake. Jake moved his head slightly and tapped his ear, the one with the earphone. Quinn was on his way. Davi could feel her heart beat faster and a blush coming on. She felt like a teenager all over again. A hand touched her shoulder and she jumped.

"Sorry, love. I didn't mean to scare you." Quinn sat down beside her and gave her his smile, the one that touched his sparkling blue eyes.

Davi leaned into him for a kiss. He kissed her softly and then released her.

"I couldn't let you leave without seeing you."

Quinn got up and walked around the table. "You must be the one and only Maggie. I have been looking forward to meeting you."

Quinn didn't give Maggie a chance to respond. He picked her up and kissed her on the mouth. Maggie's tiny build made her look like a rag doll in Quinn's arms.

Davi laughed at the sight. "Maggie, this is Quinn, in case you didn't know."

"It's very nice to meet you, Quinn." Maggie's eyes sparkled with excitement as her feet touched the ground.

"Did you have a successful day?"

Sarah answered for all of them, "It was very successful, Quinn. And before you try to find out anything, Jake was nowhere near the dresses, so he didn't see anything."

"It's true. I didn't see anything but shoes. The shoes are nice if you're into that kind of thing."

"And the three of us won't say one word. You'll just have to wait it out."

"So is everything done now? Can you ladies relax?" Quinn winked at Davi.

"Relax? I don't think so. Davi was lucky to get the marriage license yesterday. They had a backlog of appointments, and she would have had to wait at least another week before she could get the damn thing. We couldn't confirm anything until we knew we had that blasted piece of paper. Now we have to get the floral arrangements confirmed and invite everyone. I don't think we're going to be relaxed for quite a while." Maggie took a deep breath once she finished venting.

Quinn gazed down at Maggie. There was no Hollywood smile or the blue bedroom eyes for her. He gave her the gaze of a man who was truly thankful for her hard work. "Thank you, Maggie. I appreciate everything you have done for Davi."

The softness of his voice calmed her as its sincerity touched her to her core.

"You're welcome."

"I'm sorry to interrupt you, but they want you back on set, Quinn. Your break is over."

Quinn walked over to Davi. She stood up and faced him.

His hand caressed her face as he said, "I have to go. I'll see you on Friday. Come early if you can and spend the day."

Davi answered softly, "I'll see what I can do."

Quinn put his arms around her and pulled her in tight for a kiss. She could feel it instantly. He was giving her her kiss. Her legs weakened. A tingling sensation started in her toes and worked its way quickly up her body. Her hands instinctively reached for his head and her fingers wove through his hair pulling him in closer. Just as she could feel a moan coming from deep within her, Quinn released her.

"Wow," they both whispered to each other.

"Quinn, it's time," Jake reminded him.

"I'm coming," he said over his shoulder. Still looking at Davi, he said, "I will talk to you tonight. I have the photographer. I'll tell you all about it." He kissed her on the nose and then turned to Maggie.

"Maggie, it was a pleasure to meet you. Thank you again for all you've done for us."

Quinn didn't wait for a reply. He turned and walked away with Jake, calling back to Sarah as he walked, "Thanks, Sarah."

Davi sat down in her chair, smiling.

Maggie leaned toward Davi. "May I ask you something? It's personal."

"When have you not asked me something personal, Maggie? You know you can ask me anything. Go ahead."

"When he kisses you like that, it looks like you're about to, you know . . ."

"Sometimes I do. He's that good."

"Wow."

"Wow indeed."

Chapter 27

♥

On Friday, Davi flew in to attend the wrap-up party of Quinn's latest movie. Jake met Davi once she came through customs. His warm broad smile always touched her heart.

"Hi, Jake, this is getting to be a habit," she chuckled as she hugged him and gave him a kiss on the cheek.

"This habit doesn't need to be broken, dear lady. I don't mind this one bit."

He walked her to the waiting limo and opened the back door. Inside on the seat were a single rose and a wrapped box.

"Presents for me?" she asked with excitement.

"There's nonalcoholic champagne there for you too. The glass is already filled for you. They're from Quinn, in case you were wondering."

"I'm glad you told me, Jake. I thought they were from you."

Davi smelled the rose's perfume and then turned her attention to the box. She undid the ribbon and removed the lid. Inside were Belgian chocolates and raspberries with a note that read, "Happy Three Weeks—love, Quinn."

Davi smiled and took a bite of the chocolate. It was sweet. She had a taste of the champagne. The bubbles tickled her nose.

"He must be in a really good mood today, Jake, with the movie finishing up today."

"The movie has nothing to do with it, Davi, and you know it. He's been on cloud nine knowing that you were coming today and that in one week you two are tying the knot. That's all he's been talking about. I'm surprised he could say his lines this week."

"Did you hear about the photographer he lined up to do our wedding pictures? It's the head photographer from *Vanity Fair*. In exchange for some photos for the magazine, *Vanity Fair*'s going to do the whole wedding. They're going to be featuring David Paul's designs, and they offered to donate to one of Quinn's charities. I can't believe it!"

"Quinn said that some of the celebrity magazines put in a bid for your wedding shots."

"I wouldn't let anyone take my wedding pictures. I have a bad feeling about celebrity gossip magazines. Every time they feature a star's wedding, the couple usually splits up after a year."

Davi had another sip of her champagne. She offered some chocolate to Jake, but he declined.

"I have to watch my waistline, Davi. I have to fit into my tux for the wedding."

"Maybe I should cut back too. I wasn't thinking."

"You look fine. Enjoy every one of those raspberries and chocolates. They are yours."

The limo stopped.

"We're here, lovely lady," Jake announced as he got out and opened the door for her.

Davi looked toward the entrance to the restaurant and saw Quinn waiting for her.

"Have a good time. I'll pick you two up later."

"Thanks, Jake."

Davi walked toward Quinn. He leaned casually against a light post with a glass of scotch in his hand. He was dressed in a black suit with a white silk shirt unbuttoned at the neck. His eyes were riveted on her. Davi could feel her body tingle. Just one look from him and she was instantly aroused.

"Did you know that drinking scotch is just like having great sex?"

"Tell me about it," he answered without taking his eyes off her.

"It burns and you can take your time with it. There's no rush."

"What about the hair it puts on your chest?"

"A real man can handle it."

"And a real woman?"

"She can handle the scotch and the man."

Quinn laughed. His eyes sparkled. "Woman, you are something else!" He put his glass down on a nearby bench and took her in his arms. His kiss was hard. She could taste the scotch on his lips and smell it on his breath. He pulled her in closer. She could feel his arousal.

"How many have you had, Quinn?"

"Just one. I'm finished now that you're here. You are my drug of choice."

"Thank you for my presents. I enjoyed them on my way here."

"I have another present for you, love."

"I know. I can feel it pressing against me."

Quinn chuckled. "Not that, silly woman. That will go away soon. Just stay close for a minute or two. I have a real present for you."

Quinn reached into the inside pocket of his jacket and pulled out a jewelry case.

"This is for you. I was looking at rings and this caught my eye." He handed her the case. "Open it, please."

Davi took the case and stared at it. "You didn't have to give me anything, Quinn."

"Just open it, woman."

Davi opened the box to find a diamond bracelet. It sparkled in the outdoor lights. "Oh, Quinn, it's beautiful. Thank you," she said excitedly as she took it out of the box and put it on her wrist.

"I remembered that three weeks ago today, you wore sparkling diamonds. I thought you needed a bracelet to go with them. I see you're wearing the diamonds tonight. Perfect."

Davi kissed Quinn on the lips. It was a soft kiss. "You have a great memory."

"Come on, let's go in. There are people waiting to meet you."

Quinn pocketed the empty box and then took Davi by the hand and led her into the restaurant. The hostess greeted them and asked for Davi's coat. As she took it off, Davi could hear Quinn take in a deep breath. She turned to look at him.

She looked like a movie star, wearing the dress David Paul had given her just days ago. The dress was short, black, and very form fitting. Its neckline plunged to her waistline but did not expose her breasts fully. Her high heels accentuated her long legs, and her hair, in an up do, showed off her elegant neck. She wore her diamond earrings and necklace to finish the look. Davi's simple elegance was breathtaking.

"Woman, that dress should be illegal," he said with obvious lustful thoughts running through his mind.

"Is it too much?" she asked innocently.

"Yes, but I promise to not ravish you until we are at home. I will be the envy of every man here tonight. You're not getting out of my sight."

Quinn put a protective arm around Davi's waist as he walked her in to the private party room. It was loud and jam packed with everyone associated with the making of the movie. Davi could feel everyone's eyes on them.

"They're all staring at us, Quinn," she whispered in his ear.

"Can you blame them? Davi, you're the most beautiful woman in this room tonight. They're probably wondering what you're doing with me."

"I thought it was the other way around." She laughed.

"Never," Quinn said as he walked her to the bar. "What would you like to drink, Davi? Sparkling water?"

"Please."

Quinn placed the order. "Two sparkling waters, please."

"Not drinking?"

"No. I need to keep my wits about me tonight. You've got me in protector mode." He winked at her.

"Why don't you just call Jake? I know he can look after me, if you're so concerned," Davi teased.

Quinn leaned into Davi. "Woman, I'm serious. I don't trust any man around you tonight. You are not leaving my side."

Davi shook her head and said, "You're impossible."

Quinn and Davi took their drinks and wandered through the crowd in search of the director, Guy Tremblant. Quinn found him at a table, holding court over some of the younger members of the crew. Guy stood up as soon as he saw Davi. He offered his hand to her.

"Hello, I'm Guy."

"Hi, I'm Davi."

Davi shook his hand. It was a weak and clammy handshake. Davi cringed inside.

"Everyone's been talking about Quinn's latest acquisition, but no one described you accurately, Davi. You're beautiful," he said as his eyes took in every inch of her body.

"I'm not an acquisition, but thank you for the compliment."

Davi didn't appreciate Guy's tone or his ogling. Immediately, the magazine article she had read about him came to mind. It said something about an overblown ego and wandering hands.

Guy motioned for the couple to sit down.

"So, Davi, are you an actress? Have I seen your work?"

"No, I'm not in the business."

"Are you a singer?"

"No, I'm a farmer who writes."

Guy's face went blank, and then he laughed as though he just caught on to a joke. "Very funny, you're a farmer!"

"Guy, she is a farmer. She's not in our business." Quinn pulled Davi's business card from his wallet and handed it to him.

Idiot! Davi screamed silently at Quinn. *Why would you give him my card?* She looked at Quinn with disbelief.

Guy looked at it quickly. "You really are a farmer and you write? Anything I know?" He sounded mildly interested.

"I wrote *Second Harvest*. It is being made into a film this year. Quinn's in it."

"I've heard of it. It could be a great movie if it's done right. Good luck to both of you," he said as his eyes focused on Davi's breasts.

"Thank you." Davi smiled through gritted teeth. *The man's a pig.*

"So you're not in the movie business at all? You should be. I'd cast you in one of my films."

"Thanks, but I'm not interested. I don't have the attention span for this business. I'd be bored pretty fast." Davi laughed weakly. *Work with you? Not a chance.*

"So what are you doing with this man if you think making movies is boring?"

"The business is boring. Quinn is never boring."

Quinn smiled at her. "Thank you."

Davi felt a leg rub against hers under the table, and it wasn't Quinn's. She pulled her legs back and tucked them under her chair.

"Do you think my movies are boring?" Guy asked her, flashing yellowed teeth.

"No. I am interested to see how this movie turns out. I liked the scenes I saw Quinn film."

"You were here? And I didn't see you?" Guy looked genuinely shocked.

"I think you were busy making a movie. I sat on the sidelines and watched."

"Quinn, you invited Davi to the set and didn't introduce us?" Guy glared at Quinn as though he had given Guy a great insult.

"We were kind of busy, Guy, and I was more focused on Davi than I was on you, if you can understand that."

Guy made a sickly laugh. "I'd be focusing on her too, Quinn. I'm surprised you were able to work with Davi on the set." His eyes ran over her one more time. "Come to think of it, I think it was best that I didn't know she was there."

Quinn glared at Guy. "We've got to move on, Guy. I told Sarah that we'd have a drink with her." Quinn got up and pulled Davi with him. "We'll catch you later." He didn't give Guy the chance to say another word.

"What took you so long?" Davi snapped at him. "He wouldn't take his eyes off my breasts, and he was rubbing his leg against mine. Damn it, Quinn, if he weren't your director, I would have thrown my drink in his face."

"I'm sorry, love. It took me a while to catch on. He's married. I didn't think he'd talk to you that way."

"Do you not read the magazines?" Davi asked incredulously. "He's got a reputation for being too free with his eyes and his hands."

"I thought we agreed the magazines lie, Davi," Quinn bristled at being chastised.

"Not in this case. Put me in that man's company again and you'll regret it. Mark my words."

"Davi! I haven't seen you in ages!" Sarah pounced on Davi and gave her a hug and kiss. "Is this from David Paul? You look fabulous, girl!" Sarah looked at Quinn and then whispered in his ear, "How are you holding out, sweetie? Been able to keep it in your pants with her looking like this?"

Quinn answered lustily, "It's been hard, Sarah, really hard."

Sarah laughed at the double meaning. Davi smiled and shook her head.

Davi tried to forget about Guy. Quinn introduced her to the cast and crew. Quinn kept close to her, keeping his arm around her at all times. He promised her protective mode, and he'd already failed by letting Guy near her. He wouldn't make that mistake again.

Quinn had to pee. The sparkling water was going right though him.

He whispered to Sarah, "Stay with Davi and don't let her out of your sight. I'll be right back."

Before Sarah could answer, Quinn was gone.

"He's a bit overprotective tonight, isn't he?" Sarah teased. "Well, who could blame him? That dress, Davi—"

"Is breathtaking," Guy answered from behind her. "Dance with me, Davi."

Before she could turn him down, Guy whisked Davi onto the dance floor. Guy held her tight to his small round body.

"You and I need to have a talk." He was serious and drunk.

"Isn't it customary to wait for the woman to accept the invitation to dance before you take her?" Davi asked, clearly peeved.

Guy ignored the question. "I want you to dump Quinn for me. I'm much better for you."

"Excuse me?"

"He may have the looks, but I have the connections, the money, and the personality. I can give you everything that he can't or won't."

"No," she said quickly.

"I want you, Davi."

He pulled her in close. Davi cringed as she felt his arousal press against her. She thought quickly. Guy was clearly drunk. Perhaps she could talk her way out of this without causing a scene.

"Give me your best pickup line, Guy. If it's better than Quinn's, I'll leave him. If you don't match his, you'll turn around and walk away and we won't talk about this again."

Guy stopped.

"A pickup line? You mean what I'd say to get you to go to bed with me?" He didn't know whether to take her seriously or not.

"Yes, that kind of pickup line. If yours beats Quinn's, you get me. If it doesn't, you'll walk away and promise not to hit on me ever again. Is it a deal?"

"I can use anything on you? I don't have to make up a new one?"

"Hell, Guy, I don't care if it's original or not. It just has to work. So go for it now or walk away." Davi stood there without moving. Her eyes burned into Guy.

"Let me think. How much time do I get?"

"When Quinn gets back, you're out of time. You'd better hurry, Guy."

"This isn't fair."

"You're a writer, think of something." Davi found it hard not to smile. She knew she had him beat. She knew that he knew it too.

"You're the most beautiful woman in the world. I love you. They broke the mold when they made you." Beads of sweat formed on his brow. "Your dress is beautiful on you, but it would look better on my bedroom floor."

Davi laughed. "Funny, but not good enough."

"Hey, Davi, what's going on?" Quinn appeared at her side. His arm wrapped immediately around her waist and pulled her away from Guy.

"Guy's trying to come up with a pickup line that's better than yours. If he wins, I dump you for him. If he loses, he promises to never hit on me again."

"Should I be nervous?" Quinn asked as he tamped down the urge to hit Guy where he stood.

"Not with what he's coming up with so far. Time's up, Guy."

Guy cursed in French. "This wasn't fair, Davi. You didn't give me much time."

"I don't think Quinn had much time to think about his line and it sounded like he really meant it. Did you mean it, Quinn?"

"Of course I meant it, every word." Quinn's voice was low and threatening.

Davi could feel his taut body against hers, protecting her from Guy. She tingled from his touch.

"Tell me what it was!" Guy demanded angrily.

"No. I'm not going to tell you because you won't mean it if you say it, and I won't help you lie to any woman. Come on, Quinn, I'm sure there's someone else we should be talking to."

Davi pulled Quinn away from him.

"I remember everything I ever said to you, love, but I didn't use any pickup line. I meant every word I said," he whispered in her ear.

Davi stopped and looked Quinn in the eyes. "I know that. But what's the first thing you said to me that hooked me."

Quinn closed his eyes and then said, "I hope I didn't disturb you, but I was enjoying watching you work. You're very sexy when you're reading."

"No. It wasn't that. It was, 'Quinn Thomas Hot Sex Now.' You had me after that."

Quinn and Davi left the party soon after their run-in with Guy. The couple kept catching Guy staring at Davi as he followed them around the room. The man made Quinn edgy. He didn't want to have to hit Guy to get him to leave Davi alone. It was best to leave while they were still on good terms.

Jake picked them up and asked them about their night.

"Davi's got a new admirer. Guy couldn't keep his eyes or his hands off her all night. He was asking for a fight."

"Getting some competition, Quinn? Davi's got a week to back out."

Davi groaned. "The man is a creep, Jake. He made me feel uncomfortable, but I had to be careful. I didn't want Quinn to hit him and cause problems between them."

"So you got it sorted out?"

"Davi put him in his place without any help from me. She's quick on her feet, Jake."

"I know. I've seen her magic in action. Kind of bruises the male ego though, huh, Quinn?"

"Oh please! There was no need for a fight, especially with that man. If Quinn were to fight over me, please let it be with someone worth it!"

Quinn looked at Davi with bemusement. "Who would be worth it? Who would you like me to fight over you, woman?"

"I don't know! No one. Forget about it." She looked away from him.

Quinn put a finger on her chin and turned her face toward him. "No. You can't throw out that line and then drop it. Come on, tell us. Who would it be? Who's your fantasy guy?" His eyes burned into her.

"Ryan Reynolds. But I haven't thought about him since I met you." Davi smiled up at Quinn. "You're my only fantasy guy now."

"Do you think she's lying, Jake? Should I believe her?" Quinn teased.

"Leave me out of this."

"Okay, woman, I'll believe you for now. But I'll be keeping my eyes on you."

"Promise?" She smiled.

"Forever."

Chapter 28

♥

Davi padded out to the kitchen in the dark. She was hungry and thirsty. Quinn had kept her busy with lovemaking since they arrived at his hotel suite. He finally fell asleep, but sleep evaded her. She wasn't thinking of anything in particular. Her mind refused to shut off for sleep to come.

Davi poured herself a glass of juice and opened a bag of raw almonds. She saw one of Quinn's hooded jackets draped on the back of a chair and put it on to cover her nakedness. Once comfortable on the couch she turned on the television. Having no interest in the shopping channels or infomercials that filled late night television, she flipped through the channels until she came across the movie channel. It was playing an old black-and-white war movie. Davi settled in to watch it. She hadn't seen this movie in a few years.

The movie brought back memories of when she and Ross would stay up late on a Friday night and watch the old movies on the local PBS station. They would cuddle on the couch with a blanket covering them, drinking wine and enjoying cheese and crackers. It was their big date night. Sometimes Davi would fall asleep watching the movie. Ross would wake her when it was time to head up to bed, and she'd fall back to sleep in his arms.

When she was able to stay awake through the whole movie, those were the best dates. The movie would finish, they'd turn down the lights, spread the blanket on the floor in front of the fire, and make love. Afterward, they would cuddle in front of the fire, wrapped in their blanket, and talk about their dreams for the future and their children. The dreams were always the same. The kids would take over the running of the farm, and Davi and Ross would travel. She dreamed of hot beaches in the south, while he dreamed of traveling to historical sites across the globe. They agreed to compromise. They would do both. Then everything changed.

Davi started to cry. They were gentle tears. With *Second Harvest*, Davi was able to let go of her grief and the pain, but the memories still reminded her of the loss.

Quinn walked into the room and saw Davi crying as she watched the movie. Quietly, he sat down beside her and took her in his arms. Quinn reached for the remote.

"No. Don't turn it off, please." Davi sniffled.

"Are you okay?"

"I'm fine. I get this way every time I watch this movie. It brings back memories, but they're good memories of Ross."

"Tell me about them." Quinn closed his eyes and tried to imagine Davi and Ross as she talked about them.

"We were so good together. We were a team. We did everything together as a couple and as business partners. We talked about everything, and we made every decision together."

"The two of you built up an amazing farm business, Davi." Quinn's voice was warm and soothing. He could feel Davi relax in his arms. "How were you as a family?"

"The kids adored Ross. He tried to be there for them, but it was difficult when he was busy with the farm. When they got older, they all got their turns riding with him in the big tractor or the combine just to have special time with him. I was the one who took them to their games. Ross was the one who taught them about farming. We were happy. At least I thought we were until . . ." Davi's breath hitched.

"He cheated on you," Quinn said softly.

"Yes. He was willing to risk all that we had for casual sex. He broke my heart."

"It still upsets you."

Davi pushed away from Quinn to see his face. "Yes, but I know that I have to take some of the blame. I wasn't there for him when he needed me."

"That's no excuse to cheat, Davi."

"I pulled away from him. The kids were away at school. I remember feeling lost without having them around, so I got involved with volunteer work. You name it, I was on the committee—my women's church group, community services, and the local hospice. I buried myself in them. Instead of looking after my husband's needs, I looked after everyone else's."

"We all make mistakes."

"Yes, but we could have lost so much." Davi closed her eyes and shuddered. "I didn't realize that we were both unhappy and feeling lost. I thought it was all part of married life—the almost nonexistent sex life and the beginning of two separate lives. I was so naive."

"You said you tried counseling."

"We were getting there, but the cheating was a major road block. It's hard to learn to trust again once you've been cheated on." Davi sat up straight and wiped her eyes with the back of her sleeve. "That's not why I'm crying, though. It's his loss I cry for and everything that he is missing—the kids' graduating from university, the farm's success, and everything that will happen. He's missing out on so much."

Quinn wiped away a stray tear on Davi's cheek. "He's missing out on a great life with you."

Davi smiled weakly. "Yes, he is. He's still with me, though. I'm reminded of him every day when I'm with the kids. You think they're like me, but they are so much like him."

"It's too bad we didn't meet. I'd have hit him for cheating on you, but I still would have liked to have met him."

Davi shook her head. "We wouldn't be here if Ross were still alive."

"How do you know that?"

"Because I wouldn't have written my book, silly, and I wouldn't have been on that plane for us to meet."

"What if you had written a book, something else that was being made into a movie? What if you had sat beside me on the plane and you were still married? Would I have had a chance with you?" Quinn's gaze fixed on her as though he were willing her to give the right answer.

"No," Davi said as she looked away from him.

Quinn turned her face to him. "Is that definitely no or maybe no?"

"Definitely no."

"Are you sure?" He gave her his wicked smile.

"Why are you asking me this? If I say that I would have fallen for you, what does it say about my character? Could you want someone who would leave her husband and family for you after just meeting you?"

"If it were you, my answer is yes."

"No, that's not you. You wouldn't want a woman who is that fickle that she'd leave her marriage without a second thought. Give your head a shake, Quinn."

Quinn shook his head in fun, saying, "He was cheating on you."

"I keep my promises. I'd have stayed faithful."

"And been miserable. I would have still wanted you. Nothing would be different."

"Except for the tabloids, my kids' support, and your reputation."

"I wouldn't care about the tabloids, I'd win your kids over, and my character would remain unscathed."

"You're sure of yourself."

"For you I have to be."

Quinn kissed Davi softly. "You are my plan A, Davi. There is no plan B for me. If we'd met on a plane and you had told me you were married, I would have pursued you. It would still have been love at first sight, and I would have been miserable until I made you mine. I would like to think that you would have been immediately attracted to me and that you'd have given in to me right away, but that's a fantasy. I know you would have needed more time to fall for me, but I would have succeeded. Hollywood heartthrob or not, I would have won you over. And I would have done anything to win."

"Keep thinking that, stud, whatever makes you happy."

"I will and it's you who makes me happy, only you."

Davi yawned. "It's time to go back to bed."

Quinn turned off the television and led Davi back to bed. He made love to Davi, and when he was finished, he held her in his arms as they both fell asleep.

Chapter 29

♥

Jake leaned against the limo, sipping a coffee while waiting for Davi and Quinn to appear. He smiled warmly as Davi approached. She kissed him on his cheek.

"Good morning, Jake. Thanks again for offering to drive us around today. It's very sweet of you. The girls will be thrilled."

"Thanks for letting me tag along. It will give me a chance to get to know your girls."

"Sue doesn't mind you working on a Saturday?' Quinn teased as he and Davi got into the backseat.

"She's meeting with a decorator, and she doesn't want my input," Jake laughed, relieved that he didn't have to spend the day looking at fabric samples.

Traffic was light on the way to the airport. Jake pulled into the waiting area, and Quinn and Davi got out and headed to arrivals. Jake and Quinn agreed that Quinn wouldn't need his assistance in meeting the girls. Quinn could always phone if there were a problem. Quinn had his arm around Davi's waist as they walked through the airport. They noticed the stares, but no one approached them. It wasn't until they stopped at the arrivals area that they were mobbed.

There were the usual questions: What brings you here? What are the wedding plans? How did the filming of your last movie go? Are you looking forward to your next film?

Quinn answered them easily and in a relaxed manner, enjoying himself.

Then out of nowhere came the question, "Quinn, any comment on Guy Tremblant hitting on Davi at last night's wrap-up party? They say he got way out of line."

Quinn looked at the reporter. His answer came quickly and calmly. "Davi was stunning last night. Any man would have hit on her. Guy was the only one who dared, and Davi handled it. I didn't need to get involved. As far as we're concerned, the matter is settled." Quinn pulled Davi in tighter. "I think that's enough questions for now." Quinn dismissed them and turned to watch for the girls.

"Nothing escapes them," Davi whispered to Quinn.

The doors opened and out came Tigger and Cat. They were laughing and their eyes sparkled. Davi waved to them. They waved back as they walked toward them. Davi held her arms open to the girls for a family hug.

"Hey, Mom, you're looking good."

Then they hugged Quinn. "How's it going, Quinn?"

"Hi, girls, did you have a good flight?"

"Super," they chorused.

Quinn took their bags, and the foursome made their way to the limo.

Jake stood by the limo, smiling at them. He stood back from Davi's daughters, looking at each one carefully. He marveled at the remarkable resemblance of the two young women.

"Which one is which? You two look so much alike."

"I'm Cat. This is Tigger," Cat answered for them. "I wear a lot of red. Tigger usually wears purple or green. That's what we tell people to look for."

"It's great to meet you." Tigger smiled up at Jake.

"Thanks. It's great to meet you too."

Jake walked around to the trunk of the limo and opened it. Quinn put the girls' bags inside.

Quinn opened the back door for them. "Ladies?" he asked as he invited them inside.

The girls slid into the backseat. Quinn and Davi sat in the seat opposite them.

"Is this The Limo?"

Davi looked out the window. She knew where this was heading. The girls got off the plane running. They had no mercy.

"The Limo?" Quinn asked. He wasn't ready for them. "This is my limo. Why?"

Quinn looked at Davi, who was obviously avoiding him. He searched his brain, desperate for an answer. Surely, she wouldn't have told them that he had a fantasy about having sex with her in the limo. No, but she would have told them about how she sucked him into believing that magazine article about him having sex with starlets in the backseat.

Quinn swore under his breath, "Yes, it's The Limo."

The girls broke out into laughter.

Davi looked at Quinn. "They have no mercy. Be on your guard at all times."

"You women are wicked, very wicked." Quinn smiled at them.

The girls chatted with Quinn all the way to David Paul's studio. They asked him about the Hollywood gossip they had read about in the magazines and on the Internet. They asked what it was really like making a movie and what his favorite movie was. Davi sat back and enjoyed the conversation. They were so relaxed with each other.

The limo stopped. Jake got out and opened the door for them.

"Can't Quinn open his own door, Jake?" Cat asked as she got out first.

"It's a childproof lock on the door. It can only be opened from the outside," Jake explained with a serious face. "It's for his protection."

"But if it were for his protection, shouldn't it only open from the inside?" asked Tigger.

"Shh. It's our secret. Don't tell him," he whispered to them.

"Are you telling stories about me, Jake?" Quinn asked. "You know, ever since you came into my life, woman, Jake's taken too many liberties with our working relationship. He's forgotten who the boss is." Quinn winked at her.

"I don't think you were ever the boss, Quinn. But you keep thinking that if it makes you feel better," Davi teased.

They were all laughing as they walked through the entrance to the studio where David Paul waited to greet them.

"Welcome, everyone. It is so good to see you." He hugged and kissed the women, Jake and Quinn too.

David Paul stepped back to look at the girls. "You look just like your mother. I am so excited that you are wearing my creations. Come with me. Quinn and Jake, you go over there and try on your tuxedos."

The men were taken to a room away from the women. Davi and her daughters were taken to the back. David Paul's assistants brought out the dresses that Davi and Maggie thought the girls would like. They took to them immediately.

"Try them on," Davi said. "We've got the shoes to go with them too. I hope you don't mind, but they were the last pairs left in the store, and we couldn't take the chance that they'd still be here today."

Cat and Tigger went to the fitting room. Davi could hear them shriek with delight when they saw their reflections in the mirror.

"Come out and show us, girls."

Davi and David Paul were eager to see them. The girls made their entrance, looking absolutely stunning.

"What do you think? Do you like the dresses?" David Paul tried to contain his excitement.

"They are gorgeous, and you chose the right dress for both of us. Good job, Mom."

David Paul examined the fit of the dresses on the girls. He made some minor adjustments with some pins.

"This won't take long to fix. Why don't you try on the wedding dress, Davi, and let your girls see it on you."

Davi could feel her heart race. She was excited to see the wedding dress again. The girls went back to their fitting room. David Paul had robes for them while they waited for the dresses to be altered. The girls made their way to Davi's fitting room, where David Paul's assistants were helping her put on the dress. Davi turned to them to show them her wedding dress.

"Wow, Mom, you're beautiful. It's the perfect dress for you," the girls chorused.

"Do you really like it?" Davi asked with excitement.

"We love it. Has Quinn seen it?"

"Of course not. Not until the wedding!"

David Paul returned with the girls' dresses.

"Try them on and stand with your mother. Let's see how you look together. My model has on Maggie's dress, so you can see the whole effect."

The girls quickly put on their dresses and came back to join Davi. They stood beside each other with the model in front of a large mirror. They were a striking foursome.

"Wow," they chorused.

David Paul had one more look at the dresses, making sure they fit perfectly, and then he left to check on Quinn. The girls and Davi changed and were out in the showroom a few minutes before Jake and Quinn joined them.

"So how did you like your dresses? Are they nice?"

"They're beautiful, Quinn. Thanks so much for arranging for us to get them. And Mom's dress is stunning!" Tigger hugged him.

David Paul came out and handed them their garment bags.

"Have a wonderful wedding. Congratulations to both of you."

"Thank you, David Paul." Davi gave him her best smile and kissed him on the cheek. "Thank you for everything."

"My pleasure."

"Where to now?" Jake asked once everyone was in the limo.

"Tiffany's, Jake. We have rings to buy."

The girls shrieked with delight.

"You'd think you two had never been shopping before? Do you always get so excited?" Quinn teased.

"It's Tiffany's, Quinn. I bet you were excited the first time you ever shopped there," Cat countered.

Quinn gazed at Davi as he answered her, "You're right. I was excited, but it wasn't the store that excited me, it was what I was buying and for whom I was buying it. It was one of the biggest thrills of my life." He kissed her when he finished.

"Hey, none of that, you two. There are children present."

"You aren't children. I can kiss your mother anytime I want. If you can't handle it—tough."

Quinn went back to kissing Davi. Davi laughed as he pulled her in close.

"We're here," Jake announced.

The girls shrieked one more time. Quinn winced. Davi laughed.

"I hope you realize that they're doing this to get to you."

The girls exited the limo. Quinn pulled the door closed and locked it.

"Quinn, what are you doing?"

"I'm getting a quiet moment with my woman."

He pulled her close and kissed her. His hands moved over her body and down her legs. There was light tapping on the window.

Quinn released Davi. "Do they take naps at this age?"

"Quinn"—Davi laughed—"they're in their twenties. I think nap time is long gone."

Quinn unlocked the door and opened it for Davi. They both got out smiling.

"Get a room, Quinn."

"I've got one, girls. It's called my Limo."

"Oh, gross." The girls turned and walked toward the store.

"I'll be here." Jake chuckled as he watched the girls leave. "It's almost lunchtime. Do you have plans for afterward?"

"No, Jake, we haven't. Could I pay you to take the girls for an hour or two?"

Davi poked Quinn in the ribs. "You are so bad. We're keeping the girls with us. Get used to them."

"We shouldn't be long, Jake."

Quinn escorted Davi into Tiffany's. The girls were off somewhere. Quinn sighed in relief. He wanted some privacy with Davi when he showed her the rings he had picked out for them.

The manager stepped out and greeted him by name, "Mr. Thomas. It's so nice to see you again." He held out his hand to Quinn and shook it. "Ms. Stuart. It is a pleasure to meet you."

"Thank you," Davi replied.

The manager led them to a desk. "Please sit here. I'll bring you out your selection."

Quinn held out a chair for Davi and then sat down. "I had some free time, and I popped in here. I found the ring that I want to wear. I hope you like its mate."

"Why wouldn't I like it?"

"You had a definite idea of what you wanted your engagement ring to be. I didn't know if you had a set idea for your wedding band."

Davi's engagement ring was unusual. The diamonds were inlaid in platinum, giving it a smooth surface. She wanted a ring she could wear without worrying she'd catch it on something when she worked on the farm.

The manager returned with a tray of rings.

"This is the wedding band that Mr. Thomas has chosen for himself," he said as he offered the ring to Quinn to try on.

"What do you think, Davi?" he asked her as he showed her his hand.

The ring was made of platinum, just like Davi's. It was a plain band that fit his large hand perfectly.

"I don't want anything fancy. I'm not that kind of guy. I only want the ring, your ring."

The manager offered the mate to Davi, saying, "This would be your ring, if you like it."

She pulled off her engagement ring and slid the band on. It was a smaller and narrower version of Quinn's. She put her engagement ring back on to look at the two together.

"It's perfect." Davi looked at Quinn and smiled.

"We'll take them," Quinn said.

"Would you like them engraved? Normally, couples have their wedding date engraved with their initials, or you can have whatever you would like. Here's a pad of paper and pen if you want to try some things out."

"I'd like Davi's name on my ring with no date."

"No date?" Davi asked.

"I'm wearing your ring, Davi. That's all I want."

Davi touched Quinn's face. "I love you."

Davi wrote their names out on a piece of paper and then handed it to the manager, saying, "I'll have Quinn's name on mine."

"Wonderful. We can have them engraved now if you care to wait. It should only take twenty minutes at most."

"That would be great. Then we can take the rings with us. One less thing to think about," agreed Davi. "We'll look for the girls. They should be here somewhere."

Davi and Quinn found the girls looking at the women's jewelry with the assistance of a sales clerk.

"See anything you like?" Quinn asked as he walked up behind them.

The sales clerk blushed as she recognized Quinn.

"Everything is so beautiful," Cat gushed.

"And expensive," added Tigger.

Quinn whispered to Davi, "Do they have anything to wear with their dresses for the wedding?"

Davi's face paled. "No, but they'll need something, but not from here, Quinn. It's too expensive," she whispered back.

Quinn ignored Davi's protests. "These beautiful women need something for a special event. I don't know what they are wearing, but I'm sure they have a good idea as to what they need. What do you say, ladies, earrings and a necklace for you and Maggie?"

"Are you serious?"

"Yes. Find something to wear for the wedding. Your mom will help you. I'll go check on the rings."

"Nothing too expensive, girls," Davi warned them.

"Perhaps you can tell me what they are wearing and then we'll know what to look for," offered the sales clerk.

"I think I'll go get the dresses. It will be easier to find something that way."

"Good idea," agreed the sales clerk.

Davi went out to the limo. She found Jake talking on his cell phone.

"Hold on. Davi's right here, I'll ask her." Jake smiled at Davi. "Sue asked if you wanted to come over for a late lunch when we're finished here. She'd like to meet Quinn's tormentors in person."

"That would be great, Jake. We're waiting on the rings to be engraved, and Quinn is buying the girls something. We shouldn't be too long."

"We're coming, Sue. I think we'll be there in about an hour. See you then." Jake closed his phone. "Do you need something?"

"I need the garment bag for the dresses. We need to make sure the jewelry suits the dresses."

Jake opened the door and handed him the bag. Davi returned to the saleswoman. She peeked inside at the three dresses and smiled.

"I think I have just the thing for you."

The sales woman led them to a counter with a new designer's jewelry. She pulled out a few pieces and held them against the material of the three dresses. They matched perfectly.

"Try them on," she urged the girls. "See how you like them."

The girls were quiet as they took in their image in the mirror. "Wow."

"They are beautiful," remarked Davi.

Quinn appeared. "Let's have a look. Very nice," he commented. "Do you want these?"

"Yes, but . . ."

"Will Maggie wear the same, or does she need something different? She's the one who has put the wedding together. I want to make sure she has the right jewelry."

"She'll love this, Quinn."

"Are you trying to buy her affection, Quinn?" Cat teased.

"Me? No. I know how much she's done for your mother and me. Will she like the same jewelry as yours or do you think she needs something different? She's your friend, Davi. You know what she'd wear."

"Quinn, these pieces are exquisite. She'll love them. I know she will. Thank you."

"We'll take them. Here's my card." He handed the sales clerk his credit card and smiled.

Davi whispered in his ear. "You don't know how much they cost! There's no price tag on them! Aren't you even going to ask?"

"There's no limit when it comes to our wedding day, woman. Those pieces are classic. They'll wear them more than just once. Indulge me. Let me do this."

Davi sighed. There was no arguing with him. His eyes melted any resistance she had.

The girls wrapped their arms around Quinn and kissed him on the cheek. "Thank you, Quinn. You're the best!"

"Best what?" He smiled at them.

"Best best friend."

Cat explained, "We've been talking about this with Rich. You're too young to be our stepdad, we're almost the same age, and we don't think you really want to be that to us either. You'll be Mom's husband, but you'll be our best best friend with family benefits. How does that sound?"

Quinn thought about it. "I like it."

"I like it too." Davi smiled. Sometimes her family surprised her.

The sales clerk returned with the jewelry boxed and gift wrapped and Quinn's credit card. Quinn signed the receipt and thanked her.

"We're having lunch at Jake's. Sue invited us," Davi informed them.

Quinn put his arm around Davi. "Let's go. I need a drink."

The drive to Jake's was quiet. The girls enjoyed watching the scenery from their windows. Davi leaned against Quinn and held his hand. Quinn's thoughts were on the baby. He hoped they would have a boy. He'd love a daughter, but he thought a son would be easier. He knew a daughter would have him wrapped around her tiny finger the moment she took her first breath. *Oh, who am I kidding? My son will do the same. Any child of Davi's will have my heart completely. They already do.*

The limo stopped again. The girls opened the door before Jake got to it. "We'll give you some privacy," they chimed as they closed the door.

"They've got your number, Quinn."

"Do you think they'd mind if I kept you for a bit longer?"

He pulled her onto his lap. His lips covered hers. His hands massaged her breasts. Davi could feel his arousal.

"Easy, stud," she said as she pulled away. "You'll have to put those thoughts on hold."

Quinn groaned, "I want you."

"You were awfully quiet on the ride here. Is that what you were thinking about? Sex?"

"I was thinking I'd like to have a son. He wouldn't have me wrapped around his finger like a daughter would."

"Is that what you think?"

"I did for a brief moment. Then I realized that any child of ours would have me wrapped around his or her finger the moment they take their first breath. Your girls already do."

"Not Rich?"

"He's low maintenance. I could buy him beer and he'd be happy."

Davi laughed. "They love you too, you know. And it's not because of what you bought for them."

"I know. They are like their mother in every good way." Quinn breathed in Davi's scent. "I still want you."

"I promise that you can have me, but it has to be later. We're not doing anything with an audience waiting outside the door." Davi slid off Quinn's lap and ran her hands through her hair. "I'll go in with Jake and the girls. You can stay here until you simmer down. What will it take? Half an hour?"

Quinn groaned. "Not funny. I'm coming. I've already simmered down."

Davi opened the door. "You really shouldn't lock me in there with him, you know. Next time I may not be able to escape."

"You're damn right," Quinn swore as he slammed the limo door.

Jake put his arm around his friend. "You're getting it bad today, Quinn. I think there's scotch waiting for you with your name on it. Come on, let's go find it."

Chapter 30

♥

They ended up staying for lunch and supper. Sue had enough food to feed an army. Afterward, Jake drove the foursome back to the hotel. The girls slept during the ride back.

"This has been nice being together like this."

"Yes, it has," Quinn agreed as he held Davi in his arms.

When they arrived back at the hotel suite, Davi's girls were reenergized. Davi took her girls to their room. Quinn could hear their laughter between loud whispers. He smiled to himself as he thought about living with Davi's daughters. Would he ever get to relax? Would there ever be quiet?

"We're not tired. Do you mind if we watch a movie?" the girls asked when they returned to the living room.

Without thinking, Quinn said, "Go ahead. Watch whatever you want."

Davi looked at Quinn quickly. He made it too easy for them. Quinn sat on the sofa, nursing his scotch. He patted the space beside him, motioning to Davi to sit beside him. Davi snuggled into Quinn's shoulder.

"Have you found anything?"

Cat and Tigger had their backs to Davi and Quinn as they raced through the movie menu.

"Got it," they announced together.

They turned around and smiled at Quinn. He knew that smile. It was Davi's wicked smile.

"No," he said, realizing what they had chosen.

"You said whatever we wanted, and we want this." Tigger sat down at her mom's feet as Cat sat down beside Quinn. "You're not embarrassed, are you, Quinn?"

Davi looked at the screen. The girls had selected one of Quinn's earliest movies, *Hometown Hero*. She laughed. "I haven't seen this in ages. I didn't think they still showed it. Good choice, girls."

"You don't expect me to sit through this, do you?" Quinn grumbled.

Davi's voice was calm and soothing. "Please. It will be fun. You can talk through it and tell us about it, if it makes it any better."

"Why is your fun always at my expense?"

"Because you can handle it, and you'll do anything for Mom," Tigger offered.

"You've got three against one here, so deal with it," Cat said as she turned up the volume.

Quinn pulled Davi in close to him. "Will it always be like this?"

"Yes. Are you having second thoughts?"

"No. I think I'll just throw out my TV the next time they decide to visit."

"What about at the farm?"

"Can I throw them out?"

"Shh! If it's not about the movie, you can't talk. And you're not throwing us out. You'd miss us."

Quinn actually enjoyed watching the movie with Davi and her daughters. It was a sports movie with a romance that appealed to both men and women. *Hometown Hero* was Quinn's first blockbuster movie. Quinn's acting made the movie a success. He played the role of a young football player trying to make it in pro sports while finding love along the way. Quinn changed his physical appearance for his role. He trained endlessly to build up his body mass to look like a football player. When the movie was over, he and everyone else liked his new look. Quinn decided to keep it.

"This was the movie that got me started. I look so young in it."

"You are young," Davi teased.

Tigger looked up at Quinn. "Did you know how to play football?"

"Not one clue, but I learned how to play it quickly. It's not so hard once you have someone show you how. I was never into sports, but my coach told me that I was a natural."

"Obviously, he was right," Cat remarked.

"What makes you say that?"

"Because you look like you're a natural. You look like you stepped off the field and into that movie. Didn't anyone ever tell you that?"

"No. It was called good acting."

"Idiots," Cat mumbled.

Davi smiled as she listened to Cat complimenting Quinn. She hoped Quinn realized that Cat wasn't one to give out compliments without merit. She really did notice what he was doing on the screen.

Tigger covered her face when the love scenes came up. She was always embarrassed to watch love scenes with other people in the room. This time, it was especially hard with Quinn and Davi in the room.

"Tigs, open your eyes. Watch this!" Cat teased her. "Look, they're getting naked!"

"No!"

Quinn laughed. "She does this every time?"

Davi nodded yes.

"I'm with you, Tigger. I close my eyes too. It's much better doing it with your mom than with anyone on-screen."

"Eww, too much information there, Quinn," Cat said as she jabbed him in the ribs.

Davi poked him on the other side.

"Ow! No attacking the movie star."

"You didn't say that, did you?" Davi asked in disbelief.

"What?"

"You called yourself a movie star."

"Well, I am. Look, you wanted to watch this movie and I agreed. We're talking about my movie, and I'm telling you bits of information about the making of it. So in this case, I can call myself the movie star."

"He's right, Mom. Right now, he is the movie star. When the movie's over, he's back to being the annoying fiancé."

"Annoying?"

"Yes, annoying. You're the incredibly gorgeous hunk with the smile, the hair, the body, and the bedroom eyes that are only for our mother. That's what we call annoying."

"I like that. How much does it annoy you?"

"Not enough that we're moving out when you get married."

"Are we going to watch this movie?" Davi asked.

The group went silent until the next scene.

"Did you play a real game? How long did it take to film this?"

"We filmed a lot of different scenes at once making full use of the stadium. I think we filmed four or five scenes at the stadium over one day. If you look closely, you can see that the crowd is the same. They didn't bother to move anyone around. They weren't quite on the ball when they were shooting some of the close-ups. Did you notice one of the players wearing a watch in the huddle? And one of them is wearing different socks than the other players."

"What about you? Did you do anything different?"

"No. I never thought about it. I waited until my third or fourth movie before I started trying things, but the crew was better at making sure everything was exactly the same every take. Sarah was onto me too. She'd go over my wardrobe every time, making sure buttons were buttoned, socks were on and the right color. She'd even make sure I was wearing underwear."

"Underwear?"

"Don't even go there," Davi warned her daughters. "Behave," she said to Quinn.

The girls laughed at Davi's embarrassment while Quinn kissed the top of Davi's head. They turned their attention back to the movie. No one said another word during the movie.

Davi looked over at Cat. Her head rested against Quinn's shoulder as she slept. Tigger was asleep too.

"We've lost them," Davi announced. "The kiddies have crashed."

"So what do we do now? I'm being held captive here."

She shook Tigger's shoulder gently. "Tigs, it's time for bed. You fell asleep, love."

Slowly, Tigger got up and made her way to the bedroom. "Good night, Mom. Good night, Quinn."

Cat stirred as she heard Tigger. "Missed the ending, huh? Don't tell me, you got the girl." She got up off the sofa and hugged Davi. "Good night, Mom. We had a great day." She leaned down and kissed Quinn on his forehead. "You've been super. Thanks for a great day." She walked off to their bedroom.

Davi sat down and snuggled into Quinn's chest. "They adore you. You've won them over."

"So all I have to do is take them shopping and they're mine?"

"No. The shopping had nothing to do with it. You showed them the real you today."

"I told you, Davi, there's no Hollywood once I leave the set."

"I know that and now the girls do. They've seen the real deal today, and they liked what they saw."

"Did the shopping make any impact?"

"Probably. What woman doesn't like to shop at Tiffany's with someone else paying the bill?" Davi got up from the sofa. "I'm going to check on them. I'll see you in the bedroom?"

Quinn got the hint. "I'll be waiting for you."

Davi checked on her daughters. Both were lying in their beds, almost asleep. Davi kissed them softly on their foreheads.

"I can't remember when I last tucked you in." She chuckled.

"That's okay, Mom, we won't tell anyone," yawned Cat.

"I had a great time today. I hope you did too."

"Mom, you know we did," Tigger said sleepily.

"Mom?"

"Yes, Cat?"

"You did all right."

"Quinn. He's okay, Mom. You did all right. You can keep him," Tigger added.

"Thanks. He'll be happy to hear that."

"Does Quinn have any single male friends our age? They don't have to be movie stars. See what he can do in that department," Cat said as she drifted into sleep.

"I'll get right on it."

Davi closed their door as she left them.

Quinn scanned through a script while he waited for Davi as she prepared for bed. He tossed the script to the floor when she got into bed beside him.

"So are they all tucked in and fast asleep?"

Davi cuddled into Quinn's chest. "Yes, they are. They told me that I did all right with you and that I can keep you. You're okay."

"Just okay?"

"Okay is good. They also wanted to know if you had any single male friends their age. They don't have to be movie stars. I told them I'd get right on it."

Quinn laughed before he answered, "Do I have single male friends? Yes, I have them, but no one I would want to get involved with your girls. Davi, do you know how weird it would be for one of my friends to date one of your daughters? What if they became serious? No, I couldn't let that happen."

"It would be weird, wouldn't it?"

"Let's not even go there." Quinn pulled Davi onto him. "I know somewhere I would like to go though."

"Where's that?"

"Just follow my lead."

Chapter 31

♥

Davi awoke to the smell of brewing coffee. Quinn was gone. Davi knew he'd be off at the gym. He had to fit in a workout whenever he could. Davi stretched and groaned quietly. She wondered what they would do today with the girls before it was time to head home. Davi got out of bed and put on her bathrobe. She padded out to the kitchen. The suite was quiet. The girls weren't up yet. Davi poured herself a cup of coffee and then headed back to the bedroom, leaving her door open so that the girls would know she was up.

She headed for the bathroom and had a shower. It felt good to have cold water flow over her. She loved the extra boost it gave her in the morning. By the time Davi made it back to the bedroom, Cat and Tigger were in her bed, waiting for her.

"Good morning."

"Where's Quinn?" Cat asked. "He's not going to walk in naked, is he?"

"I hope not." Davi smiled. "He's working out in the hotel's gym. Did you have a good sleep?"

"Yes," they said together.

Tigger pulled back the covers so that Davi could get in the middle with them.

"This bed is huge, Mom. You could have a party in here."

Davi laughed. "Check out the shower then if you want to see something."

Both Cat and Tigger jumped out of the bed and ran for the bathroom. Davi smiled when she heard them shriek. She heard the shower door open and close, and then she heard the stereo blare when they turned it on. The girls returned to the bed laughing.

"Does he really need a shower that big?"

"Ask him. I think it comes with the suite."

"Did he ever party in it?"

"Ask him. He'll let you know."

"Let you know what?"

Quinn stood in the doorway, wearing only track pants and sneakers. A towel hung around his neck. The girls stopped as they stared at his physique—his well-formed pectorals, his rippled abs, and his strong arms. His skin glistened from sweat.

"It's huge," Tigger said.

"Really huge," Cat added.

"Unbelievably huge," Davi said lustily.

"What's huge?" Quinn reddened, feeling three sets of female eyes on him.

"Your shower is huge. Do you ever party in it?" Cat explained.

"Oh." Quinn laughed, relieved. "Your mom asked me the same thing. What do you consider a party?"

"You and about six luscious babes."

"Oh, that's easy. No, I haven't had six luscious babes in the shower with me."

"But you have had some luscious babes in the shower with you?" Cat pressed.

Quinn's eyes sparkled at Davi. "I've had only one luscious babe in that shower, and she's all I ever needed. Now if you'll excuse me, I'm off to have a shower by myself. I'll see you later."

Quinn walked off to the bathroom and closed the door behind him.

"He really loves you, Mom. Do you see the way his eyes sparkle at you? No one else gets that. No one."

Tigger sighed. "I hope that when someone falls for me, I'll see the same sparkle in his eyes. That sparkle will tell me everything."

"You will get that sparkle. I promise you that." Davi hugged both of her girls. "Now I think you better get out of here so Quinn can get dressed. Do you want to do anything today?"

"No. Just hang out. Whatever you and Quinn want to do is fine with us."

The girls left Davi and closed the door behind them. Davi got out of bed and went to check on Quinn in the bathroom. He was still in the shower. Davi stripped off her robe and then opened the door and joined him under the hot water.

"I wasn't sure you'd be joining me."

"How could I resist those eyes?"

"My secret weapon?" Quinn smiled.

"They're not a secret. The girls noticed them. They hope their dream man has the same sparkle for them."

"Am I your dream man?"

"No. You're my man. You're real, not a dream."

Davi wrapped her arms around Quinn's waist. Quinn held her tight and kissed her.

"Are you here for a party?"

"Not today. Continue with your shower."

"I'm all done, and if we're not going to have a party, I am going to get out now. I'm starving."

Quinn turned off the water and got out of the shower. Davi followed him.

"Did you have a good workout?" she asked as she dried herself.

"Yes. It felt good this morning. I think I ate and drank too much yesterday. I have to watch it."

"Yes, you'd better. You can't disappoint all of those lusting fans."

"It's not for the fans, woman, it's for you. You're the only one that matters."

"I hope you realize that although your looks are a tremendous benefit, I'm not marrying you for your looks."

"You aren't?" Quinn's eyes sparkled.

"No, it's because of what you have in here"—Davi touched over Quinn's heart and then his head—"and here. They are what matter most to me."

"Not because I'm a movie star?" he teased.

"Please," Davi groaned.

"What about my lovemaking skills? Are you marrying me for them?"

"I wouldn't marry you if it were just for sex. I would have kept you on as my boy toy." Davi playfully grabbed Quinn's package.

"You want me," he murmured lustfully as he pulled her against him.

"Yes, but it will have to wait for another time, stud. The girls are waiting for us."

"Five minutes?"

"No. Not today."

"You're leaving me today," he murmured as he held her tighter.

"You'll manage, though. You're getting better."

Davi pulled away from Quinn and walked into the bedroom. She got dressed quickly as Quinn stood in the doorway and watched her.

"One more week, and then we'll be together."

"That is the only thing that is keeping me sane, knowing that we won't have to be saying good-bye all the time. You'll be with me."

"Or you'll be with me. Now get dressed."

Davi and the girls were having coffee when Quinn walked out of the bedroom.

"Do you girls really want to meet some of my single male friends?"

"You have some?"

"Of course I do. Can you play flag football?"

"Yes. Why?"

"I've been invited to a pickup game of flag football. It's coed, so you girls can play." Quinn smiled at Davi. "You're welcome to play too, Davi. It's noncontact. It's in an hour. We'll play a game, then go out to a bar and have a beer and some lunch. What do you say? Are you up for it?"

"Who's going to be there?"

"It's a surprise. We never know who is playing until everyone shows up. The games are always last minute. It keeps the paparazzi away, most of the time anyway. Should I tell them we're coming?"

"Yes!"

Davi suggested that Quinn take the girls into the bedroom and help find them something to wear while she made a quick snack. The girls came back with their game clothes in their arms. They were identical.

"Going for the twin look again, I see," Davi said with amusement.

"Of course. It might help to confuse the opposition. One of us is better at running, and the other is better at blocking. They'll not be able to tell us apart."

"Quinn? What are you wearing?"

"Why? Does it matter?"

"No, but if I were a betting person, I would say you had the same outfit. Gray was your only color for quite a while."

"You are smart. I knew there was a reason I was marrying you." Quinn gave Davi a kiss on the top of her head before he handed the plates to the girls.

"Won't you tell us who is going to be there?" the girls pleaded.

"No. I can't even say for sure. The person who texted me is someone you definitely know, and he's single. At least he was the last time I heard."

The foursome managed to squeeze into Quinn's black Beetle. It was a nice warm October day, so Quinn drove with the top down. The stereo blared eighties music, much to the delight of the girls. Quinn drove to an old section of the city where ancient tall trees lined the streets of old brownstone homes.

"Isn't this Jake's neighborhood?"

"The park's across the road." Quinn motioned with his head. "It's a convenient spot, and I have my own security across the street if I ever need it."

"Have you ever needed it?" Cat asked.

"Not yet, but I'm sure the day is coming when I will. Maybe today will be our lucky day."

"You don't mean that, do you?" Davi asked, concerned for her daughters' safety.

"Relax. I won't let anything happen. We're here to have fun."

Quinn got out of the car and let the girls out. Davi waited for Quinn to open her door.

Quinn pulled her in for a hug as she stood up. "Relax, woman. It's going to be fun, and your girls will be talking about this for days. Maybe you will too." Quinn kissed her softly. "I love you."

"Just keep my girls safe. I don't want any broken bones before the wedding. That means you too."

Jake and Sue came out their front door and walked down their stairs toward Quinn and Davi. Quinn was busy putting up the roof of the car. He couldn't risk anyone trying to steal anything from the car.

"Looks like the girls came to play," Jake remarked as he hugged Davi. "What about Mom?"

"I'm undecided. I want to wait and see who the competition is."

"Smart girl." Sue nodded knowingly. "Sometimes it's more fun to watch them play. Come on, let's head over. Looks like the girls are on their way."

"Quinn promised they'd meet some single males, but he wouldn't say who."

"When they see who's here, you'll hear them scream from here." Sue put her arm around Davi and led her to the park.

Davi could see a group gathering, but she couldn't make out anyone. Her girls slowed down as they neared the group. Quinn and Jake caught up to Davi and Sue.

"Do you think they've recognized anyone?"

"I can't tell. I don't recognize anyone," Davi admitted.

"You will, love."

Quinn took Davi's hand. Cat and Tigger ran to Quinn and Davi. They had the biggest smiles Davi had ever seen.

"Who is it?" Davi asked, trying not to sound too excited.

"They're all here, Mom. All of them."

Davi had no idea who the mystery men were. She looked to Quinn for help. Quinn's blue eyes were sparkling at her, his Cheshire cat smile working overtime.

"They're the guys from the movie, *Coyote.* We get together whenever we can."

Davi remembered them. They were all good-looking men, even Quinn gorgeous. "You're friends with the whole cast?"

"Buddies is more like it. Come on, I'll introduce you."

"And they're all single?"

"I don't know for sure, but at least they're the girls' age and they're good guys."

"I thought you said you didn't have any single male friends for the girls to meet."

"It was dating, but these guys are okay, honest."

Quinn made the introductions. Of course, the girls already knew the men's names, but Davi didn't. There were a couple of other women. Davi noticed them staring at Quinn. Then she noticed a resemblance between the girls and one of the men. He'd brought his sisters. *Way to go on scoring brother points.*

The group split into teams. Davi, Sue, Cat, and Tigger stayed with Jake and Quinn. A few of the men joined them. Once the teams were even, the game began. Quinn won the coin toss, giving his team possession of the ball. He played the quarterback position, and Davi handed him the ball. Jake blocked and the rest chose their positions.

In the first play, Quinn threw the ball to Cat, and she ran with it. She scored a touchdown, much to everyone's amazement. Quinn picked her up and hugged her while he congratulated her on her scoring. The other team got the ball, and it was their turn to try to score. Quinn and Jake were both fast to pull the flags out of the opposition's belts. Tigger was great at blocking too. Quinn was amazed at her tenacity. The game was played for an hour, after which Quinn's team won by one touchdown. It was a close game and everyone played well.

"You're joining us at O'Malley's for lunch?" one of the hunks asked Quinn.

"Of course."

The group walked to the bar from the park. It was only a block away, and parking was difficult there. Tigger and Cat were with the group ahead of Davi, Quinn, Jake, and Sue. Davi could hear them laughing as they walked.

"You've made their day, Quinn. You were right. They'll be talking about this for days."

"Sue talks about it for the whole week then finds someone else to fantasize about," Jake teased. "It used to be Quinn, but that stopped once he met you, Davi."

Sue slapped at Jake. "I never talked about Quinn that way. You know I didn't."

"You were always trying to hook him up with someone, fantasizing about which star he should date. That's the truth, Sue."

"Who did you think he should be with?" Davi asked, intrigued.

"Oh, I don't know. No one seemed like his type or mine. I pictured being friends with these stars, and it never worked out. I knew his ladylove had to be special. That's why we were so happy when he brought you to meet us. No one could take your place, Davi."

Quinn pulled Davi in close. "I told you that you've replaced me. You're number one."

The gang settled in the bar, taking up most of the tables at one end. Cat and Tigger were in the middle of it all, enjoying themselves.

One of the young hunks came over and spoke to Quinn. "The girls say you're going to be their stepfather. Is that true?"

"Yes, but I'm not going to be their stepdad. I'm going to be their best best friend."

"Their mother lets you take them out?" The hunk looked at Davi, obviously unaware of who she was. "You're taking a big risk, aren't you? Socializing with women while your fiancée is stuck at home? What if the paparazzi publicize this?"

"Chas, before you make a complete idiot of yourself, let me introduce you to Davi Stuart, my fiancée and the girls' mother. Davi, this is my idiot friend, Chas Elliot. We worked together on *Coyote.*"

"Hey, Chas, it's nice to meet you." Davi held out her hand to him.

"Oh, god, I'm so sorry. I knew Quinn was marrying an older woman, but you don't look like an older woman. I thought maybe you were the girls' older sister or something."

"Thanks, I appreciate that."

"You could have told me, Quinn."

"No, I like watching you make an idiot of yourself."

Chas ignored the comment. "So if one of us wants to take one of the girls out, do we have to ask your permission, Quinn?"

Davi answered for him, "You'd have to ask them. They're adults and can speak for themselves, but they live in Canada. You may have to come up our way."

"And where is that exactly?"

"Canada?" Quinn asked.

"No, asshole. Where do they live in Canada?"

"About forty minutes from the Toronto airport."

"You'll be living there, Quinn? You're actually leaving us then? No more last-minute football games?"

"It all depends on what my schedule is. If I'm here, I'll play."

Chas was called back to the group.

He held out his hand to Davi one more time. "Nice meeting you, Davi. Keep an eye on this one." He turned to Quinn. "Lucky bastard, only you would wind up with a gorgeous wife and two beautiful daughters just like that. I can't wait until you're out of the market and give the rest of us a chance."

"You wish. My being out of the market isn't going to help you!"

The two men shook hands, and then Chas walked away.

"He's a good guy. He's got a big heart."

"What about my daughters?"

"They'll be fine. Don't worry. I doubt if they'll ever see these guys again or at least not for a long time. They'll be too busy to think about the girls. They're in a musical here in town."

"So they'll be in New York."

"Yes."

"Just like you," Davi pointed out. "So that means nothing."

Quinn laughed. "Not everyone is like me. Some men don't like long-distance relationships."

"Right, so they marry the woman as soon as they can."

"So you're marrying your daughters off now before they even date? I thought you didn't want to rush things."

"I'm a storyteller, Quinn. I know how this story can go. I'm just thinking of the possibilities."

Chapter 32

♥

It was Friday morning, the day before the wedding. Davi woke up at her usual time. She lay in bed, staring at the ceiling as she ran through her day's itinerary in her head. *Go for a walk, have breakfast, shower, then head to the spa for me time, return from spa and get ready for wedding rehearsal, rehearsal dinner, then bed.* It seemed like a straightforward day.

Davi smiled as she remembered her conversation with Quinn the previous day. He was begging to join her at the spa. He wanted a massage and a manicure and pedicure too. He even volunteered to have his toenails painted red if Davi would let him come. He was desperate to spend time with her.

"This is my time for me, Quinn. There will be no time for me on Saturday, and I don't think I'll have me time for a long time after that. Let me have my time, please."

Quinn backed down, but Davi could hear the disappointment in his voice. He would stick to the plan and fly out with the gang early Friday afternoon. She hoped that Luke and Jake would be able to keep him busy until then.

Davi looked out her bedroom window. She had a clear view of the road in front of the farm. There were cars and vans parked along the side of the road. She could see people with cameras lined up along the fence line, watching her house. She could also see police cars and security guards. *Wonderful.* She could cross taking a walk off her list. Davi had a quick shower and then headed downstairs for breakfast.

The telephone rang. Davi looked at the call display. The caller ID was blocked.

"Hello?"

"Hello, Davina. I've missed you. How are you?" The voice was soft and low.

Davi didn't recognize the caller. "I'm fine. How are you?"

"Much better now that I can hear your voice. Have you thought of me?"

"I'm sorry but I don't recognize your voice. You have me at a disadvantage."

"It's Guy Tremblant. You remember me, don't you?"

Davi's stomach churned. "Yes, I remember you, Guy."

"I thought so. Did my present arrive for you? I'm calling to make sure it arrived safely."

"To be honest, Guy, I don't know. So many packages have arrived in the last couple of days that I haven't been able to keep up with them. Nothing has been opened. Quinn and I will open them after the wedding."

"It's not for the two of you. It's for you, Davina. I'd like you to open it before the wedding."

"May I ask what it is?" Davi asked as she headed to the dining room, where the unopened gifts were stored.

"No. Open it when you're alone. It's for your eyes only. I suggest you open it today, Davina. I really do." His voice was too smooth, too confident.

"You're not going to tell me what it is, are you?" she said as she started searching through the piles.

"What good is a surprise if I tell you what it is? No. You'll have to find out for yourself."

Davi wanted to hang up. Guy made her feel very uneasy. "Guy, I have to go. Thank you for calling, and thank you for the gift."

"Open the gift, Davina. That's all I ask."

"I will. I have to go. Thank you." She hung up the phone. Her hands were clammy, and her body had broken out into a sweat. "What the hell is he up to?"

She went through every package, looking for something with Guy's name on it. Finally, in the last pile, Davi found a box with Guy Tremblant's name and return address on it. Davi ripped open the box. Inside were a card and a small jewelry box. Davi opened the card. It read: "Can he give you this? There's more than you ever dreamed of waiting for you

when you join me." Davi dropped the card and opened the jewelry box.
Inside was an airline ticket to Paris, leaving tonight. She gasped as she
looked under the ticket. There was a matching set of ruby and diamond
earrings and necklace. They were exquisite. She closed the box, picked
the card up from the floor, and put them back in the shipping box. Davi
walked back into the kitchen and sat down at the table. She picked up
her phone and dialed.

"Hello?"

"Jake, it's Davi. Can we talk?"

"Go ahead. What is it?"

"It's Guy Tremblant. He sent me a very inappropriate wedding gift,
and I need to return it without Quinn knowing about it. Will you look
after it for me?"

"Of course."

"I need to make sure he comes nowhere near the wedding. I have a
feeling he's going to try something."

"Definitely."

"Quinn's with you, isn't he?"

"Definitely."

"Damn it." Davi took a deep breath. "I'm going to be gone most of
the day. I don't know when you're arriving. If I put the package under
my bed, will you have the chance to get it? I don't want anyone finding it,
Jake. If Quinn finds out about it, I'm afraid of what he might do."

"No. Take it with you."

"To the spa?"

"Yes, your security guard will look after you. Don't worry."

Davi could hear Jake say something to Quinn, something about Davi
wanting to know if she could use the pool at the spa. She didn't know if
the security guard would let her go for a swim.

"Nice lie," she teased Jake. "You're good at that."

"All part of the job, Davi. I'll call you later. Keep your phone on."

"I will. Thanks. Bye."

Talking to Jake made her feel better. Even though he couldn't say much
with Quinn being there, she knew that he'd look after things. He was her
protector and Quinn's. He'd make everything right. He just had to.

Davi left her breakfast untouched. She cursed Guy Tremblant for
pulling such a stunt. She'd spent five minutes with the man. Had he
become obsessed with her? *Get a life, Guy*, she thought as she got herself
ready to head out to the spa.

There was a knock at the door. Davi jumped in surprise. It was a
security guard at the door.

"Ms. Stuart? I'm Bryan. I'll be your driver today."

"Hi, Bryan. Thanks so much for doing this. I feel embarrassed needing a security guard to go get my nails done."

"Don't feel embarrassed. It's all part of my job. Do you have a package for me?"

"Yes, it's right here." *Wow, Jake was fast,* Davi thought to herself as she handed him the package.

Bryan opened the door for Davi and escorted her to the waiting limo. He opened the back door for her. Davi still felt self-conscious every time she got into one.

The limo headed down the laneway. At the fence line, Davi could see the security guards making the crowd move their vehicles. A police officer waved the limo into traffic.

Davi looked out her window. It was a bright sunny day. The forecast for the Thanksgiving weekend was good. She hoped it wouldn't rain tomorrow, even though Maggie told her rain brought good luck. Davi loved this time of year. The crops were almost ready for harvest; the soybean plants were turning brown, and the corn stalks were dying. She'd miss being home for the harvest. She would be spending the next week or two with Quinn in New York.

The limo stopped. They had arrived at the spa.

"I was told you have to spend the day here with me. Are you coming in, or do you wait out here in the car? I'm new to this. I don't know what the protocol is."

"Oh, I come in with you. There's probably a place where I can sit and wait for you. I'll have to keep my eye on the entrance to make sure no one tries to sneak in and take a picture of you or try anything else."

Davi shuddered as she thought of what the anything else could be—Guy Tremblant. Davi led the way into the spa. It was part of an old country inn Davi and her sisters frequented a few times a year to rejuvenate and reconnect. Davi loved its peacefulness.

The receptionist greeted her, "Ms. Stuart, welcome!"

"Hi, I have a favor to ask. I have a security guard with me today. Is there a place where he can stay and wait for me? I'd really appreciate it if you could look after him too." Davi looked at Bryan. "Would you like some coffee, something to eat?"

"We've done this kind of thing before," the receptionist replied cheerfully. "We'll be happy to look after your guard for you. Now if you'd both like to come with me, I can show you where Ms. Stuart will be and the various accesses we have to the building. There are only two so that should make it easy for you. There's a lounge right there." She pointed off to the side. "You can wait there and enjoy any of our refreshments."

Davi and Bryan followed the receptionist through to the spa. Bryan had a look around. He checked the fire door. No one would be coming through it. The spa passed his inspection. He left Davi and made his way back to the lounge.

"So tomorrow is your wedding day! I'm so excited for you. What a great way to get energized for the wedding. Having a spa day all to yourself."

Davi admired the receptionist's energy. Davi would need that energy for tomorrow, but for now, she wanted to relax and enjoy whatever peace and quiet she could get. A one-hour massage was followed by a manicure and pedicure. Davi thoroughly enjoyed her few hours of pampering. There was no rush for her to change and go home. She wanted to stay and enjoy another hour or two in solitude. She hoped Bryan had been looked after.

Davi called an assistant over. "I have someone waiting for me down in the lounge. I was wondering if anyone has looked after him. He's been down there a long time."

"He's been looked after. There's nothing to be worried about."

"Thank you."

"I've been asked to bring you to the dining room for lunch whenever you are ready. You don't have to change. You're fine in your robe."

"The dining room? Do you know who arranged this?"

"I can't say, Ms. Stuart. I was only told to escort you to the dining room when you were ready."

Thoughts of Guy flashed through Davi's mind. *Could it be him? Was he planning something? No, Bryan would have noticed. No one would be allowed near me without him knowing.* Davi closed her eyes and pushed all thoughts of Guy away. *Damn you, Guy.* It was past noon, and she was hungry.

"Let's go then. I have no idea what's going on here, and I'm dying to find out."

Davi followed the assistant to the inn's dining room. It had its original old stone walls and a rustic fireplace that burned in the middle of the room. There was a table set for two at the back of the room by a window overlooking the river. This was Davi's favorite table in the restaurant. *Who would have known this,* she wondered.

Davi sat down. She looked around her but saw no one. She felt a bit awkward in her robe, but her curiosity overruled that feeling. Davi heard someone approaching from behind. She forced herself not to turn around and look. She closed her eyes waiting for the sound of the footsteps to stop. When they did, she opened her eyes.

"Quinn."

"Davina," he murmured.

"I should have known it was you, but you promised you wouldn't come, that I could have my time for me."

"And you did. You had your massage, your manicure, and your pedicure all without my company. I had my nails done while I waited for you. I had my very own secret room just to stay away from you." Quinn flashed his nails for Davi to see. "Now I want some me time with you. We don't have to talk. We can just enjoy our lunch and each other's company."

"Why do you want quiet time with me?"

Their server appeared with drinks and salads for both of them.

"I ordered for us. I hope you don't mind."

"No. It's fine. Go on."

"I realized that I haven't had any quiet time with you. Not since the day I first met you. We have been on the go constantly, I've been busy with my movie, you've been catching planes to fly home, or we've been surrounded by other people. The only quiet time we've had together has been in bed. Not that I mind that, but I need the chance to be with you just like this with no rush, no one else, and no expectation of sex."

"No expectation of sex?" Davi raised an eyebrow in disbelief.

Quinn winked at her. "For once, and maybe for the only time, I have no expectation of having sex with you, woman. I only want your company. I want to have me time with you, just the way you described it the other day—no thinking of the wedding or the next day. We don't even have to talk. Let me do nothing with you."

"I like that idea. I would love to do nothing with you."

Quinn smiled at her. "I'm glad you said yes. I don't know what I'd do if you sent me away."

"No plan B?"

"There's never a plan B with you, woman. It's all or nothing," Quinn said as he took a forkful of his salad.

"I feel the same way. I can't imagine loving you any differently. In less than one month, we've sped through everything—dating, getting married, starting a family, and yet I know that we couldn't have slowed it down if we tried."

"Do you think we'll ever do anything at normal speed, whatever normal is?" He searched her eyes for an answer.

"Everything is going to speed up now, Quinn. You have no idea. The baby will be here before you know it. Your life will be forever changed. You'll be wondering where the time went. Time going by quickly will be the new normal."

"Are you trying to scare me?"

"I'm speaking from experience. If it weren't for our children, we'd never feel time passing us by. We would always feel the same and probably act the same. Maybe even look the same, with some help from plastic surgery. Children remind us every day that we're getting older. It's bittersweet, but I wouldn't have it any other way."

"So our child will make you feel—"

"Incredibly young and old at the same time. I hope I feel young more than I do old." Davi reached for his hand. "You make me feel young too."

"You are young. I can see it in your eyes."

"I've heard that one before." She laughed. "Some stud told me that on a speed date."

"Did you believe him?"

"No, but he was so hot I thought what the hell and let him seduce me."

"How'd that work out for you?"

"Like my ring?" Davi waved her finger in his face.

"You are one wicked woman."

"Only for you, my love."

Quinn leaned over the table and kissed her softly on the lips and then reached for Davi's hands. "Nice nails. French manicure?"

"Oui, monsieur."

"And your toes?"

"As per your request." Davi slipped her foot out of the slipper and wiggled her red toes at him.

"Thank you."

"If that's all I need to keep you happy, I will have red toes every day of my life."

"Promise me."

Davi laughed. "Are you serious? You want me to have red toes every day?"

"Yes, I want you to have red toes until I ask for another shade. Promise me you'll color your toes red for me every day."

How could she resist those blue eyes? "I promise. Forever."

Quinn and Davi finished their lunch late in the afternoon. Quinn had booked the restaurant for the entire afternoon. The couple enjoyed the quiet of their surroundings. It was nice to sit and talk about anything and everything.

"It's getting late, Quinn. We should be going," Davi said reluctantly.

"I know. Jake's going to be wondering what we've been up to."

"Jake?"

"He took over from the security guard who brought you here."

"Oh! I forgot all about him! How could I do that?" Davi was embarrassed by her forgetfulness.

"Don't worry about it. It's all part of the job. He won't mind too much." He winked at her.

"But Jake, he's been waiting all of this time? Quinn! How could you do that to your best friend?"

"He offered to take over. He helped me plan this whole afternoon. He wouldn't have helped me if he didn't want to wait for us for four hours."

Davi stood up. She looked at her robe. "Oh my, I forgot what I was wearing. I can't believe this." Her face reddened from embarrassment.

Quinn stood in front of her and smiled. "No one will care. You're in a spa."

"Correction, I was in a spa four hours ago. Now I'm in a five-star restaurant in a bathrobe."

"Silly woman, what am I going to do with you?"

Quinn put his arm around Davi's waist and led her back to the spa.

Davi raced into the locker room to change. She pulled her gym bag out of the locker. She phoned Jake. It would be her only chance to talk to him alone.

"Hello?"

"Jake, it's Davi. Did you get the package?"

"Nice gift. Are you sure you don't want to keep the gems and go to Paris?"

"No! And I don't want him anywhere near Quinn or me."

"We're on it, Davi. I have everyone on the lookout for him. If he steps anywhere near the church or the farm, we'll get him. But I really don't think he'll show his face."

"Why's that?"

"He's sure you're going to meet him at the airport tonight. He'll be waiting for you. When you don't show up, he'll be back for you tomorrow, that is if he doesn't get the message. But he will get the message. I promise you that."

"You're not going to kill him, are you?" Davi could feel the panic flow through her. "Tell me you won't kill him."

"Lovely lady, we don't kill people. We just make them understand that what they want to do isn't the right choice for them. We'll talk to him. Make him see that what he's doing is a bad idea. That's all." Jake listened to the silence. He could tell Davi was quite shaken. "Davi, listen to me. This man is a whack job. We have to get him out of the picture so he doesn't harm you or Quinn. We'll get him on that plane to Paris tonight. He won't be back to bother you. Don't worry about it. He won't be killed. No one will be doing anything illegal."

Davi breathed a sigh of relief. "Thank you, Jake."

"You are welcome. Now hurry up and get out of that locker room. I can see Quinn, and he's pacing the floor outside. He'll be barging in soon to drag you out of there."

"I'm on my way."

Davi picked up her bag and walked out the door.

"You took your time," Quinn said as he met her in the hallway.

"I was enjoying the last of my me time." Davi smiled at him.

Quinn took Davi's bag from her and walked with her to the lobby.

"I'll settle up my bill now," Davi said to the receptionist.

"Oh, no need, Ms. Stuart. Mr. Thomas has looked after everything."

"What a surprise." Davi smiled at Quinn. "Thank you."

Quinn led her out to where Jake stood waiting for them.

"Hey, lovely lady."

"Hey, Jake, are you allowed to work in Canada too?" she teased. She didn't care. She was glad he was here. Davi hugged him.

Jake hugged her back and whispered in her ear, "Don't worry." Then in a louder voice said, "This isn't work. I just borrowed the car. Get in." He smiled at her as he opened the back door for them.

Jake looked at her through his rearview mirror and asked, "How was your day at the spa?"

"Wonderful." Davi snuggled into Quinn's arms. "I had the most wonderful surprise. I wore my bathrobe in a five-star restaurant and had a delicious lunch. I've never done that before. It was quite the experience."

Jake laughed.

"So if the two of you are here, where is everyone else?"

"They're at the hotel. Quinn wanted to come here to surprise you, and everyone was able to leave early, so we're all here. I'll drop Quinn off at your place and head back to pick up the rest of the crew. It's nice that Maggie invited us all back to her place after the rehearsal. Sarah's told them all about Maggie."

Jake pulled into the laneway. The security guards let him pass. Davi looked out the window. People were lined up along the fence line. They were screaming and waving posters. Camera crews were spread out, ready to catch a shot of the couple.

"They've been here all day," Davi groaned.

"And they'll be here all night right through tomorrow," Jake added. "We've hired extra security to be safe."

Quinn got out of the limo with Davi.

"Go back to the hotel and spend some time with Sue. We'll see you later."

No one was home. It would be a half hour before the girls got back from work, and Rich would be another hour. There were flowers and various wedding gifts left on the kitchen table. Davi walked right by them and headed to the stairway, leading Quinn by the hand.

"Are we going somewhere?"

"Yes. I have some expectations of you. Don't disappoint me."

Davi closed the bedroom door behind them. She turned to Quinn and kissed him. Her hands deftly undid the buttons of his shirt. Davi brought her face to his chest.

She inhaled deeply and moaned, "I love your scent."

Davi's hands moved to Quinn's pants, quickly unfastening his belt, unbuttoning his pants, and unzipping the fly in seconds. Quinn's pants fell to the floor. He was wearing his black boxer briefs.

"Nice," Davi remarked.

"I promised I'd wear underwear for the wedding, so I thought I'd better wear some for tonight's rehearsal." He winked at her.

Quinn stepped out of his pants and underwear and let his shirt fall to the floor.

"It's your turn, love," Quinn whispered to her as he undid her shirt.

His lips kissed her exposed skin where he undid the buttons. Davi gasped at the sensation. Quinn eased Davi's shirt off her shoulders and kissed them. Davi shuddered.

"Is this what you expected?" he asked softly.

"No. It's better."

Quinn undid Davi's jeans, and she kicked them off. She stood in front of him, dressed only in her underwear, one of Quinn's purchases from Victoria's Secret.

"I remember these," he murmured. "I remember that whole day. I wanted you more than I wanted anyone or anything in my entire life. I proposed to you and you said yes."

Quinn scooped Davi up in his arms and carried her to the bed. "You said yes," he repeated as he lay down with her on the bed. His mouth came down hard on hers. His tongue forced her lips open, and he took her mouth. It was Quinn's turn to devour Davi. Her arms wrapped around his neck and pulled him in tighter. His hands were all over her body, exploring every part of her. Davi moaned with delight.

Quinn released Davi from the kiss. "You drive me crazy, woman. I want all of you."

He had to have her now. Quinn pushed aside Davi's panties and was inside her instantly. She was hot and wet for him. They both shuddered at the sensation. His powerful thrusts penetrated her deeper than she had ever felt before. She raised her hips and wrapped her legs around his back to take all of him in. Davi threw her head back, letting the pleasure run through her body.

"Harder, Quinn," she commanded.

Quinn moaned as he slammed into Davi with his thrusts. He gave her everything he had, and she took it, wanting more. Davi raised her head to look at Quinn.

She smiled at him, taunting him. "Is that all you've got, stud?"

"You are wicked, woman," he groaned.

Quinn pinned her body to the bed. She couldn't move. His lips kissed her forcefully. His cock rammed into her. He thought he was going to explode. Davi was shaking under his grip. Her eyes closed as she let out a loud moan. Quinn kept on thrusting. He closed his eyes and let the pleasure flow through him. He thought of Davi and her beautiful body beneath him; he thought of her lips kissing him and her scent. That scent, that amazing scent. Quinn breathed in deeply. Davi's scent filled him. He trembled at the sensation. There was no holding back now. Quinn gave a slow shudder and exploded into Davi and then collapsed onto her.

Davi looked at the bedside clock and cursed, "Damn. We have to be at the church in twenty minutes."

Davi rolled out of the bed and ran for the bathroom. She put the shower on. To be kind, she let the water run warm. Quickly, she put her hair into a ponytail. Quinn was right behind her. Davi washed herself in thirty seconds. She scooted out of the shower while Quinn stayed in and raised the temperature. It didn't take her long to get ready. She was putting on her shoes by the time Quinn stepped out of the bathroom, completely naked.

"I don't have anything here to change into, and I don't have my shaving kit here either."

"Just wear what you had on, Quinn. I can get you a toothbrush, and maybe Rich has a razor you can use. But you've got to hurry."

"Next time I'll have my own stuff here."

"Next time we won't be running late for our wedding rehearsal."

"Next time you'll be my wife."

Davi chuckled. "Next time you'll be my husband."

Quinn stopped and stared at her. "Say that word again."

Davi knew exactly what word he meant. "Husband." Davi walked to Quinn and cupped his face with her hands. "That's what you've wanted to be called and couldn't. Isn't it?"

"Yes." His blue eyes bore into hers. "I have been aching for that."

"Tomorrow, love."

"I can't wait."

There was a knock at the door.

"We're going to be late! Wedding rehearsal is for the ceremony, not the wedding night, kids!"

Quinn put on his pants as Davi opened the bedroom door.

"Rich. Just the person I wanted to see."

"Hey, Momsie, whatcha doing?" He smiled at her mischievously.

"Quinn needs a razor. Do you have anything he can use?" Davi smiled at him sweetly, ignoring his question.

"Sure. I'll be right back."

Davi walked to the bathroom and found a new toothbrush for Quinn. Quinn put on his shirt and then combed his hands through his hair.

Rich walked in and handed him a razor and a can of shaving foam.

"Here you go, Quinn. I hope this is okay for you."

"Thanks, Rich. It will do the job."

Quinn took the offering and walked off to the bathroom.

"Mom, you look great. Was it the day at the spa or . . . ?"

Davi threw a pillow at her son, laughing. "You are so bad."

"And you love it. Come on, Quinn, it's time to hit the road," he shouted at the bathroom door.

Quinn opened the bathroom door and walked out. Davi sighed as her heart skipped a beat.

"Mom, it's only Quinn. Get a grip. You'd think you'd seen a movie star or something." He laughed as he left the room.

Quinn looked at Davi. "I hope I always see that look in your eyes when you look at me."

"You will. I promise."

"Come on, woman." Quinn took Davi's hand. "Let's go practice getting married."

Jake waited for them in the kitchen. Cat and Tigger were laughing and joking with him.

"Hey, you two, I was wondering if you decided to elope. You didn't answer your phone, Quinn."

Quinn smiled guiltily. "I had it turned off. Something came up. What's it like outside? Is it any better?"

"Worse."

Jake led the way out to the limo. There was plenty of room for all of them. The church was only minutes from the farm. When Jake pulled into the parking lot, there were police cars blocking both entrances and security guards covering the surrounding grounds.

"Isn't this a bit much?" Cat asked.

"You'd be surprised at what happens when there isn't security, Cat. Buildings are vandalized for souvenirs, the wedding decorations disappear, fans hide out in the church waiting for a chance to see the stars, and paparazzi try to get in to the ceremony. It's better to overdo it than not have enough."

Everyone got out of the limo and hurried into the church.

The minister was standing at the altar, talking with the organist. Maggie was busy checking on the decorations. The flowers would be delivered in the morning. Quinn's group of friends sat in the back pews out of the way.

Davi took Quinn's hand and led him to the minister. Davi's heart was racing. She was nervous. *Here comes the moment of truth,* she thought. *What if he says he won't marry us? Why would he say no? Because he can. He's the minister.* Davi's mind raced with pessimistic thoughts.

The minister and Quinn were looking at her with bemusement.

"Davi," Quinn said softly as he squeezed her hand.

"I'm sorry, my mind was elsewhere," Davi stammered. "Quinn, this is Reverend Samuel. Reverend Samuel, this is Quinn, finally, in the flesh."

Quinn and the minister shook hands.

"It's great to finally meet the man who swept Davi off her feet."

"Thank you. It's a pleasure meeting you."

The minister called for all of the members of the wedding party to come forward. Luke, Rich, Jake, Maggie, Cat, and Tigger assembled beside Quinn and Davi. He went through the order of service with them. Luke, Jake, and Quinn practiced standing at the altar. The girls and Maggie practiced their walk down the aisle to the music Davi had chosen. Rich and Davi waited for their cue and then walked down the aisle arm in arm. Quinn smiled at Davi the entire time.

"Why are you smiling at me?" Davi whispered to him.

"I'm practicing for tomorrow. This is a rehearsal, you know." He winked at her.

Davi and Quinn stood beside each other as the minister went through the service with them. Quinn held Davi's hand and squeezed it. She could feel the tension leave her body.

"And that's everything."

"I have something, but I'd like to speak with you in private if I may, Reverend," said Quinn.

"Of course. Come to my office if you'd like."

"I won't be long," Quinn whispered to Davi.

The girls looked at Davi.

She shrugged. "I have no idea what he wants."

Davi walked over to the organist.

"Do you mind playing for me? I'd like to hear the music tonight. I know I won't hear a thing tomorrow."

The organist played. Davi closed her eyes as she heard Pachelbel's *Canon in D Major* for when she came down the aisle. He played Beethoven's *Ode to Joy* for when she and Quinn walked up the aisle as husband and wife. Davi sighed when the music was over.

"Thank you. That was lovely."

Davi looked around. Quinn and the minister had not returned. She went to the back of the church to talk with everyone as they waited for him.

"So are you getting nervous?" Sue asked.

"I was, but then it just disappeared. Quinn smiled at me and that was it."

"Don't tell him that, Davi. He doesn't need any encouragement regarding the powers of his charm," Sarah teased.

"What is he doing?" the girls whined playfully.

"I don't know. He wanted to talk with the minister. They haven't met before. Maybe he wanted to fully introduce himself."

Maggie put her arm around Davi's waist. "Davi, I'll head home now and get ready for you to join us. There's no point in me hanging around here."

"Why doesn't everyone go with you, and I'll wait here for Quinn. You might as well get the party going," suggested Davi.

"I'll stay here with you. Everyone else can go," offered Jake.

Once the group had left, Davi took Jake's hand and said, "You're always the protector, Jake."

"Always. Don't worry about Guy. I have men waiting at the airport for him. When he shows up, and he will, they'll deal with him."

"Thank you."

"You can't fault him though. He's got amazing taste in women and gems."

Davi smiled at Jake's attempt at humor. "He's sick and he gives me the willies. I hope I never have to lay eyes on him again."

"I hear you." Jake squeezed Davi's hand. "So are you up for this, lovely lady? No second thoughts in marrying Quinn?"

"I'm ready, Jake. I can't believe I'm doing this. But I'm ready."

"You know that he's ready for this too."

"He should be!" she exclaimed. "He's the one who wanted to get married right away. I've never known a man to be so . . ."

"Romantic? Crazy? Infatuated? In love? Obsessed? Stubborn? You can tell me when I say the right word."

"They're all right. He's all of that and more."

"What am I?" Quinn asked as he walked toward them.

"You're you and I wouldn't have it any other way. Are you ready?"

"Yes. Let's go. Reverend Samuel will meet up with us shortly. He has a few things he has to finish up."

"So what did you talk about?" Davi whispered to Quinn once the limo pulled out of the parking lot.

"I thought we should get to know each other a bit and he agreed."

Maggie's house was located in the local village. It was a new home, large and spacious. Its rustic exterior allowed it to fit right in with the older homes surrounding it.

Davi, Quinn, and Jake got out of the limo and made their way to the front door. The outside lights were bright. They could hear laughter and loud conversation coming from behind the front door. Davi opened the door and walked right in. She never knocked on Maggie's door. It was always open.

"Finally!" Maggie was upon them as soon as they closed the front door behind them. "The appetizers are almost gone. We have a hungry crowd here. Get yourselves a drink, and then you can start the buffet. Quinn, look after Davi." She gave him the eye before leading Jake to where the others were.

"What does that mean?" Quinn asked. "Look after Davi?"

"I have no idea. Just be on your guard. That's all I can say."

"You make it sound like I'm in enemy territory."

"Not enemy territory, but watch out for friendly fire."

Quinn laughed. "As long as she lets me marry you tomorrow, I'll take whatever comes my way. Come on, let's go see the gang."

"Quinn!" his friends greeted him in the familiar way.

Quinn smiled at them. "Hey guys, leave any food for us?"

Quinn looked around the room. It was beautiful. Maggie had great taste. He could live in a house like this. It was spacious and warm. He could feel its hominess. Off to the side, he noticed a large table covered with family photographs. Quinn went closer to have a look at them. There were pictures of Maggie and her family, quite a few of her children at different ages, grandparents, and siblings, he guessed. There were also pictures of Davi and her family with Maggie's and by themselves. Quinn realized the closeness between the two women.

Davi hugged Quinn from behind. "Nice pictures, huh?"

"I didn't realize you were so close to Maggie, but the pictures tell the story."

"We've known each other forever. Our kids have grown up together. Holidays aren't the same if we don't spend time together."

"It's a good thing Maggie likes me or else I'd be spending my holidays alone."

"She's loves you."

"Davi, Quinn was supposed to be looking after you. How come you aren't eating?" Maggie asked as she stood with her arms crossed, frowning at Quinn.

"We're going!" Davi groaned.

Quinn turned and winked at Maggie.

The food was delicious. Maggie had outdone herself. The wine flowed freely, and so did the chocolate milk.

"Everyone, there is dessert and coffee for you. Please help yourselves," announced Maggie.

"There's more food? I don't think I can eat any more." Quinn patted his full stomach. "Maggie, you are an amazing cook."

Maggie appeared with a dessert plate filled with cake and a steaming cup of coffee.

"Quinn, this is for you. I'll get my coffee. Then we'll talk." It was an order more than a request. Maggie pointed to where she wanted him to sit.

Maggie stood in front of Quinn and Davi, while the guests found their seats.

"Be nice, Maggie, I really want to marry this one."

"What do you mean by that? I really want to marry this one?" Quinn turned to look at Davi.

Davi smiled wickedly at him.

"Quinn, Davi and I have known each other for a very long time. Our children have grown up together. We've shared in each other's joy and heartbreak. We've trusted each other with our secrets and our fears. When I read her cards before she went to California, I had no idea that you would be the love that she would find. The cards read love and success. There was no sign of a movie star."

"A gorgeous movie star," one of the women called out.

The group laughed.

"But the cards are never wrong. So when Davi came home to tell me about you, I wasn't surprised. I could see it in her eyes. She was in love and she was happy. Thank you, Quinn, for making our Davi happy again and bringing love back into her life."

Quinn stood up and hugged Maggie. "Thank you," he whispered in her ear. Quinn turned his gaze to Davi. "I've always believed in fate. I've always known that I would find the woman of my dreams, and I've always known that Davi was that woman."

The female guests sighed.

"She fought me," Quinn continued. "She wasn't easy to win over. She gave me every chance to walk away, but I wouldn't because I knew that she loved me just as much as I loved her. I didn't need the cards to tell me that. Her eyes told me everything I needed to know. From the moment I first saw her, her eyes told me she would be mine. Forever."

Quinn held his hand out to Davi, and she took it. He pulled her up to stand in front of him.

"I promise now, in front of our friends and family, that I will always love you." He kissed her softly on the mouth.

"Don't you do that tomorrow at the wedding?" Jake called out.

Everyone laughed.

"I'll make her that promise every day if I want to." Quinn's gaze didn't leave her face.

"I love you," Davi whispered. "Forever."

Jake looked at his watch.

"It's time, ladies and gentlemen. We need to be heading off."

"Thanks so much, Maggie. This was a wonderful party. We'll see you tomorrow," Davi said as she hugged her best friend and her husband good night.

Good-byes were said all around.

Quinn took Davi's hand. "Come on, woman, we've got to get you home before midnight for some insane reason."

Jake stood by their limo.

"It's your last time to be alone for a long time. Enjoy it, you two."

"Kiss me, stud."

Davi moved her mouth to his. Quinn pulled her in close and gave her a long hard kiss. His hand moved down her back and pressed on her lower spine. Davi moved onto Quinn's lap, straddling him. She could feel his arousal.

"I thought limo sex was off-limits," he said against her lips.

"For your fantasy, stud, not mine." Her breath was warm against his lips.

Davi found his zipper and undid it, releasing him. She raised her hips and guided him into her.

Quinn murmured, "Commando?"

"Just in case we had an opportunity for one last time before we're married. Add this to your memory bank."

Davi rode Quinn. He held on to her hips and guided her up and down his shaft. His mouth sought hers. He kissed her without release. He absorbed everything coming from her—her breath, her scent, and her moans. Davi drove him crazy. He wanted this to last forever, but he knew it wouldn't. Just as he thought it, it was over. He climaxed as Davi stopped riding him. Davi held on to him, staying motionless.

The limo stopped. Jake tapped lightly on the window. "We're here. Take your time."

Davi got off Quinn's lap and sat down beside him. She opened her purse and pulled out her compact and a hairbrush. A few strokes of the brush through her hair and a touch of lipstick and she was good to go. Quinn leaned his head back against the headrest, eyes closed. Davi tucked him back into his pants.

"Good night, love. I'll see you tomorrow." She kissed him lightly on the lips.

"Good night, woman. I will most definitely be seeing you tomorrow." His eyes opened, and he winked at her.

Davi opened the door and got out. "Good night, Jake. Thanks for everything." Davi gave Jake a kiss on the cheek. "You get some rest too. I'll see you in the morning."

"Good night, lovely lady. Sweet dreams."

Davi got ready for bed. She climbed into her warm bed; the sheets were still a mess from her earlier lovemaking session with Quinn. She could smell his scent on the pillow. She hugged it tight and reached for her phone.

"Hey, woman."

"I can't sleep."

"I know what you mean. I'm sitting here having a drink and wondering how I'm going to last until I see you again."

"You'll do it just like you do it every day. Pull out one of your memories."

"Ahh, that's the problem. There are too many to choose from, and none of them seems to be doing the trick."

"Can you picture us in the future, Quinn? Do you have something you can think of in that way?"

"I think of us all the time and our future together. Do you want to hear about one of my thoughts?"

"Please."

"The most current thought I've had and it seems so real is you and me with our baby boy. We're walking through the park, enjoying the day, just like normal happy families do."

"We're having a boy? Is that what you want, Quinn, a son?"

"No, I don't know. It's just that my thoughts always take me to a boy, and his name is Jack."

"Jack? That's my father's name. Is that the reason for naming our son Jack?"

"No. I didn't think of that. It's just that the name sounds good. Jack Thomas. It's got that masculine thing going for it."

"Just like Quinn the Hunter."

"Yes, but this time it would be Jack the Man. He could be a superspy, an actor, author, or farmer, anything he wanted with that name. It's a name without expectations. He can be anything he wants. He would make his name—his name wouldn't make him."

"Is that what you think about your name? That you had to be an actor to live up to its expectation?"

"Quinn isn't your everyday name. How many Quinns do you know other than me? I felt obligated to do something with my name. I know it sounds crazy, but I know my parents gave me that name so I would become somebody."

"So if it weren't for your name, we probably would never have met. I'll have to thank your parents. Do you have a girl's name? Do you ever think of us having a girl?"

"Sorry, nothing yet, but I have plenty of time to dream of that. Eight months."

Davi yawned. "I think I'd better try to get some sleep. Maybe I'll dream about Jack tonight. It would be a big change for me."

"Really? Why is that?"

"I dream about you every night. You stay with me until it's time to wake up. I thought you knew that."

"I know it now. Thank you. Good night, love. I'll see you at the altar at exactly four o'clock."

"I'll be there. And remember, Quinn, wear underwear."

Quinn laughed. "I will. Go to sleep."

Davi put the phone down on her bedside table and cuddled with her pillow. She fell asleep soon after. Her dream started with Quinn, but for the first time, she dreamt of a baby boy named Jack.

Chapter 33

♥

Davi woke up at eight o'clock. She could hear the girls out in the hallway.

"I'm up," she yelled so that they would hear her.

Davi's door burst open. Cat and Tigger jumped on her bed and crawled under the covers with her, sandwiching her between them.

"Mom, this might be the last time we can do this. After today, Quinn's going to be in here with you."

Davi kissed the top of their heads. "He won't be here all of the time. We'll still have the chance to have our Saturday morning cuddle. I'm not in any hurry to end this. No matter how old you two get, you'll still be my babies."

"He really loves you, Mom. What he said last night . . ." Cat paused.

"It was so romantic," Tigger finished for her.

"Do you think we'll ever find someone like that?"

"I know you will, or you may have already. You'll know when you find someone that loves you like that. I believe we all have someone out there for us to love. You can't sit back and wish for it to happen. It will happen when you least expect it. Don't go looking for him because you might not recognize him when you first see him. Always keep your heart and your eyes open."

"Is that what you did, Mom, with Quinn? You kept your heart open for him?"

Davi shook her head. "My heart was closed and blind. I wasn't looking for love, and I wasn't seeing it. It was all Quinn. He was persistent enough to get me to open my heart. I've only known one other man as stubborn and determined as Quinn, and that was your father. I could never say no to him either. You two have a bit of that in you too, especially the determination. Nothing has ever stopped you from getting what you set your sights on."

"Speaking of sights," said Cat, "the clock says we're going to be late if we don't get out of this bed right away. Come on, Tigger, time to hit the shower."

Davi smiled as she watched them race for the bathroom. Her thoughts were interrupted by her cell phone ringing.

"Hello?"

"Davi, it's Jake. How are you?" His tone was unusually serious.

Davi sat up in her bed. "It's Guy, isn't it?"

"He didn't show up for the flight. My men waited, but he was a no show."

Davi closed her eyes.

"It doesn't mean he's here, Davi. He could be in Paris waiting for you. He may have been so confident that you'd leave Quinn that he was already in Paris when he called you."

"Do you really think that, Jake?"

"I honestly don't know. I've doubled our security. There's no way he can get into the church or the reception. I don't know what he's thinking. He could be anywhere waiting to make an appearance, or he may have given up. We just won't know until something happens."

"Or doesn't."

"Or doesn't. I'm sorry."

"It's not your fault. You're not the crazy one trying to steal me away from Quinn. I can't see him wanting to hurt me, Jake. He's just obsessed with me." Davi shook her head as if she were ridding herself of any thought of Guy. "I can't worry about it today. Once Quinn and I are married, Guy will have to give it up. I'm not leaving Quinn for him. Not for anything or anyone."

"You'll be okay?"

"I am more than okay. I'm getting married today to the man I love. Nothing and no one will ruin today for me."

"I won't let anything happen to change that."

"I know you won't. Now if you'll excuse me, I have to get ready for my wedding."

Davi stood in front of the hallway mirror. She didn't recognize her reflection. She knew it was hers, but it was so different. Her hair was swept up softly off her shoulders. Her blue eyes sparkled brighter than the blue sapphire earrings and necklace she wore. The wedding dress fit her perfectly. Every curve was gracefully accentuated as the dress flowed over her body.

"Wow."

"Wow, indeed. If you thought Quinn had separation issues before, they are nothing compared to what he's going to be like when he sees you like this. He'll grab on to you and never let go," Maggie said as she stood beside her friend, admiring her.

Davi smiled. "I think he can make it through the day, Maggie. He has to."

There was a knock at the door. The photographer had arrived.

"Showtime," announced Davi

The photographer was indeed a professional. He was relaxed, and he kept the women smiling. Quinn had made the right choice in asking him to take their wedding photos. He hadn't done weddings in years, but he had a great eye for stunning shots. They set up in the living room, where there was plenty of space and great light. Davi felt like she was in a photo shoot more than she was posing for her wedding pictures. The assistant coached Davi for the right facial expressions. In some she smiled; in some she looked thoughtful. She looked at the camera, or she looked away. This was hard work.

The girls loved it when they were included in the photos. They were relaxed and easy to work with. Their smiles were so natural and uplifting. The assistant praised them on their being so photogenic. Maggie soon joined in the photos and then Rich.

"What a great-looking family," Jake said as he looked in from the doorway.

"Don't you look smart," Davi said as she admired him.

"The wife thinks I clean up well. Thanks."

"Will you take a picture of me with Jake, please?"

"No, Davi, that's not necessary." Jake waved off the request.

"Yes, it is. I want a picture with you."

The photographer pulled Jake into the room and stood him beside Davi.

"Don't look at the camera. Look at each other. That's right."

He took a few pictures.

"That's it for in here. Now Quinn asked that I take some shots with you and the Ladies. He said you'd know who they were. I take it you three aren't the Ladies?"

Davi smiled, while the other three laughed knowingly. "He wants me to pose with the cows. They are the Ladies."

"Cows? He wants you to pose with cows?" The photographer thought about it. "This could be very interesting. Will we be going in a barn or are they outside?"

"I hope we can do it outside. I don't want to smell like the barn for my wedding. Come on people, let's go find the Ladies."

Jake walked with them. He hadn't seen the farm yet, and he was intrigued by Quinn's request for a picture of Davi with the cows. They stopped outside of the maternity barn. The weather was still warm enough that the half wall was still open. A few cows had their heads hanging over the top of the wall, watching Davi and her entourage.

"I can't stand too close to them or else they'll lick me. How close do you need me to stand?"

"We'll keep them in the background."

The photographer's assistant helped Davi stand in the right position. Davi held out her bridal bouquet. The cows stretched their necks to sniff the flowers. The photographer clicked away. Davi moved in closer but stood off to the side. The cows followed her with their heads. It was a great shot. Everyone joined Davi for more pictures. All of them found it hard to keep a straight face, and their laughter added to the uniqueness of the pictures. Davi didn't know it at the time, but these would be the main photos used in the *Vanity Fair* publication.

The limo drove down the farm laneway slowly. The crowd was huge.

"I should wave to them to let them know that I appreciate their support."

Jake groaned. "It's five minutes to four, Davi. You can put your windows down in the back, and we will stop. But you're not getting out of the limo."

"Thanks, Jake. Smile girls. Look happy," Davi encouraged them.

The limo windows went down. The screaming was deafening. Davi smiled her best and waved. She yelled thank you to the well-wishers. Jake drove away. The limo slowed as it approached the church. Cars were parked on both sides of the road. People were lined up against them, hoping for a view of Davi or Quinn.

"I'm glad our family and friends took us up on our offer and used the limo service. They'd never get near here otherwise," commented Davi.

The limo pulled into the church parking lot and stopped by the front entranceway.

"Wait for me before you get out. I'm going to check to see if we're going to be starting on schedule."

Jake entered the church. Davi put her window down. The crowd screamed for her. There were banners wishing Davi and Quinn good luck. Some read: "We love you, Quinn."

I love him too, Davi said to herself as she waved.

Jake approached the limo door with Rich and opened the door. "Ladies, it is showtime. We are one minute to the hour. Is everyone ready?"

"Yes!" the girls answered together.

"Davi?"

"I promised to meet Quinn at four. I can't keep him waiting."

The crowd went ballistic when they saw Davi exit the limo. She turned and waved to them for about ten seconds. That was all the time Jake allowed her. Rich offered his arm to his mother, and then the group walked into the church. Jake walked up to the front of the church to join Quinn.

Davi could hear the music playing. It was Pachelbel's *Canon in D Major.* Tigger started down the aisle first. Cat followed after, and then a few steps later, Maggie followed. The guests stood for the procession. Rich waited until the girls had made it to their positions at the altar before he walked with his mother.

"I love you, Momsie," he whispered in her ear.

"I love you too."

"My new best friend is waiting for you. Let's go."

The church was decorated with the beautiful colors of fall. White bows hung on the aisle side of the pews. Orange, gold, and white fall flowers filled large urns standing on pedestals at the altar. Large white pillar candles on stands burned brightly. Davi could smell the floral bouquet as she entered the church.

Rich and Davi walked down the aisle slowly. Davi smiled at her friends and family. She didn't cry. She was eager to get to the altar and stand with Quinn. Davi could feel her heart beat increasing.

Settle down, Davi, she told herself. *Take your time. Enjoy the moment. Make a memory.*

They reached the end of the aisle. Davi looked to her right at Quinn, all six foot three gorgeous inches of him. His blue eyes were sparkling as he smiled at her. Davi smiled back at him. Rich stopped in front of the minister. Davi was an inch from Quinn. She could feel the electricity coming from him. She tingled.

The minister welcomed the guests.

Then he looked at Davi's children and asked, "Who supports this woman in her marriage to this man?"

Cat, Tigger, and Rich answered, "We do."

Davi placed her hand in Quinn's. He gave it a squeeze. The tingle worked its way up her hand through her body.

"We will now exchange the wedding vows and rings." The minister motioned to Quinn to start.

Quinn turned to face Davi, taking both of her hands in his. "I, Quinn Thomas, take you, Davina Stuart, to be my wife, my partner in life, and my one true love. I will cherish our union and love you more each day than I did the day before. I offer you my solemn vow to be your faithful partner in sickness and in health, in good times and in bad, and in joy as well as in sorrow. I give you my hand, my heart, and my love, from this day forward for as long as we both shall live."

Davi then made the same vows to Quinn.

"We'll now have the exchange of rings," the minister announced.

Quinn slipped the wedding band on Davi's finger as he said, "I give you this ring as a visible and constant symbol of my promise to love you and be yours forever."

Davi repeated the lines as she slipped the wedding band on Quinn's finger.

"Friends, we were going to sing a hymn, but last night, the groom asked if he could sing to his bride. Quinn, when you're ready." The minister stepped back.

Davi looked at Quinn with surprise. This was unexpected. She could feel a blush coming on. *Get a grip, Davi*, she told herself. *Just breathe.*

Quinn looked at Davi. His gaze burned into her as he took her hands in his. Quinn's warm tenor voice mesmerized her. Davi cried as he sang to her.

> *Maybe it's intuition, but some things you just don't question*
> *Like in your eyes, I see my future in an instant*
> *And there it goes, I think I found my best friend . . .*

Davi knew the song. Quinn sang it beautifully.

> *I knew I loved you before I met you*
> *I think I dreamed you into life*
> *I knew I loved you before I met you*
> *I have been waiting all my life . . .*

When Quinn finished singing, he kissed her tears away. "I love you, Davi," he whispered to her.

The minister then announced, "The couple will now sign their marriage license."

After they signed the license, the minister said a prayer for the couple.

"Now that Davina and Quinn have given themselves to each other by the promises they have exchanged, I pronounce them to be husband and wife, in the name of the Father and the Son and of the Holy Spirit. Amen. You may now kiss the bride."

Quinn and Davi gazed into each other's eyes. Quinn leaned down and kissed her softly on the lips. Davi wrapped her arms around his neck and pulled him in tight. After a moment, Quinn pulled away, winking at Davi as he did.

"It is my pleasure to introduce to you, Mr. and Mrs. Quinn Thomas!"

Everyone applauded.

Davi and Quinn both smiled as they held hands and walked up the aisle to the front door. Davi didn't hear the music or the congratulations. She was married to Quinn Thomas. Forever.

Chapter 34

♥

The crowd cheered as Davi and Quinn exited the church. The couple stopped on the top step and kissed as the photographer took their picture. Quinn and Davi didn't hear or see anyone. It took a tap on Quinn's shoulder by Luke to get them to separate.

"Congratulations, Quinn," Luke said as he shook Quinn's hand.

"Thanks, Luke."

"Davi, you are beautiful," Luke said before he kissed her on the cheek.

"Thank you."

In seconds, friends and family surrounded the couple. Quinn held on tight to his new bride. He wasn't about to let her go, not yet anyway.

The photographer approached them. "If it's all right with you, I'd like us to go back to the farm and take pictures of the wedding party out by the barn. I looked at the shots we took earlier and they're quite good. We should go now while the light is still good."

Davi smiled at Quinn. "Nice idea there. I'd never have thought of it."

"You had to have a picture taken with the Ladies. You talk about them all of the time. It wouldn't have been right to leave them out." He smiled at her.

Quinn waved Luke and Jake over to tell them of the plans.

Jake shook his head. "We're going to drive back through that mob? Why not? I'll round up the rest of the group."

When Davi and Quinn got into the limo, Quinn gave her a long and deep kiss.

"You take my breath away," he said when he released her.

"Thank you for my song. It was beautiful. What made you decide to do it?"

"It is my wedding gift to you. I wanted the ceremony to be more personal, if it could be."

"Promise you'll sing to me again. I love your voice."

"I promise."

The limo stopped. Davi looked out the window. She wasn't surprised to see the size of the crowd now. Jake slowly inched his way through the crowd. Security was trying to push people back, but it was difficult. Finally, they made it through. Jake drove the limo right up to the barn. Davi and Quinn slid out of the backseat with Quinn holding her hand.

"We had some great shots here earlier," said the photographer, "so we'll give this another try. There's also a spot over there that will work out well. I think you'll like how these turn out."

Davi and Quinn posed in various positions. Quinn was a natural. It was obvious he was comfortable in front of the camera. Quinn spouted off trivia about cows to the photographer as he took pictures of them. Davi laughed. She didn't know he knew so much about cows.

"The Internet, Davi. What do you think I do when you're not around?"

By this time, the other members of the bridal party had arrived as well as members of the families.

Davi rushed through introducing Quinn to her siblings, nieces, and nephews. "You can stop and chat later. We need to get these pictures taken."

Quinn put his arm around Davi. He stood close to her as the various members of Davi's family positioned themselves around them. Davi could feel the heat coming from Quinn. Her heart started to race.

"Déjà vu," she whispered.

"I'm thinking the same thing," Quinn whispered back as he held on to her. "Don't worry, love, I've got you."

The photographer shot away. Davi felt a pressure along her hip. She gave out a quick laugh.

"When he's finished, don't move. I'll make it look like I'm talking to you. Just go with it," Quinn whispered to her. "I've got to get my other brain to settle down. Your scent is driving me crazy."

"Everyone, thank you for your patience. We'll take some more shots at the reception. We've lost our light now that it's starting to get dark," the photographer announced.

The group gradually dispersed.

Quinn held on to Davi, slowly whispering in her ear, "Partly skimmed milk, sugar, glucose, fructose . . ."

Davi tingled as she listened to his voice. It was low and incredibly sexy.

"Cocoa, salt, carrageenan, color, artificial flavor . . ."

Could anything sound more sinful? She felt a blush come to her cheeks.

"Vitamin A, palmitate, vitamin D."

"You memorized the ingredient label for chocolate milk?"

"It's one of your favorite drinks next to scotch and coffee."

"Yes, but why would you memorize the ingredients?"

"I read the carton once. Anyway, it did the job. We can go now." Quinn released her from his hold and kissed her again.

"You might need to stay away from me if I'm going to have that effect on you all day. It could become embarrassing," she teased.

"Woman, I am not letting you out of my sight. I can handle embarrassing. I cannot handle being without you." Quinn opened the limo door for her. "Mrs. Thomas."

"Say that again."

"Mrs. Thomas." Quinn looked down at her, smiling.

"I like that name. I think I'll keep it."

Quinn and Davi cuddled in the backseat of the limo. Quinn kissed her tenderly.

"I really like your dress," he murmured.

"Thank you. I love it. What did you think about the girls' and Maggie's dresses?"

"I didn't notice them. I'll have to let you know later."

"You didn't notice three beautiful females walking down the aisle, standing beside us at the altar, standing beside us for our wedding pictures?"

"No. I'll pay better attention later. I was focused on the fourth woman."

"Well, make sure you notice them when we get to the reception. Please."

"I will." Quinn's fingers played with Davi's wedding ring. "Nice ring, Mrs. Thomas."

Davi reached for Quinn's ring hand. "Nice ring, Mr. Thomas."

The limo pulled up to the entranceway of the reception hall.

"It's showtime again," Davi announced.

Davi and Quinn went through another round of having their pictures taken with family. Davi was starting to see spots.

"How do you put up with the flashes? All I can see is spots."

"They'll go away soon. This isn't bad, you know. Wait until you're on the red carpet with me. Then you'll see spots."

"I feel like I'm with you on the red carpet already."

"No, I am on the red carpet with you today. You're the star. I'm just the tagalong."

"Nice tagalong."

"I try."

Maggie caught up with them.

"It's time for the receiving line, you two. It's good to see you've still got your smile on, Davi."

Maggie took Davi by the hand and led her to her spot. Quinn followed holding on to Davi's other hand.

Davi turned to look at Quinn. His eyes were sparkling and his smile was bright. He looked gorgeous, movie star gorgeous. She sighed.

Quinn knew that look. He winked at her.

The guests started through the line. The first to go through were Sue and Jake.

"Davi, you look fabulous. The service was wonderful." She kissed Davi on the cheek. "Way to add to your perfection, Quinn, singing to your bride. It was so romantic." Sue kissed Quinn.

Jake hugged Davi.

She pulled away and kissed him. "Thanks for everything."

"My pleasure, lovely lady."

Jake shook Quinn's hand. "Be good to her. Remember, we'll be watching you."

Quinn laughed. "How could I forget? I promise."

Chas Elliot and Taylor Mann were next through the line.

"You two?" Quinn asked, surprised.

"Congratulations, Quinn. It seems the bridesmaids needed dates for today and we were available. We wouldn't have missed this for anything. What a great service, Quinn." Chas hugged Davi. "You are beautiful, Mrs. Thomas. Congratulations. Thank you for inviting us."

"You'll have to explain why they're here," whispered Quinn.

"Later," Davi whispered back.

Davi's family followed through the line next. Close to forty family members in total. Davi's sisters led the line.

"Baby sister, you look amazing. Great wedding!" they chimed together as they had a group hug.

"Bev, Babs, just in case you didn't meet him earlier, this is Quinn." Davi laughed as the two women fawned over him.

They both stretched to give him a kiss. Neither one made it to his shoulder.

"We have heard so much about you, Quinn. Welcome to the family."

"Save me a dance for later?" he asked them.

Davi saw her sisters blush.

"Nice one, stud. That will keep them happy for months," she whispered.

Davi's brothers-in-law, nieces, nephews, and their children followed. Davi got the hug and kiss, but it was Quinn they wanted to talk to.

"Tagalong, huh?" she muttered to him once her family left the line.

Quinn's parents were the last to come through the line.

"Congratulations, Quinn and Davi," Quinn's mother said happily, glowing with pride. "You two make a wonderful couple, and the ceremony was so touching." She hugged both of them.

"Well done, son." Quinn's father shook his hand. "Welcome to the family, Davi." He kissed her on the cheek.

"Thank you." Davi smiled.

"Your mother is parched, so we're going to go check out the bar." Quinn's dad winked at them and led his wife away.

"Now I know where you got that wink from! Very interesting." Davi chuckled. "Is there anything else you inherited from your father?"

"You'll just have to wait and see." He winked at her.

Davi looked over to the entranceway to their banquet room. "I want to look at the seating arrangement. The girls and Maggie looked after it all by themselves." Davi led Quinn over to the board with the seating plan posted on it.

"Man!" Quinn laughed. "I should have known there'd be no truce, especially on our wedding day."

Instead of being numbered, each table had a name assigned to it. Each one was named after one of Quinn's movies. The head table even had a name, *The Engagement.*

"Why am I not surprised?" Davi shook her head. "I wonder what the tables look like. Do you think Maggie will let us sneak in and have a look?"

Quinn looked around him, everyone was gathered around the bar or sitting in the lounge, eating finger food. "Let's live on the edge and sneak in."

They slipped into the reception room and were stunned immediately by what they saw. Each table had a beautiful floral centerpiece. To show the name of the table, there was a miniature movie poster of that movie, each one was signed by Quinn.

"I signed these last week. Luke told me it was for a charity. I can't believe I fell for it."

In front of each place setting was a miniature stuffed Holstein cow, a shot glass filled with Quinn's favorite scotch, and a glass of chocolate milk.

"They didn't miss a thing," Davi commented. "That's us."

"Definitely," he agreed. "Come on, we better get back out there." He took Davi by the hand and led her back out to the crowd.

"There you are," Maggie admonished them. "You snuck a peak, didn't you?"

"It's fantastic, Maggie. You and the girls did a fabulous job with the tables. Thank you."

"The girls had fun with it. I had to rein them in. You wouldn't believe the ideas they had. It's time to go in. The DJ is ready to play your entrance songs, and the kitchen is eager to get your dinner served."

The doors to the dining room opened, and the guests filed in. The bridal party stayed behind for their grand entrance.

"Mom, Quinn, we've picked our entrance music. The DJ is going to play a medley of songs for the wedding party. When it's your turn to come in, it will be your own song. You can walk, run, or dance to the music. It's totally up to you," Rich informed them.

"Is it going to be embarrassing?" Davi grimaced. "I am your mother, remember?"

"I promise. It's all good, nothing embarrassing."

"Rich, best friend, if you're lying, you lose your status as new best friend. You realize that," Quinn warned him.

"Nothing to fear. I told you, it's all good."

The music started to play. Davi and Quinn recognized the music instantly. It was a medley of the theme songs from Quinn's movies. The songs had all made it to the top ten lists when they were released. The girls, Maggie, Luke, Jake, and Rich made their way to the head table, dancing to the music. The guests clapped and cheered as they danced. When they were seated, the music changed to Davi and Quinn's song.

"I don't believe it." Quinn smiled. "It's the love song from *The Engagement*. We're going to dance this one in, woman. How's your two-step?"

"A bit rusty but I think I can manage."

"Just follow my lead."

Quinn took Davi in his arms and danced her into the room. Instead of heading straight to their table, he circled the floor.

"Keep smiling. You look beautiful, love," he whispered in her ear.

The song was a country and western tune. It won best song of the year at the Country Music awards. Quinn danced to this song in his movie. He was repeating the dance with Davi. For two and a half minutes, Quinn guided his bride across the dance floor. Everyone applauded the newlyweds. They looked as though they had been dancing together forever. Quinn timed it perfectly. By the time the music was ending, he and Davi were at the head table. The music stopped and Quinn kissed Davi. Everyone cheered. The party was on.

Davi could feel her heart racing. She looked up at Quinn.

"Wow."

He winked at her as he offered her her chair.

The first course seemed to pass by quickly. The clinking of glasses kept the couple busy. Quinn didn't mind. He'd kiss Davi all night and never let her go if it were up to him.

Dessert was about to be served. Davi got up and walked over to the DJ. She talked to him, and he nodded his head in agreement. Davi looked over at Quinn and motioned with one finger for him to come to her. Everyone who noticed hooted and hollered. Quinn's smile was filled with mischief even though he had no idea what Davi had planned for him.

Davi pulled out a chair. "Sit," she ordered Quinn.

Quinn sat obediently, facing the guests. He smiled broadly.

Davi spoke into a microphone. "My husband sang to me at our wedding. It was a complete surprise to me, and I thank him for that wonderful gift. Now I have a song for him. Since I met Quinn, everyone has asked me, 'What makes him so special, Davi? He's an average-looking guy. He has all of his hair, his body isn't too bad for a guy his age, he's got an okay career, and he drives a nice car. What is it that you see in this guy?' This song should explain everything to you. Hit it, Mr. DJ."

The DJ played the instrumental only to "The Kiss". Davi knew the words by heart. She stood in front of Quinn as she sang to him. Her hand stroked his face, gently caressing his lips.

It's the way you love me
It's a feeling like this . . .

Then she'd run a hand through his hair, teasing him. Every time she was at the chorus, she made sure her fingers were on his lips.

This kiss, this kiss . . .

Quinn kept his eyes riveted on Davi. They smoldered as she touched his face. A few times, he reached out for her, but Davi avoided his grasp. She made sure that she was on his lap by the time the song finished. Quinn wrapped his arms around Davi as she put her arms around his neck. They gave each other a long kiss. Everyone applauded Davi's performance.

Davi released Quinn and gazed into his eyes. "Forever," she whispered.

"Forever," he replied.

"Okay, everyone, it's time for the bride and groom to cut the cake. Afterward, we'll have the bride and groom's first dance, and you are all invited to join them once they've made a lap or two."

Davi led Quinn to the cake.

"What kind of cake is it?" Quinn asked.

"I have absolutely no idea. I left it up to the planning committee. It will be a surprise for both of us."

Davi and Quinn stood by the cake with the knife. Some of the guests gathered around them to take a picture. Quinn put his hand over Davi's as she cut into the cake. It was a rich chocolate cake covered by a creamy icing. Davi ran her finger over the side of the knife and tasted it. It was dark chocolate with raspberry filling.

"Do they know everything about us?"

Quinn laughed. "Not everything, I hope."

A waiter came and wheeled the cake away. Davi and Quinn stayed on the dance floor, waiting for their first dance.

"Are you going to tell me what we'll be dancing to?"

"No, but I know you can do it. You're a terrific dancer, Mrs. Thomas."

"Friends and family, Davi and Quinn will now have their first dance."

The music started to play.

> *Oh, my love, my darling*
> *I've hungered for your touch . . .*

Davi tensed as Quinn took her in his arms and set off on the dance floor. In seconds, Quinn knew something was wrong. He looked down at her face. There was no smile. Her eyes were forming tears as she bit down on her lip. Immediately, Quinn knew the problem. He danced toward the door with her and then out into the lobby in a mad dash to escape her torment.

"Oh, Davi, of all the songs I could have chosen, I chose your song with Ross. I'm so sorry." Quinn pulled her against his chest. "I should have checked with you."

"Stop it, Quinn. It's not your fault. I never thought for an instant that this would happen." Davi dabbed at her eyes.

Maggie came tearing out of the dining room, looking for them. "Davi, Quinn, what's wrong?"

"We're fine. Quinn got me out of there before I lost it. Ross and I danced to the same song." Davi took a deep breath. "I'm good. If anyone asks you, say that I suddenly felt overwhelmed, and Quinn got me out of there so I could calm down. No one needs to know the reason why."

"What do we do now?"

"Plan B. What's your favorite song, Davi?"

"'Always and Forever.' It's a great song."

Quinn nodded in agreement. "'Always and Forever' it is then. Maggie, go in and have the DJ play that song. I'll have Davi twirling on the dance floor as soon as I hear it start."

"How do I look? Is my face okay?"

"Davi, it's perfect. I'll see you in there." Maggie smiled at her.

Quinn walked Davi close to the dining room entrance.

"Davi, I'm going to make you forget the last five minutes. There'll be no memory of them. I promise."

"You can't promise me that, but don't worry, I'm fine.

As soon as he heard the music, Quinn had Davi on the dance floor.

Always and forever
Each moment with you
Is just like a dream to me
That somehow came true . . .

He held her close and guided her around the dance floor. Davi couldn't help but smile at him. Quinn made her feel like she was dancing on air. After their third time around the floor, their guests joined the couple in finishing their dance. Quinn felt Davi relax in his arms. He cursed himself for what he had done to her.

Davi looked at Quinn. She could see the concern in his face. "Sometime, we'll look back on this and laugh. What are the odds that you would choose the exact same song Ross chose for our first dance?"

"I don't think it's funny, Davi. The look on your face scared the hell out of me."

"I'm sorry. I should have told you what our song was. It doesn't matter now. It's over."

"Just like that?" He found it difficult to believe that his bride was over the ordeal.

"I won't waste any more time thinking about it, and neither should you. Focus on the positive. It's our wedding day, husband. Let's celebrate."

Jake tapped Quinn's shoulder. "Mind if I cut in?"

The two men switched partners.

"So?" Jake asked.

"What?" Davi knew what he wanted to know.

"You weren't really overwhelmed, were you? It was the wrong song."

"It was pretty obvious, wasn't it, Jake?"

"No, I don't think so. Quinn gave it away in his face. It wasn't concern as if you were upset. It was absolute panic. He's a great actor, Davi, but when it comes to you, he can't act worth a damn."

"It was our song twenty-seven years ago. I never thought to tell Quinn. What are the odds that he would pick the very same song?" Davi shook her head. "I was stupid. It's my fault. We're okay now."

They danced in silence until Jake thought it was safe to talk without being overheard. "There's been no sign of Guy. I've got security all around the building. If he's in the area, he's not getting in here."

"The man's obsessed. He needs help. I'm not even thinking of him, Jake. He can't do anything now. Quinn and I are married. He'll give up. He has to."

Quinn and Sue twirled by them just at that moment. Once again, Sue's face was red from excitement. Davi laughed at them while Jake shook his head.

"My sisters will be waiting for their chance with Quinn. They want some of that."

Jake smiled knowingly. "The line has already started, Davi. Look over there."

He pointed to a group of women standing on the side of the dance floor watching Quinn's every move. They were all related to Davi.

"He's going to have a long night ahead of him."

"This is a great party, Davi. Your DJ is playing all the right music. No one's going to want to stop dancing."

Jake moved Davi across the dance floor. He was a large man but very nimble on his feet.

"Did you and Quinn take dancing lessons together? You're both very good."

"Thanks, but no. Dancing keeps me quick on my feet and balanced. I need to have that for my job. I took up dancing years ago. My mother said it would be a good investment when I started to date. She was right."

"Mother's usually are."

The song ended. Davi was asked to dance by one of her brothers-in-law. Davi looked for Quinn while she danced. He was dancing with one of her sisters. The difference in their height was comical, but Quinn managed remarkably well. Davi would have thought he'd wait for a fast song, but then she realized that Quinn knew they'd all want a slow dance with him. Quinn smiled at Davi as he danced by her.

The song ended. Rich had the microphone in his hand trying to get everyone's attention.

"Hi, everyone. I have it from a very reliable source that Quinn's really big on karaoke, and he loves singing country. So Quinn, if you would, please come up and join me."

Davi looked for Quinn. He was laughing as he made his way to the microphone.

Quinn took the microphone from Rich. "I have absolutely no idea what I'm singing, but I'm game. So, Rich, tell me what we're singing."

"Well, Quinn, you're Big and I'm Rich."

Rich laughed as Quinn took in the meaning. Rich put a Stetson cowboy hat on Quinn and then one on himself.

Everyone cheered, "Go guys!"

The music started. It was a well-known country song.

> Well, I walk into the room
> Passing out hundred-dollar bills
> And it kills and it thrills like the horns on my Silverado grill . . .

Davi stood in front of her two favorite men. She danced to the music, her gaze never leaving them. They were very good, and they were having fun.

"And so it continues. The family goes on," Maggie whispered in Davi's ear.

"Yes, it does." Davi put her arm around her friend's waist and held her close. "We're going to be a great family." Davi thought for a moment and then sighed. "Ross would have loved this party."

"Right," Maggie snorted, "except for the fact that this wouldn't be happening if he were still around."

"Oh, I know, but if he's looking down on us right now, I'm sure he's having a great time watching us. He's probably dancing with some angel right now."

"And he'd be happy for you like we all are. You deserve this, Davi. You deserve, Quinn."

Quinn and Rich finished their song. Davi applauded and cheered as they bowed. Quinn smiled at Davi. He clapped Rich on the back, said something to him and then went to Davi, still wearing his Stetson.

"Nice hat, Big."

"It's a great hat. It's mine, a gift from my new best friend. All I need now is the boots."

"You don't have cowboy boots? I'm shocked."

"Take me shopping for some. I really want a pair."

"I promise."

"I hear our song playing." Quinn scooped Davi in his arms and danced her onto the dance floor. "I'm having a great time. This is a great party."

"I was thinking the same thing." Davi kissed Quinn's cheek. "So how many more ladies do you have to dance with tonight? There was a long line at the side of the dance floor last time I checked."

"I don't know. They just keep coming at me. I'll dance two without you, and then I'll dance with you for the third. How does that sound?"

"Like a plan, Mr. Thomas."

"Thank you, Mrs. Thomas." Quinn kissed Davi softly on the mouth and then smiled. "This is all I've ever wanted, to be married to you. The rest is just a bonus."

When the next song started, Quinn released Davi. "See you soon."

Chapter 35

Davi needed to use the washroom. She headed out the doors and down the hallway. The ladies' room was empty and quiet. Davi liked the sound of quiet. When she was finished, she looked in the mirror and checked out her makeup.

"You're as beautiful as the night I met you."

Davi turned her head. Guy Tremblant stood at the door. Davi could see that he'd locked the bolt behind him. His hands were behind his back.

"Guy."

"You didn't come to the airport. I don't blame you. It was foolish of me. You wanted me to come rescue you. I see that now. You needed me to prove my love for you and I failed you. I'm here now. I have a taxi waiting." His voice oozed confidence.

"Guy, Quinn and I are married now. There's nothing you can do." *Keep calm, Davi.*

"Nonsense. You only married him because I didn't show you the man that I am. But I can show you now."

Guy walked toward Davi. Davi stood still. If she backed away from him, she knew he would know she was afraid, and she couldn't let him have the upper hand.

"I don't need to be shown what kind of man you are, Guy. It's quite obvious."

"It is?" He sounded genuinely surprised.

"Yes, it is. You're handsome, intelligent, and very talented. You're very sensitive too, maybe too sensitive. I'm sorry if I gave you the wrong impression."

"What wrong impression?"

"That I had feelings for you. We've only just met." *Keep cool, Davi.*

"But you do have feelings for me. The moment we met, I knew you were the one for me. I felt it in your hand when you offered it to me. We had a connection. Tell me you felt it too."

"I did feel something." Davi remembered the handshake. It was weak and clammy, and it gave her the shivers. "Are you sure it's love you feel for me?"

"If he can fall in love with you at first sight, why can't I? Why do you accept his love and not mine? Why?"

A knock at the door interrupted them.

"Davi? Are you in there? It's Sue. Why is this door locked? Davi?"

"Sue, I'm okay," Davi called out to her. She didn't want to risk upsetting Guy. She had no idea what he held behind his back. She had to get a message to Jake.

"What are you doing in there?"

"I need to be by myself. Jake and I had words. He said some things . . ."

"Jake? What the hell did he say to you? I'll kill him."

Davi smiled inside. Sue was reacting the way she was supposed to.

"Tell him he's obsessed and needs help. Keep him away from me, Sue. I'm not that kind of woman. Go tell your husband that."

"Okay, I will," she shouted angrily through the door. "Then I'll kill the bastard!"

Guy and Davi stared at each other. He cocked his head as he watched her. Davi could see his confusion.

"Why didn't you cry out for help?"

"Do I need help? Am I in danger?"

"Of course not. I would never hurt you. I love you."

Sue stormed into the reception room, searching for Jake. She found him talking with Luke.

"I'll kill you, Jake! What the hell did you say to Davi? She's really upset."

"I didn't say anything. What's going on?"

"She's locked herself in the ladies' room. She says it's because of you. She said that you're obsessed and that you need help."

Jake knew instantly what was wrong.

"What the hell did you say to her?" Sue said angrily.

Jake took a firm grip of Sue's shoulders, looking her right in the eyes. "Calm down. I didn't do anything. Davi's in trouble." Jake straightened. "Luke, get Quinn. Sue, have the DJ play something that gets everyone on the dance floor. Keep everyone inside this room. Do whatever you have to. I don't care if you have to lock the doors. No one leaves this room."

Jake pulled out his cell phone and barked orders into it to his security team while he rushed to the ladies' room. Luke grabbed Quinn, and they followed close behind. They caught up with Jake as he listened at the door. He raised a hand to caution them to be quiet.

Quinn waited impatiently for Jake to tell him what was going on. Luke held him back.

"Jake," Luke whispered, "what the hell is going on?"

Jake walked back to them.

"It's Guy Tremblant. He's in there with Davi. He has the door locked from the inside."

"What the hell? What's he doing here?"

Quinn made a move to rush the door. Jake grabbed him and pulled him to a stop.

"He wants Davi. He came to take her away," he said through gritted teeth.

Jake's answer shocked Quinn. "How do you know that?" He didn't wait for an answer. "We have to get her out of there, Jake. We'll break the door down."

"We can't. It's solid and bolted from the inside."

Quinn's every thought told him to protect his wife, to fight for her. Jake could see it in his face. He kept his eyes fixed on Quinn. He had to make Quinn see how crucial it was that he stay calm, think before acting.

"What do you suggest we do? Sit and wait until he kills her, then tries to escape?"

"He's not going to kill her. Davi wouldn't have been able to talk to Sue if that's what he wanted to do. He wants to leave with her. We have to let him."

"What?" Luke asked, incredulous at Jake's suggestion.

"I can get her out of this safely, Quinn, but you have to trust me. Do you trust me enough to let me do it?" His voice was strong with confidence.

"Yes," Quinn answered. Quinn raked his hands through his hair as he tried to focus on staying calm. "Tell me what you're planning."

"We have to get him out of there. Then we can take him. I'm going to talk to her. Stay here." Jake knew he had to keep it together. Davi's life may depend on it. *Don't blow it, man. You can do this.*

He walked up to the door and knocked, calling out to her, "Davi, it's Jake. I'm sorry I hurt your feelings, but I was only looking out for Quinn. He's my best friend, and I can't stand by and watch you hurt him."

Davi wanted to cry when she heard Jake's voice through the door. He was there to save her, and he knew what to do. Now if only she could get Guy to believe him.

"You said terrible things to me, Jake. You accused me of having an affair with Guy!" she shouted back at him.

"I'm sorry. But when I saw the jewelry and the airline ticket, I jumped to the wrong conclusion."

"You weren't wrong, Jake. We're not having an affair, but I'm leaving Quinn. I want to be with Guy. He's made me promises, and I know he can keep them."

Quinn walked closer to the door. Jake cautioned him to be quiet.

"But it's your wedding day. You're leaving Quinn now?" Jake feigned disbelief.

"I have to. I should have done it yesterday, but you wouldn't let me. It's your fault, Jake. If you hadn't stopped me, I'd be in Paris by now." Davi's voice was strong and even.

Her lies were convincing, even to Quinn.

"What the hell?" Quinn mumbled under his breath.

Jake cautioned him to be quiet.

"Do you really want to leave and break Quinn's heart?"

"He doesn't love me. Not like Guy. I want to be with Guy. He's here to take me away with him, Jake."

"Should I go get Quinn? Do you want to say good-bye?"

"No. Just let us leave now. We have a taxi waiting."

Jake couldn't believe Guy would let Davi tell him there was a taxi waiting. Guy was definitely not thinking straight. Jake hoped it would be to their advantage. Jake spoke quietly into his cell phone. His men confirmed that they had the driver and the taxi under control.

Jake called out to Davi, "Davi, are you ready to come out now? No one's here to see you. They're all dancing. Can you hear the music?"

"Yes. I don't want to see anyone, Jake."

"I have to see you, Davi. I have to be the one to tell Quinn you left him. Let me see you off, okay?"

There was the longest silence.

Davi called out, "Okay. Give us a minute."

"Get out of here, Quinn," Jake said quickly. "He can't see you. Trust me. She'll be okay."

"I can't. She's my wife. I should be the one saving her."

"Pride won't keep you warm at night if he kills her, man. Davi trusts me. You said you did too." Jake stared Quinn down. It was the hardest thing he'd ever had to do to his friend.

"Keep her safe, Jake," his friend warned as he backed into a doorway out of view.

The door opened. Davi walked out with Guy holding her hand. She looked composed. Quinn could see her from where he stood. His heart ached for her. It was all he could do not to run to her.

"Davi," Jake said calmly. "You're missing a great party."

"We'll have one in Paris." She smiled weakly.

"Guy, you've got some pair of balls to come here and claim Davi. Congratulations." Jake smiled as he approached them.

"Thank you. I have a taxi waiting. We have to go." Guy turned to walk away with Davi.

"Hold on," Jake called out. "Let me shake your hand. Thanks for taking Davi. She wasn't going to fit in. Quinn will be disappointed that she left, but he'll get over her. He's got women on the sidelines waiting for him."

Jake held out his hand to Guy. Davi could see the other hand making a fist. As Guy reached out to shake his offered hand, Jake let fly with a left hook. Guy was on the floor instantly. Jake scooped Davi up in his arms and moved her out of the way. Security guards were on top of Guy in an instant, dragging him out the door.

Quinn raced to Davi and pulled her in tight. "Are you all right? What the hell is going on?"

Davi looked up at Quinn. "I guess you're not the only one who believes in love at first sight. His wedding present for me was to take me away to Paris without you."

"Did he hurt you?" Quinn's hands ran over her body as his eyes looked for evidence of her being harmed.

"No. It wasn't like that. I'm okay. Please, let's not give this man any more of our time. I want to go back to the party. It's our wedding." Davi's voice was strong and even.

"What?" Quinn asked, amazed at her composure.

"You heard me. He didn't hurt me. We just talked. I want to forget about it for now. I want to get back to my party. Will you join me, love?" She held out her hand to him.

"Are you sure?" Quinn searched her face, trying to confirm that she was fine.

"Dance with me, Quinn. I'm sure it's my turn by now."

"I'll look after Guy," Jake said.

Quinn and Davi walked back to their table. Davi had a long drink of water. Quinn reached for the first glass he could find. He downed a glass of chocolate milk and choked.

Davi's girls came running up to her and pleaded with her, "Come on, Mom, our song is coming up. You have to dance with us. Everyone's dancing."

Cat took Davi by the hand and pulled her to the dance floor to join Davi's sisters and nieces. Abba's "Dancing Queen" played. They all knew the steps to this song. Davi's family took over the dance floor.

Quinn stood back and watched. Luke joined him.

"What the hell happened, Luke? She's practically abducted, and now she's on the floor dancing to 'Dancing Queen.'"

"She's your wife. You should know how she thinks."

"I will never know how that woman thinks. Do you think she's crazy?"

"Is she crazy to marry you? Yes. Is she crazy-crazy? No. She's tough, Quinn. She can handle anything. You've got a real rock there."

Quinn marveled at the way Davi moved on the floor, her lack of inhibition, her carefree laugh, and endless smile. He found he loved her more, and he didn't think that was possible.

Luke put his arm around Quinn's shoulders and offered him a scotch. "This will be your first. I think you need it."

Quinn took the drink and then chuckled. "I just choked down a glass of chocolate milk to calm my nerves."

"Did it work?"

"It must have. Maybe that's why she's calm all the time. I'll have to start drinking that brown stuff now too." Quinn pointed at Davi with his drink. "How can she do that? Walk away from almost being kidnapped and dance to Abba?" He couldn't let it go.

"Settle man. Everything's okay. Jake got Guy and Davi wasn't hurt. Life is good. Finish your drink."

"I need to talk to Jake. I need to know what's going on."

"He's busy. He'll talk to you when he's free. He and Davi were amazing. Did you hear them? It was as though they had a script. They knew exactly what to say to get Guy to come out of there."

"That's why I need to talk to Jake. How did they know what to say to each other? Why didn't they tell me about Guy wanting Davi? How the hell did he get in here?"

"They'll tell you when they can, but right now, your wife doesn't want to think about it. She's the one who went through the whole ordeal, and she's willing to put it on hold so that her guests can still party. Can you do the same? Maybe you should have another drink, get a buzz, and enjoy yourself."

Quinn raked his hand through his hair and took a deep breath. "I haven't missed the drinking tonight. Not one drop. There's my scotch right there, Luke." He nodded toward Davi. "I just have to look at her and I'm buzzed. I had the same feeling when I first saw her on the plane."

"You've got it bad, man."

"Tell me about it. I rarely have nightmares, but when I do, it's of her saying no to me on the plane and I have no plan B. I don't have a comeback, a second chance to win her. I'm stuck on this plane, and I watch her walk away. I wake up in a sweat. It really terrifies me."

"Well, those nightmares should be over now." Luke stopped himself from mentioning Guy. "She said yes and you are hers just like you wanted."

Quinn gulped down his drink. "Amen to that, Luke." He handed Luke his empty glass. "I've got another dance partner to find before I get to be with my wife. I'll see you around."

Quinn looked around him and found Maggie talking with some friends. Quinn swooped in behind her and carried her off to the dance floor.

"You are mine, my Irish beauty, at least for the next song." He smiled at her.

"What took you so long?"

"There's been a line up. Didn't you notice? This Hollywood heartthrob has been in big demand tonight."

"I noticed. You and Davi will be here all night if you have to dance with every female here."

"I don't mind and I know that she won't either. She told me that I have obligations to perform tonight. It's part of my job as husband and star."

"Just make sure that husband takes priority over star."

"You're very protective of her, aren't you?"

"Yes."

"Thank you for that. I promise that my role as husband will be my only priority. Being a movie star will be a sideline from now on."

"Don't promise that. I don't want you to disappoint your fans around the world. Be who you are. Just remember Davi."

"How could I forget her?" Quinn looked down at Maggie and smiled. "I meant it when I thanked you for all you've done. Davi thinks the world of you. I do too."

"We've been friends for a very long time." Maggie smiled at Quinn. "Thank you."

"For what?"

"All of this, my dress and my jewelry. You didn't have to do it."

"But I wanted to and you are most welcome. I owe you, Maggie, more than you'll ever know. You're the one who told Davi she'd find love. You opened her eyes to the possibility. If it weren't for your card reading, I don't know if she would have let me in."

Maggie shook her head. "Davi doesn't believe in the cards! She only humors me by letting me read them for her."

"She gives you more credit than she lets on. Believe me. Your forecast gave her the push she needed to go out with me. I am eternally grateful."

Davi looked for a place to sit. She saw Sue and Jake waving to her and joined them.

Jake got up from his seat and hugged her. "How are you, lovely lady?"

"I'm fine, thank you. I will never kid you again about being our protector, Jake. You have my utmost respect." She kissed him on the cheek.

Davi sat down beside Sue and squeezed her hand. "Thanks for wanting to kill Jake. It was the only way I could call for help. I knew he'd know what to do."

"I was so scared for you. Why didn't you tell us Guy was coming for you?"

"We didn't know he was. Honest. Jake and I thought we had him all figured out."

"Well, you didn't, and you almost gave me a heart attack. And poor Quinn, I don't know what went through his head." Sue's face reddened as she thought about it.

"He'll be fine," Jake assured her. "His pride was bruised, but he'll understand once he hears the whole story."

"His pride?" Sue asked angrily. "He could have lost Davi and I could have lost you and all he was concerned about was his pride?"

"Sue," Davi said firmly. "What man wouldn't want to jump in and save his wife? I don't care if it was love or pride that made him want to rescue me. Quinn didn't need to prove anything to me. All that mattered was that he was man enough to let Jake have control of the situation."

Davi, Quinn, Jake, and Sue were the last to leave the reception. Quinn wore his Stetson, one hand clutched a stuffed cow and the other held Davi's hand. They sat in the lounge. Quinn refused to leave.

"I don't want to take this home with me. Tell me what the hell went on tonight." His gaze moved from Jake to Davi.

Davi's eyes held Quinn's gaze as she spoke. She told Quinn about the phone call and the wedding present. She explained how she and Jake thought that Guy wouldn't try for Davi again, but they were wrong.

"I didn't want you to worry about this. I'm sorry for not telling you, but I wasn't going to let him take control of our wedding day. Jake and I had him figured out. Guy didn't want to hurt me. He just wanted me to be with him. He wasn't thinking clearly. If he had, he would have had a real gun."

"What?" Quinn asked his voice loud and filled with anger. "He had a gun?"

"It was a toy gun," Davi explained. "He was going to use it to threaten Jake if he had to."

"Did you know it was a toy gun?" Quinn glared at Davi. God help him, he should be relieved that she wasn't harmed, but she was taking this all too lightly.

Davi shook her head. "I didn't know what he had. He kept his hands behind his back. When he opened the door, I realized he was holding a toy gun. He'd forgotten to take the dollar store sticker off it."

"The man's a fucking idiot," Quinn cursed.

"No, you're my one and only idiot, Quinn." Davi smiled at him, trying to calm him. "Guy is sick. He's obsessed with me, and no matter what I tried he wouldn't leave me alone. He thought if I could love you, I could love him."

"You're my obsession. I didn't give up on you either."

"I guess that's the weird and wonderful part about love at first sight. If the person you fall in love with loves you back, it's a blessing. But if the person doesn't love you back . . ."

"You become Guy Tremblant," Sue finished for her.

"Thanks for giving me up so easily, Jake. I hope you didn't mean it." Davi poked him.

"We're never giving you up, Davi. Please don't think about anything I said to Guy. My men called. Guy's been put on a plane to Paris. His wife's been called. She assures us that she'll be there to meet him at the airport."

"You think she can set him straight?" Davi asked.

"She's his bankroll," Quinn answered. "Without her family's money, he wouldn't have the backing to get a movie made in Hollywood. *Untitled* is his first big-budget film since the scandal."

"You mean all that stuff about him is true?" Sue asked incredulous. "And you still agreed to work with him?"

"He's a brilliant director," Quinn answered defensively.

"But a lousy human being who tried to kidnap your wife," Sue chastised him.

"Easy there, Sue," Jake said as he pulled Sue toward him. "It's over now. We have our happy ending."

"Can we go now? It's been a long day." Davi squeezed Quinn's hand.

"I want to say something. Then that's it. No more talk about Guy and what happened here tonight. Ever. Jake, thanks for keeping a cool head and getting Davi away from Guy. I was so afraid of losing Davi that I would have done anything to rescue her. I could have made things worse. And you, wife of mine"—Quinn looked into her eyes, amazed at the strength he saw in them—"you really are a rock. I don't know how you kept your cool through this whole ordeal. From now on, you tell me everything. No more secrets." Quinn didn't wait for Davi's answer. "Let's go home."

Jake and Sue joined them in the backseat of the limo. It was a shorter ride than Davi had expected.

"We're at your stop," Jake announced.

The limo driver opened the door, and Davi looked out. They were at the farm.

"Aren't we supposed to be going to the hotel?" she asked, puzzled.

"Change in plan, love. I'll explain it to you later."

Quinn exited the limo and then offered Davi his hand.

Quinn poked his head back into the limo. "Good night, you two. Enjoy the backseat. We'll see you tomorrow," he said before he closed the door.

Davi waited for him at the kitchen door. The door was unlocked, and the lights were on. Quinn scooped Davi up and carried her over the threshold. Davi laughed with delight. Quinn put her down and then kissed her.

"I want our first night to be here, in our home. I hope you don't mind."

"I don't mind at all. I'm rather relieved not to spend a night in a hotel bed. Where are the kids?"

"They came by and picked up their stuff. They're spending the night at the hotel."

"You think of everything, don't you?" Davi smiled at Quinn, her eyes melting into his.

"I try."

"So what do we do now, if you've thought of everything?"

"If my best friends did as they promised, everything is waiting for us upstairs. We only have to lock the door, turn off the lights, and go to our bedroom."

Quinn locked the kitchen door and turned off the kitchen lights. He picked Davi up and carried her to their bedroom. Davi switched off the lights as they passed the switches. Their bedroom door was open. Soft music played from Davi's stereo. A bottle of scotch, an ice bucket with a carton of chocolate milk, and two glasses were on the bedside table. A flickering glow came from the bathroom.

"Candles?" Davi asked.

"For the Jacuzzi. I thought we could have a soak before bed."

"Mmm, sounds lovely. I'll need help with my dress first."

"May I?"

Quinn turned Davi around and undid her buttons. Davi kicked off her shoes and stepped out of her dress and then laid it across one of her armchairs. She turned to face Quinn. His blue eyes were sparkling. He wanted her as much as she wanted him.

"Kiss me," she breathed.

Quinn kissed her softly. Davi responded with urgency. Her arms wrapped around his neck and pulled him in tight. Quinn gave her the kiss she wanted and then pulled back.

"Not yet, woman, be patient."

"I want you now, please." She had never had to beg before.

He smiled at her. "I want to enjoy you. I want to pleasure you. I don't want this night to end." His eyes were now on fire. "Wait here, wife."

He walked off to the bathroom. Davi could hear water running into the Jacuzzi. She sat down on the side of the bed. She poured a shot of scotch for Quinn and a glass of chocolate milk for herself. Quinn walked back to the bed. Davi marveled at his naked body.

"You definitely deserve the name Big."

"I'm glad you think so." Quinn took the offered scotch. "To us," he toasted as he touched his glass to hers.

"To us. Forever."

"Come, our bath awaits us."

Davi brought her drink with her. The lights were dimmed. The tub was surrounded with candles. Quinn dropped to one knee to undress Davi. With careful deliberation, he undid her garters and rolled her stockings down her legs. Davi lifted each foot for him to remove the stocking. Then he undid the garter belt and placed it on the floor. Quinn stood and unclasped Davi's bra. He tossed the bra on top of the garter belt. Davi took off her panties.

Quinn offered his hand to Davi to help her into the tub. Once she had sat down, Quinn got in behind her. He pulled her close and kept one arm around her waist while the other held on to his drink. Davi's head rested on his chest as the hot water bubbled around them.

"Remind me to thank Maggie for making me put this in."

"We'll owe her our thanks for years to come. Think she'll forget?"

"Maggie never forgets. She'll only mention it when it's to her advantage."

"Tell me your top three moments of today," Quinn asked her, his lips brushing the top of her head.

"Top three? I don't know. Let me think." Davi closed her eyes. "When you sang to me in the church, when we were declared husband and wife and I knew you were mine forever, and when I sang to you. What were yours?"

"Being married to you, when you sang to me—no one has ever done that to me before—and every time I danced with you."

"I loved the dancing. I'm glad you could fit me in."

"It was close there. I thought I'd have a few unhappy fans or family members before the night was through. I didn't realize there is a pecking order in your family. I was told in no uncertain terms with whom to dance and when."

Davi laughed. "There is no pecking order, Quinn. They were having fun with you."

"Can I trust no one in your family? Will I always be played for the fool?"

"No. You'll catch on. You've got time."

They sat in silence for a moment. Davi could feel Quinn tense as he held her.

"Don't," she said. "Don't think about Guy ever again. Don't give him that power over you."

"How did you know I was thinking about him?"

"I could tell." Davi turned to face Quinn. "Don't think you did anything wrong either. It's not your fault for what that man is." Davi could see the look of regret on Quinn's face. "And don't think I was wishing you to come in and rescue me. You did the right thing. You let Jake do his job. Everything worked out fine."

"You didn't want me to be your hero?" A weak smile crossed his face.

"Do you need to be my hero?" she asked him, a wicked smile forming on her face.

"Yes," he murmured. "I need to be your hero."

"Okay then. When I need a hero, you can fight Ryan Reynolds for me, but don't beat him up too much. He has such a pretty face."

Quinn finished the last of his scotch with one gulp and then placed the emptied glass on the ledge of the tub. Quinn pulled Davi in to him.

"So you think I'd win?" His eyes were on fire.

"It would be close, but you'd win." She smiled wickedly.

Davi knelt between Quinn's legs and took hold of his shaft with both hands under the water. Davi gently played with him as she moved into Quinn to kiss him. Quinn's mouth was ready for her. As her lips touched his, his mouth opened and his tongue greeted hers. His right arm came down her back and put pressure on her lower spine as his left hand cradled the back of her head and kept her close to him. Davi increased her pressure on Quinn's cock. She could feel it growing under her grasp. She wanted it.

The tingling sensation started to run its course through Davi's body as Quinn gave her her kiss. She knew she would come if she continued kissing him like this, but it was time to give to Quinn. Davi pulled her mouth away from Quinn and smiled.

"Let's try something," she cooed as she straddled Quinn's legs so that he could enter her.

Quinn needed no coaching as he guided himself into her.

Davi gasped as he entered her. "I feel you."

"You're supposed to feel me, love." Quinn smiled.

"No. I mean I really feel you, all of you. It's as though you're three times as big as you usually are. It's incredible."

"Do you want me to stop?"

"Don't you dare!"

"Just checking." He winked.

Quinn placed his hands on Davi's hips and guided their movement as she rode him. The hot water still bubbled around them. Davi smiled as she thought of the men's karaoke performance.

She started to sing to Quinn, "Save a horse . . ."

"You've got it, woman. Ride me."

Davi leaned back slightly to change the pressure point. She took a sharp breath when she found it. Quinn noticed it right away. Davi's legs gripped him harder. Quinn didn't move. He let Davi take control and ride him. Her head fell back, and her mouth opened slightly. Quinn held back on his own pleasure, concerned with giving Davi hers. As she neared her climax, Quinn gave in to his own excitement. He concentrated on Davis breasts as they teased him, not far from his mouth. Davi's nipples were hard, and they pointed at Quinn, taunting him. Quinn looked down to where he and Davi joined. The bubbling water hid it. He could get a glimpse of Davi's navel as she rode him. He longed to see the small mound of hair that hid her sex, her hidden treasure. Quinn's mind focused on that treasure, the one that gave him so much pleasure. His thrusts increased, he had to see it. Davi quivered on top of him, moaning as she climaxed. Her moans filled his head. He had to have that too.

He wanted all of her. Quinn gave into the pleasure, thrusting until he thought he'd explode.

Quinn moaned from deep inside his throat. His climax took its time. It felt like his seed was dribbling from him instead of exploding into her. Davi stayed with him, waiting for him to open his eyes, to let her know that he was spent. Quinn pulled Davi in close and hugged her. His face buried in her breasts, taking deep breaths.

"Hey, stud. Are you okay?" she teased.

Quinn shook his head no. "Woman, I wanted you again before I even finished the first time. It was doing my head in."

"What am I going to do with you?" Davi kissed the top of his head.

"Love me, woman. Love me again."

Chapter 36

♥

Sunday was exhausting. Davi and Quinn's family and friends gathered at the farmhouse to celebrate the Canadian Thanksgiving. It was a full day of celebration with too much food, too much alcohol, and too much storytelling about the bride and groom.

That night, Quinn and Davi said good-bye to the family and flew to New York with Quinn's entourage.

"So what are your plans while you're in New York, Davi?" Sue asked excitedly as they rode in the backseat of the limo from the airport. "Sightseeing? Shopping? Lots of sex?"

"Lots of sex," Quinn answered for her.

Davi poked him in the side. "I don't know what Quinn's schedule is. He hasn't enlightened me."

"I'll be at the studio from eight until five every day, unless something comes up. We'll be going through the readings and get fitted for wardrobe. I'll be home by six every night, and at that time, we will go out and do something exciting to celebrate our honeymoon."

"Do you have it all planned?" Sue asked him.

"Not at all, but I'll think of something. We are definitely having lots of honeymoon sex." He winked at Sue. Quinn remembered an unfinished conversation at the wedding. "Speaking of plans, what's the story with Chas and Taylor and the girls? No one told me they were invited to our wedding."

"The girls invited them. They didn't have dates for the wedding, and they knew these fellows could dance. They've been talking with each other on the phone and e-mailing all the time since they played flag football. I didn't think you'd mind since they are your friends and you introduced them to the girls. I don't know if they'll see them again. We'll have to wait and see."

"Is Quinn jealous?" Sue teased.

"No. I'm being protective. The girls are my responsibility now."

Davi sighed as she played with her wedding band. "They're adults. Let them enjoy themselves and get a taste of Hollywood men."

"Get a taste of Hollywood men?" Quinn asked as he shifted in his seat.

Sue tried desperately to stifle a laugh as she stayed out of the conversation.

"It's an acquired taste, love. They may not want to have it on the menu every day."

Quinn sat up straight, glaring at Davi. "What the hell does that mean?"

"You know what I mean—the gorgeous looks, the wicked smile, the come-on eyes, and the great sex. It's not for everyone." Davi winked at him.

Quinn's glare softened immediately into a smile as he said, "You are wicked."

Davi woke to kisses, tender kisses on her lips and forehead. She slowly opened her eyes. Quinn sat on the bed beside her. He was shirtless and wearing jeans. His face was its usual sexy gorgeous, with blue eyes sparkling, tousled hair, and a smile that touched his eyes.

"Good morning, wife."

"Good morning, husband. What time is it?"

"It's time for breakfast in bed. Sit up and we'll get started."

Davi sat up and folded the covers down by her waist, exposing her bare breasts. Quinn placed the tray on her lap and then dropped his pants and got into bed beside her. He had cooked scrambled eggs, made toast, and a pot of herbal tea.

"I didn't hear you get up. What time is it?"

"It's seven thirty. I got up half an hour ago. I couldn't sleep."

"We didn't get to sleep until after three. I should be sleeping, Quinn." Davi took a bite of her eggs.

"I thought you'd want to come to the studio with me today."

"Today I plan to stay in bed as long as possible. I have important sleep to catch up on, so. I'll take a rain check on the studio thingy."

"You're making me jealous."

"No, I'm not. You find it very difficult to stay in bed. It's a necessity for you—getting your sleep and getting laid, but lounging around in bed all day is not your thing. That's why you're going to work."

"Woman, your language." Quinn chuckled.

Davi waved her left hand in front of him and smiled. "Now that I have the ring, I don't have to watch what I say."

"You are wicked."

"Only for you, love."

Quinn leaned over and kissed her. Davi cupped his face with her hands and held him to her. He licked the jam off her lips.

Davi smiled. "Later," she said.

"Later," he replied.

Quinn returned to the suite promptly at 6:00 p.m. He walked immediately to the bedroom. The bed was unmade, and he could hear Davi singing in the bathroom.

"Hello, wife, busy day?" he asked her as he leaned against the doorframe.

"Hello, husband," Davi murmured seductively from the Jacuzzi. "I slept all day. It's my first time ever, and I feel so good."

"What about dinner? Would you like to go out?"

"Can we stay in? I just got in here, and I'd like to stay. You could join me." She gave him her best come-on smile as she flicked water at him.

Quinn didn't hesitate. He picked up the bathroom phone and called room service.

"I like how you hunt, Quinn Thomas," Davi teased. "What else can you do that I'd like?"

"Everything," he answered lustfully as he stripped off his clothes and then eased himself into the tub and faced her.

"This feels good," he sighed as the hot water washed over him.

"It does, doesn't it?" Davi caressed him with her foot.

Quinn caught her foot and kissed the toes, murmuring, "I love red nail polish. It's so sexy."

"I gather that." She offered Quinn her other foot. "This one is lonely."

Quinn smiled and took the offering. He kissed the toes and then sucked on them.

Davi laughed at the sensation. His hands moved up her legs. He grabbed hold of them and pulled Davi toward him. Davi gasped as she slid down the tub. Quinn caught her before she fell back into the water.

"Smooth move, stud. You've done that one before."

"You'll never know, wife."

Davi wrapped her arms around his neck. "I don't mind. I've got the ring."

Quinn laughed. "Is that going to be your answer to everything?"

"Do you mind? You know I don't mean what it implies. It's just a joke."

"I love it. It's so wicked and so not you. I'm the one who wanted the ring. It should be my line, but it is totally yours."

Quinn nuzzled Davi's neck. He loved her scent.

"I missed you today. It took everything I had to not leave the studio and come back here to you. I hope you're well rested, wife. No more time off for you."

Room service knocked at the door.

"Later." He winked at her before he got out of the tub.

Quinn wrapped his robe around him and left to answer the door. He returned a few minutes later.

"Your dinner has arrived, Mrs. Thomas. Would you care to join me?" Quinn offered his hand to her.

Davi stood up and took Quinn's hand. She stepped out of the tub and put her robe on. A table for two was set in the living room. The lights had been dimmed and candles lit. Quinn held out a chair for Davi. She sat down and waited for him to join her.

Their plates were covered with silver domes. Quinn removed the one over Davi's plate first and then removed his. Davi smiled. She was looking at a burger and onion rings. Quinn had a burger and fries.

"This hotel makes one of the best burgers in town. I hope you like it."

"You gave me onion rings."

"You prefer them to fries. I did my homework."

"And my burger?"

"Well done, relish and mustard, no ketchup. I left out the onion, but I had them add their secret sauce. It's my favorite. Give it a try."

Davi took a bite. It was delicious. She nodded her head in approval as she chewed her food.

Quinn poured her a glass of water.

"There's a bit of after bite to it. Be prepared."

Davi's eyes bugged out. "What sort of after bite?" Davi hated surprises with her food. As soon as she asked the question, her tongue started to tingle. Davi waited. The tingle turned to a bit of a burn and then subsided. "Is that it? Or does it kick in later?"

"No that's it. It's just a tingle. I thought you could handle it."

"I love tingles," she said as she took a bite of her onion rings.

Quinn devoured his burger and fries. The man had quite the appetite. Davi cut her burger in half and offered it to him.

"Are you sure?"

"You need it more than I do, and I know half will fill me. Have some of my onion rings too."

Davi finished her burger, sat back in her chair, and watched Quinn eat. He was thoroughly enjoying his meal. She smiled at him.

"What?"

"I'm thinking of the simple things in life that make you happy—a good burger, scotch, and red toenails."

Davi lifted her legs and draped them over Quinn's thigh. Quinn picked up her feet and kissed every red toe.

"What are the really good things in life that make me happy?"

"A really good single malt scotch, sex, and me."

"Not in that order, though," he said as he reached for an onion ring.

"Of course not."

Quinn's hand stroked Davi's legs.

"So if I were to guess for you, the simple things in life that make you happy are your family, your friends, and the Ladies. The really good things that make you happy are your family, your friends, and me. They are almost the same except that I outrank the cows on the really-good list."

"Good guess. How do you know the lists are almost the same?"

"Because you don't categorize the things you love. Everything and everyone is valued equally. Everything is important to you just as everyone in your life is important to you. I'm lucky that you value me just above your cows."

"It's close, so don't take it too lightly."

"I won't."

Supper was definitely over. Davi slid her legs off Quinn's lap and then straddled him, facing him. She let her robe fall open, fully exposing her nakedness to him.

"It's time," she said softly.

"Time for what?" he asked as he gazed into her eyes.

"It's time to show me why you beat out the cows."

Chapter 37

♥

Davi spent the next day shopping with Sue. Sue's kids spent the day with the grandparents on Tuesdays, making it ideal for a girls-only get-together of shopping, pampering, and gossip.

Sue found Davi the perfect dress for New York's nightlife. It was a Dolce&Gabbana strapless minidress in shimmering black. Davi thought it was over the top, but Sue convinced her it was the right dress for her.

"Trust me, Davi. You have the legs and the body for this dress. You'll thank me for making you buy this. Of course, you'll need the shoes now and the accessories. We'll get them next."

When they finally sat down to have lunch, Sue had a look at Davi's nails and sighed. "You'll have to get a manicure before we head back. You can't go out with your nails looking like that. Why don't you get your hair styled while you're at it? Have some professional get you all dolled up for your date tonight."

"What date tonight?" Davi asked, confused.

"I know nothing. Quinn and Jake know I can't keep a secret. You're going out, and Quinn wants you looking fabulous."

"And why didn't he tell me about this?"

"Don't shoot the messenger, Davi. I'm sure you'll love the surprise, whatever it is."

Davi sang along with the music blaring from the stereo. She was happy and felt truly blessed. She had spent a wonderful day shopping with Sue, and now she was getting ready to go out on a date with her husband, her incredibly gorgeous, sexy, and talented husband.

Davi could feel the heat in her cheeks as she remembered their lovemaking from last night. She thought she'd done everything in her twenty-five years with Ross, but Quinn proved her wrong repeatedly. Quinn deserved an Oscar for Best Bedroom Performance.

Davi took her time getting ready. She had a quick bath so that she wouldn't mess up her hair. Her makeup had been applied at the salon. She only needed to touch up her lipstick. She massaged her favorite body lotion into her skin and then dabbed on her perfume. As she dressed, Davi enjoyed the feeling of rolling the silk stockings up her legs and the feel of the satin and lace against her skin. Davi stepped into her new dress. She loved how it sparkled in the light. Her new shoes were beautiful. The four-inch heels were a bit much, but the shoe was comfortable. Davi could walk in them with confidence, especially if Quinn were by her side. Davi put on her earrings. They were dangly and funky. They went well with her dress. She needed no other jewelry. She bought an evening bag and filled it with her necessities. She was ready.

The door opened and Quinn walked in. Davi stood up to greet him.

"Wow, wife, you look fantastic." Quinn pulled Davi close and kissed her.

"I have absolutely no idea where I am going tonight. I hope Sue had the good sense to dress me appropriately or else I will never forgive her."

"You are perfect. Trust me."

"I've done a lot of that today. It may wear out soon."

"Just another couple of hours and you'll know everything."

Quinn released her and walked into the bedroom, undressing as he walked.

Davi sat in one of the armchairs and watched him strip. She loved looking at his body. Quinn winked at her, acknowledging the attention.

"Did you have a good day at the studio today, dear?" she asked playfully.

"Yes, I did, wife. We have a new secretary who is trying to seduce me, and I think the producers are giving me a promotion. I've been given a parking spot closer to the front door, so I know I'm on my way up the Hollywood ladder."

Quinn made his way into the bathroom. Davi followed him and stood in the doorway.

She ignored the comment about the secretary, confident that nothing would come of it. "Ooh, a new parking spot. I'm so excited for you."

"Why don't we go out and celebrate?" Quinn called out from the shower.

"Where would you like to go for dinner?"

"I've already made the reservations. We have a table waiting for us."

Quinn came out of the shower. Davi offered him a towel. He rubbed his hair with it and then dried his body. He let the towel fall to the floor. Quinn could see Davi watching him from her reflection in the mirror. He winked at her and then started to shave.

Davi went back and sat in the bedroom, waiting for Quinn. What he wore tonight might give her a hint as to where they were going. She crossed her fingers for luck.

"Why are you crossing your fingers?

"I'm hoping that I can tell what we're doing when you get dressed. I'm hoping for a clue."

Quinn laughed. "Good luck."

Quinn put on his boxer briefs and black socks. He looked at Davi after each item was put on, teasing her. Quinn reached into his closet. He pulled out a white tuxedo shirt.

"Oh, oh," breathed Davi.

"What does a tuxedo tell you?" he teased as he put on the pants.

"It's a big deal."

"What kind of big deal?" he asked as he expertly put the studs in his shirt.

"A red-carpet big deal?" she gasped.

"What kind of red-carpet big deal?" he asked as he tied his bow tie.

"I have absolutely no idea."

"So it will still be a surprise then. Good."

The limo stopped. Jake got out and opened the door for them.

"Will you tell me where we are, Quinn? Shouldn't I know where I am before I get out of this limo? You're throwing me to the wolves here."

"You're right I should tell you. We're at the Vanity Fair Charity Gala. It raises money for various children's charities across the world. I was asked to make a presentation. This is a relatively small red-carpet event. I thought it would be perfect for your first time."

"So what do we do here?"

"We smile, we walk around and look at pictures, talk to people, get our picture taken a lot, and we help raise money for charity."

"I can do that."

"I know you can. Now let's go."

Davi stepped out of the limo with Quinn right behind her. The crowd went ballistic. Davi and Quinn waved and smiled. Jake gave Quinn the signal to call him when he was ready to leave, and then he drove off.

Quinn put his arm around Davi's waist and led her up the red carpet. It was long and led to an entrance further down the street. Davi looked ahead and could see where celebrities were stopping for interviews and picture taking. She took a deep breath to steady her nerves.

"I can understand why you thought you'd surprise me with this. I don't know if I would have agreed to do this so soon."

"You'll be fine. Just smile. You look stunning."

Quinn stopped at the first reporter. "Quinn and Davina Thomas, congratulations on your recent marriage."

"Thank you."

"This is your first time on the red carpet, Davina. How does it feel?"

"It feels good. I'm very happy to be here this evening."

"You two make quite the attractive couple."

"Thank you."

Quinn moved on with Davi.

"You're doing great, wife," he whispered in her ear.

"Quinn, over here! Quinn!" photographers were calling out to him to stop for a picture.

Quinn stopped and posed with Davi. He was such a natural. Davi only hoped she came across looking the same way. She smiled as she held on tight to Quinn. It took them twenty minutes to reach the entrance to the gala. Davi thought they would never get there. They were greeted immediately by a representative for *Vanity Fair*.

"Good evening, I'm so happy that you were able to make this on such short notice. We're so excited about our exhibition, and I hope you are too. The photographs are amazing. Come with me, please."

Quinn and Davi didn't have a chance to respond. Quinn was relieved. If Davi wondered what the rep was talking about, she didn't let on.

"Would you like to see the photographs now or wait until the unveiling?"

"Oh, we can wait along with everyone else," Davi offered. She looked at Quinn. "Is that okay with you, or do you want to see them now?"

"We can wait. That's fine." Quinn looked around. "Will you show us to our table?"

"Right this way."

Quinn and Davi followed her. Quinn had a tighter grip on Davi. She could feel his tension.

"When do they unveil the photographs? Will it be soon?" Davi asked.

"After dinner."

Quinn ordered a double scotch and a sparkling water for Davi from a waiter once they were seated. They were the first to sit at their table. Davi looked at the name cards. She didn't recognize anyone's name except for the photographer who had taken their wedding photos.

"This is part of the surprise too," Davi said softly.

"Yes." Quinn kept his voice low to match hers.

"You know what the photographs are, don't you?" she asked, her voice still soft.

"Yes." Quinn took a gulp of his scotch.

"Have you seen them?"

"Yes."

"Are they good?"

"They're fantastic."

"Then that's all I need to know. I'm looking forward to my surprise."

Davi sipped her sparkling water and looked around. She was hoping to see some celebrities.

"Do you know anyone here?"

"I know a lot of people here, Davi." Quinn looked at her, bemused.

"Good. Then introduce me to them." Davi stood up and offered Quinn her hand. "Show them whose ring you wear." She winked at him.

Quinn took her hand as he stood up. He kissed it softly.

"You are a constant amazement to me, love."

"Why is that?"

"Because you know me all too well, and I have so much to learn about you." His blue eyes sparkled as he spoke to her.

"Read my Web site," she teased.

"It lies. I read your age."

Quinn didn't wait for Davi to respond. He took her hand and led her through a crowd of people.

"Quinn Thomas," a well-known television host called out. "Congratulations! Introduce me to your lovely bride!"

Quinn stopped and made the introductions, "John, this is my wife, Davi. Davi this is John."

"Nice to meet you, John." Davi smiled at him politely as she extended her hand. "I'm a big fan of yours."

"Thanks," John beamed at her as he shook her hand. "It's a pleasure to meet you. I've read your book. I hope this guy doesn't wreck it by acting in the movie."

"Me too." Quinn laughed as he pulled Davi in close to his side. "It could mean the end of my marriage."

Davi could feel the tension leave Quinn's body the more he introduced her to his friends and colleagues. This is what he'd been looking forward to, wanting everyone to meet his wife, the woman to whom he belonged. She hoped she could remember everyone's name, but she knew that it would be impossible. She met photographers, journalists, screenwriters, and directors. There were other actors there as well, from television, cinema, and the theater. This evening was a magnet for all of the big names in the business.

Davi was thrilled when recognized as the author of *Second Harvest*. Many had enjoyed her book and asked whether she had plans to write another book. When Davi told them that she had recently completed the first draft of her second book, they wished her success with it.

"Is Quinn in your next book?" a female journalist asked her. "That would make the New York Times Best Sellers list for sure."

Davi smiled appreciatively. "No, he's not in it, but the ending came to me after I met him. I have to thank him for that."

"So is Quinn your muse?" she pressed.

"If anyone's a muse, it's Davi," Quinn answered for her. "She's my inspiration. She keeps me focused."

"How so?"

"Just knowing that she's near me keeps me settled," Quinn explained. "Knowing that I am hers makes the world a better place for me."

"You didn't have to say that," Davi whispered in Quinn's ear as they walked away.

"Why not? It's the truth," Quinn said with sincerity.

"They're going to think I've got some kind of spell on you or something."

"You do have a spell on me, woman. Don't ever take it away." Quinn kissed her.

Since their arrival, Guy Tremblant had been watching Davi from the sidelines. He followed her as Quinn moved her through the crowd, introducing her to various people. Davi's beauty captivated him. He hadn't forgotten how stunning she looked a few days ago at that sham of a wedding. If it weren't for that lying head of security, Guy and Davina would be in Paris now, making love. Guy was determined to make Davina Stuart his no matter what. She belonged with him.

Guy downed his fourth shot of vodka, his liquid courage. He now felt emboldened to talk to Davi. When she saw him, she would run into his arms. She would beg him to take her away with him. She would spit on Quinn and leave him to look like the fool he was. Guy made his way through the crowd.

"Davina Stuart," he whispered in her ear. "They couldn't make me stay away. I've come for you."

Davi felt the blood leave her face. Her stomach instantly cramped. *Stay calm, Davi. He won't hurt you.* She forced herself to turn around.

"Guy, how are you?" Davi held out her hand to be polite. "I thought you were in Paris with your wife."

Guy took her hand and kissed it. "I am much better now that I have seen you. I was in Paris for a very short time, and I consider myself no longer married. I am free to marry you, my love." He held on tight to Davi's hand.

Davi could smell the alcohol on his breath. Guy's hands were cold and clammy. She looked for Quinn. His back was to her as he was engaged in a conversation with a famous director. She could only think of one thing to do. She had to break it off with Guy; maybe that would work if he actually thought they were in a relationship.

"Guy, I can't. Things have changed. I've changed my mind. I'm staying with Quinn. I'm sorry. We can't do this any longer. It's over."

"It's not over," he said with indignation. "I won't let it be over. You're mine!"

Davi turned to leave. Guy grabbed her arm and yanked her around to face him again. Davi could hear people gasp around her as they witnessed the scene. Quinn was beside her in an instant, with his arm around her as his free hand took hold of Guy's wrist.

"Let go of my wife, Guy," he said through gritted teeth. Quinn towered over Guy. His eyes were fixed on him. "It's over. Whatever sick ideas you have about my wife, they end now. Do you hear me? No more."

Guy looked angry as he let go of Davi's arm. He didn't apologize. He walked away.

"Are you okay?"

"I'm fine. I told him it was over. I thought he might believe me if I actually broke it off with him. I don't know if he'll ever give up. He really is sick."

"I won't let you out of my sight for the rest of the evening. If he comes near you again, I don't know if I'll be able to control myself. He's asking for a fight. Come on, let's get back to our table. It's about to start."

Quinn ordered two sparkling waters from a passing waiter. He couldn't afford to have another scotch, not with Guy stalking Davi. Quinn kept close to Davi when they returned to their table. The other guests were sitting down as well. Davi smiled at them. They had been with her earlier and had witnessed Guy's performance. No one mentioned it. Instead, they kept the conversation light as they enjoyed their meal.

"Ladies and gentlemen, it is my pleasure to welcome you here tonight."

Davi didn't hear another word. She tried, but her scene with Guy weighed heavily on her. She knew it wouldn't be the last time she heard from him. The man gave her the chills. Davi shook her head and tried to focus on the speaker.

"It gives me great pleasure to showcase some of our outstanding photographs taken in the last year. We were honored when Quinn Thomas asked us to take the photographs of his wedding this past week. Most of these pictures will be shown here tonight and in our next issue of *Vanity Fair*. Some of our photographs will be offered in our live auction. Quinn Thomas has generously offered to match the highest bid received from tonight's auction. As you know, proceeds will be going to our children's charities. Thank you, Quinn."

There was a round of applause. Davi smiled at Quinn. He hadn't told her he was doing this.

"Quinn and Davina, please come and join me now. Please honor us by officially opening our showcase of photographs."

Quinn stood and offered his hand to Davi. They walked up to the podium. Davi accepted the offered ceremonial scissors and then cut the ribbon as Quinn declared the showcase open. Everyone applauded. Davi and Quinn posed for pictures.

"I'd like to see the photographs. May we go in now?"

"We're expected to be the first in. Allow me, madam," Quinn said as he offered his arm to Davi.

They walked into the gallery. Davi tried to be polite and look at every photograph displayed. Each one was remarkable. She was particularly impressed with the black-and-white photos. She came across two of Quinn. They were taken during an interview for his last movie, *Untitled*.

"Nice pictures of you, Quinn. You've got that lonely look in your eyes. The photographer captured it very well. I'm so glad you don't have that look anymore."

"You're not the only one, wife. I have you to thank for that."

Davi and Quinn turned a corner and came across their wedding photos.

Davi gasped. "Oh my, look at us! Look at the Ladies! Everyone looks beautiful!"

Tears came to her eyes. She had never expected the pictures to come out looking so breathtaking. Most of them were in black and white. The cows were a perfect backdrop to the wedding party. There were quite a few photos of Quinn and Davi. Davi ran her finger over them.

"You're gorgeous, Quinn. Look at you. Your eyes—you can see them sparkle in the picture. There's no touch-up there."

"Look at your eyes too. We both look so much in love. The camera captured it perfectly."

Davi smiled as she looked at her face in the picture. She never saw herself looking so beautiful before. It didn't register that it was actually her. They moved on to the next picture. It was of her children. She touched it lovingly.

"My babies," she whispered.

Davi took her time looking at every picture.

"These are amazing. When do we get to see the rest?"

"They've made up an album for us and a disc with all of the photos. We'll be taking them home with us tonight."

Fellow guests gave them compliments. "Great pictures, Quinn and Davi."

"Very unusual but beautiful. How did you get the cows to pose like that?"

Davi laughed. Quinn led her back to their table.

"I could go home now," she sighed. "My day has been perfect."

"I'm glad you think so, but we have to stick around for the auction. It should be happening soon."

Quinn looked around the room, searching for Guy. If he knew what was best for him, Guy would be long gone from here. Quinn could feel the tension in his shoulders.

"Ladies and gentlemen, we'll now have our auction. Please remember that all proceeds go toward children's charities. Our first item is . . ."

The auction seemed to go on forever. Davi didn't see anything of interest. She wanted to take her wedding album and go home. Quinn took part in the bidding but didn't buy anything. He did his best to get the bids up.

Finally, the last item was up for auction. It was a framed black-and-white photograph of Quinn. It had been taken when Quinn was first making his way in Hollywood. *Vanity Fair* had featured him as an up-and-coming star. Davi noticed that his build was slightly smaller, although he was still just as gorgeous. His eyes sizzled at the camera. His tousled hair had that sexy bed-head look. The picture called out to her. *Come and get me.*

"Do you have a copy of it?" she asked immediately.

"I've never seen that picture before."

"I want it," Davi said with complete seriousness.

"Bid on it then. I'll cover you." He winked at her.

"Thanks for the offer, but I have my own money." She turned away from him and settled in her chair, ready for serious bidding.

Davi opened the bid at one thousand dollars. It was low compared to bids on the other photos. Her bid was instantly over bid by one thousand dollars. Another bidder entered the bidding war, raising the bid to three thousand dollars. Davi had a hard time getting her bid in. Seven women were bidding against her. The bids were increasing drastically.

"I really want that picture," she muttered. "It's for my eyes only." Davi yelled out to the auctioneer, "Fifteen thousand."

The room went quiet.

The auctioneer called out, "I hear fifteen thousand, going once, twice . . ."

"Twenty thousand," another female voice called out.

There were loud gasps throughout the room. People turned to stare at Davi.

"I'm not backing down. You're mine," Davi said under her breath. She called out, "Twenty-five thousand."

"I hear twenty-five thousand, going once, twice—sold for twenty-five thousand dollars."

Davi turned and faced Quinn. "You're mine," she said with obvious satisfaction.

"You just cost me fifty thousand dollars, wife."

"Correction, husband, that photo is mine, and I will be paying for it all by myself. You just pay what you owe."

"Davi, you—"

"We'll talk about it later. I'm going to pay for my picture."

Quinn smiled at her. He wasn't going to win this one. Davi got up to get her picture. She handed over her credit card to pay for it. The picture was wrapped for her, and the young aide handed her the wedding album that was also wrapped for easy carrying. Davi was a happy woman. She had her photograph of her sexy husband, and she had her wedding pictures.

Quinn waited for her. His smile touched his eyes.

"Where are you planning to hang me?" he teased "Over our bed?"

"In my office, if you must know. I want those eyes burning for me and only me."

"They do," he murmured as he pulled her close to him.

"Don't you have a check to write?"

"They'll send me the bill. Come on, let's get you home."

Quinn kept his arm around Davi as they walked out of the building. Most of the guests were leaving. It was getting late. Quinn spotted Jake, who was parked further down the street than Quinn had hoped. He didn't like to be too exposed with fans still gathered in large groups on both sides of the street.

"Damn," he grumbled.

"What is it?"

"I don't like being out in the open like this. Come on, Davi, we'll walk."

"We can wait."

"No, it's too cold. Let's go."

Davi kept tight against Quinn's side. The air was cold, and her wrap wasn't offering much protection. She could hear Quinn's name being called out. He waved with his free hand, but he wasn't about to stop.

Quinn and Davi were six feet from the limo. Jake stood with the back door open, watching them approach. Davi saw Jake's expression turn to alarm as he stepped toward them.

"Quinn!" Jake yelled.

Quinn pushed Davi forward into Jake's arms. Jake caught her and shoved her into the limo. He slammed the door and was gone. Davi sat up in the backseat, her heart racing, panic working its way through her. She could hear yelling and people screaming.

"Quinn," she moaned as she felt like she had been punched in the stomach.

Davi opened the door and got out. She saw Jake kneeling on the sidewalk with Quinn's head in his hands, his body motionless. Davi screamed Quinn's name as she ran to him.

Davi fell to her knees beside Quinn. "What happened?" she cried out, her hands touching Quinn's chest.

No one answered her.

"Jake! What happened?" she yelled at him.

"It was Guy. He came out of nowhere. Quinn didn't have a chance."

Davi could hear the blaring of sirens. She put her fingers on Quinn's neck.

"He has a pulse, Jake, and he's breathing."

Quinn's eyes were closed. Davi touched his face.

"Quinn, love, it's Davi. Stay with us, love. You hear me? Stay with us."

Davi didn't see or hear the commotion behind them. A group of people had Guy Tremblant pinned to the sidewalk. A bloodied pipe lay beside him.

"You'll never have her!" he shouted. "Never!"

The ambulance arrived first. Jake had to let go of Quinn to let the paramedics work on him. It was then that Davi saw Jake covered in Quinn's blood. Davi stood up.

"Jake you're covered in blood. What happened?"

Jake didn't take his eyes off Quinn when he answered, "That maniac came out of nowhere. He had something in his hand, and he just kept swinging at Quinn. He got two or three good blows in before he was tackled. I should have been there."

Davi put her hands to her mouth, forcing back the bile rising from her stomach. She started to shake. Jake pulled her in tight to his side to comfort her.

"He'll be fine," Jake lied.

Davi hadn't seen the back of Quinn's head or felt his broken skull in her hands. Jake pulled out his cell phone. He called his men to tell them of the situation and to have security waiting at the hospital for Quinn and Davi. Next, he phoned Luke. Luke had to know about this.

"Luke, it's Jake. Get out here now, man. It's Quinn. Tremblant attacked him." There was a brief silence. "Davi's with me. We'll talk later. Just get out here."

Davi watched the paramedics as they put Quinn on the stretcher and then into the ambulance.

"I'm his wife. I'm coming with you," she called out to them. No one was going to keep her away from Quinn.

One paramedic offered his hand to Davi and helped her into the back of the ambulance. Davi sat still on the bench while Quinn was readied for transport. She couldn't touch Quinn; he had IV's stuck into him, an oxygen mask covering his mouth, and a monitor hooked up to his chest. In an instant, the doors closed and the ambulance was on its way to the hospital.

The ride to the hospital seemed to take forever. Once they arrived at the hospital, Davi stayed by Quinn's side as long as she could. He was rushed into an examination room, and she was told to wait outside. Davi stood helpless out in the hallway, rubbing at her wedding band as she prayed for Quinn. Through the glass in the door, she could see doctors and nurses working on him. Quinn was hooked up to more monitors. More doctors raced into the room.

Davi forced herself not to panic. *He needs me,* she told herself. *You can lose it later. You've done that before.* Davi shook her head. *Focus.*

Davi didn't know how much time she had spent out in the hallway when Jake came barreling into the emergency ward. His face was flushed, his suit covered in blood.

"Jake."

"How is he? Any word?" he asked as he hugged her.

"Nothing. They haven't stopped working on him since he got here. So many doctors have gone in there, Jake." Davi started to cry.

"He's a fighter, Davi, and stubborn. He'll be okay," he said as he hugged her tighter.

"I can't lose him, Jake. I just can't."

A doctor came out of the room and approached them. "Are you with Quinn Thomas?"

"Yes," Davi wiped her tears away with the back of her hand. "I'm his wife."

"Mr. Thomas has had severe blows to the head. He has a depressed skull fracture, meaning he has broken skull imbedded in his brain . . ."

Davi didn't hear anything else. She stared at the doctor's lips, but she didn't hear one word. Her ears buzzed, her hands tingled, and her legs weakened. She held on tighter to Jake.

"Davi?" Jake's voice pulled her back.

Davi looked up at Jake.

"Did you hear the doctor? Quinn needs surgery to save his life."

"Do it," she responded without hesitation.

"Would you like to be with him before we head out? He's unconscious. You can talk to him. He may hear you."

The doctor led them to Quinn. Davi could hear Jake exhale loudly as he saw Quinn's swollen face and the tubes running into him. Davi took Quinn's only free hand and held it. She kissed him softly on his mouth.

"It's Davi, Quinn. I'm here for you, and Jake's here too. The doctors are doing their best for you. You need to be strong. I'll be here waiting for you. I won't leave you." Davi squeezed his hand. She felt a tingle.

"It's time. We have to move him now," the nurse advised them.

Davi kissed Quinn once more and then let go of his hand.

"I can show you up to the waiting area. You'll be more comfortable up there."

Jake and Davi took the elevator with the nurse. Davi didn't pay attention to the floor they were on or where they were going. They were shown to a quiet room with comfortable furniture and soft lighting. Davi and Jake sat down.

"There's a kitchen off to the side where you can make yourself something to drink if you want. If you need anything, there's a buzzer by the door."

"Thank you." Davi smiled at her. She appreciated her kindness.

"I should call Sue. I'll be right back."

Jake walked out into the hallway, leaving Davi alone. Davi closed her eyes and prayed for Quinn.

"Sue's coming. She's bringing you a change of clothes and a clean shirt for me," Jake said when he returned. He crumpled into a chair. "I'm so sorry. I thought we got rid of Tremblant. I thought he was gone for good."

"Guy was at the fund-raiser. He wanted to take me away with him, and he caused a scene. I knew he'd be back, but I never thought he'd do something like this." Davi looked at Jake, focusing on the bloodstains on his shirt and jacket. There was so much blood.

"When you asked if I was going to have him killed, I should have done that. This is my fault."

"Don't," Davi said as she held up her hand to make him stop. "I can't deal with this right now."

"I should have had more security for him. If I'd only been six feet closer—"

"Shut up, Jake!" she yelled at him, her voice filled with anger. Davi got up out of her seat and stood over him. Her body shook as she stared down at him. "I don't need to hear how guilty you feel, and I don't need to hear the what-ifs. Quinn is fighting for his life right now, and I'm fighting to keep myself together. If you can't be supportive and be positive, then get the hell out of this room and leave me alone."

Jake couldn't look away from Davi. Her eyes flashed fire as she chastised him.

"I'm sorry," he said softly. "You have my support. Tell me what you want me to do."

Instantly, Davi burst into tears. "Hold me, Jake, and tell me he won't die."

"Here you are!" Sue cried out as she rushed into the room.

Jake and Davi both startled at the sound of her voice. Jake got out of his chair to greet his wife. Davi stayed sitting on the sofa.

"How is Quinn? Has there been any news?"

"He's still in surgery," Davi answered. "I don't know when we'll hear anything."

Sue sat down beside her. "He'll come out of this. Quinn's a fighter."

"Thanks," Davi said softly as she tried to hold back the tears.

"I brought you a change of clothes, Davi. I thought you'd feel better in something more comfortable, and I threw in some things I knew you'd want. Go change. There's a washroom over there. Go."

"Thanks," she said as she clutched the bag to her chest.

When Davi walked off to the washroom, Sue stood up to hug Jake.

"Careful, I'm covered in blood. Let me change my shirt."

Jake took off his bloodstained jacket and shirt and tossed them into a nearby garbage can. He then put on the clean shirt Sue had brought for him. Jake led Sue to the sofa, and they sat down together.

"How are you? I've been so worried."

"I'm fine. He didn't touch me. That maniac didn't even fight fair. He attacked Quinn from behind while Quinn was holding Davi."

"How is Quinn, really?"

"I think it's bad, but I'm not a doctor, so I don't know for sure."

"How is Davi holding up?"

"Barely," Jake answered sadly. "She's barely holding on."

Davi took her time changing. She wanted alone time, and she knew that Jake and Sue needed time together. Davi stripped off her clothing and threw it all in the garbage. She wanted no reminder of tonight's events. Davi looked in the bag. Sue had thought of everything Davi would need, including a T-shirt of Quinn's and toiletries.

Jake and Sue anxiously awaited Davi's return. Davi smiled weakly at them as she walked into the room.

"Thanks, Sue. You thought of everything. I think you've been through this before."

"Something happened to Jake a long time ago, and I was stuck in the hospital with none of my own things. I knew you'd want these. I have the feeling you'll be camping out here."

"I'm going to check on security. I'll be back soon." Jake left before anyone could reply.

"He did everything he could, Sue. He's blaming himself for what happened."

"It's his job, Davi. He's supposed to be on top of things, and to have this happen to his best friend is torture. If you crossed the street and got hit by a car, Jake would blame himself even if you were far away in another city. He's the protector. You know that."

"Of course I do."

"How are you feeling? Nothing happened to you?"

"No. I'm fine."

Davi went silent. She could hear talking outside the door. The voices got louder, and then they were gone. Jake walked in a few minutes later, his face beet red.

"A reporter made it through security. Someone was just about to come in here when I stopped him. I have a man outside this door now and one outside of the surgery entrance. They'll keep trying all night."

Davi cried out, "You can't let them get to Quinn, Jake. If they get to me, I can deal with it, but they can't take a picture of Quinn. They just can't."

Sue wrapped her arm around Davi to comfort her.

Jake knelt down in front of them. He took Davi's hand in his.

"No one will get to Quinn. I promise."

Davi dozed on the sofa while she waited for news on Quinn. It was another two hours before the doctor made it to them.

Sue took Davi's hand and squeezed it.

"We fixed the skull fracture. There was no swelling to the brain, and that is very good news. He had more bleeding than we thought so it took us longer to get that stopped. We'll be monitoring Mr. Thomas for blood clots. It's standard procedure after surgery of this type. We've run an EEG, and there doesn't appear to be any brain damage. He is a very lucky man."

"When can we see him?" Davi asked eagerly.

"He's being moved to ICU right now. You can see him there. He'll be unconscious for quite a while."

"Thank you, doctor."

"You're welcome. I'll check on your husband later."

Davi hugged Jake and Sue and cried, "He's going to be all right."

Jake led the way to the ICU. It was a frightening ward. Every patient was hooked up to monitors and intravenous machines. The constant beeping and buzzing of machines was disquieting. The ward nurse led the trio to Quinn's room.

"You can't stay for long. Mrs. Thomas can, but that's it. He'll look worse than he actually is. The swelling and bruising will go away, and the hair will grow back."

"Hair?" asked Jake.

"They had to shave his head. They don't normally do it, but in this case, they had to shave it all off to get to the break."

Davi walked to Quinn's bedside. She gazed at his swollen face. She kissed his lips softly.

"Hey, Quinn," she whispered in his ear, "your woman is here. I'm with you, love. You're going to be okay. The doctor said the surgery went well. Rest then come back to me, love. I'll be here."

Davi ran her fingers over Quinn's shaved head. The tape from the bandage at the back of his head stopped where his sideburns would have been.

"He's even gorgeous without his hair," she said softly. "I knew he would be."

Sue and Jake came up on the other side of his bed. Sue looked like she was about to cry. Jake put his arm around her to comfort her.

"Hey, Quinn, it's Jake. We're here for you, man, and we're looking after your lady for you. You get your rest and feel better soon." He touched Quinn's hand and gave it a squeeze.

"Are you okay for a while, Davi? I think I should take Sue home. It's getting late. I'll be back soon."

"I'll be fine, you two. Sue brought everything I need. Go home, both of you. Get some sleep, Jake. I won't be going anywhere."

Sue could barely look at Davi without crying. Davi hugged her and thanked her for her help. She needed Sue to go before she herself started to cry. Davi watched them walk down the corridor. She turned back to Quinn. She pulled up a chair and sat beside his bed. Davi held his hand, the one without the wires and intravenous. She could feel his warmth, but most of all, she could feel a tingle. He would be fine. He just had to be.

Chapter 38

♥

Davi woke with a start. Alarms were going off around her. Something was happening to Quinn. Davi jumped out of her chair as the nursing staff rushed in. She backed out of their way.

"He's having a seizure," she heard one of them call out.

Davi watched as her husband's body convulsed on the bed. The nurses held him down while another administered something into his intravenous. His seizure stopped. All but one of the nurses left. She turned to Davi.

"He had a seizure. Sometimes it happens after surgery such as his. We caught it in time. The doctor will be here later to check on your husband. Can I get you anything?"

"No thanks. Will he be okay?"

"Let's wait for the doctor to check him out."

The nurse left the room. Davi pulled her chair back up to Quinn's bed. She took his hand and squeezed it. She could feel his tingle though it was weaker than before.

"Quinn, love, you need to be strong. You have to come back to us. I'm here. I'll do all I can, but you have to do your part too. Come back to us."

She listened to the sounds of Quinn's machines and watched the intravenous bag drip into the line. She tried to ignore the catheter running out from under his sheet into a urine bag. She watched as his chest rose with every breath. Davi stared at his eyes for the longest time, willing them to open. If only she could see that sparkle one more time.

"Remember when you told me about how you make memories?" she asked Quinn as though he would answer her. "I did that on our wedding day. I remember everything about that day. I remember walking down the aisle and seeing everyone watching me and smiling at me. The strange part was that I didn't care that they were there. All I wanted was to walk down that aisle to you. You were waiting for me, and I had to be with you."

Davi got up out of her chair. She leaned into Quinn and kissed him.

"I'm right here with you, Quinn, and I'm going to think about us. You've given me great memories, and I'm expecting a lot more. You promised me forever, and I'm going to hold you to it. Think of your memories too. Think of everything wonderful that has happened, and maybe by the time you're finished, it will be time to wake up and make new ones."

Sometime in the morning, the doctor came in to see Quinn. "I hear Mr. Thomas had a slight seizure."

"Please call him Quinn, doctor."

He looked at Quinn's EEG as he spoke to Davi. "The seizure he had can be normal for his type of injury. His brain waves are normal. Everything looks fine. The nurses have been checking on him every hour, and his vitals are good. He should be waking up sometime today. I'll be back later to check on him."

Davi breathed a sigh of relief. She squeezed Quinn's hand.

"Wake up soon, Quinn. Please wake up soon."

Davi startled as she heard a slight rap on the doorframe. She turned to see two police officers. She stood up to greet them.

"Hello, I'm Davi Thomas. You're here about Quinn's attack?"

"Yes, we're sorry about the delay. We were busy with Mr. Tremblant for most of the night. We came here as soon as we could."

Davi looked around. There weren't any chairs for them to sit in.

"I'm sorry, I don't want to leave Quinn, and there doesn't seem to be any chairs. Do you mind standing?"

"Not at all."

The police officers introduced themselves and gave Davi their card.

"Would you mind telling us about last night?"

Davi sat down in her chair. She told them about her first encounter with Guy Tremblant, his wedding gift, and his appearance at their wedding. Then she told them about last night. Davi was tired but not too tired that she didn't notice that she was asked the same questions, but in different ways. The police needed to verify that she was telling the truth.

"So the first time you met Guy Tremblant was at the wrap-up party?"

"Yes. I had seen him once or twice during the filming of the movie, but I had never met him."

"And you said it was love at first sight for him?"

Davi shuddered at the thought. "That's what he told me."

"Did you believe him?"

"I believed he was drunk."

"You gave him no encouragement?"

Davi ran her hands through her hair as the realization hit her. "Yes, I did." Davi stood up quickly from her chair. "Oh, god, what did I do?"

"Tell us, Mrs. Thomas. Tell us everything."

Davi looked down at Quinn and then back at the police officers.

"It was at the wrap-up party. Guy wanted me to leave the party with him. I thought I could blow him off without causing a scene."

"What did you say to him?"

"I told him that if he could come up with a better pickup line than Quinn's, I would leave with him. I thought when I told him he'd lost, he would leave me alone."

"And did he?"

Davi pointed to Quinn and cried, "Would he be there if Guy had left me alone? We deluded ourselves thinking that he would give up. The man's obsessed." Davi fell down into her chair.

The police officers put their notepads away. "Thank you, Mrs. Thomas, for your help."

"What happens now?" Davi asked as she wiped at her tears.

"We'll do our best to keep Guy Tremblant locked up."

As they were leaving, Luke arrived. He gave Davi a hug and then went to have a look at his friend. Davi could hear Luke hold back a sob. She put her arms around him.

"Thanks for coming."

"I could kill that maniac."

"That won't help Quinn. Let the police look after it."

"You look exhausted. Did you get any sleep here?"

Luke looked around at all of the noisy machines.

"I got a bit of sleep. I'll be fine. He had a seizure, but the doctor says it's all part of the post-op recovery. He'll be back to check on Quinn later today."

"Have you had anything to eat?"

"I'm starved, but I don't want to leave Quinn alone. He should have company."

"I'll stay with him while you go look after yourself. I won't leave him."

"Talk to him, Luke. I don't know if he can hear us, but I know I feel better when I talk to him. You may find that too."

Davi took her purse and left Luke with Quinn. As she walked down the corridor, she realized that she needed to phone her kids. Davi went to the waiting room and pulled out her phone. She turned it on. It was filled with text messages and voice mail. She scanned through them quickly. They were all from her family. Davi phoned home. Her call was answered on the first ring.

"Mom!"

"Hi. I'm sorry I didn't call earlier."

"How's Quinn, Mom. How are you?"

"He came through surgery okay. He should wake up sometime today. I'm okay. Just a bit tired."

"What happened, Mom? The news said he was attacked by his director."

"Yes, it's true. I don't want to talk about it right now. Just focus your thoughts on Quinn. Can you do that for me?"

"Of course we can. Do you want us to come out?"

"No. Let's wait until the weekend. There's nothing you can do. I'll let you know about Quinn as soon as I know anything. I need to get back to him. I love you. I'll talk to you soon."

"We love you, Mom. Give Quinn our love."

"I will. Bye."

Davi ended the call and turned her phone off. She didn't want to talk to anyone else. She headed into the nearest washroom to freshen up. She looked a mess. She did her best to clean her face and fix her hair. She stared at her reflection. *Be strong, Davi. Be strong for him.*

The hospital cafeteria was quiet. It was still early for the morning crowd. Davi was relieved. Maybe she could slip through without being recognized. She took out a tray. Chocolate milk, coffee, scrambled eggs, and sausage made up her breakfast. She paid for her food and found a quiet corner to sit in. Davi didn't taste her food. It didn't matter to her. She knew she needed to keep up her energy. The next few days were bound to be hard.

Davi felt herself being pulled to Quinn. She had to leave. She left her unfinished food on the table and hurried back to the ICU.

The ride in the elevator was torture. Did it have to stop at every floor? *Damn it!* Davi cursed as the elevator stopped for the third time.

Finally, the elevator doors opened for her floor. There was a commotion going on outside of Quinn's room.

"No," Davi moaned as though she had been punched in the stomach.

Davi hurried to the room. Luke stood outside the door, visibly upset.

"Luke! What happened?"

"Quinn started having a seizure. He was going wild, Davi. They're trying to stop it, but they can't. It's serious."

Davi ran into Quinn's room. She pushed her way past a nurse and grabbed Quinn's hand, squeezing it tight.

She leaned into his ear and spoke to him, "Quinn, it's Davi. I'm here. Be strong, Quinn. Stay with me, Quinn, stay with me. I won't leave you. Be strong." Davi said the words over and over.

Quinn's seizure lasted for minutes. Davi cried silently as the nurses tried to stop it. Through it all, she held on to his hand, desperate to keep their connection and terrified of losing him.

The seizure stopped. Davi could feel Quinn squeeze her hand. She felt a tingle.

"That's good, Quinn. Rest now. I won't leave you. I won't let you go." She kissed his forehead.

The nurses made sure Quinn was stable before they left the room.

Davi fell into her chair, still holding Quinn's hand.

"How is he?" Luke asked from the doorway.

"He's quiet now." Davi's voice was calm and soothing. "You can come in now."

"The seizures . . ." Luke's voice broke.

"I don't know, Luke. We'll have to wait for the doctor to let us know."

Davi gazed at Quinn and gave him a weak smile. "You won't let me leave you, will you, husband? That's okay. I'll be here for you." Davi didn't take her eyes off Quinn. "How do you like his new look, Luke? He looks quite handsome bald."

Luke walked up behind Davi and looked down on Quinn. "You're right. He could handle that look. But I prefer him with hair."

"So do I. He looks younger bald, and I don't need a younger-looking husband. I bet I look ancient next to him now."

"Don't even think about it, Davi. You're beautiful and always will be." Luke looked around the room. "I'm going to find a chair. I'll keep you company."

Davi didn't let go of Quinn's hand. She would squeeze it every few minutes to let Quinn know she was with him. She talked in a normal voice so that he could hear her.

"I've got something for you, Davi. We should have done this earlier, but we didn't have the time. Quinn wanted to marry you so fast that he had me jump through hoops for you."

"What kind of hoops? I don't understand."

"Quinn doesn't want any claim to your assets. He told me in no uncertain terms, 'Make sure Davi knows I don't want her spread.'"

Davi smiled. "He remembered."

"I've brought his power of attorney for you and his living will."

"Luke, I don't want to talk about this now. He's not dead, and he's not dying."

"We have to talk about this, Davi," Luke's voice was soft, but insistent.

"Not now, Luke." Davi's eyes flashed at him. "He's going to come through this. There's no plan B."

"You're stubborn, just like him."

"I don't know if it's stubborn. I just know what matters and what doesn't. I only focus on the positive. You should do that too."

An easy silence enveloped them.

A thought came to her and she smiled. "I do like his Bug, though," she said in a teasing voice. "I have no use for his Porsche, but his Bug would make me happy." She felt Quinn squeeze her hand. "He heard that." She smiled.

"How do you know? He's still unconscious."

"I felt it. That's all I can tell you."

Quinn's doctor came by to check on him. He looked at Quinn's chart, and then he examined Quinn's bandaged head, his pupils, and checked his heartbeat.

"He seems to be doing well. The seizures he experienced were mild and did no harm to him. If he hasn't woken up by the end of today, we'll try to stimulate him tomorrow to get him to waken." The doctor smiled at Davi. "How are you holding up?"

"I'm fine. I'm tired, but I can handle it."

"Make sure you get some rest and try to eat. We don't want to be admitting you as a patient as well."

"I'll try," she promised.

Luke got up to stretch. "I need to make some phone calls. Will you be okay by yourself?"

"Of course I will. Can you give me a minute? I'll use the washroom before you leave. I've had too much coffee."

"Go. Take your time."

Davi leaned into Quinn. "Quinn, love, I have to leave you for a few minutes. Luke is here with you. Be good until I get back." Davi let go of his hand. She looked at Luke. "He likes to have his hand held, but you don't have to do it if you don't want to. I'll be right back."

Luke sat beside Quinn. He didn't feel comfortable holding Quinn's hand, but he did talk to him. Luke decided to talk about the latest Patriots football game.

Davi walked down the hall to the washroom. It felt good to stretch her legs. She wasn't gone for long. When she returned to Quinn's room, she could tell that something wasn't right. Luke stood beside Quinn's bed as a nurse worked on the other side, trying to calm Quinn. His eyes were closed. He was unconscious, but he was obviously distressed.

"What happened?" Davi's hand was on Quinn's immediately.

"I don't know. I was talking to him and all of a sudden, he started thrashing around. It's like he's having a nightmare."

Davi talked to Quinn, "Easy, Quinn, it's Davi. I'm here. Nothing's going to hurt you. I'm here, Quinn."

The thrashing continued. Davi didn't know what to do for him. Tears streaked down her face.

"What scares him, Luke? Does he tell you about his nightmares? He only tells me about his good dreams." Davi searched Luke's face for an answer.

Luke raked his fingers through his hair, trying desperately to remember what Quinn had told him. "Something about you saying no to him on the plane and he has no plan B. Does that make any sense?"

Davi turned to Quinn. "Quinn, I'm giving you a second chance. Talk to me, Quinn. I'm sitting with you on the plane, and I'm not going to leave. You have a plan B, and it's going to work. You're talking to me, and I'm falling in love with you. Talk to me, Quinn." Her free hand caressed his face. "We're holding hands. We're together, Quinn, forever. I'm not going anywhere."

Quinn settled. Sweat covered his brow. The nurse dabbed at it with a towel.

"He's resting now."

Davi sat down in the chair thoroughly exhausted and sighed. "I hope he wakes up soon. I don't know how much more of this I can take."

"How do you know what to say to him?" Luke asked as he sat down across from her. "You seem to settle him."

"I know how he thinks. I know what he dreams about—at least I know his good dreams. Quinn told me that he goes through his memories of me when we're apart. Maybe he's got to go through all of them before he can wake up."

"Why would he have to do that?"

"Maybe it's part of the healing process. I don't know, but I have to be here for him. I have to let him know that I'm here waiting for him when he wakes up."

"But the bad dream he just had . . ."

"I wasn't holding his hand. He lost me. I have to be with him. I can't let go of him until he's back with us." Davi turned her gaze to Quinn.

"You can't be serious."

"What's going on here?" Jake asked from the doorway.

Jake hadn't slept while he was away. His clothes may have been fresh, but his day-old stubble and his tired eyes gave him away.

"Davi needs to go back to the hotel and get some sleep."

Luke stood up to shake Jake's hand.

"What's the problem? Is it Quinn?" Jake looked over Luke's shoulder at Quinn.

"Of course it's Quinn. She says he won't come back to us unless she holds his hand. She's got some sort of magic that will work wonders on him."

Jake didn't laugh. "I know she's got magic, Luke, I've seen it in action, so don't go blowing it off. Although Davi would never say she's got magic. What's the real story here, lovely lady?"

Davi looked up at Jake. He could see that she was tired, but her eyes were full of fire.

"I can feel Quinn. He's not ready to wake up yet, but he's aware of me being here. If I let go of his hand, he has a seizure or a nightmare. I can't break the connection with him. I have to stay here."

"Isn't that just insane?" Luke stared at Davi in disbelief.

"She's right. You haven't seen them together, Luke. I have. They have a connection I've never seen before. If Davi says she's staying here holding on to Quinn's hand, then I'm going to do my best to support her. You can give her your support or leave. It's your decision."

"It doesn't make any sense to me."

"It doesn't have to make sense. Do it for Quinn. He's the only one that matters."

Luke looked at Quinn lying in the bed, helpless.

"What do you need me to do?"

Chapter 39

♥

Quinn's new room was bigger and brighter with a wider bed. It was more like a hotel suite than a hospital room. Luke's power of persuasion and a sizable donation to the children's ward got Davi what she needed for Quinn.

Quinn had a final once-over by the nurses in the ICU. His vitals were normal. Quinn's doctor approved the move. Quinn would receive the same care in his new room as he would in the ICU. The only difference was that the doctor took Quinn off his pain meds and sedatives. It was time to wake him up.

Jake and Davi stayed with Quinn while he was moved to the new room. Luke was busy issuing a press release on Quinn's status. He thought Davi and Jake were wrong about Quinn, but he wasn't going to fight them. He would wait and see what happened with his best friend.

"So what's your plan now, lovely lady? You had Luke jump through hoops for you to get Quinn settled in here. Do we just sit and wait for him to wake up?"

"That's all we can do, Jake. At least we can all be more comfortable, and we can keep Quinn comfortable. We have a television, a couch to relax on, comfortable chairs for visitors, and our own washroom. Everything is good."

Jake left Davi to bring back food from the cafeteria.

Davi sat on the bed beside Quinn. She caressed his face and then kissed his forehead.

"I wonder what you're remembering now."

Quinn's hand gripped hers tighter. She could feel him tensing.

"The doctor cut back on your meds. He wants you to wake up. Breathe through it. Think of something good so you can't feel the pain. I don't know where you are in your memories. Maybe we can go through one together. Remember when I sent you the text that I was pregnant? You couldn't wait to see me, and you flew to Toronto to surprise me. You met my kids, and they fell in love with you instantly, at least the girls did. You met the Ladies." Davi moved in closer to whisper in his ear, "Remember how we made love that night? You were amazing in bed. Not that you aren't always, but the way you loved me . . . You were so loving and tender. Do you remember how I cried in your arms afterward? Do you remember kissing my tears away?"

Davi wiped away her tears with her free hand. She lay down beside Quinn on the side without the tubes and wires. Her hand stroked his shaved head as she snuggled into his side. She could feel his warmth. He was comfortable.

"Come back to me soon, husband. Wipe my tears away." Davi closed her eyes and fell asleep.

Jake came back to the room, carrying a tray filled with food for the two of them. He almost dropped it as he saw Quinn put his finger over his mouth, warning him to be quiet. Davi was fast asleep against Quinn with his arm wrapped around her. Jake put the tray down on the table and went to Quinn.

"Hey, Quinn, welcome back," he said quietly.

"Hey, Jake, I guess something happened to me. I don't remember a thing, and my head is killing me."

Jake pulled up a chair close to Quinn. He nodded to Davi. "She hasn't left your side, man. Every time she does, even if it's to go to the bathroom, you have a bad reaction. She's been keeping you quiet."

"I know. I felt her and I could hear her talking to me, but I didn't know why. She said something about my Beetle and flying on a plane. Tell me what happened."

"What's the last thing you remember? Do you remember going to the Vanity Fair Charity Gala?"

"I remember going there with Davi. I remember walking along the red carpet, but I don't remember anything past that. It's just blank."

"Tremblant was there too. He made a scene with Davi and you stepped in. There wasn't a fight or anything. Apparently, it was over as quickly as it started. Anyway, as you were leaving, he came up from behind you and hit you with a pipe. I didn't see him until it was too late. I called to you, but all you had time for was to push Davi to me, and then you were down. You had to have some surgery to repair your broken skull. I'm sorry I didn't get to you in time to stop him."

"Davi's okay, though? She wasn't hurt?"

Quinn looked down on his sleeping wife.

"She's fine."

"Then that's all that matters. You did your best, Jake."

"No, I didn't. I should have taken that maniac to the police the night of your wedding. He shouldn't have been let go."

"Is he in jail now?"

"Yes."

"Then it's okay. Focus on the positive, Jake."

Jake shook his head. "Davi said the same thing."

"She's always right."

"She has been so far."

Quinn tried to move his head so that he could kiss the top of Davi's head, but he couldn't. His head throbbed.

"How long have I been out?"

"You were attacked two days ago. They've been trying to get you to wake up. Davi was awake when I left her, so I think she's only been out for twenty minutes or so."

"You'd better call the nurse and let her know I'm awake. I'd love something to eat if I can."

"Sure thing," Jake got up and walked out of the room. He didn't want to use the intercom and waken Davi.

An excited nurse walked in with Jake.

"Mr. Thomas, it's good to have you awake. How are you feeling?"

Quinn smiled his Hollywood smile. "My head hurts a bit, but I'm really hungry. Do you think I can have something to eat?"

"Let me check you out first. I see your wife is sleeping. I'll try not to wake her. She's been up with you since you got here. You've been keeping her busy."

"So I've been told. I knew she was here. She told me not to wake up until I was ready. I ran out of dreams. It was time to wake up."

"You seem to be fine. I'll notify the doctor that you're conscious. He'll want to check you over before I can give you anything to eat. Would you like a drink? You can have some water or juice while you wait."

"Water will be fine. Thanks."

Davi stirred. She felt Quinn's arm around her. It wasn't there before. She snuggled in closer to his chest. This felt good. She brought her hand up to caress Quinn's face. As she touched his lips, she felt him kiss her. Davi opened her eyes and sat up.

"Hey there, husband." She smiled at him sleepily. "Welcome back."

"Hey, wife, it's good to be back."

Davi kissed him softly on the lips and then asked, "How are you feeling? They've taken you off your pain meds."

"I have a headache, but it's nothing I can't handle. Thanks for looking after me."

"You're welcome. Does the nurse know you're awake?"

"She's been and gone, Davi. She'll get the doctor to check Quinn out before he can have something to eat. I brought something for you if you want it."

Jake got up from his chair and moved toward the untouched tray.

"Maybe I should wait until Quinn can eat. It doesn't seem fair . . ."

"Eat, woman. I can manage, and Jack's depending on you to look after yourself. Go ahead. I'll be fine."

"Jack? Who's Jack?"

"The baby. Quinn had a dream that the baby is a boy named Jack, so we call the baby Jack. Boy or girl, the baby will be called Jack."

"It figures. Why give your daughter a normal name now?" Jake chuckled.

"Exactly," Davi agreed.

"You look tired," Quinn said as he gazed into Davi's eyes.

"And you look gorgeous. Bald suits you, but I want you to grow your hair back, husband."

Quinn reached up to touch his head. His face showed his shock as he felt his shaved head.

"Show me."

"You look great, Quinn." Davi smiled. "Trust me."

Quinn held out his hand to Jake, ignoring Davi's assurance. "Jake?"

Jake looked in the bedside table and found a mirror. He handed it to Quinn.

"Nice," he said sarcastically as he examined his head in the mirror.

"I think you look just as gorgeous as before, but it makes you look a lot younger. I can't have you looking younger, Quinn. It won't work for me." Davi smiled at him affectionately.

"It's not working for me either, love." Quinn tossed the mirror onto the bed. "What does the back look like? The scar, I mean."

"I haven't seen it. I'm sure your hair will cover it once it grows back."

Quinn leaned back into his pillow and closed his eyes.

"Maybe I should go and leave you two alone for a while," Jake offered.

"No. Stay, Jake. You brought food. We're eating. Quinn can rest for a bit."

Davi jumped off the bed and walked over to the tray of food. She took her plate and sat down on the couch.

"Mmm, good choice, Jake. Thanks," she said when she tasted her salad with grilled chicken.

"Eat, Jake. Please."

Jake sat down next to Davi. He started on his club sandwich. He looked at Quinn with concern.

"He's okay, Jake. He's dealing with it. Losing his hair seems harder to handle than almost being killed."

Jake stared at her. Now was not the time to be pushing Quinn.

"I can understand it too. I mean, Quinn's hair means so much to him. It makes him a sex symbol. Who can resist that just-out-of-bed look? I mean, it makes me hot. What am I going to run my fingers through now? How am I going to pull him closer for a kiss when we're making love? I guess our love life is over for a while." She winked at Jake.

Quinn opened his eyes and glared at her. "That's not funny."

"I think it is. You're more than your hair, husband. At least, you are to me. It will grow back. Get over it. We were all sick with worry over the thought of losing you, and all you can think about is your shaved head. You're better than that."

"You won't allow me a pity party? Not even for one minute?" he grumbled.

"No. Life's too short. Make a joke about your head and move on."

"You are wicked."

"Only for you, love. That's why you gave me your ring."

"That's not the only reason. Come here, please."

Davi walked over to Quinn's bed. She stood by his free hand and took it in hers.

"You could have died, Quinn. I told myself that you had to be okay. You had to come back to me because I have no plan B. I don't know what I would have done if I'd lost you. I would have died too." Davi burst into tears as she crawled on to Quinn's bed.

Quinn pulled her in close with his arm and consoled her. "It's okay, woman. I'm fine. You looked after me. You brought me back. I'm not going to leave you. I promised you forever, and I meant it. You're not going to get rid of me that easily." Quinn kissed the top of her head. "I love you."

"I love you too," Davi said through her sobs.

"Cry it out, love. You deserve it. Cry it out all you want," Quinn whispered to her.

Jake made his way out of the room. He phoned Sue and Luke to let them know the good news. He gave Quinn and Davi time to be alone.

Davi spent the rest of the week in the hospital with Quinn. His doctor wanted to be sure that he was ready to go home and the seizures had ceased. Quinn walked the halls with help from Jake until he regained his balance. Davi didn't mind giving that job to Jake.

Stubble started to sprout on Quinn's head. Davi liked to run her hand over it. Quinn enjoyed the attention.

"Soon you'll have something to hold on to," he teased.

Jake drove Quinn and Davi back to the hotel when Quinn was finally discharged from the hospital. He escorted them to their penthouse, walking close to Quinn since he was unsure Quinn could handle the distance.

"I'm okay, Jake. I think I can walk to the elevator and down the hall."

"No complaining. Your wife wants me here. Make her happy."

Davi walked behind them, carrying her plastic hospital bag filled with their belongings. It felt like they'd been away for months, not days.

Davi cut in front of them as they neared the door to their suite. She slid the key through the slot and opened the door. Panic went through Davi's mind as she imagined that their friends could be inside for a welcome home party. Neither one of them was up for it. *Please let me be wrong*, she prayed. There was silence. The room was dark. Davi sighed, relieved.

"Let me sit down on the couch. I'm going to ignore bed for a while, if you don't mind. I've been on my back too long," Quinn nodded toward the living room.

"Are you sure you don't want me to stay? I don't want Davi to strain herself trying to help you on to your feet. I'd feel better if you were in bed." Jake winked at Davi.

"No thanks, Jake. We can take it from here. Thanks for all you've done. We just need to relax and settle in. We'll call you later." Quinn groaned loudly as he sat down on the couch.

Davi walked Jake to the door to thank him for his help. She kissed him on the cheek.

"Go home and take it easy. He's not going anywhere for a while."

Jake smiled down on Davi. "And we both know why that is, don't we? Take care, lovely lady. You need your rest too. Remind him of that."

"Good-bye, Quinn. Take it easy," Jake called over Davi's shoulder. He winked at Davi.

Davi closed the door behind Jake and locked the door.

"That was the worst bit of acting I've ever seen, 'I've been on my back too long.'"

"I think he bought it." Quinn said with confidence.

"Not a chance, stud. Jake was on to you and so was I."

"Woman, it's been almost a week. I need you. The doctor said we could have sex."

Quinn gave her his best bedroom eyes. His hands reached for her and pulled her down onto the couch.

"I have nothing to hold on to, husband."

"Grab my ears, I don't care," Quinn murmured as he worked on her buttons.

"I need a shower, I stink."

"So do I," he said as he removed her shirt. "We'll shower later, before we have more sex."

"I'm exhausted."

"I'm not. You can lie there, and I'll do all the work. I owe you that much."

Quinn pulled off her jeans. He looked down at her belly. He caressed it and then kissed it.

"Do you think Jack will mind if Daddy loves Mommy for a while?"

"No, but don't be too loud. You might scare him or the neighbors."

"I can try . . ."

Chapter 40

♥

Quinn took a medical leave of absence. He gave the studio a choice. Give him three weeks off or find a replacement. He didn't care. The studio did. Quinn and Davi had become a hot commodity. The studio filmed around Quinn for the next three weeks.

Once Quinn got the go-ahead from his doctor, he and Davi flew back to Toronto.

"Mom! Quinn!" The girls cried when they met them at the airport.

Davi didn't mind that the girls hugged and kissed Quinn first. They'd been terrified at the thought of losing him. Every night they called him to make sure he was feeling better. Once they were reassured, they'd talk to Davi and give her the latest news, especially where two hot actors from New York were concerned.

Cat hugged Davi. "Mom, you look terrible."

"Thanks, hon."

"You and Quinn need to go on a honeymoon somewhere safe."

"We'll think about it. For now, all we want is to be at home."

"Your mom wants to sleep," Quinn told them as they walked through the airport.

"What about you?" Tigger asked.

"I'm all yours, as long as I don't have to get off the couch."

Davi laughed as Quinn offered himself up to the girls like a sacrificial lamb. She hoped he wouldn't be crying for mercy too soon.

When they got home, Davi went to bed and slept. Quinn spent the afternoon with the girls on the couch, watching movies. Quinn got first choice, and much to the girls' surprise, he chose *The Proposal*, one of Ryan Reynolds' latest movies. Quinn had to keep tabs on the competition.

"So girls, tell me what you think about Ryan?" Quinn asked casually.

Cat looked at him with disbelief. "You're not jealous, are you?"

"What? Me?"

"He's younger than you," Tigger pointed out.

"By one year," Cat added.

"And he's Canadian," Tigger offered.

"A definite bonus there," Cat agreed.

"And he's hot," they both said together.

"Your point being?" Quinn asked, not sure if he wanted to hear the answer.

"Mom's not trading you in."

"And you're still the better actor."

"Honest?"

"At least one of us is telling the truth, Quinn. You figure it out."

Davi's prenatal checkup was the next day. She wouldn't let Quinn go with her. "Nothing's going to happen, and you don't need to be going anywhere. My blood pressure is checked, and I am weighed. That's it, Quinn. I wouldn't lie to you. It's the next appointment that you won't want to miss. It's the ultrasound. You can see Jack in all his glory."

"You promise?"

"I promise. If I'm wrong, I will phone you and have one of the girls drive you over to the doctor's immediately. That's the best I can do."

"Fine. Next time, then."

Davi had a long visit with her doctor. Her doctor was aware of the attack on Quinn. Davi had many questions for her about the baby and Quinn.

"They shaved his head." Davi smiled. "He looks gorgeous, but now he looks so much younger. He makes me look like a cradle robber."

Her doctor laughed. "I don't think so."

"It's true. He has to grow that hair back ASAP."

"What about you? How are you?"

"I'm good or at least I'm getting there. I need my honeymoon. I need rest with nothing to do but soak up some sun. We wanted to have this appointment to make sure both the baby and I were okay before we went away."

"So you've decided on keeping the baby?"

"Definitely. I still want the tests run, but we're having this baby. We've named him Jack."

"You're convinced it's a boy?"

"No, but its name is Jack. Quinn picked the name, and it stuck with me. If it's a girl, we may have to reconsider, but for now it's Jack."

"Well, Davi, you're fine. A honeymoon will be the best thing for you and the baby. Rest and have fun with your husband. Come back healthy. In a month's time, we'll check in on you again. We'll do an ultrasound and know a lot more about Jack by then."

Davi returned home happy and relaxed. She needed the visit with her doctor to put her mind at ease about Jack and Quinn. As she walked into the kitchen, she saw one of her suitcases and her travel bag sitting by the door. Quinn's smaller suitcase was next to them.

"What's this?"

The girls ran to Davi and hugged her. "Bon voyage," they cheered. "You're going on your honeymoon. Quinn booked it while you were at the doctor's office. Your flight is in four hours and your bag is packed."

"No hints?" Davi asked

Quinn smiled at her. "No. Not until you absolutely need to know. Just make sure you have your passport."

"It never leaves my purse. I've been traveling too much lately." Davi looked at the girls. "You won't embarrass me? You packed all the right things?"

"Quinn oversaw us. Everything in your bag was given his approval or was suggested by him."

"I repeat, you won't embarrass me?"

"No," they said in unison.

"You've got everything you need, and if you don't, we'll buy it for you there. Come on, wife, we need to go."

"I'm getting tired of surprises," Davi moaned.

"This will make up for it, Davi. I promise." Quinn hugged her. "We both need this. Let's go. The girls will drive us to the airport."

The next day, Davi was lying on a beach bed on a secluded beachfront patio in Aruba. It was hot, and the sun was beating down on her as Quinn applied suntan lotion to her white skin.

"Mmm, that feels so good. Thank you." Davi made a rumbling noise in her throat.

"Are you okay, wife?" Quinn laughed.

Davi peered over her sunglasses. "I'm purring. Or at least I'm trying to."

"You can stop trying. It sounds more like you're trying to cough up a hair ball."

"Sorry. I told you I don't purr."

"It's okay. You tried," Quinn said as he continued massaging the lotion into her skin.

"I can't believe you got me into a bikini. This is so embarrassing."

"Hush, wife. You are beautiful. There is no one more beautiful to me."

Davi reached for Quinn and pulled him in for a kiss.

"If I remember correctly, this is where the fantasy ends and forever begins. What do you think, husband?"

"Oh, most definitely, wife, this is definitely forever."

Epilogue

♥

Maggie sat in the local coffee shop, staring at her herbal tea. *If only the tea leaves could tell me what I want to know, maybe I could let this go and be happy for them.*

A young woman walked in through the entrance and approached her table.

"Are you Maggie?" she asked. "Of course you are." She smiled as she sat down.

"Alannah," Maggie said with excitement, "thank you so much for meeting with me."

She had heard great things about this medium. No one came close to seeing what she saw. Maggie was desperate for her guidance.

"Don't thank me until you've heard what I tell you," the medium said, her eyes serious. "Thanks for meeting me here. I have class in thirty minutes, and I'm booked all day."

The medium watched as the server brought her a cup of Americano coffee.

She took a sip and sighed appreciatively. "The caffeine helps me see," she explained. "Tell me what's troubling you."

Maggie took a sip of her tea as though she needed it for courage.

"It's my friend," she explained. "We have a strong bond, stronger than I ever imagined. When I read her cards, everything is clear. There is no second-guessing. It happens."

"What's the problem?"

"I'm seeing her no matter whose cards I'm reading. She's coming through to me constantly. I can't shut it off, and the message is always the same. It's—"

Alannah put up her hand to stop Maggie.

"Don't tell me. Let me see it for myself. Did you bring me something that belongs to your friend?" She held out her hand, knowing that the answer would be yes.

"It's her diamond bracelet. He gave it to her. She wore it on her wedding day."

Maggie dropped the bracelet in the medium's hand.

"Perfect."

The medium closed her eyes as she ran her fingers over the stones. She did this for a minute in silence. Maggie didn't dare sip her tea in case she disturbed her.

A brief smile crossed her face as she nodded in recognition. "I love his movies." Then her expression changed to complete seriousness. "You can't tell her, Maggie," she said, her eyes still closed. "It's not your news to tell."

"Do you see it too?' Maggie asked with trepidation.

"Do I see two hearts beating? Yes. She's pregnant with twins."

"What else?" Maggie leaned in closer to her.

"It's not her decision to make. It's his."

She opened her eyes and reached for her coffee.

Maggie wanted to ask more, to push for what she really wanted to hear. Instead, she waited anxiously while the medium drank her coffee in silence.

"What happens to them is meant to happen. You can't play with their fate, Maggie. I know what you've seen, and it's going to happen. Let the cards play out. To interfere could cause more harm than you could ever imagine."

"But the darkness. Surely you saw the darkness?" Maggie stammered, fearful of what she saw.

"Yes, I saw the darkness and the light that follows. The light will return."

"They're my friends. I can't sit back and do nothing."

"Doing nothing is the best thing you can do. Their love is strong. Let the cards play out the way they should." She returned the bracelet to Maggie. "You're a good friend, Maggie. Be there for them. Know that it will work out."

"If I say nothing," Maggie said somberly.

"Only if you say nothing."